THE SHEIKH'S ROYAL ANNOUNCEMENT

SHARON KENDRICK

CLAIMING HIS OUT-OF-BOUNDS BRIDE

ANNIE WEST

MILLS & BOON

First Published in Great Britain 2020
by Mills & Boon, an imprint of HarperCollins*Publishers*
1 London Bridge Street, London, SE1 9GF

The Sheikh's Royal Announcement © 2020 Sharon Kendrick

Claiming His Out-of-Bounds Bride © 2020 Annie West

ISBN: 978-0-263-27825-5

Printed and bound in Spain
by CPI, Barcelona

THE SHEIKH'S ROYAL ANNOUNCEMENT

SHARON KENDRICK

This book is dedicated to Clelia Accardi,
who is a proud Sicilian with a great sense of humour.

Clelia gave me invaluable help with my book *Cinderella in the Sicilian's World...*

Grazie mille!

CHAPTER ONE

THE MOMENT CAITLIN walked into the room she could scent danger. It lingered like stale perfume in the fancy salon. It impregnated the plush velvets which covered the squashy chairs. A pulse of warning thudded at her temple because this wasn't the first time it had happened. The strange and indefinable feeling that somehow she was being *watched*—that alien eyes were following her. Several times lately she had found herself whirling around, expecting to see something or someone out of the ordinary behind her—but there had been nothing and afterwards Caitlin had scolded herself for being so jumpy.

Yet now her skin prickled with apprehension as she stood alone and looked around. At tall, mullioned windows, which gazed onto the wet bloom of an autumn garden currently bathed in soft light. She tugged at the sleeve of her home-knitted sweater and was grateful for her thick, woollen tights, which she'd worn because these big old Scottish hotels were always draughty, no matter how grand they might be. And this one was certainly grand, judging by its imposing exterior and soaring position over the city.

As instructed, she had arrived just before eleven and the clock was striking the hour as she was taken into what was obviously the most important room in the hotel by a polite manager with a curiously expressionless face. For the past ten minutes she had been waiting with increasing nervousness, wondering who on earth she was going to meet and what they were going to offer her.

A job, hopefully. Actually, 'the job of a lifetime', as the agency had excitedly informed her—offering the kind of salary which usually only featured in fairy tales. And if it had sounded too good to be true that hadn't been enough to deter her—because who was ever put off by something like *that*? Certainly not Caitlin, who had a hungry mouth to feed and nothing in the way of security for the future. Why wouldn't she explore every opportunity which came her way when opportunities were increasingly rare for a single mother who lived on a remote Scottish island?

She was just studying a rather depressing oil painting of a stag standing against a background of blurry purple heather when she heard the sound of a door being opened behind her. Pinning her most polite smile to her lips, Caitlin turned to greet her prospective employer— but the smile withered and died, like a dried-up leaf thrown onto the blaze of a bonfire, as she stared at a man behind whom the heavy doors were now being closed. She felt faint. Then dizzy. Then faint, all over again.

Kadir Al Marara.

It couldn't be him.

Please let it not be him.

But it was. Oh, it was. There could be no mistaking the aura of raw masculinity which radiated from the powerful figure who stood before her, owning every atom of the space around him. Caitlin felt the blood drain from her cheeks as she stared into a dark face which had haunted her dreams and her conscience for five long years, no matter how hard she had tried to keep it at bay. But the flesh-and-blood version of the man was even more disturbing than the image which crept into her mind when she was least expecting it. And one question circled round and round in her mind, like a dark spectre.

What was he doing here?

For a moment she couldn't move, so great was her shock at seeing him again. It was only when her heart had stopped missing every other beat that she allowed her gaze to travel over him—the man she'd never thought she'd see again. The man who looked like no other, with his darkly exotic good looks and imposing presence. His face was the most beautiful she'd ever seen, with eyes of glittering jet set in skin the colour of beaten gold. She reacquainted herself with his distinctive hawklike nose and the carved cheekbones which illustrated his noble lineage. And now she wondered how she could have been so trusting when she'd first met him. How could she have been taken in by his explanation that he was nothing but a businessman, when his royal pedigree shimmered from every atom of his impressive frame?

Did he *know*? she wondered. Did he realise he had a small son who was the spitting image of him? And if he did—what then? Was he going to storm into her life again and change it out of all recognition, as he had done once before?

Paralysing fear crept over her as she stood there, not knowing what to do or say, because Kadir's appearance was throwing her senses into disarray—and not just because it was so unexpected. Because he looked so…*different* from the man she had known for that brief snatch of time. His jet-black hair was obscured by a pure white *keffiyeh* headdress, which seemed only to emphasise the olive-hued beauty of his face. And he was wearing robes. Flowing robes of soft silk, which whispered against the hard contours of his muscular body. She half shook her head in confusion. What had happed to the elegant Italian suit? To the silk shirt and vibrant cobalt tie which he had slung with careless impatience to lie on the bedroom floor along with her discarded panties?

That had been his *disguise*, she reminded herself bitterly. Modern, western clothes worn to send out mixed messages, so that she—and probably countless other women like her—wouldn't be able to guess his true identity. If he had been dressed this way when she'd met him, would she have been so eager to fall into his arms and his bed? Caitlin wondered. But she would never know the answer to that. Their gazes had connected and a powerful mutual attraction had surged between them. And because of that, her life had changed for ever.

He hadn't told her he was a powerful desert king. There were plenty of things he hadn't told her. Things which would have filled her with horror if she'd been aware of them at the time. She had only found out about them afterwards, when she had tried to track him down. When she had discovered what a stupid fool she had been. And the power of that memory allowed her to suppress her fear and the nagging sense of guilt that she could have done this all so differently.

'Kadir,' she said, and somehow the word slipped from her lips as easily as breathing. It sounded almost calm—and so very different from the last time she'd said it, when it had shuddered from her lips in another cry of helpless passion. She licked her lips as a wave of nausea washed over her.

Because what if he *did* know? What if he had discovered the truth she had fought so hard to conceal? She thought about Cameron, safely at home with Morag, and, despite her thick sweater, Caitlin could feel another shiver begin to ripple over her skin and it took everything she knew to stop her teeth from chattering. Wasn't it her duty to discover Kadir's intentions before she even thought about telling him? Or maybe she was just dragging her feet, knowing that once she told him the truth, nothing would ever be the same again. She tried to keep her voice cool, as befitted a woman who had been deceived as badly as she had. 'What on earth are you doing here?'

Kadir didn't respond to Caitlin's question immediately, but then he didn't have to because he was King and could make people hang on to his every word. The most powerful king in the Middle East, or so it was said. He owned rich lands and lavish palaces, which many envied, as well as countless servants and trusted aides who would walk over burning coals to do his royal bidding. Why, up until a few short weeks ago, he would have agreed with those who commended him for his many attributes. For having his finger on the international pulse after all his hard-won battles to regain a lasting peace in his sometimes primitive homeland. To many, he had everything a king could possibly desire.

And yet...

He felt the flicker of heat on his skin.

Yet this woman had kept from him the most precious thing a man could possess. The fruit of his loins and rightful heir to the vast region over which he ruled. She had denied him four precious years of his son's life. Four years he could never get back.

And never had he felt such an all-consuming rage.

But he would not show it. He knew only too well that concealing emotion was the only sure way to triumph in this strange business they called life. Because emotion was just another word for weakness and it rendered a man as powerless as sexual desire. It could make him do things which were abhorrent to him. Things which could take your destiny hurtling towards an unwanted destination and that was a feeling he couldn't afford to have. Not ever again. Celibacy had made him strong and powerful—which was why he would ignore the soft gleam of sunshine which made Caitlin Fraser's hair look like a fall of bright flame. He would disregard her pale skin and gentle curves and the memories of what it felt like to be deep inside her, and on her, and next to her. He would forget the fact that once she had made him feel as strong and invincible as a lion. Instead, he would lay the bait and let her walk into her own, doomed trap...

'You seem surprised to see me, Caitlin,' he observed coolly.

She furrowed her freckled brow. 'That's something

of an understatement. Of course I'm surprised. You
disappeared without a word five years ago. You crept
away in the middle of night and now you've turned up
without any kind of warning,' she said and then added,
as if the thought had only just occurred to her, 'How
did you find me?'

He shrugged. 'Such tasks are not a problem.'

'For someone like you, you mean,' she accused.

Steadily, he met her gaze. 'Someone like me?'

'A desert king! A royal sheikh! Something you didn't
bother telling me at the time!'

Kadir did not comment on her furious allegation.
Instead, he continued to stare at her with that same
unruffled curiosity. Let her condemn herself with her
own words, he thought bitterly.

'I don't understand why you've just suddenly appeared like this,' she was saying. 'Is this some kind
of set-up?'

'A set-up?' he questioned coldly, his fury growing as
she continued to act the innocent and, oh, didn't she do
it so well? Did women learn the art of deception in the
cradle? he wondered bitterly. Might that explain why
they were so damned good at it?

She nodded her bright head. 'I came here expecting
to meet a prospective employer.'

'Someone you did not know?' he probed.

'That's right,' she agreed.

'Someone you did not know,' he repeated. 'And yet
still you agreed to keep the appointment?'

Her soft lips opened in protest, as if she had correctly picked up on the censure in his voice. 'Well, yes.
Why wouldn't I?'

'Even though it could have been anyone? Tell me, Caitlin, do you often arrange to meet up with strangers in hotel rooms?' His eyes narrowed with a sudden dark flare of contempt. 'Although I suppose you do have some kind of track record for that, don't you?'

Her pale cheeks flushed. 'I could say the same of you,' she returned. 'But this was no romantic rendezvous. This was supposed to be a business meeting and perfectly legitimate. It was arranged for me by an employment agency and I take every opportunity I can to find work because I happen to need the money.' She glared. 'Now that might be something which is so far off your own radar that you can't understand what it feels like, but I can assure you—it certainly isn't a crime.'

'No,' he gritted out, his voice growing harsh, and suddenly Kadir knew he couldn't play this game any longer—no matter how tempted he was to see how far she would go to conceal the truth from him. To count how many lies she told him before he wheedled it out of her at last. 'The crime is that you became pregnant with my child and didn't bother to tell me. That you bore my son four years ago without my knowledge—and I have missed out on every precious moment of his life ever since. That is quite some crime, Caitlin.'

Caitlin's heart was crashing so hard that it felt as if it might burst from her chest, but she forced herself to focus on the facts rather than the pain which was coursing through her. He *did* know! Of course he knew. Why *else* would he be here? He certainly hadn't thought twice about her since the night he'd seduced her with all that abundant charm, and crept out some time during the night while she'd been sleeping, without even bothering to say goodbye. She remembered waking up feeling dreamy and half in love until it had dawned on her that there was no sign of the man to whom she had given herself so wholeheartedly, other than the traces of his seed which had already dried on the bedsheets. It hadn't been until later, when she'd discovered she was carrying his baby, that she'd realised just why he'd been so eager to leave so surreptitiously.

Anger coursed through her in a bitter wave.

And that was what she needed to hang on to. The memory of his betrayal—and her own stupidity. The realisation that she had allowed history to repeat itself—and had allowed herself to be treated like a fool. But she also knew the bitter consequences which could befall women who buckled under the strain of a situation like this and she wasn't going to let that happen. Not to her and not to her son. She couldn't allow this powerful sheikh to just swan in and take control of her life, with that arrogant look of condemnation hardening his sculpted features every time he looked at her. She didn't need his approval. She needed to be strong. For Cameron's sake as much as her own.

Because hot on her anger came an even more debilitating wave of fear. A dark flicker of dread as she started worrying about what he was going to do about his discovery. And, more importantly, what he was *capable* of doing. About the worrying consequences of having kept this secret for so long. Because nobody else knew that the Sheikh of Xulhabi was the father of her son.

'I did try to contact you, Kadir. As soon as I knew I was carrying your baby, I attempted to track you down.

At first I couldn't quite believe it when I discovered your true identity, but once I had got my head around it—I still continued with my search.' She shook her head and could feel the heavy sway of hair as it brushed against her neck. 'And believe me, it isn't easy for an unknown commoner to try to make contact with a powerful ruler of a foreign country. There are mechanisms in place to thwart you every step of the way.'

'But you *didn't* make contact with me, did you, Caitlin?' he accused. 'There were aides and ambassadors with whom you could have left a message, but no such message was received.'

'No. Because during my search I discovered what you had failed to tell me.' Briefly, Caitlin closed her eyes and when she opened them again she prayed that her face showed no traces of the terrible despair she had felt at the time. 'You had no r-right to sleep with me that night,' she continued, in a voice which wouldn't seem to stop trembling. 'Oh, I'm not just talking about the fact you didn't mention you were a royal sheikh and made out you were a commoner, because maybe that was some game you liked to play and you used to get off on it. Maybe it turned you on to deceive women in such a way.'

'You talk to *me* of deception?' he demanded witheringly.

'No. I'm talking about something else. Something much worse.' She sucked in a breath and it scorched at her throat like a blowtorch, her words taking her back to a place she rarely allowed herself to visit because it was still painful. Too painful to bear. The discovery of his deception had carried an even greater significance for Caitlin, for it had been like a dark echo from her own past. A reminder of just how easily men could cheat on women. She remembered the sense of foolishness and regret which had washed through her veins in a putrid flow—along with the realisation that, for all the blame she used to fling at her own mother, maybe she really wasn't that different after all. She had certainly been hoodwinked in exactly the same way.

'Because you were a married man, weren't you?' she accused, and now her voice was shaking with shame and anger and guilt. 'You had a wife back home at your palace in Xulhabi, but you didn't bother mentioning that on the night you spent with me, did you, Kadir Al Marara? Tell me, how many times did you break your marriage vows by having sex with other women?'

CHAPTER TWO

KADIR STARED AT the woman whose bitter words had just
come hurtling through the air towards him like a swarm
of bees, but they did not sting his flesh or cause him
to flinch. Because any remorse he might have felt was
diluted by the nature of her accusation and his mouth
tightened with anger. She might have fared better if she
had stuck to the facts. Why hadn't she just taken her
share of the blame? Admitted that they had both been
carried along on a wave of passion—their bodies taken
over by a chemistry so powerful that it had been irresistible, even though he had done his damnedest and tried.

But instead she had played the guilt card and turned
him into a stereotype of a man. The dark and brooding sheikh, like a character from one of those flicker-
ing black-and-white films he had once seen. And being
categorised in such a way had happened much too often
in the past for it not to have touched a raw nerve. How
many times? she had asked him—and the answer to
that question was just once, with her. But he would not
give her the pleasure of knowing that—because might
that not lead her to believe she meant something special to him?

'You begged me to have sex with you. *Begged* me,' he reiterated cruelly, and so great was his fury that he actually found himself enjoying her embarrassed flush of recognition. 'You know you did. Would you like me to remind you of the words you used, Caitlin?'

'No! I don't... I don't want to talk about that night.'

He stared her down. 'Well, maybe I do. Maybe I want to relive it minute by minute.'

Her face had drained of colour and quickly she stared down at her freckled fingers, which were knotted together as if she were praying for divine intervention, before slowly lifting her gaze to his. And for a second, Kadir found himself lost in the sky-washed hue of those pale, Scottish eyes. How had he forgotten their quiet blue beauty? The way they seemed able to look deep inside you, as if they could see into your troubled soul and offer it some kind of temporary solace. He had forgotten because he'd had no choice—because the possibility of how good she had made him feel had been incompatible with his life and his world. And he needed to forget it now.

Which was why he continued to stare at her, without saying a word. Silence was a tactic which had always worked well for him in the past. If you allowed it to grow for long enough, the other person would always break it first. Because people didn't like silence. They were frightened of it. They didn't like listening to the noisy clatter of their own thoughts.

'Just tell me,' she burst out at last. 'Tell me why you're here.'

Now it was Kadir's turn to pause. What *did* he want? To rewind the clock, perhaps? To have carried on walking around the sweeping Scottish estate he'd been considering buying and not been distracted by her bright hair or the curve of her hips, or the darkening of her extraordinary eyes when she had turned around to look at him? Would he prefer not to have participated in the passionate night which had followed, even though his actions had afterwards appalled him? No. He did not want that, even if such a thing were possible—for how could he wish his son never to have been born?

'Why do you think I'm here?' he demanded. 'Because I want to see him. I want to see my son.'

She flinched, as if he had asked her for something impossible. He could see the moment of indecision which froze her slender frame, like a deer in the forest which had just discovered itself in the presence of the hunter. And then gradually, life seemed to flow back into her body and she shook her head a little, like somebody who had just awoken from a bad nightmare.

'Yes,' she said slowly. 'I suppose you do.' She reached down towards a green leather satchel the colour of a wine bottle, which she lifted with trembling fingers from the chair on which she must have placed it. Silently, Kadir watched as she withdrew a rather battered wallet and flicked behind a bank card, before drawing out a photo, which she handed to him. 'Here. Take this.'

He didn't look at it immediately. Just continued to fix his gaze on her. 'You think I will be satisfied with a picture?' he demanded witheringly.

'Won't it do for the time being, at least?'

Unable to hold back for a second longer, he swiped it from her fingers, taking great care not to make contact with her skin—as if he could not trust himself to touch her. And then he willed himself to stay strong and not give in to the sudden sense of despair which washed over him as he steeled himself to examine the first picture of his son. The aide who had discovered his existence had offered to get photographic evidence, but Kadir had stopped him because he had a deep loathing of the paparazzi and was loath to replicate their predatory behaviour. Information about the child's age and appearance had indicated that he was indeed the father, but it was instinct which made him certain and these days he trusted his instincts far more than he would looking at some snatched photo, taken from behind a tree.

Yet no amount of mental preparation could make him immune to the feelings which bombarded him as he stared down at a pair of jet-dark eyes so like his own. He walked over to the window, so that he could study it properly in the autumnal light. Judging from the bland background it was a formal shot, though the little boy's silky black hair flopped untidily over his forehead, as if no amount of careful brushing could tame it. Kadir narrowed his eyes as he noticed a tiny chip on one of the child's front teeth and a rush of indignation heated his blood. Had he fallen and hurt himself? he wondered. And why had nobody been there to protect him?

He turned away from the window to find Caitlin's eyes on him, the uncertainty of that blue gaze clearly seeking some kind of reassurance. And didn't it fill him with a vengeful amount of pleasure to discover that he wasn't going to provide her with any?

His lips flattened.

None at all.

'I want to see him in the flesh,' he clipped out. 'And as soon as possible.'

Caitlin nodded, her heart sinking as she heard his words, even though she'd been expecting him to say that. Of course she had. What else could he possibly say in the circumstances? Her heart twisted with a complex mixture of emotions, though she was ashamed of the one which was dominant. Which bubbled to the surface in a dark and angry tide and had nothing to do with her little boy but everything to do with *her*.

Jealousy.

Hot and black and potent.

'And what about your wife?' The words rushed from her lips and she could feel her cheeks flush. 'Will she want to see him, too?'

There was the briefest of pauses as his face darkened but his voice was devoid of emotion as he delivered his response.

'My wife is dead.'

And wasn't Caitlin appalled by the primitive rush of relief which flooded her body on receipt of these words? 'I'm sorry,' she said automatically.

'No, you're not.'

'I am sorry for every person's loss,' she defended truthfully. 'But mostly I'm sorry I ever slept with you, without knowing you were a married man!'

'That's history, Caitlin,' he ground out. 'I'm not concerned about the past. The present is what occupies me. I am not leaving here—and neither are you, by the way—until you have agreed a date for me to meet my boy.'

'Cameron,' she corrected automatically.

'Cameron,' Kadir repeated and Caitlin thought how his rich voice made the traditional Scottish name sound somehow exotic and distinguished.

And wasn't that one simple fact enough to make fear whisper through her body, as she acknowledged his power and might? Because not only did he *look* different from the man into whose arms she had fallen so willingly, he *sounded* different, too. Along with the flowing robes and headdress, he seemed to have acquired a steely patina, which made him seem distant and aloof. Influence radiated from every pore of his muscular body and instinct told her that he would take total control of the situation if she let him. So don't. State your terms, she told herself fiercely. Show him you won't be pushed around by anyone. She wasn't one of his subjects. She was a free and independent woman and, moreover, they were in *her* country.

'Of course you must meet, but I would like it to be on neutral territory,' she said, as it occurred to her that maybe she was ashamed of her little croft cottage. Scared how tiny it would look in contrast to his soaring palaces. Or was it because she couldn't bear the thought of Kadir's powerful presence stamping itself on her humble surroundings like a dark smash of stone? So that when he left—as leave he inevitably would—the place would somehow seem empty and diminished without him? 'How about here in Edinburgh? That would be as good a place as any.'

'I'm sure it would, but I'm afraid that doesn't fit in with my schedule. I have to be in London this week,' he said coldly. 'You can meet me there.'

'London?' repeated Caitlin.

'There's no need to make it sound like Mars,' he purred. 'It's no great distance. Just over an hour by plane, in fact. My business interests are centred there and my time in your country is short.'

'It is?' she verified, unable to keep the hope from her voice.

'Indeed it is.' He inclined his head, almost courteously, as if he hadn't noticed her telltale slip of the tongue, but the flashing of his black eyes indicated that maybe he had. 'Bring Cameron to London. Is he familiar with the city?'

'No,' said Caitlin, acknowledging the humble limitations of Cameron's upbringing. He'd never even been out of Scotland before, let alone flown to London. But that had been deliberate. She'd wanted to shelter him from the world and from people. She'd wanted to protect him from the harsher side of life.

And hadn't there been part of her which had thought that if she hid herself away successfully, then a scenario like this would never have arisen? 'No, he's never been there.'

'Well, then, that's decided. I'm sure it will be an exciting destination for one so young, and there will be much to entertain him.' He flickered her a businesslike smile. 'I will arrange for my plane to collect you.'

Caitlin blinked. His *plane*? He had his own plane? Well, of course he did—could she really imagine the king of one of the wealthiest countries in the world standing in line with ordinary people at the airport? She licked lips which suddenly felt dry. 'It's very kind of you to offer,' she said stiffly. 'But I'm perfectly capable of getting to London under my own steam.'

His black gaze slanted over her sweater and, briefly, travelled down her knee-length tweed skirt, his lips curving slightly as he registered her woolly grey tights. 'But presumably not with any kind of style?' he offered cruelly.

His observation—actually it was more of a judgement—irritated her, even if it happened to be true. But Caitlin told herself it was better to be irritated than passive. He hadn't objected to her no-nonsense clothes last time around, had he? He'd been more concerned with removing them than providing some kind of fashion critique. But she wasn't going to start going down *that* road. It was going to be difficult enough negotiating the emotional minefield which lay ahead, without remembering how it had felt to lie in Kadir's arms while he rained sensual kisses all over her mouth.

'I believed I was coming here today for an interview about future photographic work,' she returned briskly. 'And as far as I was aware, holding a camera in often inclement weather requires practical rather than fancy clothing.' She hesitated. 'As for your proposed trip to London, I'd like to bring Morag along, if she can be persuaded to make the journey.'

He frowned. 'Who's Morag?'

'She's an ex-nurse who has known me since I was a child. She's retired now and helps look after Cameron when I'm working.'

'And how often does that happen?' he demanded. 'How often do you have to leave our son in the hands of this woman?'

It was a totally unfair accusation and the possessive note in his voice was more than a little worrying, but

Caitlin told herself he was angry and people said all kinds of things when they were angry. Drawing in a deep breath, she met his hostile gaze with one of manufactured calm. 'I never leave him unless it's absolutely essential and I choose my work carefully. I don't take on jobs just for the sake of it, because I'm trying to grow my reputation. I do a lot of photographic work for an agency which is, I suppose, how you were successfully able to lure me to this hotel with the promise of a job. Which I'm guessing doesn't really exist.' She gave a bitter laugh. 'There is no job, is there, Kadir?'

The brief shake of his head gave her his answer, but as their gazes locked she saw the smoky flash of fire in the depths of his eyes, which his thick lashes couldn't quite conceal. Was she imagining the faint sigh which escaped his lips, which made her focus on them unwillingly, only to recall how it had felt to be kissed by him? And then a whole batch of memories came rushing back and there seemed to be nothing she could do to keep them at bay.

She wondered if he ever thought about the circumstances in which they'd met, when she'd been trying to capture the image of a golden eagle and he'd told her afterwards that he'd never been so mesmerised by a woman's neck. Or her bottom. Apparently, he'd been thinking of purchasing the vast Scottish estate she was in the process of photographing, though the sale had never happened. She'd often wondered if he might have gone ahead and bought it if he hadn't met her, or whether his infidelity had nudged his conscience and made him change his mind. Surely she was the last person he would ever want to bump into. She gave a bitter smile. Unless she was flattering herself by thinking she was his *only* extra-marital dalliance...

He gave a sudden click of his fingers, and that impatient gesture told her much more than words ever could. For the first time Caitlin caught a glimpse of the imperious sense of entitlement which marked him out from ordinary mortals and, again, she wondered how she could have ever believed he was a *commoner*.

'Of course there is no job,' he said coolly. 'Have Cameron ready to leave first thing tomorrow morning. One of my aides will arrive on the island to escort you both to Edinburgh.' There was a pause. 'And what will you tell him, Caitlin? How are you going to explain me to my son?'

'I haven't decided yet. I need to give it some thought.'

'Does he know who his father is?'

'No.' She shook her head. 'He's never asked.'

'Are you sure?'

'Yes! I swear to you.'

She heard a low hiss of air being expelled from his lungs.

'How can I believe you?' he demanded. 'Despite the hand you lay so convincingly over your heart!'

'Believe me or don't,' she bit back. 'But it's the truth!'

He studied her from between narrowed eyes. 'Come equipped for a stay of several nights.'

'Is that really necessary?'

His laugh was soft and low and taunting. 'Oh, Caitlin, can you really be that short-sighted? Do you think I'm prepared to be briefly slotted in to your schedule, like an unwanted dental appointment? That a few hours would be adequate for me to meet the child whose existence I have only just discovered?'

She hadn't given it any thought at all—it had all happened so quickly that Caitlin felt as if she'd jumped onto a merry-go-round. Only now she was even more scared than before. Scared of Kadir's power and his potential to completely wreck her life, but equally scared of the way he could make her feel. Because why, after all this time, did she find herself reacting to him in a way which shouldn't be happening? Her body felt as if it were coming alive under that searing gaze, in a way it hadn't done since the last time he'd looked at her. It was as if her senses had lain dormant all this time—like the bulbs which lay beneath the unforgiving earth of winter before being brought to life by the first warm flush of spring.

He was staring at her with an arrogant air of propriety, yet righteous indignation was the last thing on her mind. She could feel the prickle of heat to her breasts and the low coil of hunger which was tightening deeply at her core. Flickers of awareness were twanging low in her belly and her throat felt desert-dry. She'd always had the artist's way of looking at the world—of seeing her surroundings in terms of light and shade and variants of colour. But now it felt as if she'd been wearing blinkers which had just been removed and, suddenly, her vision had become crystal-clear. And she found herself looking at Kadir Al Marara as if she had never really seen him before.

She noticed the faint shadow of new beard at his jaw and found herself wondering how often he shaved. She didn't know. Just as she didn't know what he liked to eat for breakfast, or how he spent his days. She didn't know anything about his mother or his father and very little about his dead wife. His *wife*, she reminded herself bitterly. The woman he was married to when he slid your panties down before giving a low laugh of exultant pleasure as he discovered your molten heat. The memory filled her with shame—shame that she had done it and shame that it still had the power to turn her on.

This man is nothing but a stranger to me, she realised. I may have borne his child, but I don't *know* him. Just as he didn't know her. To him she was just a woman he'd bedded one night in a tiny Scottish town. A woman who had pressed her body close to his and murmured against his mouth, *'Please. Oh, please...'*

Shuddering with self-recrimination, she found herself wishing she could close her eyes and, when she opened them again, discover that this whole meeting had been nothing but a bad dream.

But that wouldn't be fair on Cameron, would it?

She couldn't keep hiding the truth about his father's past, no matter how much it suited her. She had been without a father during her own childhood and had been bitterly aware of the great gaping hole that had left in her life. Did she really wish the same for her child?

She wondered if her misgivings were showing on her face and if it was that which prompted the speculative look which Kadir iced at her.

'There's something else we need to discuss, Caitlin,' he added silkily. 'Just in case you were thinking of concocting some kind of disappearing act, I would strongly advise against it. Because not only would it be a complete waste of your time, it would also make

me angry and that is never a good idea. And besides,'
he finished, his voice dipping to a husky note so that it
sounded like smoke on velvet, 'no matter where in the
world you go with my son, be sure that I will seek you
out and find you.'

CHAPTER THREE

CAITLIN'S PULSE WAS hammering as she fled the hotel for the ferry terminal to catch the boat taking her back to her tiny island home. Usually, on one of her rare trips to the city, she would treat herself to a detour. A little relaxation and luxury and a contrast to her very basic life on Cronarty. She would peer into the windows of the big, bright shops before treating herself to a hot chocolate with whipped cream and marshmallows floating on the top as she watched the tourists bustle by. But today her mind was so full and her heart so heavy that she couldn't face it. How could she possibly relax in the light of what she'd just learned? She needed to get home—and as quickly as possible.

On board the ferry she stared straight ahead, breathing in the cold, clean air in an attempt to calm herself. But nothing could stop the thoughts which rattled through her head as she saw the craggy peaks of Cronarty in the distance. She'd been born on this island. Been schooled here. She'd grown up watching her mother dream her foolish dreams, then watched as those dreams had been smashed—over and over again. As her mother had gone to pieces, Caitlin had internalised it all with the acquired bravado of the only child, refusing to show any pain, even when that pain had become unbearable. And although she had been glad to escape to the big city once the long battle had ended, Cronarty had been the only place she had thought of coming to when she'd discovered she was pregnant and alone. The island had felt safe, with its soaring clifftops and stunning beaches, against which the mighty, foam-capped waves of the Atlantic crashed.

But suddenly it didn't feel safe any more.

She shook her head, as if that might somehow dislodge the memory of the dark and brooding sheikh, but his image seemed to be firmly rooted in her mind.

Stepping off the ferry, Caitlin began to walk towards her tiny cottage, the chill wind whipping around her. Sometimes Morag brought Cameron to meet the boat if she'd been away but they wouldn't be expecting her back until later. What on earth was she going to *say* to them? How could she possibly explain to her sensible babysitter that her son's father was a powerful desert sheikh with whom she'd had a one-night stand? More importantly, how was she going to tell Cameron himself? She bit her lip. She hadn't lied to him. She *never* lied to him—she'd answered any questions he put to her but there hadn't been many. He'd been too busy kicking a ball or swimming in the cold waters down by the bothy to pay much attention to his ancestors. Children on this remote place weren't into tablets or mobile phones. Why, she didn't even own a television set!

And Cronarty inspired its own particular form of loyalty—so that when Caitlin Fraser had returned to its shores, her belly huge and swollen with child, nobody had interrogated her about where the father was. In a way, living there was a bit like living in a capsule that time had forgotten. Cameron hadn't yet started school on the mainland, so his upbringing had been beautifully unspoiled. And yes, she was sure people occasionally wondered why the pale and fey Caitlin Fraser had a wee boy whose hair was as black as the night and whose skin possessed the deep gleam of polished gold. But they never asked.

And now?

Caitlin stared up at the sky, where heavy clouds as dark as iron were massing ominously on the horizon.

Now the outside world was about to burst in on their quiet little life like an unexpected explosion detonating the night sky. Her son was soon to discover that his father was one of the most powerful kings of the desert and tomorrow they were being flown to London so he could meet him. How did you even begin to frame something as monumental as that?

Guilt had riddled her heart for years whenever she'd thought about the lack of a father in Cameron's life— a guilt which had been quickly absolved by recalling Kadir's marital status and reminding herself that men were capable of great deception. Yet Kadir's wife was now dead. There no longer existed a reason why her son could legitimately be kept from his father. Not even her own sense of hurt at having been so badly deceived...

She shivered as she saw the outline of her home in the distance, but suddenly it wasn't her little cottage she was seeing, but an altogether different view. A treeless landscape, with distant hills. And a woman with her own dreams of becoming a successful photographer, whose life was about to be turned upside down.

She had been leaning on a five-bar gate, steadying her hand to get the perfect shot of the golden eagle circling overhead. The shot had been perfectly framed when an exotic voice of silk and smoke had disturbed her and the bird—which had swooped away out of focus. Caitlin had whirled round to remonstrate, but the words had died on her lips as she'd found herself staring at the owner of the voice.

Who wouldn't have been speechless if they were confronted by a man like Kadir Al Marara who had just appeared out of nowhere? A towering figure of a man, with jet-dark hair and skin the colour of burnished metal? Who stood out from the rusty browns of the Scottish landscape with the effortless dominance of a mighty mountain peak rising up in front of you? His black eyes had glittered with an expression she hadn't recognised, something she'd momentarily thought was haunted. It was only afterwards that she realised she had probably been right. He had studied her for a moment in silence, in a way which should have felt insolent but, instead, it had felt as if she had been waiting all her life for a man to look at her that way.

'I have disturbed you,' he had observed.

'Yes. You've frightened the eagle away.'

'It will return.' His voice had sounded assured, like no voice she'd ever heard before, and Caitlin had been fascinated by his exotic accent and the woven fabric of his words. When he'd spoken, it had sounded like poetry.

'Do you know about eagles, then?' she had asked him curiously.

The shrug of his shoulders had simply drawn atten-

tion to their power and Catlin had been so mesmerised
by the play of muscles beneath his fine suit jacket that
suddenly she hadn't cared whether or not he was an
ornithological expert or that her perfect shot was now
a distant memory.

'I know a great deal about falcons, for we have many
in my country, and all birds of prey share familiar traits.'

'What country is that?'

'Xulhabi.' Dark eyebrows had been raised.

'I've never heard of it.'

He had smiled again but this time the smile had been
tinged with darkness. 'Few people have.'

It hadn't been the most conventional of beginnings,
yet what had happened next had followed a time-hon-
oured pattern—although it had certainly never happened to Caitlin before. The atmosphere between them
had been electric. Off the scale. She'd wanted him to
touch her. She'd longed to feel his lips on hers and the
weave of his fingers through her hair. Even though she'd
tried to tell herself it was wrong to feel that way towards a total stranger, she hadn't seemed able to walk
away from him. She didn't remember what they'd talked
about, only that it had felt like the best conversation of
her life. At last, she had glanced at her watch, saying
she really needed to be on her way, but he had seemed
to share her reluctance to leave. And when she'd explained she was driving back to Edinburgh, he had offered to meet her halfway, for dinner. There was a place
he'd known...

She'd known it, too. The food was famous and the
views to die for. She remembered protesting that he
couldn't possibly get a table at such short notice, but

of course he had. He was a sheikh, wasn't he? A fact he had neglected to tell her during the delicious meal they'd barely touched or the ecstatic night which had followed. But she remembered that when they'd found themselves in a softly lit bedroom, he'd seemed to have second thoughts. Suddenly, he had drawn back, with a stricken look on his face, which should have warned her.

'I should go,' he had ground out harshly.

She should have listened to him. She should have let him beat a hasty departure—but desire had made her into a creature she barely recognised. A creature which had been hungry and yearning and craving her first experience of sex. But it had been more than that. She had wanted to comfort him, too. Had wanted to wipe that tortured look from his face and replace it with a smile again.

'Please. Stay.' Her words had been little more than a whisper but his answering kiss had told her that his doubts had fled. She remembered the way he had undressed her. His slow exploration and her own wondering reaction as he had taken her to the stars and back. Why, it had been so easy between them that he hadn't even noticed she was a virgin.

'Caitlin! There you are!'

She'd been so lost in her thoughts that she almost jumped out of her skin as Morag appeared in front of her, her greeting splintering Caitlin's erotic introspection. But something was missing, because the childminder didn't have her precious charge with her...

Caitlin blinked in alarm. 'Where's Cameron?'

Had Morag detected the sudden panic in her

voice—was that what prompted her perplexed frown? 'He's gone to play with little Rory MacIntosh today, remember?'

'Yes. Yes, of course. Silly of me. I don't know what I was thinking of.' Caitlin shunted out a sigh of relief but the concern hadn't left Morag's usually cheery face. And wasn't it an indication of her unsettled state that her first thought had been that Kadir must have somehow arrived here before her, to spirit Cameron away, right from under everyone's noses?

She looked at the kindly woman she'd known all her life and wondered how she was going to explain everything, knowing she needed to tell the ex-nurse the truth and nothing but the truth. She needed to tell *someone*.

'Have you got time for a cup of tea before you go?'

Briefly, Morag's eyes narrowed, before her face crinkled into a smile. 'Tea? I thought you'd never ask!

'If you would like to follow me, Miss Fraser?'

Caitlin nodded as she trailed the Sheikh's aide through the huge and intimidating house, aware of Cameron's hand held tightly in hers. Her own heart was pounding with apprehension but she thought her son seemed more excited than nervous. Maybe that wasn't so surprising. It wasn't every day a four-year-old got to fly on a private jet. Or to travel in the chauffeur-driven limousine which had been waiting for them when they'd touched down in London. She'd thought he might have been overwhelmed by a bombardment of new and very luxurious experiences, but the little boy had seemed to take them all in his stride.

'Where are we going, Mummy?' he'd asked at one point and Caitlin had known this was the moment of truth.

Looking directly into jet-dark eyes, which were so achingly like his father's, she had swallowed the lump in her throat. Just keep it simple, Morag had advised her earlier, and Caitlin had clung on to the ex-nurse's words like a lifeline.

'We're going to meet your daddy, Cameron. Remember, I told you about him last night? He's come to England from a land a long way away so that he can see you.'

This information had been received with a wriggle of Cameron's shoulders—a gesture which had hinted at anticipation rather than suspicion and Caitlin had told herself she was glad. But she hadn't really been glad, had she? She had been afraid of so many things—some vague, some not. Because what if he was as blown away by his father as she had once been? What if he looked at her and found her dreary and poor and dull in comparison to his more dazzling parent?

And now they were here at Kadir's home—or, rather, one of his many international properties, as his aide, Makim, had coolly explained. Caitlin had received this particular piece of news with a sinking heart. She'd been hoping the meeting might take place in another hotel. She had wanted the reassurance of being on neutral territory, knowing that at any minute she could just walk out with her son and that nobody would be able to stop her. But the car had brought them to the most beautiful house she'd ever seen—tall and white and elegant, sitting on a prestigious edge of London's Regent's Park.

In the extensive grounds she had spotted several stony-faced guards with suspicious-looking bulges in their suit jackets and walkie-talkies within easy reach. A couple of hungry-looking guard dogs had been patrolling the perimeter and she had successfully dissuaded Cameron from going up to pet them. It certainly wasn't the sort of place you could just walk away from.

She wished Morag were there to provide a little moral support, but the babysitter had been summoned away by a female servant and was currently in the kitchen drinking fresh mint tea.

'Mummy! Mummy, look!' exclaimed Cameron, letting go of her hand to point at a pair of stone cheetahs, which stood at either side of a huge set of ornate doors, as if they were guarding it. The two statues were gilded and their narrowed eyes glittered green, like real emeralds. Maybe they *were* emeralds, Caitlin thought faintly as Makim rapped on the doors, which were opened by a robed servant.

But she barely noticed the servant, she was too mesmerised by the man walking towards them, his eyes fixed intently on the small boy who was gazing around the stately salon in wonder. For a moment Cameron seemed too preoccupied by the vaulted ceilings, the jewelled chandeliers and mighty portraits of robed men on horses to notice anything else. But he must have gradually become aware that someone else was in the room and Caitlin witnessed the exact moment when it happened—the beginning of an instinctive love affair between her son and the father he had never met. And that knowledge was like a sharp blade to her heart.

She saw Cameron's eyes widen as Kadir walked towards him and the robed Sheikh crouched down so that his eyes were on a level with his child's. And, far from being disorientated by this exotically dressed stranger, Cameron just gazed back at him with all the bold curiosity of a child.

'Hello, Cameron,' said Kadir softly.

'Hello.' Cameron's voice didn't hold the slightest trace of shyness.

'Do you know who I am?'

'I think so.' There was a pause. 'My daddy?'

Kadir nodded. 'Indeed I am. And it is good to meet you at long last.'

He lifted his gaze to acknowledge the watching Caitlin and she felt another stab of apprehension as she met the fleeting look of anger in his eyes. She told herself it would soon pass and the best way to facilitate that was not to react to his rage—though her resolve was tested when Kadir rose to his feet and held his hand out to Cameron.

And Cameron took it.

'Shall I show you some of the pictures in the room and explain who they are?' the Sheikh was asking.

'Yes, please.'

It was astonishing—and Caitlin's lips flopped open. When it came to family, it had only ever been her and Cameron. He had never grown up in the bosom of a big, extended clan, with aunts and cousins and grandparents—perhaps that was what made him such a contained child. But there was no such containment now. He went to Kadir automatically and held up his hand to the Sheikh, who curled his olive-dark fingers around it. Almost jealously, Caitlin watched as they moved around the room in perfect symmetry, achingly aware of the physical similarities between them as they stopped in front of the largest portrait of all. Had she deliberately blinded herself to the parallels between them, because it had been less painful that way?

'Do you see that man on the horse…the man with the crown on his head? That is your great-grandfather.'

'*Is* it?'

'Indeed it is. He was a very famous warrior and also a great scholar. And you see those tall mountains behind him, with snow on them? They are the high mountain ranges of Xulhabi, where sometimes you can see snow leopards, if you are quiet enough and look carefully enough.'

'Can *I* look for them?'

'I certainly hope so.'

'Kadir—'

Caitlin had opened her mouth to protest. She wanted to tell him to tread carefully. Not to promise things which might never happen and fill a small boy's head with tales of snow leopards and warriors—but Kadir acted as if she hadn't spoken. As if she had suddenly acquired invisibility.

'Tell me, Cameron, do you play chess?' he was saying.

Cameron shook his head. 'I don't know what that is!'

'It's a game. A game with kings and queens and knights. It is a game of strategy and plotting—both of which are very necessary if you wish to get on in the world and which I will teach you.'

'Now?'

Kadir smiled. 'No, not now. Now I think it is time for you to have something to drink, for you must be thirsty after your long journey and we have a lot to do this afternoon.'

As if on cue—which Caitlin supposed it was—the double doors opened and a beautiful young woman appeared, with Morag following close behind, looking curiously unfazed by this unexpected turn of events. The moment Cameron spotted his childhood nanny, he gave a squeal of pleasure, running straight into her waiting arms as she scooped him up.

'Morag, Morag! I'm going to learn how to play chest!'

'Chess,' corrected Morag affectionately as she ruffled his hair.

'My daddy is going to teach me how to play!'

'Is he now?'

Morag looked across the room at Caitlin, a complicit look which obviously didn't escape Kadir's notice, for he drew his shoulders back and appeared to grow even more statuesque.

'Morag, why don't you and Cameron go with Armina?' he suggested evenly. 'I think she might have some Xulhabian candy for you to try with your drink. Have you ever eaten chocolate flavoured with rose petals and passionfruit?'

The sound of Cameron's whooped delight would usually have warmed Caitlin's heart, but her abiding emotion was one of *vulnerability* as he went off with Morag without a backward glance, leaving her alone with the man she was terrified of being alone with, for all kinds of reasons.

Not just because he had bonded with his son with an ease she hadn't been expecting. Or because his interaction with Cameron had left her feeling strangely excluded. No, it was more basic than that. It was the discovery that she was far from immune to him, even after all this time.

She still wanted him. She still ached for him. Still lusted for his lips hard on hers and his arms tightly around her, making her feel as if she'd found a place she'd been searching for all her life.

Without doing a single thing, Kadir Al Marara was making her feel things she'd thought had died a long time ago.

Today he was wearing soft robes the colour of mercury—their bright, silvery hue contrasting with the darkness of his hair and making his eyes appear as impenetrable as a night without stars. Outwardly modest, the outfit covered his body from neck to foot, but no material in the world could have disguised the undeniable power of the muscular body which lay beneath. With an effort, she forced herself to meet his black eyes, though the faint spark she read in them suggested he was perfectly aware of what lay behind her silent scrutiny.

She cleared her throat. 'I thought the meeting went very well.'

'I thought so, too. Though perhaps you were hoping for a different outcome,' he mused. 'For Cameron to take an instant dislike to me and refuse to see me again, perhaps?'

She shook her head. 'Of course not.'

'Really?' His dark brows shot upwards. 'Wouldn't it be easier all round if that were the case?'

She wasn't going to argue with *that*—how could she, when just having him this close was sending her senses into a spin, so that she couldn't think straight? For a moment she stared down at the rug, trying to concentrate on the precise patterns of cobalt and claret. Knowing it was wrong to feel like this and trying like mad to put a brake on her emotions. But when she looked up again she encountered a steely gleam of comprehension in the depths of his black eyes.

'Yes,' he observed. 'Desire can be extremely inconvenient, can't it, Caitlin?'

Her heart was pounding so loudly she was surprised he couldn't hear it. 'I'm sorry?'

'Please. Do not insult my intelligence. I may not have seen you for five years but if I held a mirror up to your face, you would behold the expression of a woman who wants me to kiss her,' he concluded softly.

'How dare you?' she said.

'I dare because it is the truth,' he breathed, and now his black eyes had grown smoky. 'And what is the point in playing games? Be honest, Caitlin. If not with me, then at least with yourself.'

She shook her head and when she spoke, the words felt like rocks in her throat. 'You seem to hold the truth in very high regard, but only when it suits you. Did your wife know what was going on the night you slept with me, Kadir?' she croaked. 'Maybe you even discussed it with her afterwards and gave me marks out of ten. I don't know. I don't have much knowledge of this kind of thing, but did you have what some people call an open marriage?'

CHAPTER FOUR

KADIR FROZE, FOR her choked and wounded words hurt and he had not expected them to hurt. Because his night with her and its aftermath had been nothing like her bald accusation about having an open marriage. In fact, she was so far off the mark it was almost funny, except that this was no laughing matter. And although he had ignored her earlier allegations of infidelity because he'd been angry about having been kept in the dark about his son, he realised he was going to have to explain himself.

But it wasn't easy. Few people knew the truth about his late wife and there was very little on record—deliberately so. It had been hushed up by the palace both during and after her short and tragic life. Nobody would ever have dared ask the question which Caitlin Fraser had just asked and if they had, he would have shut down the conversation immediately, telling them it was none of their business and that nobody had the right to question the King.

Yet Caitlin *did* have the right. He could see that. She obviously perceived him as some kind of monster—perhaps with good reason, he conceded reluctantly—and that unsavoury character assessment could not be allowed to continue, not if his ambitions were to be realised. He needed her to revise her opinion of him but he must tread carefully if he wanted her to agree to his plan to allow Cameron to travel to Xulhabi.

Because that was the reason she was here today. The only reason.

'It's true that I was legally married when I had sex with you.'

'You'll have to do better than that, Kadir,' she said coldly. 'Surely all marriage is legal?'

He gestured towards one of the most comfortable chairs. 'Won't you sit down?'

'I'd prefer to stand.'

'Please,' he said obdurately, for her face had grown very white and he felt a flicker of concern for her welfare. But despite her initial refusal, she sank into the chair and he thought how out of place she looked in this lavish setting, in her well-worn clothes. Yet there was something so gloriously accessible about her, too—for she possessed a luminous quality which transcended the faded jeans and heather-coloured sweater. Was it that jog to his memory which made him recall a similar sweater, peeled off to reveal a thermal vest beneath and the rare sound of his own laughter as he had wondered aloud how long it would take him to reach her bare flesh. Hadn't he laughed more during those twelve hours than at any other time he could remember? He felt a sudden tension in his body as he acknowledged how seriously he had underestimated the earthy appeal of humour.

And perhaps Caitlin had sensed the unwanted erotic path of his thoughts. Perhaps that was why she suddenly thrust her chin forward with a look of pure challenge, her eyes flashing ice blue fire.

'I've asked you a straight question and I'd appreciate a straight answer,' she snapped. 'So please don't bother concocting any lies just to spare my feelings.'

Kadir began to pace the priceless Persian rug, the walls of the huge salon suddenly feeling as if they were closing in on him. How long since he had examined this particular subject? How long since he had wanted to, or dared to? He shook his head. 'It is difficult to know where to start—'

'I don't think it's difficult at all,' she said, her face taking on an intense expression, as if someone were digging a sharp object into her flesh but she was determined not to show how much it hurt. 'I thought we were talking about your *wife*. That's the woman you were married to on the night you had sex with me, in case you need me to jog your memory for you.'

Kadir recognised that he deserved her condemnation for what he had done, yet surely nobody could condemn him quite as ruthlessly as he had done himself. How many times had he woken in the middle of the night, plagued by the guilt of his actions—a guilt compounded by the realisation that he had been powerless to stop himself.

This woman alone had the power to override his will and his best intentions—and wasn't that an ongoing threat which he needed to guard himself against?

He cleared his throat. 'I think it's important you understand some of my background before I get to the subject of marriage.'

'In Scotland, that's what we'd call time-wasting.'

'I was brought up as the only child of the King in very turbulent times,' he continued roughly. 'As the sole heir to the throne, a strong sense of duty was instilled in me since birth. My destiny has hung heavy on my shoulders for as long as I can remember. It still does.' He paused. 'It is the tradition of Kings from the Al Marara bloodline to marry women of similar pedigree—'

'Like breeding racehorses, you mean?'

He shot her a look. 'Look, Caitlin, we aren't going to get very far if you continue to be obstructive.'

The tone of his voice was suddenly censorious and Caitlin suspected it would have intimidated many people. But she was way beyond intimidation. Way beyond anything she recognised as normal behaviour. Instinctively, she realised she was fighting for something—she just didn't know what it was.

'All right. Go on,' she said stonily, though she couldn't imagine ever wanting to hear a story unfold less than she did this one.

'My father had broken the mould of his ancestors, who had always married for duty. Instead, he married my mother for *love*.' He bit the word out like a curse. 'And paid a heavy price for it.'

'What do you mean?'

'I don't want to go into details about my parents' marriage, Caitlin. Suffice to say it wasn't a happy one and certainly not one I ever wanted to emulate. I saw this thing called love as nothing but a trap—and one which I was determined never to fall into.' He gave a bitter smile. 'So when the time came for me to take a bride, I was perfectly willing to wed the princess who had been selected for me by the palace elders. To ac-

cept that we had much in common by virtue of our upbringing and royal blood, and to enter into the marriage
wholeheartedly.'

'And, was she beautiful?' she asked suddenly.

Kadir narrowed his eyes, for it struck him as a highly
irrelevant question. Until he remembered his last sight-
ing of his mother and the way plastic surgery had transformed her into a monster he barely recognised. And
wasn't that what women were all about? he reminded
himself bitterly. Shallowness and vanity, and a gro-
tesque desire to stay young for ever?

'Yes, she was beautiful,' he said slowly, but felt no
sympathy when Caitlin flinched.

You shouldn't have asked me, he thought. You should
never ask a question if you are unable to cope with an
answer you don't like.

'But for me, the most important thing was that she
wanted to be a royal queen and to be my wife. She was
eager to embrace all the challenges which came with
that role. Or so she told me.'

His words tailed off and he would have given any
amount of gold from his vast vaults not to have continued with this conversation. But Caitlin was looking at him expectantly, those wide blue eyes stirring
yet another forbidden memory, and he forced himself
to plough on with his sorry tale instead of recalling
how soft she had felt in his arms. 'But the reality was
that Adiya had no interest in ruling by my side. Nor in
learning how to be a good wife and, in time, to produce children who could inherit my kingdom. She had
but one interest...'

He couldn't bring himself to continue and shook his head, afraid that the words might choke him.

'Do you want to tell me what that is?' questioned Caitlin, breaking the fraught silence. Only now her voice contained some of the gentleness which had lured him in so willingly the first time he'd met her—and didn't that almost forgotten quality of sweetness tug painfully at his heart?

'And that interest was drugs,' he said baldly.

'Drugs? *Drugs?*' She stared at him at first with consternation and then with dismay. 'You mean—'

'I mean heroin, to be precise—although I understand she started off with cocaine,' he supplied bluntly. 'Don't look so shocked, Caitlin. Did you think the west had some kind of monopoly on addictive substances? Apparently, one of her cousins gave it to her to try and she liked it. A lot.'

'But didn't you… I mean, didn't you *notice* anything which might have made you suspicious, before you married her?' she questioned, seeming to have forgotten her antipathy towards him, at least for the time being.

'How could I?' he demanded. 'I had no experience of such things and our times together were limited because of *propriety*. Often she was veiled, her eyes downcast because of supposed *modesty*—at least that was my assumption, although afterwards I was to discover it was because the pupils of her eyes were like pinpoints and she wished to conceal that from me. Obviously, she was careful enough not to be really *high* during our chaperoned meetings before the marriage, but all such caution fled once the ceremony was over when I discovered I'd married a junkie.'

'Oh, Kadir,' she breathed. 'What on earth did you *do*?'

'What could I do? I wanted to help her, and for her to get better. I tried to ensure her supply was cut off, but somehow she always managed to get hold of more. I employed the finest addiction therapists in the world to treat her,' he added bitterly. 'But in order for someone to get better, they have to want to try. And Adiya didn't. She liked it too much. She liked lying around in a chemically induced state of bliss.' There was a pause and his words came out as a ragged whisper, as if the walls were listening. 'Until one day she overdosed, then lay in a deep coma until she died.'

For a few seconds, Caitlin felt as if she had been robbed of the ability to move, but it wasn't just that which made her feel as if her blood had turned to ice. Because Kadir's face had grown so ravaged that she wanted to get up and go to him. To put her arms around him and comfort him. But she was so shocked she didn't think she'd be able to get out of the chair and maybe that was a good thing, because it certainly wasn't her place to offer him solace at a time like this. Her mind was spilling over with questions she wasn't sure were wise to ask, but one was hovering like a dark spectre at the edge of a nightmare and refusing to be silenced.

'So when you...when we...when we had sex together,' she said haltingly, because she wasn't going to try to make it sound like something it wasn't, 'was she—?'

'Adiya was already in a coma, yes, and had been for some time,' he said harshly. 'She had no idea that I was breaking our marriage vows, although I knew, of course. And I...'

His words tailed off and the bitterness and self-recrimination which had darkened his face were hard to witness. And despite Caitlin's determination to remain impartial and not get sucked into some messy emotional quagmire, she couldn't seem to let the subject go.

'You should have told me,' she said, but she didn't tell him why. No need to explain that a lying and cheating man had provided the grim, grey backdrop to her own childhood—one twitch of its grimy fabric enough to send her mother into paroxysms of rage and regret. Because she and Kadir were not going to have the kind of relationship which invited unnecessary confidences of the type which revealed far too much of your vulnerability and inbuilt fears. 'If you'd told me I might have understood—and if I hadn't, then at least I might have felt as if my feelings had been taken into consideration, rather than you just ignoring them as if they were of no consequence. As it was, I felt second-best when I discovered the truth. As if I'd just been some vessel you had used to satisfy your lust.'

He didn't correct her. Had she wanted him to? She bit her lip. Yes, of course she had.

'Because only a very limited number of people knew about it,' he told her heatedly. 'Out of respect to Adiya's family we kept the illness completely under wraps. Even her death and subsequent burial weren't publicised, for the circumstances of her death would have carried with them too great a stigma for her family to bear, on top of her untimely death.' He paused, and when he spoke his voice sounded raw. 'And although I didn't tell you the whole story, I never made you any promises I would be unable to keep, did I, Caitlin?'

'You didn't tell me you were a king.'

'No, that's true—but was that relevant? It wasn't ever supposed to be anything other than a one-night stand—we agreed that at the time. It was supposed to be uncomplicated sex between two people. You even provided the condoms, if you remember.'

Caitlin's cheeks flushed, because hadn't that been another legacy from her own unhappy childhood? She had carried a pack of condoms in her purse since she was eighteen years old, because the thought of an unplanned pregnancy had been something she'd always feared and she was determined it would never happen to her. It had taken her another six years before she had opened that packet—maybe that was why they hadn't worked, maybe they had been out of date. She shifted awkwardly as she took her mind back to that night. What had Kadir said as his hand had slid between her thighs and he'd flicked a provocative finger against her molten heat?

'I can't offer you anything.'

No, he hadn't made any promises and now she understood why. But if he hadn't been able to offer her anything back then, what was he doing here now?

'So why did you come here?' she questioned. 'And why now? Why did you seek me out, Kadir?'

His eyes narrowed with unmistakable calculation. 'Can't you guess?' he said softly.

She shook her head. 'I'm not in the mood for guessing games.'

'I came for you because I have been fighting a war for the past two years and at times during that war, I was nearly beaten and broken and I lost... I lost much that was dear to me,' he husked. 'And sometimes, in the midst of the desert storms which raged around my troops, when my throat was raw and my body ached as if every bone I possessed had been snapped—I would think of you, Caitlin.'

'Me?' she verified, so surprised by his admission that she didn't stop to ask what it was he had lost.

'Yes, you.' He paused, his voice suddenly growing smoky as he began to walk over towards where she sat. 'I remembered how sweet and clean you had felt in my arms. I don't know how many lovers you'd had before me, but you made me feel as if I were the only one and, somehow, I could never quite forget that feeling.'

She stared at him askance as she took in the implication of his words. *How many lovers she'd had before him,* he had said, and the irony was that he had been the only one and he hadn't guessed. Not then and not now. She gave a wry smile. Maybe all that stuff about virgins being extra-tight was just the stuff of legend.

But the fact remained that he had come back because he wanted her—physically, at least. The watchfulness in his gaze had given way to a heated blaze, which Caitlin was discovering she was far from immune to, despite the shocking disclosure he had just made. Or had his bitter story made her want to offer him comfort of the most basic kind?

He was so close that she could see the pulse which flickered hectically at his temple and the way his lips had parted and it reminded her all too vividly of what she'd once had with him and still missed. No man before or since had ever made her feel the way that Kadir could and sometimes she thought that nobody ever could.

A sudden tension seemed to have descended on them, imprisoning them in a private and erotic world, and as Caitlin started to rise to her feet he reached out and pulled her into his arms. And she was so captivated by her own sense of longing that she let him. She looked up into the dark gleam of his eyes, unable to tear her hungry gaze away from them.

'I want to kiss you,' he murmured, his breath warm against her face. 'And you want that, too, don't you, Caitlin? You want it as badly as I do.'

It was a boast. A virile statement of fact, which couldn't be denied without inviting a charge of hypocrisy. And to her eternal shame Caitlin found herself whispering, *yes*—such a tiny word but one which managed to convey a broken note of yearning, which seemed to spiral up from somewhere deep inside her.

He framed her face with his hands and for a long moment just stared down at her. His eyes were like jet-dark lasers but his mouth was unsmiling as he moved closer still. As he lowered his head like a bird of prey Caitlin felt as if she were in rapid free fall, and when his lips touched hers, it was like landing in paradise all over again. A willing captive to the power of that kiss, she swayed as the Sheikh's tongue flicked into her mouth, tasting and exploring her as if he were determined to prove just how satisfying a kiss could be. And how ultimately frustrating.

Was that his intention? To kiss her for just long enough to make her respond. So that she would reach out her hands to anchor herself to him—encountering unfamiliar silk beneath her fingertips and realising how thin it was? She swallowed, rubbing at the hard flesh, his muscles so deliciously honed and powerful that she found herself longing to see him naked again. Yet despite her lack of experience, Caitlin could sense danger—only this time a much more subtle variety. She could feel her body starting to change and there was nothing she could seem to do to stop it. Her nipples were pushing urgently against the lacy scratch of her bra and that achingly familiar low coil of heat was beginning to unfurl deep inside her.

Was it the corresponding rush of desire which made her want to squirm her hips against his with unspoken invitation, as if she couldn't wait to feel him inside her again? Was that what prompted a soft murmur which was tinged with triumph? Caitlin swallowed as he smoothed his hands down over her undulating curves, as if he were reacquainting himself with her by touch alone. In just a few minutes it would be too late, because she recognised that he would go right ahead and do it to her. Here. Now. His finger was already straying to the button of her skirt. Another second and he would be skimming it down over her hips and pulling her panties down and...and...

No matter how much she ached for that to happen— she mustn't let it.

Because she was in jeopardy of reading too much into something which was purely carnal and she was much too vulnerable around Kadir, even after all this time. What chance would she have of standing up to him and fighting her corner if she submitted? How could she possibly safeguard her child if she was in thrall to the Sheikh and allowed him to weaken her with a single touch?

Her hands were trembling as she placed them over his powerful chest, tantalisingly aware of the thunder of his heart as she stepped away. Her own heart was racing so hard that she felt dizzy, particularly when she noticed the flare of frustration which backlit the ebony smoulder of his eyes. But she thought she could see something else, too. Was it surprise that she'd been able to resist him? She was pretty surprised herself.

Walking over to the window, she smoothed down her ruffled hair and adjusted her clothing before turning round to face him again, determined to keep her expression neutral.

'That's not going to happen,' she said.

'It very nearly did.' His black eyes glittered. 'You're surely not denying you wanted to?'

She shook her head. 'How could I? But want and need are two very different beasts, Kadir. I may have just fallen into your bed last time around, but there's too much at stake this time. We need...' She swallowed. 'We need to talk about the future. About what is best for Cameron—and I don't want any unnecessary complications.'

Her words filtered into Kadir's mind and he allowed himself to mull them over. A complication, was that how she saw him? As an obstacle or an impediment best avoided? Hadn't his mother thought exactly the same? He felt his blood turn cold but maybe it was easier this way. Easier to do what he needed to do. For all their sakes, but most of all for the sake of his child. Deliberately, he kept his next words casual and to most people they would have sounded like nothing more than an aside. But if any of his aides had been present they would have been instantly alerted to the anger which was simmering away inside him.

'I agree,' he said. 'The future is what matters now, not the past. I no longer wish to be a stranger to the child who shares my DNA and who will one day rule Xulhabi. Which means that Cameron will obviously need to spend time there.'

'You mean…in the holidays?'

'Not really. There is too much to be crammed into the odd week, here and there. He needs to understand his heritage and history, and be schooled in the many arts of kingship. I want to take my son back to Xulhabi with me, to introduce him to the land he will one day inherit.'

'Are you completely insane?' she breathed. 'Do you really think I'd let Cameron go anywhere with you until I've got to know you better?'

'Don't worry, Caitlin. I fully intend for you to accompany him. And before you look at me with such horror in your eyes, what possible objections could you have? You don't have a nine-to-five job and even if you did, I could easily compensate for any time lost at work.'

She was shaking her head. 'Well, I can tell you right now that's not going to happen. At least, not yet—and certainly not now. This has been a lot for a little boy to take in. Can you imagine what would happen if we flew him out to the desert? He'd be completely overwhelmed.'

'I can imagine it all too well, yes—but I don't share your opinion. I think any young boy would enjoy the experience.'

She glared at him. 'Well, I think it would make him lose all track of what is normal.'

Should he tell her that Cameron's life was never going to be normal again? Kadir felt almost sorry for her as he made himself appear to consider her words. But he could read the fierce determination which blazed from her blue eyes and so he made himself go through the motion of shrugging. 'Very well. If those are your wishes, then I suppose I will be forced to comply.'

'They are,' she said, looking at him with suspicion— as if she couldn't quite believe he was agreeing so easily. 'We can start out slowly,' she added placatingly. 'Little by little, bit by bit. We'll get some dates in the diary. How does that sound?'

'Wonderful,' he said sardonically, reaching towards a bell to summon a servant. 'I shall leave you now to get ready for dinner. We will eat early so that Cameron can join us.'

'Dinner?' she echoed blankly.

'Of course.' Kadir felt a rush of pure pleasure as he registered the discomfiture on her face. 'You agreed to stay for a couple of days, didn't you? Surely you haven't forgotten?'

He could see her long neck quiver as she swallowed, before appearing to regain some of her customary fire. 'I'm not going to reconsider letting Cameron go to Xulhabi with you,' she warned. 'If that's what you're thinking.'

'Fortunately my thoughts are something you will never be privy to,' he answered smoothly. 'Though I cannot deny how disappointed I am that you have stubbornly refused to see the matter from my point of view.'

CHAPTER FIVE

'DO WE *HAVE* to go, Mummy?'

Caitlin gritted a smile which hopefully conveyed a sense of calm she was far from feeling. 'Of course we do, darling. We'd only ever planned to stay in London for a couple of days, remember? And someone needs to get back to Scotland to feed your hamster!'

With fingers which were trying very hard not to tremble, Caitlin did up the final button of Cameron's brand-new coat, having to battle feelings of pride and resentment as the soft cashmere brushed against her skin. It suited him very well, as did all the other clothes Kadir had insisted on buying from one of the city's best-known stores—a bizarre shopping trip, by any stretch of the imagination, mainly because they had shut the shop especially for him. And although natural maternal pride made Caitlin acknowledge how cute her son looked in his new outfits, she'd been aware of feeling as if she had somehow failed him by bringing him up in such frugal circumstances. How she had blushed when one of the many fawning shop assistants had gingerly picked up Cameron's old anorak and questioned whether or not madam would be keeping it. Madam had declined, of course, though she'd been unable to rid herself of a stupid sense of disloyalty as she did so.

If only she could dislodge the uncomfortable feelings which were swirling around inside her, because this weird trip to London was making her realise that, physically at least, she was still in thrall to the father of her child. One touch from the arrogant Sheikh and she'd been all melting compliance. How weak was that? But you don't have to see him again for a while, she told herself fiercely—and there was nothing to stop her building up some kind of immunity to him.

Giving Cameron an encouraging smile, she ruffled his hair. 'The plane will be leaving soon and so we'd better go and find your…daddy to say goodbye.'

'I don't want to say goodbye!' Cameron shouted, in a tone she'd never heard him use before.

'It will only be for a little while,' came a velvety voice from the doorway and Caitlin looked up in alarm to see Kadir standing there, his quiet tone of reason worlds away from the look of fury he was flashing at her. How long had he been standing there? she wondered. Long enough to have heard Cameron cooing that this house was nice and warm? The implication being that the fire which blazed in their little sitting room in Cronarty never quite managed to eliminate all the icy drafts which whistled through the house in the dead of winter.

'Daddy! Daddy!' Cameron ran across the salon and hurled himself at the Sheikh, flinging his little arms around the legs of the golden-robed figure who laughed indulgently at his son.

And once again, Caitlin felt like the outsider. The

usurper. The spoilsport who wouldn't allow what father and son both clearly wanted—for Cameron to accompany the Sheikh to Xulhabi. She had been forced to listen while Kadir had waxed lyrical about his land. His poetic words had created vivid images of the country's capital city of Azraq, where apparently a pair of red-footed falcons—the rarest of all the falcons—lived amid the soaring golden towers of the palace. He had regaled Cameron with tales of horse-riding and archery and how, when he was just seven years old, he had learned to sword-fight.

'Can *I* learn to sword-fight, Daddy?' Cameron had asked plaintively and Caitlin's natural fears had made her wonder aloud about danger, before Kadir had given her a withering look, which had scorched across the room over his son's dark head.

'You think I would put him in *danger*?' he had demanded. 'Don't you realise that in some countries boys learn to sword-fight as young as five?'

'Not in Scotland, they don't!'

'Then all I can say is—it's a pity for Scotland!'

And that was how it had gone on. Their two-day stay in the Sheikh's luxury home had been difficult, to say the least—well, for her anyway. Not for Cameron, that was for sure. He had been happy enough to participate in the dizzying array of treats which had been planned for him and had quickly adapted to the bizarre concept of discovering that his previously unknown father was a powerful king of the desert.

Maybe children weren't as aware of status as adults were, she thought. Cameron hadn't commented on the fact that Kadir's house was so big you could have fitted ten of their tiny cottages into its extensive space. Or that countless servants could constantly be seen gliding past, or silently lurking in corners—always ready to do the Sheikh's bidding. And he certainly hadn't raised any objections when they were whisked around London in yet another fancy car, with a professional guide who had been hired for their stay. Though in truth she thought that Kadir could have qualified for guide status himself, he seemed to know so much about the city.

'Xulhabi does a lot of trade with the world's major cities—so naturally I make it my business to know as much about them as possible,' he had replied, in answer to Morag's question. But he had followed this up with a smile which had made the middle-aged nanny melt—as usual. A smile which was also doled out on regular occasions to Cameron.

But never to her.

For her he reserved his best icy expression—a look as chilly as the wild winds which howled around the shores of Cronarty. Was he still angry that she had refused to allow Cameron to go back to Xulhabi with him, when surely he must realise that her reasons were perfectly valid? Or were they?

Weren't they based on fear? A nebulous fear she couldn't quite grasp and certainly couldn't articulate?

It had been a shock to find out about his late wife's drug addiction and her subsequent coma, but in a way it had added to the confusion of her feelings. The reasons for his infidelity no longer seemed so black and white, but that didn't change the fact that he had kept his identity and marital status secret from her. She just needed some time alone to make sense of all she had learned and then to come to some acceptable decision about their future.

Standing beside their small suitcase, Caitlin waited patiently while Cameron said his final goodbyes, but she could do nothing about the twist in her heart as the Sheikh gently disengaged Cameron's arms and crouched down to look deep into his son's eyes.

'We will see each other again very soon, my boy,' he said gently. 'I promise.'

Cameron nodded fiercely and before Caitlin knew it, the limousine was outside waiting and ready to go.

She was quiet during the journey to the airfield, where the plane was waiting to take them back to Edinburgh—and the fact that the aircraft was much bigger and shinier than the one they'd flown in before obviously cheered Cameron up. But Caitlin's heart remained heavy as they were taken through to a roomy cabin at the back of the aircraft and told to make themselves comfortable. Busying herself, she buckled up her son's seat belt, then watched as he gazed through the window at the thick clouds outside.

As the engines began to power into life, she turned to Morag, needing some kind of reassurance. Wanting someone to tell her that everything was going to be okay—because why was some inexplicable sinking sensation in her stomach making her feel strangely *doomed*? 'That didn't go so badly,' she observed quietly, more in an effort to convince herself. 'Considering how difficult it *might* have been.'

'No. Not bad at all. I like him,' Morag added, and then, after a pause, her brogue grew very gruff. 'I like him a lot.'

Caitlin wondered if she was imagining the faint reprimand behind the nanny's praise, or was that just her own paranoia getting the better of her? A childish urge to grit out a litany of complaints about the Sheikh was making her face feel hot and flushed, but she suspected that Morag would have no truck with her objections. Why, she'd even been understanding when Caitlin had briefly explained that Kadir's wife had been in a coma for most of their short marriage, though she didn't explain why. If she had been expecting the middle-aged nanny to make a negative judgement about his illicit night with her, then she was destined to be disappointed.

'Poor man,' had been Morag's only comment.

Poor man? What about *her*? Caitlin had wanted to ask. Didn't her feelings come into it? Didn't Morag realise how difficult it was going to be to adapt their lives in the light of the Sheikh's dramatic reappearance? Already she was fretting about how many days of the year Kadir would expect to see his son.

But Morag's words forced Caitlin to take a step back and try to look at the matter from a different perspective. It had made her realise that Kadir was not all bad, just as she was not all good. And that insight didn't sit particularly comfortably with her. As soon as she got back to the island, she resolved to contact him. She would tell him that they needed to work out—in as civilised a way as possible—a timetable for future meetings. She needed to get past her own feeling of having been duped by his omission to tell her about his marital status. She had to move on from the way it had made her feel when she'd discovered it. They all did.

Yet still her nagging feeling of disquiet wouldn't shift.

The plane provided every conceivable luxury and they were offered delicious drinks, fruit and pastries—but although Cameron and Morag tucked in with alacrity, Caitlin had no appetite for hers. Instead, she found her gaze wandering around the cabin, noticing the exquisite surroundings of the royal aircraft. It was fitted out with sandalwood furniture adorned with Xulhabian insignia and featuring those two striking sitting cheetahs.

A glossy US magazine was lying on one of the tables with the Sheikh's stark image dominating the cover and Caitlin could do nothing about the sudden leap of her heart as she picked it up. Enigmatic and darkly regal, Kadir was wearing a traditional white garment, and on his arm sat a falcon—its beady eyes gleaming with faint menace at the camera. Caitlin flicked through the pages and started reading the article, which heaped praise on the 'notoriously private' ruler's attempts to establish a peaceful state in the desert region after so much warfare. It spoke of his fierceness and his bravery in battle. It was hard not to be impressed and she didn't want to be impressed. In an attempt to distract herself from the glowing accounts of his diplomatic triumphs, she found herself studying a map of Xulhabi, and realising for the first time just how big a country it was. What must it be like to be King of such a place? she wondered. To have grown up knowing that, one day, all that would be yours—along with the weight of responsibility which came with such a role.

And Kadir expected Cameron to share that weight! For a boy of not yet five, surely that was too great a burden for him to have to carry?

They were over an hour into the flight before Caitlin began to sense that something was wrong and it all began with a polite enquiry made to one of the beautiful Xulhabian stewardesses, whose response was mystifying. Did she *really* not understand a simple question about what time they were expected to land in Edinburgh? Instead, the woman flashed a non-committal smile before scuttling off towards the front of the plane and Caitlin was left feeling perplexed. Moments later she glanced out of the cabin window to discover that now the clouds had cleared, her view was unimpeded, but instead of the russet tones and undulating views of Scotland, she could see…

She remembered a long-ago holiday before her son had been born and her breathless wonder as she had gazed out of the cabin window.

She closed her eyes as if to convince herself that her vision must be playing tricks on her, but when she opened them again, the scene outside was exactly the same.

She told herself not to be so stupid. Of *course* those snow-capped mountains weren't the dominating peaks of the Alps. How *could* they be?

But it was funny how you could convince yourself something wasn't true even when you knew it was. She allowed another fifteen minutes to pass, but the stunning vista below them showed no sign of magically giving way to the much lower peaks of home.

Caitlin felt dizzy.

Sick.

She wanted to blurt out her fears to someone—anyone—but Morag was busily doing some colouring with Cameron and she didn't want to alarm him. Besides, what if her fears were unwarranted? What if…?

But you wouldn't need to be an aviation expert to realise that they were way off course and Caitlin rose unsteadily to her feet. Walking to the front of the plane, she found the stewardess in a cabin almost as large as the one in which she'd left Cameron and Morag. Her head had been so full that she hadn't really noticed it while passing through at the beginning of the journey, but now she became aware that this area of the plane was almost palatial. It boasted rich velvet sofas and lacquered lamps. And a very old writing desk on which sat a beautiful emerald and silver paper knife, which was fashioned to look like a dagger.

'Could you please tell me what's going on?' Caitlin said, her crisp question belying the growing dread at the base of her stomach.

The stewardess's stunning eyes became shuttered. 'Going on?' she echoed.

Caitlin bristled because it was adding insult to injury to have the woman treat her as if she were some kind of idiot. 'I know we're flying off course,' she accused, keeping her voice deliberately low. 'And I'd like an explanation of just what is happening!'

'I'm afraid I cannot—'

'It's okay, Rania. You can leave us now.'

The velvety voice from behind them could have come from only one source and Caitlin whirled round—shock and fury washing over her, along with something else. Something powerful and all-consuming. Something which felt uncomfortably like desire as her disbelieving gaze took in the dominating figure who was standing in the doorway.

Kadir Al Marara, all-powerful and muscular, his hawklike features enigmatic.

Only his black eyes moved—for they were watchful and glittering as they raked over her. Suddenly Caitlin was reminded of the falcon she'd seen on the magazine cover—dark and still and potentially deadly—and a whisper of foreboding shivered over her skin as she returned his hooded gaze.

She was vaguely aware of Rania exiting the salon as fast as her high-heeled shoes would allow, leaving her alone with him, and her heart thumped painfully against her ribcage as she tried to make some sense out of what she was seeing.

'I don't understand,' she said. 'What are you doing here?'

He shrugged. 'Up until a few moments ago, I was flying the plane.'

His deliberate misunderstanding of her question tipped the temper she hadn't even realised she'd been holding in check and the words suddenly exploded from Caitlin's lips. 'I'm not interested in your piloting skills!' she hissed, clenching her fists by her sides as she experienced an overwhelming desire to pummel them hard against his powerful chest. 'I'd like to know why we haven't landed in Scotland.'

'Because we aren't flying to Scotland.'

'Yes, we are! You know we are! That's what we agreed!' she babbled stupidly and then her voice rose. 'Where are you taking us?'

'You know exactly where I'm taking you, Caitlin,' he informed her silkily. 'To Xulhabi.'

'You can't,' she said, her voice dropping to a disbelieving whisper. 'You can't do that. That's…that's *kidnap*!'

Kadir stared at her, steeling himself against the suddenly vulnerable tremble of her lips and the widening of her sky-washed eyes. 'That's one way of looking at it, I suppose,' he drawled. 'I would prefer to think of it as purposefully reuniting with my family.'

'How dare you?'

'I dare because I have no choice,' he told her simply. 'I owe it, not only to my people, but also to my son—to allow him to set foot on the soil of his forebears. And he cannot do that if his mother is proving unreasonably resistant, and he is stuck on some remote island far away, unable to access the skills he will require when he rules Xulhabi.'

'Will you stop saying that?' she demanded. 'You make it sound as if it's a done deal, when Cameron might not want to be the heir to your wretched country! He might want to be a…a farmer—or a vet!'

'I'm afraid that's not going to happen, Caitlin,' he replied, with a steely air of finality. 'It cannot happen. His destiny is ordained.'

She gasped as the import of his words must have dawned on her—because suddenly she was launching herself at him like a wildcat, all that vulnerability vanished as she began to pummel her fists urgently against his chest.

'Caitlin—that isn't going to do you any good,' he protested, though without the kind of conviction he might have expected. Because wasn't there a part of him which was actively *enjoying* her anger and her outrage? Wasn't the heavy throb of his erection an inevitable response to having her this close to him again and breathing in her particular scent, which made him think of soap and honey and wild Scottish moors? A sudden wild rush of yearning pulsed through him and he longed to tangle his fingers in the bright banner of her hair, but he forced himself to ignore it and confront the problem in hand. 'Stop it.'

'No! I won't stop it!' she declared, with another blow to his chest, which he barely felt, even though she was obviously putting all her weight behind it. 'Not until you direct the pilot—or do it yourself—to turn this wretched plane right round and take us to Edinburgh!'

'Sorry,' he said, with an adamant shake of his head. 'I can't do that.'

Did his words suddenly take root or did she just realise that he meant them? Was that why she stopped her rhythmic pummelling so he thought she might have ceased her attack? But, no, his guess was way off mark—or maybe he had underestimated her. For she was swooping towards the writing desk with all the force of a heat-seeking missile. And, moments later, she was back, brandishing the jewelled paper knife above him.

'Take me back home immediately, or I'll scar that beautiful face of yours!' she declared.

He wanted to kiss her. He wanted that so badly. And, judging by the hungry look which suddenly flashed from her eyes, so did she. As he caught hold of the wrist of the hand which held the jewelled dagger he could feel her tremble with something which didn't feel remotely like fear—and the instinctive parting of her lips was as powerful an invitation to kiss her as he'd ever seen. Though what did *he* know of a woman's true desires?

Kadir couldn't deny that the temptation was as powerful as any he had ever experienced, but he resisted it as he had done so many times before. Because this wasn't about sex. It was about power. His power—and hers, too. He wondered if she understood that she was in the rare position of having something he wanted. Something he hadn't been expecting to find—and which felt like the most precious gift he'd ever been presented with.

His son.

Within the veins of his child ran the true blue blood of a future king and nothing could change that unassailable fact—not Caitlin's wishes, nor his own. After so many years of warfare and disruption, the royal line of Xulhabi was more important than any one person's personal desire or agenda. It was his duty to provide an heir for his people and now it was within his ability to do so. Only Caitlin Fraser stood in his way.

Kadir knew he couldn't afford to let Cameron out of his sight for a moment because he didn't trust her. And why should he when she had seemed so eager to block all his attempts to get to know his son better? When she had spoken so primly and parsimoniously about getting *'some dates in the diary'*. As if she were some middle-aged matron scheduling in a dinner party! For all he knew, she might take it upon herself to 'disappear'—and, although he had the resources to find her, to play a cat-and-mouse game while he hunted her down would be disruptive and unpleasant for everyone concerned. Especially Cameron.

'Drop the knife, Caitlin,' he said silkily.

'I *won't*!' She wriggled within his grasp. 'Not until you agree to turn this plane round and fly us back home.'

'Drop the knife,' he repeated, trying to ignore the insistent throb of his erection and the even more insistent desire to crush his lips down over the soft quiver of her own and lose himself in her kiss. 'Drop it right now, or I shall be forced to have one of the palace doctors meet us when we land and declare you mentally unsound to care for our son.'

His words must have hit home for her grip loosened and the sound of the knife bouncing off the polished wooden floor sounded deafening as she stared up at him, her mulish expression now tinged with wariness. 'You wouldn't dare?'

'Oh, I would. I would stop at nothing to get my way on this. Believe me when I tell you that—even if that is the last thing I want to do. Because you are testing my patience just a little too far.'

'You're a fine one to talk about testing patience!' she flashed back. 'Think about it! It's not just me and Cameron you're strong-arming back to your country— there's Morag, too, over whom you have no power at all! What has she done to deserve all this? Don't you think that the first opportunity she gets, she'll be on the phone to the Foreign Office telling them what you've done and demanding they get us back home as soon as possible? And they'll come after you—you can bet your sweet life they will! The British government will lock you up and throw away the key. Hopefully for ever! Because kidnap is kidnap—no matter how high-born and mighty you are!'

'Your imagination is remarkably vivid but essentially flawed—since I suspect you might find that Morag's sympathies are very much in tune with my dilemma. She has certainly been very accommodating thus far,' he mused. 'Which begs the question: Can't you do the same—at least for the time being? Don't alarm our son by an unnecessary display of hysteria, Caitlin. Accept the situation for what it is and try to make the best of it.'

'How can I possibly do that?' she demanded. 'When I don't know even what "the situation" is!'

'But you will. In time,' he said smoothly. 'There are many issues we need to address about the future and they will be discussed in more detail when we arrive at my royal palace.'

She stared at him. 'So I don't really have a choice, do I?'

He shook his head. 'No, Caitlin. I'm afraid you don't.'

CHAPTER SIX

'You are pale, Caitlin.'

'Of course I'm pale! I've just had a severe life shock! I wasn't expecting to be hijacked while I was in the air and then flown to some wretched hellhole of a place against my will!'

'I would not describe the royal palace of Xulhabi as a hellhole and we are not going to conduct this conversation in an inflammatory manner, if that's what you're hoping.'

Kadir's voice was as soft as the warm air which scented the courtyard—the rustle of his robes the only sound Caitlin could hear above the distant tinkling of a fountain. Outside the sky was the most beautiful she'd ever seen, a deep indigo canopy punctured by stars so bright, it almost dazzled the eye to gaze upon them. But gaze on them she did, because anything was better than having to look Kadir in the eye and try to pretend that he wasn't making her pulse-rate soar with anger, outrage and that annoying ever-present throb of desire. She needed to concentrate on what he had actually *done*, which was an affront, by anyone's standards. And didn't his high-handedness and outrageous flexing of power cancel out a little of the understanding she'd been starting to feel towards him?

'What I'm hoping,' she spat out, 'is that you see sense. That you'll understand you can't just go around *kidnapping* people like some *despot*. If you let the three of us go home, before any irretrievable damage is done, then we'll just draw a line in the sand and move on.'

'I think you need to compose yourself,' he said, with infuriating calm. 'Did you like the clothes which I arranged to have sent to your suite?'

Caitlin wished he wouldn't try to change the subject, especially one which was difficult to answer without sounding *grateful*. Yet how could she fail to like the delicate tunics she'd found neatly lined up in one of the wardrobes? In rainbow colours, the fabrics were so fine that they felt like a cloud to the touch. As a gesture of defiance she had wanted to ignore the whole lot of them and just dress normally—but, despite the palace's super-efficient air-conditioning, she couldn't possibly wear her trademark sweater and sensible tweed skirt in this hot climate. So she had reluctantly slipped on one of the tunics while silently despairing at the way it managed to make her feel so ethereal and so...*feminine*. And much more aware of her own body than was usual, which, given the company she was in, could be regarded as distinctly dangerous. 'They're okay, I suppose,' she said ungraciously. 'Or at least they'll do for the time being.'

But Kadir didn't react to her clumsy rejection of his offerings, he just slanted her another devastatingly cool smile. 'Look, why don't we take a walk around the palace gardens before dinner?' he suggested. 'The grounds are very beautiful when they're floodlit and a little fresh air might make you feel better.'

'I'll tell you what would make me feel better—getting someone to drive me back to the airfield so that I can jump on a plane and not have to keep looking at your smug face!'

'Oh, Caitlin, Caitlin,' he murmured. 'Repetition is never an attractive quality. You really are going to have to find something different to talk about. No harm is going to befall you, Morag, or our child, of that I give you my word. And you wouldn't really want to fly back tonight, would you? Not when Cameron is tucked up so peacefully in bed.'

Caitlin's pulse accelerated. She wished he wouldn't *do* that either. Talk to her in that cool and measured way, as if she were an out-of-control hysteric and he were Mr Reasonable—when actually he was the one who was guilty of kidnap. An accusation she had flung at him on more than one occasion but which seemed to keep washing over him. In fact, he hadn't actually responded to *anything* she'd said to him, so far. It was like trying to demolish a brick wall by hitting it with a feather.

Maddeningly, Kadir had been nothing but diplomatic from the moment their motorcade had arrived at his impressive palace, whose soaring towers, golden cupolas and domed windows had taken her breath away yet also managed to daunt her with its sheer size and majesty. Not wishing to distress Cameron, she had forced herself to behave with exaggerated politeness towards the man who had brought them here without permission—and her own acting ability had taken her by surprise. Why, to the casual observer, she and the

Sheikh might have seemed like a pair of amicable partners as he led her through the seemingly endless marble corridors and pointed out the many attractions of
the royal palace along the way, sounding once again a
bit like the seasoned tour guide he had seemed back
in London.

'This is the recreational library, and in here are volumes in English of just about every classic book ever
written, but my staff will always be able to get their
hands on anything you can't find.'

'Thank you,' she had replied stiffly, though her eyes
had widened with anticipation on seeing rows and rows
of beautifully bound books in a stunning room which
overlooked a dramatic sculpture garden.

'And here is the film room.' He had opened the door
so that Caitlin could peer in at a luxurious space with
twenty comfortable seats and a screen as large as her
local cinema at home. 'I have arranged for many suitable children's movies to be available for Cameron,
that's if you are happy for him to watch them.'

'Thank you,' she had repeated, because it had seemed
churlish to do otherwise. But that thin veneer of civil-
ity she was presenting to the outside world didn't hint
at the bitter truth which was raging inside her like a
boiling cauldron.

*That she felt as if she had walked into a living night-
mare...forced into unwilling proximity with a man she
resented and desired in equal measure.*

Yet, Cameron had shown no such reserve, happily
greeting whoever passed him and generally behaving
as if to the manor born. As if he were used to being
surrounded by a gaggle of doting servants. As if, on

some fundamental level, he understood that one day all this would be his. How could she, his mother, have then created a scene—grabbing at the arm of the first senior official they met and demanding to be allowed to call the British Ambassador before being ferried home?

To Caitlin's fury, Kadir had also been right about Morag, who hadn't reacted to being spirited off to a far-off desert country with any of the indignation Caitlin might have expected from the middle-aged matron. In fact, she had actually smiled and remarked that nothing like this had ever happened to her before and she was quite enjoying the adventure—not to mention the prospect of spending an unspecified amount of time in a royal palace, especially one which had such beautiful gardens.

'But we're being kidnapped!' Caitlin had snapped as they had been shown into the large part of the palace which had been given over to them and whose north-western light Kadir had insisted was the best.

'Well, you keep saying that and I suppose that is one way of looking at it, dear. But Cameron doesn't seem to mind and neither do I. And the boy really *should* get to know his father, Caitlin, especially since he's a king.' Morag had given a sigh which had sounded positively girlish. 'And a desert king, at that. Why, it's like something out of a fairy story!'

Caitlin remembered blinking at her in astonishment. Whoever would have put the normally staid nanny down as a romantic?

But Morag had recently retired to her own suite of rooms which adjoined Cameron's—citing jet lag as her excuse to miss dinner and have an early night and leaving Caitlin alone with Kadir in a way which felt almost premeditated. As if he were planning to target her when she was on her own and at her most vulnerable.

Was he?

Because if that was the case she must not let him.

They needed to talk, yes. They needed to discuss 'the situation', as he had described it so infuriatingly on the plane. What they didn't need—or rather what *she* didn't need—was to wander around the dreamy-looking palace grounds, all washed in moonlight, which had painted the statues a glowing silver. Because wasn't the faux romance of her surroundings making her have thoughts which were very troubling? Thoughts which involved Kadir taking her into his arms and kissing her again—except that this time she wasn't certain she'd be able to stop it from going any further. She let out a heavy sigh. Her body felt so *responsive* when he was close—as if it had been programmed to react that way around him, and all the reasoning in the world didn't seem to make the slightest difference. And wasn't her physical vulnerability a warning sign that she needed to be on her guard against her own feelings, for fear of where they might take her?

Which was why she shook her head in answer to his suggestion—no matter how much the potent perfume of the frangipani cried out to her to inhale it long and deeply. Because she needed to be strong. She must never forget that she was on *his* territory, and he was a king. An all-powerful king with hot and cold running servants and what seemed like no contact with the outside world. And she was going to have something to say about *that*.

'No, thanks,' she said, as she heard a nearby clock beginning to toll the first of eight chimes. 'I'd rather just go straight into dinner. For this discussion about our future which we're supposed to be having.'

He inclined his robed head, his black eyes glittering and unreadable. 'As you wish. Please. Follow me.'

Kadir kept his eyes straight ahead as Caitlin accompanied him, though it was difficult not to be diverted by her athletic grace, which made the filmy material of her robe cling rather distractingly to her bottom as she walked. Stepping back, he ushered her into one of the less intimidating dining rooms, where a table had been set with crystal and gold and festooned with crimson roses. He watched as she glanced around the room, as if committing it all to memory, and once again he found himself mesmerised by the red-gold gleam of her hair, which was highlighted by the fractured gleam from the chandeliers.

He felt his pulse quicken. In truth, he could hardly believe she was here—or that his audacious plot had proved quite so effective. Such dramatic and high-blown behaviour wasn't his usual modus operandi—and he was aware that by behaving in such a way, he was helping perpetuate the common myth of desert kings being nothing but primitive men who simply stormed in and took what they wanted. Yet Kadir had seen his actions as his only option and in a crazy kind of way it had felt *right*. For hadn't he secretly enjoyed playing the powerful macho sheikh and showing the pale Scottish redhead exactly who was boss? And hadn't she brought such a drastic measure on herself? If she hadn't been so intransigent in her dealings with him, they could have worked out a far more conventional way for her to arrive in his homeland, with young Cameron in tow.

But in reality he couldn't really envisage any other solution than this. Even if she had been amenable to future visits, would he have readily waved goodbye to his son—even temporarily—and left him behind? How did he know he could trust her—and that she wouldn't try to keep his son away from him again, as she had already done for four long years?

Once again he felt a flicker of regret as he thought about how much of Cameron's young life he had missed. But coupled with that regret was a complex cocktail of feelings which did not sit comfortably with him, for he could not deny his own part in what had happened. Just as he could not deny that his desire for Caitlin was as intense as ever. It still pulsed through his body each time he saw her, despite the fact that she made no effort to adorn herself.

And she never had done, he reminded himself grimly. If she had, he might have been on his guard when he'd stumbled across her on that wild Scottish moor.

Memories came back to taunt him. The first time she had touched his naked body, he had felt as if he might dissolve. And when he had joined with her... He swallowed. When he had spread wide her glistening folds to thrust deep inside her warm and liquid heat, he hadn't known where he ended and she began. Many times he had wondered if that was the effect she had on all men.

Yet he didn't want to feel like this. As if he could explode with frustration every time she came close—a visceral need to be inside her again.

So what was the secret of her enduring appeal? he

wondered. Was it the flame of her hair, which contrasted so vividly with that pale, freckled skin? Or eyes which were the colour of a Xulhabi spring sky—the most delicate blue you could imagine? Clear, soft eyes, fringed with pale lashes. When he'd met her, she had been ignorant of his status—something which had made her unusually candid in his company—and that had been rare enough for him to be charmed by her.

Was it that simple charm combined with a powerful sexual awakening which had stamped her memory so indelibly on his mind all these years? Which had haunted him during the long years of battle so that his promise to himself had been, *If I survive this, then I must see her again.*

It had proved a powerful enticement—powerful enough for him to ignore the wound which had gushed from his thigh and the fact that he had been forced to go without water for almost two days. He had nearly died during that last battle—that long and bloody battle, during which he had lost his one true friend and ally.

Rasim had been like a brother to him. Yet despite his strength and seeming indestructibility, he had lain broken and mortal as he'd breathed his last in the Sheikh's arms. Kadir remembered staring down at the waxen death mask of his friend in shock, and the reality of that awful image had almost taken him under. But a vision of Caitlin had sustained him as he'd hovered on the edge of consciousness—her pale face and bright hair never allowing him to slip into timeless oblivion. No wonder he hadn't been able to shift her from his mind afterwards, for he had associated her with his own personal resurrection.

He made no further comment until they were seated on opposite sides of the table and he observed her glancing somewhat askance at the gleaming array of solid golden knives. 'Just work from the outside in,' he advised, with a sudden flicker of benevolence.

'I *know* that,' she replied, with force. 'I may live in the north of Scotland, but I have actually visited a restaurant before!'

He gave a sudden laugh and saw a startled servant turn and look at him, before quickly composing himself and busying himself with the drinks. And now Kadir found himself wondering how long it was since he had laughed out loud.

'Forgive me for my presumption,' he murmured.

'It's something I'm fast coming to associate with you.'

'It comes with the job—and the territory. People neither wish nor expect their leader to prevaricate. It makes them feel safer if he is prepared to go out on a limb to make the right decision,' he acknowledged drily.

'And do you?' she challenged. 'Always make the right decision?'

'Not always,' he said, in a surprisingly candid admission. 'But on balance, yes.'

'How unsurprising that your ego is so healthy, Kadir.'

Unapologetically, he shrugged and waited until the servant had filled their goblets and various dishes of local delicacies had been placed in front of them, then dismissed the hovering staff.

'So,' he began, once they had both picked at their food without much interest. 'You are happy with your accommodation, I hope?'

She gave a little *tsk* at this and her fork clattered down onto her plate with a gesture of irritation she didn't bother to hide. 'I'm hardly going to complain about a suite of rooms the size of a football stadium, am I? Or the fact that whenever I so much as cough, a servant comes running to find out whether there's anything I need.'

He inclined his head. 'I will take that as an affirmation.'

'Kadir,' she said, giving an impatient sigh as she took a sip of water. 'We can't sit here pretending that nothing's happened. I want us to go home. All of us,' she added pointedly.

He spread his hands out, the palms opening towards her in an expansive gesture. 'In theory, nothing is preventing you from leaving.'

'In theory, yes. But you are perfectly aware that I don't have the means to get myself to the airport. And although most of your servants speak English, every time I ask someone if they can arrange to have a car sent for us in the morning, they act mystified.' She drew a deep breath. 'Although I notice they understand perfectly well when I request another jug of water or for Cameron to have a slightly firmer pillow!'

'Caitlin—'

'And another thing,' she continued, barely giving herself time to draw breath. 'Every time I've tried to use my phone, it's failed to connect. And the Internet isn't working either.' She glared at him. 'Almost as if there was some malevolent blocking device at work!'

'Nothing malevolent about it, I can assure you,' he returned smoothly. 'The signal is notoriously bad here. We're in the middle of the desert, for heaven's sake!'

'My point exactly. So will you please get us out of here?' she said, from between clenched teeth. 'ASAP.'

Kadir carefully set down his goblet and leaned back to study her. 'You know I can't do that, Caitlin.'

'Can't, or won't?'

Unwillingly Kadir felt another smile tug at his lips, because her feistiness was exhilarating. Uncomfortably so. He could feel the heavy pulse of his blood and his groin had grown so hard that it was impossible to think straight. Difficult to concentrate on anything other than how much he hungered to see the splendour of her naked body again and to feel her in his arms. But he forced himself to put such distracting thoughts aside, because lust would weaken him. Would detract him from his primary purpose.

'All I'm asking for is time for Cameron to get to know me. I would like to do those things I promised him. To show him the palace stables and take him to the capital of Azraq so that he can see the mighty golden dome for himself. To teach him chess and educate him about his ancestors. There is a whole rich culture here of which he is ignorant. Is it not fair for the child to re-alise that he is part Xulhabian as well as part Scottish?'

She seemed to give this some consideration. In fact, she picked up a glistening slice of iced white peach and chewed on it thoughtfully, before speaking. It was her first obvious enjoyment of her food she had been given, he noted, and he was surprised at how good that made him feel.

'And after that you'll let us go?' she said.

His benevolence vanished and Kadir sighed, because either she wasn't getting the point or she was refusing to see it. Or perhaps he had been a little too vague. Surely she must have realised that he wasn't just going to let them go. To do what? For Caitlin to return to her old life and perhaps seek out a man willing to marry her and for their son to be brought up as an ordinary islander? His mouth twisted. Did she really imagine he would allow his only child to think of another man as a father figure?

Perhaps he needed to demonstrate to her that there could be no other father for Cameron.

And no other man for her.

He lifted a damask napkin to his lips. 'If that's what you want, then of course I will allow you to leave. All I'm asking is that you allow a little time for you and Cameron to get to know Xulhabi better.'

'How much time?' she demanded.

He studied her with calculating eyes. 'Shall we say a few weeks?'

'A few *weeks*?'

'That seems reasonable.'

'To you, maybe.'

'So you're agreed?' he said, his air of finality bringing to an end her objections.

She shunted out a breath, but the faint nod of her head indicated that she had finally seen sense. 'I suppose so.'

'Good.' He was careful to keep any sense of triumph from his voice. 'And now, let's talk about something else. We've spoken about so many things—'

'You can say that again,' she said darkly, and he might have smiled, if he weren't determined to discourage interruption.

'But one thing is still glaringly absent,' he continued smoothly.

She leaned forward, reaching towards a silver dish of salted almonds. 'Oh? And what's that?'

'So far all the information seems to have been coming from my direction. Isn't it also time you told me something about your past, Caitlin Fraser?'

CHAPTER SEVEN

CAITLIN, HER HAND hovering over a bowl of almonds, stilled. 'My past?' she echoed.

'That's right,' he agreed.

'And…' she licked her dry lips, laying the blame on the salty almonds '…what do you want to know exactly?'

'It's not too difficult. The usual things. Where you were born and how you spent your childhood.' Kadir shrugged. 'It has occurred to me that I know practically nothing about the mother of my child.'

She pushed the nuts away and glared at him. 'Didn't your spies find out for you when they were tracking me down?'

'My emissary came back with very little concrete information,' he admitted. 'He discovered you were living on a small Scottish island and had borne a son who bore an uncanny resemblance to me, and that your mother had died many years before. Other than that, nothing. There was no mention of a father on your birth certificate.'

'You looked at my *birth certificate*?'

'Why wouldn't I?' he questioned coolly. 'In the same

situation, wouldn't you have endeavoured to gather as much information as possible?'

Caitlin returned the burn of his black gaze, her heart pounding hard beneath her thin tunic. She felt fear and she felt dread, which easily eclipsed her outrage that he had gone poking around in her past. Because everyone had a secret they would prefer the world not to know, and he was about to discover hers.

If she chose to tell him.

She had never talked about it with anyone, mainly because she'd never got close enough to someone to want to confide in them. Or for the layers of her painful past to be peeled away, leaving her exposed and vulnerable. Except for this man, of course. She'd been closer to Kadir than to anyone, but it had only been a very fleeting intimacy and it had only ever been physical. It made her feel a little foolish now to realise just how spiky and unrounded she must be as a human being, that she should have considered the twelve hours she spent with Kadir as the most significant twelve hours of her life. How sad was that?

But those hours had produced a beautiful child. His child. And didn't that make his question not only understandable, but reasonable? Didn't he have the right to know something about her, as she did him? And he had already obliged by confiding in her the bitter truth about his marriage.

Nonetheless, it wasn't easy to address a subject she'd spent much of her life trying to forget, and a moment or two passed before Caitlin was ready to speak. And wasn't it funny how something could still hurt, even after all these years? It was like poking at a scar you thought had completely healed, only for it to surprise you by starting to bleed again.

'There was no mention of my father on the birth certificate because my mother didn't name him,' she began.

His eyes became shuttered so that all she could see was the ebony gleam which shone from between the thick lashes. 'Why not?'

She paused. *Say* it, she told herself. Just say it. It's not a big deal in this modern world, not like in the old days. But it still felt like a big deal to her. 'Because he already had a wife and other children and he begged her not to. In fact, he did his best to try to persuade her not to give birth to me in the first place. But fortunately, she chose to ignore his advice and incentives.' She gave a bitter laugh. 'It was the one sensible thing she did throughout the whole of my childhood.'

'Caitlin.'

The shock on his face was almost palpable as he said her name but Caitlin couldn't resist a dig, even though the comment probably hurt her far more than it could ever hurt him. 'Perhaps now you'll understand my shock when I discovered you were married.'

'I am only just beginning to realise the impact that discovery must have had on you,' he said gravely, before giving a heavy sigh. 'So your mother had a brief affair with a married man?'

Just like you.

He didn't actually come out and say that, but the words hung in the air just as clearly as if he had. Caitlin could feel her cheeks begin to burn, knowing that she didn't have to justify herself because this wasn't about her—they were supposed to be talking about her mother. But she went ahead and did it anyway.

'It was nothing like what happened with us. Because she *knew* he was married. At least she was given the choice about whether or not she wanted to get involved,' she retorted, and saw him flinch—but strangely, his obvious discomfiture gave her no pleasure. 'She used to work for him, until she got pregnant, and then she left, supposedly by mutual agreement, though basically she was told to go or she would get fired. But the affair continued for years, based on a promise my father made that he would divorce his wife and marry my mother. Which he never did, of course.'

Kadir's eyes narrowed. 'And did you ever meet him?'

'Only once, but I was too young to remember much about it, or maybe I just blocked it out. Apparently, he wasn't exactly thrilled to have a child who had been born out of wedlock—a child with the potential to upset his pampered life as a city boss. And then it all turned sour. My mother started to get needy. She...' Caitlin swallowed, because this bit she *did* remember. She wished she could have forgotten it, but the mind could prove remarkably stubborn when it came to selective memory. 'She started to make demands. Started setting ultimatums, which were never met, so she'd set another one, and then another. Then she threatened to ring his wife and tell her about me...'

'What happened?' he questioned, as her words tailed off.

'He met up with her one day and told her he had already confessed to his wife.' She vividly remembered the use of the word confession. A word associated with sin. Had that association contributed to Caitlin's failure to interact successfully with the opposite sex, once she'd come of age? She didn't know and right now it wasn't particularly relevant. All she knew was that Kadir was still looking at her with curiosity burning from those ebony eyes—and she was going to finish her story. She had to—because what good would it do if they continued to be strangers to one another? 'He told her he never wanted to see her again, nor me.'

Now why had her voice started wavering? Why did she care about the rejection of a man who had never wanted her born? She cleared her throat, drank some pomegranate juice and continued. 'And he didn't. See me, that is. We were living on Cronarty by then. My mother never really recovered from his rejection. She kind of went to pieces—and when we heard that he'd died very suddenly she insisted we go to the funeral to pay our respects.' Caitlin shivered, wishing she'd brought one of her thick Scottish sweaters down to dinner with her after all.

Her mother had been slightly drunk and very determined—and no words of Caitlin's had been able to make her see sense. At eight years old she'd been powerless to prevent her mother from taking her along to the service, where she had made the discovery that her birth father had been a very rich and powerful man indeed. She remembered the sickly scent of the white lilies which had been massed outside the huge church and the startled faces of the black-clothed mourners when they had appeared. Sobbing, her head dramatically covered with an ebony mantilla, her mother had dragged Caitlin towards the door but someone must have worked out who they were.

'And?' Kadir prompted.

Caitlin bit her lip. It had been the single most embarrassing event of her life. 'We weren't wanted there—obviously. Two women stepped forward. They were the most beautiful women I'd ever seen. They must have been a decade or so older than me. Their faces were icy and their eyes were filled with contempt. I remember they barely opened their lips as they spoke. They told us that if we didn't leave immediately of our own accord, then they would call security. I discovered afterwards that they were his daughters, too. But legitimate, of course.'

'By the desert storm!' To her surprise, Kadir had brought his fist crashing down hard on the table so that all the golden cutlery rattled. 'Why didn't you tell me this before?'

'When was I going to do that, Kadir?' she demanded. 'We didn't exactly do much talking at our first meeting, did we? Even if we'd had time, it's not really the best conversational ice-breaker in the world. And when you found me again, you were too busy being angry and taking control of all our lives for me to want to bring it up. Anyway, what difference does it make?'

Kadir shook his head and for a moment he stared straight ahead in silence, as the tall candles guttered on the table between them. He couldn't put it into words, but it *had* made a difference. He felt the unexpected clench of his heart as he imagined her pain and humiliation at being ejected from the church. He could picture only too well the inebriated mother who had dragged her there. If he had been in full possession of those facts about her past, would he still have brought her out here, without her permission? He felt a stab of guilt. He didn't know. He could never know. But surely he could show her a little consideration from here on in.

'It is late and your eyelids are growing heavy,' he said softly, rising to his feet. 'I think we've said everything there is to be said for tonight. Come, Caitlin, I shall accompany you to your suite.'

'Thank you.' For a moment she looked a little taken aback by his kindness and then, in a flurry of ice blue silk, she got to her feet.

They walked towards her suite mostly in silence, though occasionally he took the time to point out a particularly beautiful artefact and, once, to pause at the circular window which, at least twelve times a year, framed the full moon. She made all the appropriate responses to his remarks but he thought she seemed preoccupied. And when they finally reached her door, Kadir could see uncertainty clouding her freckled face, which somehow pierced his conscience far more than her defiance had done earlier.

'Can I ask you something?' she said.

Unexpectedly, the corners of his lips twitched. 'You haven't held back so far.'

'Even though nothing I say ever achieves what I want it to achieve?' she returned, before sucking in a deep breath. 'But this is different.'

'Oh?'

She twisted her ringless fingers together before looking him straight in the eye. 'It's important for us to monitor how well Cameron settles in, because I'm sure that even you...'

Her words tailed off and when she looked at him, there was something beseeching in her gaze.

'Even I, what, Caitlin?' he prompted sardonically.

'If we discover he's desperately unhappy and home-sick. If, for example, he misses Hamish—'

'Hamish?' A sudden spear of jealousy shot through him. 'Who the hell is Hamish?'

'His hamster. Mrs McTavish is looking after him at the moment. They have another two hamsters so it's no bother for her.' She hesitated. 'But if, for any reason, he really wants to go home after a few days, then you'll let him?'

Kadir knew what she was doing and thought how clever she was. For he could hardly lay claim to wanting to be a good father if he then did the very thing which would make his child unhappy, could he? Slowly, he nodded, picking his next words with care. 'How can I refuse such a request?' he questioned. 'All I ask in return, is that you will do nothing to try to influence the child in his decision.'

Their eyes met in a long moment. 'Touché!' she said softly, and then she smiled.

It was a rueful smile but it was the first one he'd seen since re-entering her life and the effect of her soft curving lips momentarily captivated him. Her ice blue gaze pulled him in like a magnet and suddenly Kadir found he couldn't look away. And neither, it seemed, could she, for she was staring at him as if she were in a trance.

Clad in the traditional tunic of a high-born Xulha-bian woman, she looked both strange and yet deeply familiar. Her long red hair tumbled all the way down her back and Kadir longed to feel those glossy tendrils trickling through his fingers once more.

He sensed that if he kissed her now he would meet no opposition. And he wanted that. He wanted that very badly. But with desire came the certain knowledge that Caitlin Fraser had once possessed the power to make him lose control, and he couldn't risk that happening again. Not right now. Not until he had achieved what he'd set out to achieve.

And that was the bottom line. This was all about Cameron and Xulhabi, not him. His own foolish and transitory desires must be sublimated for the time being. He must determine his son's claim on the land he would one day inherit and nothing could be allowed to divert him from that aim.

Because while desire ebbed and flowed like the tide, he must be nothing but steadfast when it came to the continuity of his bloodline.

CHAPTER EIGHT

CAITLIN COULDN'T SLEEP.

Despite lying between linen sheets as fine as gossamer on a spacious bed which could have slept a family of four, she was disturbed by images of Kadir's searing black gaze as he had bade her goodnight after dinner last night. She couldn't believe that she had confided in him so honestly and told him more than she'd ever confessed to another living soul, considering it to be nobody's business but her own. Even Morag knew only the very barest facts about her background.

But Kadir had lulled her into a frank disclosure about her mother and father, before walking her to her suite of rooms and then leaving her in a swirl of kingly finery. The atmosphere around them had felt loaded with tension and for a moment she'd thought he was going to kiss her again. And, when that had failed to materialise—hadn't she convinced herself she was relieved? That had been total self-delusion, of course—because she would have liked nothing more than to have been cradled within the warm power of Kadir's embrace.

After checking on a sleeping Cameron, she had gone

to bed but the night provided no immunity against forbidden thoughts, and suddenly she found herself wide awake and at the mercy of her senses. She kept remembering how it had felt to have Kadir's hands and lips on her body—brushing with devastating accuracy over her belly and breasts. At one point she awoke, her nipples aching and her skin bathed in sweat, aware of an aching deep inside her which wouldn't seem to go away. In the end she gave up chasing that elusive slumber, shutting herself in the bathroom while it was still dark outside, and standing beneath the power shower as she blitzed her body and her hair. By the time dawn was glimmering on the horizon, she was already dressed and raring to go.

Her nerves felt jangled as she waited for Cameron to wake up, forcing herself to lie back against the pillows on the huge bed and watch as the garden was gradually lit by soft shades of rose and gold. She had given Kadir her word she wouldn't attempt to influence their son in any way, but she couldn't believe her little boy would want to stay in this remote place, so far from everything he knew. She couldn't *let* herself believe it—because that offered a glimpse of a future which terrified her. A future in which her own position was uncertain. What place would she have in a culture like this? Would she become the faceless Englishwoman unwillingly tolerated because she was the mother of the future King? She swallowed. She would give it a few days, as promised, and then quietly ask Cameron what he wanted to do. And when, as expected, he complained of being homesick, she would convey his sentiments to Kadir.

The ticking of the Ottoman clock was hypnotic and she must have dozed off, because when her eyes snapped open it was fully light and she could hear the distant bustle of life in the corridors of the palace. Hastily, Caitlin barged into the adjoining suite of rooms to find Cameron's bed...

She blinked in dismay.

Empty.

Morag was in the next room and at first Caitlin didn't recognise her because her ample frame was clothed in a flowing robe instead of her usual elasticated trousers and comfy top. She was sitting alongside a veiled female servant as the two of them companionably folded unfamiliar garments into a neat pile. They looked up in slight alarm as Caitlin came bursting in through the door.

'Where's Cameron?' she demanded.

Morag smiled. 'Ach, he was awake ages ago! Running around as excited as I've ever seen him. The Sheikh has taken him down to the stables.'

'Has he had breakfast?'

'The Sheikh said they would eat upon their return.'

'Oh, did he?' questioned Caitlin, trying to keep her voice light. 'You should have woken me.'

'The Sheikh said that you must be tired after your long journey and we should let you sleep.'

'I'll bet he did.'

She wanted to ask Morag if she realised that she sounded like a tame parrot with 'the Sheikh' this and 'the Sheikh' that, but Caitlin realised that would be taking her temper out on the wrong person. And besides, she needed Morag on her side. Turning to the servant who was seated alongside her, she tried to summon the semblance of a smile. 'Do you think you could show me the way to the stables?'

'Certainly, mistress. I will go and find Makim and ask him.'

She returned minutes later with Kadir's aide by her side and he chatted equably as he led Caitlin from the suite, even though his attempts at conversation were met only with politely monosyllabic responses because she didn't trust herself to say what was really on her mind. At least—not to him.

But she was unprepared for her emotional reaction when eventually they tracked Cameron down to the state-of-the-art stables on the eastern side of the palace and Caitlin felt as if she were looking at the scene through the wrong end of a telescope, because it was so…unexpected. And never before had she felt quite so redundant as a mother. Or so excluded.

Her son was being held by his father and his little arms were locked tightly around his father's neck as Kadir crooned softly to the most beautiful horse Caitlin had ever seen, its glossy dark coat gleaming like a polished nut. It made such a perfect tableau that she almost wished she had her camera with her so that she could have captured the image, but her hands were trembling so much she doubted she'd have been able to hold the camera. Because all she could think was, *why had the Sheikh spirited away her son without telling her*?

Despite the heat she felt cold. An outsider. Someone who had no right to be there. A dark and nebulous fear began to creep over her as she took a step forward. Did they hear her enter? Was that why Kadir suddenly turned and saw her, a brief flare of something she didn't recognise in his black eyes. Was it *resolve*?

'Caitlin,' he said softly.

She hated how her skin shimmered in response to the way he said her name as he bent to put Cameron down so he could come running over to her, black hair flopping into his eyes.

'Mummy! Mummy! Daddy's going to get me a pony so I can learn to ride! He says we can go and choose one!'

He looked up at her expectantly and Caitlin's heart sank as she bent to kiss his soft little cheek. What could she say? *You won't be needing a horse, darling, because hopefully you won't be here long enough to ride it.*

But even she acknowledged that as a mean and self-ish thought. Just as she acknowledged that if she re-acted in any way other than positive, it would be like announcing to a class of excited youngsters that there was no such thing as Father Christmas.

'That's lovely, darling. I hope you said thank you,' she replied gamely.

'Indeed he did,' purred Kadir. 'The child's manners are faultless.'

And even though inside Caitlin was glowing with maternal pride at the compliment, she couldn't shake off her resentment towards the man who was making it. She felt manipulated and she wasn't quite sure how to liberate herself from that feeling. 'Good to know,' she said tightly, before turning to her son. 'Shall we go and have some breakfast now?'

Breakfast was obviously a poor substitute for being amongst a stable full of snorting thoroughbreds but

Cameron nodded and obediently took his mother's outstretched hand.

She met Kadir's eyes, hoping that her gaze managed to convey the fact that she was seriously cheesed off. And confused. And out of her depth, like a novice swimmer who had stupidly jumped into the deep end of the pool. 'Please excuse us.'

'Of course.' He inclined his head. 'Makim will show you the way back. I have some work I must attend to, if you don't mind?'

'I don't mind at all,' she said truthfully.

Because Kadir's company was the last thing she felt like right now. At least with Makim she wasn't plagued by doubts and feelings she wished would go away. Stupid, conflicting feelings which made her stupidly susceptible to the Sheikh's potent charisma, even though she resented his high-handed and deeply patrician attitude.

With Cameron chattering beside her, they returned to their expansive quarters and, once seated at the dining table, Caitlin forced herself to try and eat some breakfast. But she felt disorientated as she peeled an orange for her son and fanned the segments onto a plate. It occurred to her that she was still in a sense of shock. Everything had happened so quickly. Everything still *was* happening so quickly and she was just sitting back like a spectator and letting it. Maybe it was time she stopped being so passive around the mighty Sheikh, and started being a little proactive.

She and Cameron spent much of the morning in the swimming pool and, after lunch, Caitlin took her son on an extensive tour of the palace and the grounds.

They played ping-pong in the games room, watched a cartoon about the travails of a mermaid with very similar hair colour to her own, and were just about to sit down to an early dinner with Morag when Kadir surprised them by making a sudden, unannounced appearance—heralded by an over-the-top display of deep bowing from the attendant servants. Annoyingly, Caitlin's heart started beating out a primitive tattoo of excitement as his dark figure dominated the entrance to the lavish dining room.

'Do you mind if I join you?' he questioned.

What could Caitlin say, when any words of objection would have been drowned out by Cameron's enthusiastic squeals and Morag's smiling agreement? 'Of course not,' she said coolly. 'Though you mustn't let us disrupt your routine if you prefer to eat dinner at eight?'

The brief flicker of his black eyes indicated he'd got her message loud and clear, but he continued walking towards the table, his robes flowing like rich cream over his hard body. 'Ah, but any disruption is not only necessary, but welcome. I realise I must be open to change if I am to carve out precious time with my son,' he replied smoothly, high-fiving Cameron as he slid into the seat beside him. 'And don't all the pundits say it's better to eat earlier, rather than later?'

Caitlin opened her mouth to reply, then shut it again. He had an answer for everything! She forced herself to eat some of the delicious food on offer and to listen as Kadir talked Cameron through some of the unfamiliar dishes on the menu. At other times he chatted affably to Morag, who started telling him about her love of historical fiction, which, to his credit, he managed to look enthusiastic about.

Meanwhile Caitlin sat there in frigid silence and all while Kadir's black eyes mocked her, as if daring her to say something. But she didn't want to make small talk. She wanted to talk to him about rules of behaviour concerning their son. About setting down guidelines he must agree to conform to while they were here. Basically, to assert her maternal rights and make him realise that he couldn't just push her into the shadows.

She was relieved by the time the meal ended and Morag began to gather up her young charge to get him ready for bed. She had just ushered him out of the room, when Caitlin turned to Kadir, who was also preparing to leave. 'Could I have a word with you, please?' she said, in a low voice.

He frowned. 'But you've had the opportunity to speak to me all evening, Caitlin, and you didn't say a word.'

'That was different. I didn't want to have this discussion in front of Cameron and Morag.'

'Why not?'

She shifted uncomfortably on her feet and flailed around for a coherent explanation which wouldn't seem as if she were only pursuing her own selfish interests. 'Because... Because...'

'Look.' Lifting his arm so that silk concertinaed away from his wrist, he shot an impatient glance at his golden wristwatch. 'I have phone calls I need to make and I'm pretty tied up for the rest of the evening and most of tomorrow. Why don't we schedule in a time for Wednesday afternoon, when you might have worked out what it is you want to say to me? Come to my office. Shall we say three p.m.?'

She wanted to protest that now he was making her feel like a brainless fool, but instead Caitlin found herself nodding her agreement. Perhaps it made sense to address it that way. She would write down all her concerns in a list, just as she did when she took Cameron to the doctor. She would state her wishes calmly and clearly, so there could be no misunderstanding. And hopefully Kadir would be sensible enough to take note of them all. 'That sounds fine,' she said stiffly.

But she felt far from fine as she was led through the labyrinth of marble corridors at the appointed hour. Her nerves had been growing extremely frayed these past two days, and now her mouth was bone-dry with nerves—despite the fact that she'd gulped down a glass of iced water barely ten minutes ago. Was she really going to have the guts to lay down the law to a man like Kadir? Yes and yes and a million times yes. He might be *the* Sheikh, but he certainly wasn't *her* Sheikh.

The monarch's section of the palace was very different from her own quarters. It felt like a smooth and carefully oiled machine, with its quiet sense of purpose and people with files diligently going about their business. Passing through several outer offices, she was eventually shown into a lavish vaulted room, which was obviously the sole preserve of the King.

The room was empty and quickly she looked around, searching for clues about the man who inhabited it. A large desk dominated one side—a jewelled pot of golden pens contrasting rather comically with a computer and an array of phones. Over by some of the tall windows which overlooked the gardens was an informal area containing a luxurious divan, as well as a couple of ornate chairs. On a gleaming table stood a huge cut-glass bowl of orange roses, and on top of an inlaid bureau stood a small, framed photo of a man. And that was the only personal touch in a largely neutral room. No images of his mother were on show, she noted. Nor yet, any of Cameron.

Caitlin peered at the photo. Darkly handsome, the man wore traditional desert garb and looked about thirty. She wondered if it was an early photo of Kadir's father, but somehow it seemed too modern.

'Ah, you're here.'

The deep resonance of Kadir's voice interrupted her examination and Caitlin quickly straightened up, adjusting her tunic as she did so and wishing it were as easy to modify her racing heart. 'I am.'

Kadir waited for her to ask about the photo he'd seen her looking at, but felt a huge wave of relief when she didn't, because right now he had no desire to delve into the past. Instead he concentrated on the slightly unbelievable fact that she was here, for no woman had ever been permitted entry into what was essentially his sanctum. As a space, it had always been sacrosanct—his and his alone, apart from the occasional necessary visit by his aides. But he had wanted to meet her away from the distraction of their son and his nanny, or the curious glances of the palace servants.

'So, Caitlin,' he said coolly. 'You wanted to speak to me?'

'Yes.' She cleared her throat. 'I think we need to clear a few things up.'

He raised his eyebrows. 'Please. Elaborate.'

'Well, obviously I can't stop you from just dropping in at mealtimes—'

'That's very generous of you,' he commented sardonically.

'But in future, I'd prefer if you didn't just take Cameron riding like you did on our first morning here, without having run it by me first.'

'Your objection being *what* exactly?'

'You should have woken me.'

'Should I? You'd had a long and emotional journey the previous day and had shown no sign of stirring. But Cameron wanted to make sure you were okay before we went off together, and so he looked in on you and told me you were still sleeping. On balance, I decided it was best not to disturb you.'

'Or maybe you just wanted to stake your claim on Cameron? To get him on his own so you could start influencing him.'

'Influencing him to do *what* exactly, Caitlin?'

She shrugged, biting her lip as if trying to hold back an unwanted tremble. 'Who knows? To turn him against me, perhaps. To push me out of the picture.'

He frowned. 'You really think I would do something like that?'

'How should I know what you'd do, Kadir? You put us on a plane and flew us halfway across the world—I wouldn't put anything past you! It was his first morning in a strange place. And in a palace, no less. He's never been anywhere like this before and it could have been very confusing for him.'

'But he seemed perfectly fine with it. And Morag agreed with my suggestion.'

'Of course she did. She would pretty much agree with anything you said because you've got her wrapped around your little finger!'

'The same certainly cannot be said of you,' he observed wryly. 'So tell me, Caitlin—what's *really* troubling you?'

She gave a frustrated wiggle of her hands. 'Surely you must realise that if you start promising him things— it's only going to create problems. Don't you think this kind of treatment is unbearably seductive for a small boy? Promises of ponies and palace pools. So that when he goes back to his other life—his *normal* life, on a tiny island in the middle of the Minch—it will be unbearably difficult for him to settle back in.'

Kadir met the fierce accusation of her gaze and an unexpected feeling of sadness washed over him as he listened to her heated accusations. Couldn't she see that everything was going to be different from now on? Was she really that naïve? 'But this *is* your new normal, Caitlin,' he said gently. 'Better get used to it.'

Some of the indignation left her eyes and was replaced by a flicker of apprehension. 'What are you talking about?'

He picked his words carefully. 'People already know you are here—that much was inevitable. My aides tell me that much comment has been made of Cameron's resemblance to me and that was inevitable, too. His identity cannot be kept a secret much longer. Sooner or later, the world is going to find out that he is my son and heir.'

'And doesn't he get any say in the matter?' she demanded. 'Don't I?'

He shook his head. 'This is not a question of who says what. He is my son. His destiny is written in the stars. Do you really think Cameron can just go back to his previous life and pretend nothing has changed? That he can carry on living on Cronarty?'

'But the island is as safe as houses,' she defended. 'The people there are very loyal. They won't make any kind of fuss, if I ask them not to.'

'Oh, Caitlin.' He shook his head. 'Now you really *are* being naïve. We aren't talking about an ordinary child. We are talking about the welfare of a future king and there are security issues at stake here. Big ones. My country is now at peace, but for many years we have been fighting a perilous war—and wars always create enemies. Don't you think Cameron will be vulnerable to threats from outside sources once his identity is known? Isn't that something you ought to consider before you take him back to a place where he will be largely defenceless against malevolent forces?'

He could see her lips folding in on themselves, as if she was trying very hard not to cry and that was not his intention. He didn't want to make her cry—and not just because he wasn't sure he was equipped to cope with a woman's tears. 'Caitlin—' He held out a hand towards her but she shook it away.

'I never meant for this to happen—to give birth to a future king!' she burst out. 'But you didn't give me the choice, did you, Kadir? You didn't tell me about all this royal stuff, because if you had, I could have turned around and run in the opposite direction!'

He stared at her, and as he saw the pain in her eyes something dark and unknown nagged away at... He furrowed his brow. Not his conscience, no. Something else. Something buried away deep inside him, but an instinctive measure of self-protectiveness made him quickly push the thought away. 'Yes, I should have told you,' he agreed huskily. 'But I couldn't. It wasn't even a deliberate decision—it just happened that way. And even if I *had* told you, do you really think you would have walked, Caitlin? Don't you think I tried myself and couldn't manage it?'

She shook her head so that fiery strands of hair flew around her narrow shoulders. 'That's...irrelevant.'

'No, it's not. Not then and certainly not now. It's still there, this...*thing* between us, and it won't seem to go away.' He shook his head. 'Don't you think it's time we stopped fighting it, Caitlin?'

She stared at him. 'You're talking about...desire?'

'Of course I am. What else could it be?' he husked. 'You must know how much I want you. And you want me, too. I can see it in your eyes and in your body. Why else do you shiver whenever I come near? And don't you think I shiver, too? Well, don't you?'

Caitlin swallowed as his black eyes glittered, his words firing up everything she already felt for him and igniting the smoulder of feelings she'd been trying to keep at bay. But this wasn't a fairy tale, she reminded herself bitterly. Nobody could accuse Kadir of building her up with false hopes. He wasn't professing love, or emotion. He was spelling out exactly what he felt for her, which was lust—no more and no less. It shouldn't have been enough and yet somehow...

She closed her eyes. Would it be so wrong to be intimate with the man who had fathered her child? Wasn't she allowed to enjoy her body, like other people? Last time around she'd been vulnerable. She'd started to believe she was falling in love with him but this time that wasn't going to happen. Why would it when Kadir had expressly told her that love was a trap?

But sex. Sex she could do.

'So what do you propose we do about it?' she asked him, her voice coming out all breathy.

He stilled, as if her easy assent had taken him by surprise, but quickly he reasserted his mastery. 'I'll tell you exactly what we're going to do. First we're going to get rid of the view.' He walked across to the wall and the touch of a button made electric blinds float silently down over every window, dimming the light so that it looked like a gilded and exotic boudoir. 'And next I'm going to kiss you.'

He was walking towards her, his black eyes glittering, his steps slow and deliberate. He was giving her time to change her mind, Caitlin realised. But somehow, making her wait was only increasing the hunger she felt for him, so that by the time he stood in front of her and pulled her into his arms, she was almost on fire with need.

And suddenly he was kissing her and she was kissing him back. Kissing him hard—as if trying to imprint her mouth indelibly on his. And he was saying things against her lips—soft, urgent words in a language she didn't recognise.

'Kadir,' she whispered as his fingers curled possessively over her silk-covered breast and the nipple immediately sprang to life.

'I want you,' he said deliberately. And he picked her up and carried her across the gilded room, towards the wide divan and the powerful scent of orange roses.

CHAPTER NINE

WITH A SWIFT economy of movement, Kadir peeled off Caitlin's tunic, revealing the modest bra and pants she'd bought in a discount store in Edinburgh. As his hungry gaze raked over her, she wondered if he was used to his women wearing bewitching scraps of silk and lace and how she could possibly measure up against them. But the hot flash of his eyes and the growl which erupted from his lips seemed to imply he didn't feel in the least bit short-changed by her appearance.

He unclipped her bra and bent to slide her panties all the way down her thighs, effortlessly lifting her up so that they fluttered from her ankles, before setting her down again. He kissed her hair as he reached down to touch her breast, a slow, circling thumb making the nipple grow hard again.

'I have wanted to see you naked like this for so long,' he husked.

Her cheeks grew hot, but Caitlin was determined to match his matter-of-factness. Because emotional danger beckoned if she read too much into what was simply a biological act. 'And you,' she whispered. 'I have longed to see you naked, too.'

'Then what are you waiting for, Caitlin? Why don't you take off my clothes?'

His uneven words were coated with need and Caitlin trembled beneath their rush of elemental power. She had never undressed a man before and she'd certainly never undressed a powerful king of the desert. But there had to be a first time for everything, surely? Her hands were unsteady as they moved towards the hem of his robe, mainly because she could feel the heat of his body beneath the silk and knew what delights awaited her. Pulling the garment over his head, her fingers tightened around its voluminous folds, her breath catching in her throat as she realised that, unlike her, he was completely naked beneath.

And it was impossible not to stare at him. To feast her eyes on the broad shoulders and honed chest and gleaming olive skin. The narrow hips and muscular thighs and long, hard legs. But most of all, she couldn't seem to tear her gaze away from the thick pole of his erection which sprang from between his thighs, pale against the dark forest of hair.

'Do you like what you see, Caitlin?' he questioned softly.

She lifted her gaze to his face. He's playing a game with me, she thought, and maybe he wanted her to play it, too. Was that what long-parted lovers were supposed to do when they met up again? But what if you didn't know the rules of the game—when your only experience of sex had been one short night which had ended so abruptly? 'It's okay,' she said coolly, the fabric slipping from her fingers to the floor.

'Just okay?'

His black eyes challenged her and suddenly Caitlin wondered why she was even *trying* to flirt with someone who was light years ahead of her in terms of sexual experience. 'M-more than okay,' she admitted truthfully, the words coming out in a rush. 'Your body is beautiful.'

Was it her shaky praise which provoked the sudden tension in his body? Which made his eyes narrow before he bent to capture her lips again, searing them with a kiss which felt as if he were branding her with fire? Caitlin didn't know and somehow it didn't seem important. She just kissed him back as if her life depended on it, because hadn't she dreamt of doing this so many times during the long nights she'd spent alone, and then woken up frustrated in the morning to realise it had all been a dream?

He lifted her up and laid her down on the divan, the smoky expectation in his eyes leaving her boneless with longing as he began to stroke her. And Caitlin closed her eyes, giving herself up to the sensation as he began to explore her skin. Because last time it had all been so new and she'd been so overcome with emotion that she hadn't really had the chance to appreciate what was happening, but she wasn't going to allow that to happen this time. No way. Instead of having pointless fantasies about having found 'the man of her dreams', she was going to concentrate solely on the physical. On the way he was stroking her inner thigh with a thoroughness which quickly had her squirming with frustration. On the way his tongue was licking its way luxuriously over each nipple, so that she wriggled with pleasure. The way he groaned when she smoothed her hand over the jut of his hips and stroked his curving satin-skinned buttocks. The way his blunt tip brushed tantalisingly against her belly, and already she could feel a little bead of moisture there.

'Kadir,' she whispered.

He reached out to slide out a drawer from beneath the rose-covered table, before producing a small square of foil which glinted in the dim light. As he smoothed on the protection with a slow and provocative deliberation, she wondered if he just *happened* to keep those condoms there, or whether the whole scenario had been a set-up. Again, her cheeks grew warm and this time Kadir must have noticed, because his black eyes were curious.

'Are you blushing?' he murmured.

'Not at all. I think the air-conditioning must be failing. It's very hot in here.'

Unexpectedly, he laughed before pulling her into his arms and suddenly words were forgotten because his mouth was on hers and his hand was back between her thighs. *Where it belongs,* she thought fiercely. But then her fingertips encountered the rough ridge of a small jagged scar, which snaked across his lower abdomen, and inexplicably she felt a sharp pain shooting through her. Almost as if she were experiencing second hand the hurt he must have felt at the time. She opened her mouth to ask who had caused it, who had inflicted such a wound on him—but by then his finger was brushing against her quivering bud and her brain wasn't functioning at all.

Her body was hungry and her need was intense. Her throat dried as he straddled her and she parted her legs to accommodate him. And at last he was inside her. Easing slickly into her waiting heat and not seeming to notice the hard dig of her nails as she clung to him.

She gasped with each delicious thrust he made—her fingers sliding over his sweat-sheened skin as he took her higher and higher, until she didn't think she could bear it any more. And suddenly she was falling. Falling in slow motion through a splinter of stars, vaguely aware of Kadir's body tensing and hearing his guttural cry as he jerked inside her, before gradually growing still.

For a while they just lay there, Caitlin staring at one of the intricate lanterns which dangled from the ceiling as a great swell of emotion rose up inside her. And stupidly, she wanted to cry. To let out the tears which were building behind her eyelids, no matter how hard she tried to blink them away. Which wasn't supposed to happen. Sex was supposed to provide release and remind her what she'd been missing—not leave her racked with regret and a deep ache at the thought of what she could never have.

'Why are you crying?'

To her consternation, Kadir's question made her aware that a tear had dripped onto the velvet divan and she turned her face away from him. She wanted to deny the accusation but then he would rightly accuse her of lying, so instead she dashed an angry fist against her wet cheek. 'It doesn't matter.'

'Was it really so awful?' he persisted softly.

She gave a short laugh. 'Oh, come on. You must know it was anything but.'

'Then I am at a loss to understand.' He stroked his

finger between her breasts. 'How do men usually respond when you react like this?'

She thought about glossing over the remark, rather than opening it up for debate. But his wife had lied to him, hadn't she? And there was no reason for her to do the same. 'They don't respond in any way at all,' she said quietly. 'Because there hasn't *been* any other lover than you. I was a virgin the night I slept with you, in case you hadn't noticed. In fact, I'd never been intimate with any man before you, Kadir—and I haven't been intimate with any man since.'

There was total silence. A pause so long that time felt suspended. And when he spoke his voice sounded heavy. As if each word had been carved from some dark and unforgiving rock. 'Me neither.'

Bewildered now, Caitlin turned to look at him, but his eyes were closed, his dark lashes fringed against his olive skin, his hair startlingly black against the green velvet divan. 'Run that past me again,' she whispered.

He opened his eyes and she found herself caught in the ebony gleam of his gaze.

'Your first experience,' he said flatly. 'Well, it was mine, too. Nobody before and nobody since.'

She shook her head. 'I don't think I've understood that properly.'

'You have.'

'You're saying…are you saying I'm the only woman you've ever had sex with?'

Another pause. 'That's exactly what I'm saying.'

She hated the way the possibility of that made her feel. As if she were somehow special. As if something had marked her out and made her seem different. But that was a crazy hope without any foundation—and even giving it houseroom was dangerous. And besides, it didn't make sense. None of it did.

'I don't understand,' she whispered. 'How is it even possible? I mean, you're so...'

'So?'

In the dim light, she could feel herself blush but she was still so caught up in the thrill of that moment that she said something she probably shouldn't have done. 'So amazing,' she whispered. 'So how on earth can you have been a virgin?'

Kadir looked down at her flushed pink face and wondered why he had told her, but deep down he knew why. He owed it to her to tell her the truth, even though it was not the kind of admission most men would be happy making. Yet from the outset he had been comfortable with his sexuality and his decision to channel it as he saw fit. With his ability to discard the expectations usually associated with a virile and highly desirable man. Yet, having told her part of the story, surely it would be impossible to leave the rest of the matter unexplained. Did he really want to masquerade as something he wasn't?

'I wanted to be the greatest king there ever was,' he began, and as he saw her lips purse together he shook his head. 'No, *not* for the sake of my ego, Caitlin, but for the sake of my people, who had suffered greatly by the time I came to the throne. My forebears had served Xulhabi well—my father less so. Under his watch, this country had been subject to constant invasion and land grabs and, economically, we were lagging behind many of the other desert states.'

'Why? Did he…did he take his eye off the ball or something?' She gave an embarrassed shrug. 'I'm sorry. I don't know how this kingship thing works.'

'In a way, that's exactly what he did,' he conceded. 'But the rot set in when he married.'

'Isn't that a little…harsh?'

'Harsh, but true.' He flickered her a look. 'You may recall me telling you he married my mother for love?'

'Which you don't believe exists?'

'Oh, I believe it exists, all right,' he said slowly, his voice growing hard. 'Just not for me. Maybe the example I was shown by my parents was enough to warp my opinion for ever.'

'Tell me about them,' she said quietly, brushing a handful of hair away from her cheek.

He stared up at the ceiling. 'She was the youngest of seven sisters—beautiful and completely spoiled, by all accounts—and although my father was warned it was an unsuitable match, he would not listen. Ironic, isn't it? That I chose so carefully when selecting a bride. I wanted more than anything not to repeat the mistake of my father, which is why I picked a supposedly *suitable* princess.' He gave a bitter laugh. 'And look how that turned out. Which just goes to prove that the majority of relationships are doomed from the start.'

'So what happened?' she said.

He shrugged. 'He was completely obsessed with her and, in a way, that seemed to diminish her respect for him. And the more she played him for a fool, the more it seemed to feed his desire for her. He found himself unwilling to commit to the very demanding role of monarch because that would take him away from the wife he was so infatuated with. But she…' He stopped for a moment, wondering if there was any need to tell her this and then he thought—why wouldn't he tell her when he had come this far, when he had already broken the rule of a lifetime by confiding such intensely personal matters? 'She took a series of lovers, which broke his heart. His loyal courtiers tried to protect him—the less scrupulous ones took advantage. And he went to pieces.'

'And what about you?' she questioned cautiously. 'It must have affected you, too.'

He shook his head, determined his expression would show no sign of the pain which had hit him so hard as a child and made him feel even more isolated. 'I tried to block out as much of the chaos as possible. And then, when I was nineteen, my father died, and my mother soon afterwards, and by the time I acceded to the throne, everything was in a mess.'

She looked as if she wanted to ask him a question and he guessed that maybe she was too shy to frame the words. 'You want to know what all this has to do with celibacy?'

'Well, yes.'

'History has always acknowledged the power which abstinence from sex confers upon a man,' he said. 'Wasn't the great knight Lancelot eventually ruined by his weakness for a woman's flesh? And don't great sportsmen deprive themselves of sex before a big game, in order to achieve the highest honours in their field?'

'I guess so,' she said uncertainly.

'I vowed that I would enter my marriage without impediment, so I could offer my bride not just my untouched body and my fidelity, but intense pleasure, too.

That is why I studied erotic texts so extensively for so many years, for there are many ancient books which provide comprehensive guidance on the subject.'

There was silence for a moment while she seemed to absorb this.

'But what about your wife?' she questioned eventually. 'Surely she wanted you to consummate your marriage?'

'It never got that far. Or rather, the subject remained purely academic and there was no consummation.' His mouth twisted. 'For there is only one thing which makes addicts happy and that is their chemical of choice. Adiya simply wasn't interested in sex, not at any time during our short marriage.'

'But why...?' She looked as if she was trying to understand. 'I mean, there must have been a thousand more suitable women to choose from, so why me?'

This was, Kadir realised, what Americans sometimes called the sixty-four-thousand-dollar question. Could he put his response to Caitlin Fraser down to frustration and lust and being in the right place at the right time? Of course he could, because what other possible explanation could there be?

'Just before I met you, I'd spoken to one of Adiya's doctors, who had explained that she could live in that vegetative state for many years and it was highly unlikely she would ever recover.' He swallowed. 'And I accepted that, as my destiny.'

He had decided to embrace the life which fate had afforded him. He would be a celibate king. So he had buried his once fervent desire to sire a child and had used his energies to rescue his battered homeland, throwing himself into a series of demanding battles to reclaim the areas of his country which had been unlawfully occupied.

The war had been won but he had lost Rasim, his oldest friend, and for a while that had derailed him. And then, on a business trip to the UK, he had seen Caitlin Fraser standing on a hillside with her camera, her flame-red hair calling out to him, the soft crumple of her lips imploring him to kiss her when she turned round to reproach him for frightening the eagle away. It had been the most overwhelming temptation of his life, even though many women had propositioned him. He had resisted them—but he hadn't been able to resist her. Like some tame puppet he had asked her to meet him for dinner—made physically vulnerable by a woman in a tweed skirt and a scratchy sweater. Of *course* he hadn't known she was a virgin—he had no template with which to compare his night with her. Nor she him. Yet she had been, he recognised with a sudden unwanted rush of exultation.

She had been a virgin, too.

'And why *me*?' he said suddenly, turning the question on its head. 'There must have been men who had tried it on with you before.'

Now it was Caitlin's turn to hesitate, but she saw no reason to hide the truth from him. She wriggled up the divan a little.

'Because I had an inbuilt fear of men. My mother may have failed in many of the more accepted parental skills, but she was very good at teaching me that men were never to be trusted. That men would do you down if you gave them the chance. If you're told something enough times, then eventually you start to believe it. Oh, I went out with people from time to time, but nobody ever lit my fire.'

'And what was so different about me?'

He had been irresistible, that was what. With his towering stature and flashing black eyes, he had seemed more like someone who had stepped from the pages of a story. But what she'd felt for Kadir had transcended the physical. When she had talked to him it was as if she'd known him all her life, as if there were no barriers between them, nor ever could be. And when he had kissed her, she'd believed she could trust him with not just her body, but her heart and soul, too. The reality had been very different, of course. Maybe her mother had been right all along.

She wanted to hurt him as he had hurt her. To tell him she had fallen into bed with him because he had obviously been very rich and that had turned her on. But that wouldn't have been true and, anyway, he was the father of her child and they needed to find some way to work through this seemingly impossible situation in which they found themselves.

She reached down and touched her finger against the ridging scar which marred the perfection of his body. 'This is new,' she said quietly.

He nodded as he laid his palm over the faint stretch marks left behind after her pregnancy. 'So are these.'

It was unexpectedly poignant, this unspoken acknowledgement of the time which had passed and the ways in which they'd both changed. For a moment the atmosphere became undeniably intimate and Caitlin was fearful of the way it made her feel. 'What happened?' she said, quickly moving the conversation on.

For a moment he didn't reply and she half thought he wasn't going to. But then he spoke and she had never heard a voice sound quite so heavy, or defeated.

'It was just at the end of the war with Yusawid and the final push to reclaim our borders. I was leading from the front but I was badly wounded, and Rasim came to my assistance, and he...' His voice sounded thick. 'He saved his king but lost his own life in the process.'

'That's the man in the photo on your desk?'

He nodded. 'That's him. Rasim and I grew up together. We learned to play and fight together and he was more like a brother to me, despite the fact that his mother was a palace servant. But he was the only person who was ever there for me in an atmosphere of poison and hate.' He turned to her. 'Can you understand now why the future of Xulhabi means so much to me, Caitlin? Can't you see that if I fail to secure the continuation of the line, I will also be failing the man who gave his life, not for me, but for his country?'

Yes, she could understand all that. She bit her lip. But wasn't he asking too much of a child who was not yet five?

He had started stroking her breast again and wasn't it crazy how one minute you could literally be discussing life and death and in the next you could be opening your mouth so that your lover could put his tongue inside it? Maybe that was nature's way of protecting them from life's hardships—by making it possible for pleasure to eclipse the pain.

So many conflicting feelings were buzzing around

her head and there were still questions she needed to ask. But not now. Not when Kadir's dark head was moving towards hers.

Because how could she possibly think about anything when he was kissing her like this?

CHAPTER TEN

INDOOR SWIMMING POOLS were pretty much the same the world over, Caitlin thought. Even a grand palace version of a pool didn't differ much from what you might find in a public bath. There was still all that echo and amplification of sound. Still the glimmer and shimmer of water beneath overhead lights which made everything seem supernaturally bright.

She stood in one of the recesses of the giant complex, shadowed and unobserved as she watched the deft movements of Cameron and Kadir playing together in the turquoise water.

Father and son.

From here it was achingly obvious that there could never be any question of Cameron's parentage.

Except that there was. At least, according to the dictates of ancient Xulhabian law it had to be proved.

She felt another twist of frustration as she recalled the conversation she'd had with Kadir, early last week. A conversation which had seemed doubly insulting in view of the fact that they had just had the most amazing sex.

Apparently, a tiny sample of her son's blood had been required.

'Blood?' Caitlin remembered echoing, rolling across the expanse of rumpled sheets and looking at him as if he were some kind of moonlighting vampire.

'It's no big deal. It is simply to ensure that there can never be any legal challenge.' His voice had been smooth but explicit. 'This will cover us in case there is ever any dispute about Cameron's right to rule. A kind of insurance policy, if you like.'

Caitlin had been so taken aback that she had found herself nodding her consent, without really thinking it through. Not thinking about all the implications which lay behind that supposedly simple remark. Why had she agreed so readily? For the sake of her son, or because she and Kadir seemed to have reached a plateau of understanding—almost of peace—and she wanted to maintain that situation for as long as possible? Had she maybe been seduced by the hope—no matter how hard she tried to deny it to herself—that the intimate moments they'd been sharing were something worth building on?

But she had flinched as a tiny needle was inserted into her son's perfect skin, and it was only afterwards that Kadir's statement had sunk in properly. He was still taking it as a given that Cameron would one day inherit his crown, when they still hadn't come to an agreement about that.

'Daddy! Daddy! Look!'

She watched Cameron dive beneath the dappled surface to swim an entire underwater width of the pool. And while he might have been bathing in Cronarty's lochs since he'd been little more than a toddler, he certainly hadn't been able to do *that* before they'd arrived here. She expelled an unsteady breath. Maybe it was true that plenty of money and resources were ultimately the most effective way of teaching a child something. She continued to watch as Kadir mimicked his son's movements, except that he managed an entire *length* of the pool, which made Cameron clap his hands together in delight. Was there *anything* the desert King wasn't good at? she found herself thinking.

Yes.

He wasn't very good at making her feel *connected* to him, for all that she shared his bed each night and revelled in the mind-blowing reality of his lovemaking. Because they weren't connected. Not really. Despite their semi-shared living situation, his bed and his body were all she had of him, for the confidences shared on their first night together had never been repeated.

And maybe *lovemaking* was too optimistic a way of describing what took place every night in her bedroom, into which Kadir crept once darkness had fallen, before taking his leave as the sun was rising.

She was his secret.

Sometimes she thought she was his *guilty* secret.

'I am simply protecting your reputation,' was his reply to her studiedly casual question about her status. 'If it were openly acknowledged that you are my lover, it could create intrigue within the palace and that is always unwise. Let's leave it until we have come to a decision about where we go from here.'

And where was that? Caitlin had wanted to ask. But something held her back from asking the kind of questions which might provide difficult answers. Because while she couldn't imagine staying here, she couldn't imagine going back to Cronarty either. At least, not yet.

In an attempt to create some semblance of family life, she had joined in with the daily riding sessions which Cameron shared with his father. At first she had simply watched from the sidelines, but one morning Kadir had persuaded her onto a placid mare, even though it had been many years since she'd been in the saddle. His words had been soft and encouraging and she had found her gentle ride exhilarating—almost as exhilarating as the satisfaction in the Sheikh's eyes and Cameron's delighted whoops of excitement.

Sometimes, once the fierce heat had leached from the afternoon, Kadir would demonstrate the skills of Himyar, his prized falcon, while she and Cameron watched it circle and swoop before landing on the Sheikh's forearm, where it sat regarding the world with its clever, beady eyes. And he kept his promise to teach Cameron chess—a game which the boy was already beginning to understand and to love.

Yet sometimes Caitlin felt as if she were living in a parallel universe. To the outside world they were nothing but polite parents who were coexisting in relative harmony. Given Kadir's position of absolute power, nobody ever questioned them about their relationship. Nobody, other than the taciturn nocturnal guard, was aware that each night Kadir would slip into her darkened room and Caitlin would be on fire with unbearable desire as he took her in his arms. For two relative novices to sex, they certainly seemed intent on making up for lost time. And didn't it give her a buzz to think that

Kadir had never done this with anyone else before—that each discovered pleasure was unique to them?

If only it were so simple to regulate her mood. To keep at bay the unwanted emotions which came flooding out of nowhere to tug at her heart. Sometimes she would find herself overcome with unrealistic yearnings—partly brought about by his disclosure about Rasim's death. What a gap his friend's death must have left in his life. And, knowing his history—who could blame him for associating love with loss or betrayal and never wanting to associate himself with it again?

She had wanted to comfort him, but Kadir didn't want her comfort. Sexual satisfaction seemed to be his only goal.

She swallowed.

Sometimes she thought…

She bit her lip, reluctant to acknowledge the thought which would never quite leave the edges of her mind. Because what if the once celibate Sheikh was using his newly discovered erotic skills to make her compliant? To *subdue* her and win her over—to make her fall in with whatever plans he had for Cameron?

Well, she couldn't ignore the topic for ever, and the longer it went on, the harder it would be for her to break away from him. He had carelessly mentioned 'a few weeks' at the beginning of their stay, and that time was fast approaching. Maybe it was time she exerted a little control of her own.

Before she got in too deep to tear herself away.

She moved out from behind the mosaic pillar and wandered down to the edge of the pool and Cameron immediately dived beneath the surface to repeat his underwater width.

'Did you see me, Mummy?' he spluttered as he emerged from the water and shook tiny droplets of water from his plastered black head. 'Was that good?'

'I did see you and it was brilliant! You swim like a wee eel!'

'Do I?'

'Yes!' She lifted him from the pool and wrapped a towel around him, her fingers wiggling mischievously beneath his arms. 'And you're just as slippery!'

He giggled as she tickled him and she wondered how she could ever take him away from all this…this *ease* and privilege. Would he resent her if she did so? Her introspection was halted by Morag bustling in to supervise the dressing of her young charge before taking him away for lunch, leaving Caitlin alone with Kadir.

She had seen him naked many times, but that had always been within the closeted privacy of the bedroom. Right now it seemed surreal to see the desert King half submerged in the turquoise water, his muscular weight resting on his elbows as he leaned on the side of the pool and studied her. His black hair lay flat against his head and against the olive-skinned wetness of his face, his ebony eyes gleamed like dark jewels. And, oh, didn't her heart and her body just clench with hopeless and instinctive longing?

'Such a pity you can't come in and join me,' he murmured. 'Think what fun we could have together in the water.'

'You may be trying to propel Xulhabi into a new age

of enlightenment, but I really don't think the palace is ready for mixed bathing at this stage.'

'I make the laws, Caitlin.'

'But there are servants everywhere,' she continued, dismissing his arrogant boast with the ghost of a smile. 'It wouldn't be appropriate, even if we *were* the kind of couple who messed around during daylight hours, which we aren't. And besides, I need to talk to you.'

Kadir hauled himself out of the pool, noting the way her body instinctively tensed as he moved closer. Her awareness of him was always apparent and he knew if he laid one finger on her, she would start to fall apart in his arms, just as she always did. Yet the expression on her face suggested that sex was the last thing on her mind right now—and the new-found glint of determination he could read in those ice blue eyes made him wary.

'What do you want to talk to me about?' he questioned, holding out a hand so that a servant immediately appeared with a white towelling gown, which Kadir shrugged on over his wet shoulders.

She didn't answer until he had belted up the robe and the servant had scurried away. 'I'm not sure that now is the ideal time to be having this conversation,' she prevaricated.

'Tell me,' he commanded imperiously.

She met his gaze and drew in a deep breath. 'You must know we can't stay here indefinitely like this, Kadir. We still haven't set out any timeline for our departure and it's not fair on Morag.'

'Has Morag expressed any desire to leave?'

'Well, no. But that's not the point. She's probably just being polite.'

'You don't think it might have something to do with the friendship she has struck up with my head groom, Ghassan, which is leading her to spend so much time in the stables when she isn't caring for our son? Either that, or she's showing a late-onset interest in riding, which I somehow doubt.'

'The fact that Morag is using her time wisely is irrelevant,' she shot back. 'I happen to have some commitments of my own back in Scotland.'

He raised his eyebrows. 'What kind of commitments?'

'I have a job, in case you'd forgotten. I'm a photographer and there's a backlog of photos I'm due to take, which need to be made into greeting cards before Christmas.'

'And the entire western world will grind to a halt if these greetings cards aren't made available?'

'Don't you *dare* patronise me, Kadir Al Marara!' she returned heatedly. 'I *need* to work! I've always worked—even though my earnings were never destined to break the bank. *You* may have been born with a silver spoon in your mouth, but not all of us have had your advantages.'

There was a pause during which Kadir found himself considering what his life might have been like if he had been given the birthright of most men and the weight of his destiny had not been quite so heavy. If he had been forced to work simply to put bread in his mouth. Hadn't that been his fantasy as a child? Sometimes a royal procession would travel to Azraq and, from within the sumptuous splendour of his golden carriage, he had observed the ragged street urchins playing in the dust, and had envied them. While most boys had longed to be kings or princes, he had simply yearned to be ordinary. 'None of us has any control over the circumstances of our birth,' he observed wryly. 'We can only hope to influence what happens to us later.'

'Yes, I realise that. But you're skating round the subject, as well you know, and you can't keep ignoring it for ever. I want to go home, Kadir.'

'Do you?' he demanded.

'This isn't real,' she breathed. 'It doesn't feel real. It's like I'm living in some kind of limbo.'

Kadir felt his breath catch as her stark words took root and he realised he had been burying his head in the sand—which was all very well for ostriches, but not kings of the desert. He had been aware for days that this clandestine affair of theirs could not continue indefinitely, and that the problem was only going to get worse if he kept pushing it to the back of his mind.

Wasn't it time that he bit the bullet and did what he needed to do, even though he had once sworn that he would never go through with this particular measure again? He had vowed never to let another person get too close to him, but he could see that, with Caitlin, he was going to have his work cut out to maintain that state of affairs.

'I need to talk to you, too. But not now and not here,' he said, gesturing towards his wet hair. 'I must first dry off and get changed but also, what I am about to say to you requires a certain degree of formality.'

'Oh?' Her brow pleated into a frown. 'Now you're talking in riddles.'

'Or perhaps simply stirring your interest? It seems

to have worked, in any case.' Briefly, he lifted a hand to summon an aide, who came scurrying towards him. 'Come to my office in an hour, Caitlin.' His eyes glittered. 'I think you know the way well enough by now. I have a business proposition to put to you.'

CHAPTER ELEVEN

'WILL YOU MARRY me, Caitlin?'

Despite the generous proportions of the Sheikh's office, Caitlin felt the walls closing in on her as she stared in disbelief at the robed figure seated behind the desk who was studying her with an expression of amused speculation—as if her open-mouthed reaction was the last thing he had been expecting.

'You look shocked,' he observed, when still she said nothing.

Caitlin shook her head as she tried to absorb the enormity of the words Kadir had just uttered, but it was difficult to take it all in. She touched the polished wood of the desk—not touching it for luck but checking it was real—to reassure herself that she wasn't dreaming. 'Of course, I'm shocked.'

His eyes narrowed. 'But surely you must have considered that marriage might be an option at some point?'

Again, she shook her head, disbelief rippling through her as she stared at the desert King who'd just proposed marriage in the most unromantic of circumstances. There had been no moonlight or champagne and he certainly hadn't dropped down onto bended knee. His hair still damp from swimming, the Sheikh of Xulhabi had just asked Caitlin Fraser to be his bride, a proposition which once would have filled her with giddy delight. But delivered in the emotionless style of someone who was reading from a shopping list—even though he probably didn't even know what a shopping list was—Kadir's proposal had filled her with nothing but distrust.

But *he* was the one who had described it as a 'business proposition'. *He* wasn't building it up to be something it wasn't, was he? So maybe that was the way she ought to regard it, too.

'No,' she replied slowly. 'I can honestly say it hadn't crossed my mind that you might ask me to marry you.'

He leaned back in a highly embellished chair. 'And what do you say, now I have?'

She shrugged as she looked around the room. Golden pens were gleaming in a jewelled container in front of him and all the inlaid furniture was incredibly beautiful, but suddenly everything in the room seemed very foreign to her. Which was exactly how she felt. Foreign and alone. Like someone auditioning for a role which was never going to be right for her. 'I don't know,' she said, at last. 'What would happen, if I said yes?'

'It's very straightforward. You would be my Queen and my consort. Traditionally, such a position is a springboard for charitable works and, of course, we have the resources to make that possible. You would have your own staff. You could run your office as you see fit, for I am aware that as an independent woman—'

'Are you being sarcastic?' she questioned suspiciously.

He shook his head. 'Not at all. I am trying to make… *allowances*, Caitlin—something which I am not normally required to do. I am aware that you have a career and that perhaps…' He held out his palms in an expansive gesture she had seen him use before. 'Perhaps you might wish to continue with that career, although on a much smaller scale, of course.'

'Like how?'

'Well, it wouldn't be appropriate for you to produce Christmas cards in a country which doesn't actually celebrate that particular holiday, but there's no reason why you couldn't do some work for the Xulhabian tourist board. We're hoping to expand the travel industry and to encourage visitors in the near future and you could help promote that.'

'Wow.' She expelled a slow breath of air. 'You've got it all worked out, haven't you?'

'I have done my best to come up with a solution to our…dilemma,' he said, flicking her a shuttered black gaze. 'So what do you say, Caitlin? Is this something which might appeal to you?'

Caitlin didn't answer immediately, mainly because her thoughts were still in such a muddle. Was it typical of *all* men or just this man—that they could address all the practical concerns of an unexpected proposal of marriage, without even touching on the emotional ones? 'I don't know,' she admitted. 'Your reasons are—'

'Logical?' he supplied as he plucked one of the golden pens from the container and began to twirl it in between his thumb and forefinger. 'And lucid? Both qualities which should never be underestimated. Think about it, Caitlin, and then ask yourself, why *wouldn't* we marry? We share a son—a fine boy who will one day be King. Wouldn't parents who are wed make life so much easier for him?'

'I suppose so,' she admitted.

'He likes being here in the palace,' he continued. 'Anyone can see that. And all the time he is learning. About horses and falcons and history. About the history of Xulhabi, which will be invaluable to his future.' He paused. 'You must realise that I can offer him the finest tutors—'

'But,' she put in, like a drowning woman attempting to cling to the raft of her old life, 'I've got him down for an infant school on the mainland starting next September.

Their eyes met. 'That's not going to happen,' he said quietly. 'You must have realised that by now. Because not only do I need to marry in order to legitimise my succession, there is also the thorny subject of Cameron's security if you were to return to Scotland.'

Caitlin flinched, because those particular words struck home. Several times she'd thought what might happen if she insisted on taking Cameron back—then letting him come out to visit his father on high days and holidays. Mightn't Cameron start resenting the laughable contrast between life as a desert prince and life as an ordinary Scottish schoolboy? And what *of* the security aspect? No matter how much protection Kadir paid for, wouldn't she be forever looking over her shoulder? Jumping at every unexpected sound and terrified someone would snatch away her beloved boy?

'I can understand perfectly the reasons why you've

asked me to marry you,' she said slowly. 'But you've made no mention of *us* in all this.'

'Us?' he said, as if she had just uttered a word he couldn't comprehend.

'About…about what it would be like for us to be man and wife.'

'I think we could coexist quite—'

'Happily?' she inserted sarcastically.

'Certainly without rancour,' he amended coolly. 'Neither of us seem to have had any complaints about the physical side of our relationship and I see no reason why that shouldn't continue.'

'Is that why you seduced me, Kadir?' she questioned suddenly. 'To lull me into a state of blissful dependence, knowing that one day it might serve you well?'

There was a pause. A pause which seemed to go on as his eyes just got blacker and blacker—unless you counted the furnace-bright spark at their centre. 'I seduced you because I couldn't get you out of my mind,' he husked at last. 'Because you were like a fire in my blood which would not be doused. You still are. Because no matter how often I feed my hunger for you, it still returns—even stronger than before.' He slammed the pen down onto the desk and stared at her. 'Is that what you wanted to hear, Caitlin?'

It was the most passionate thing he'd ever said and, almost without thinking, Caitlin placed her hand over the sudden jump of her heart before quickly letting it fall back down onto her lap. But he must have seen the gesture and correctly interpreted it because his eyes suddenly lost their blazing centre and became flat—almost matt.

'But that is simply passion—or lust, depending on your definition. And if you're holding out for love—if that's what all this is about,' he added softly, 'then that I cannot do. This proposal comes unencumbered by any false promises, which will leave you permanently disappointed. Do you understand what I'm saying to you?'

And the weirdest thing was that Caitlin *could* understand. Now that he'd told her more about himself and she had pieced together some of the fragments of his past, she'd been able to work out some of the things which motivated this battle-scarred man. Born into a dysfunctional relationship which hadn't worked on any level, he had pointed the finger of blame towards the unpredictability of emotion. He had considered his father a fool because he'd married for love, rather than duty, which was why he'd made duty his priority for his own wedding to Adiya.

But in the end, both duty *and* love had let him down—no wonder he was wary about relationships.

Yet with Cameron...

Caitlin felt her throat dry, wanting to hide from the truth, but knowing she couldn't. Because the one bright element in this situation was watching Kadir's relationship with his son blossom. They had hit it off from the get-go and it had been a pretty amazing thing to observe. Couldn't the bond they shared be a new beginning, of sorts? Was it too much to hope that Kadir might come to trust those new feelings and spread them around, like the rays of light radiating from the sun?

Spread them to her?

Maybe. Maybe not. She certainly couldn't enter into marriage if her sole objective was to get Kadir to love her, because he had ruled that out most emphatically. But that didn't mean she couldn't lead by example, or that she couldn't hope things might one day change. Because how could a damaged man learn to love and trust unless he was shown the way? Couldn't she demonstrate that she was willing to forget the past and move on from it? That there was more to a relationship than the stuff which happened in the bedroom—no matter how mind-blowing the sex happened to be.

She wondered briefly if she should make him wait. Play power games designed to show him she wasn't a total pushover. But what would be the point of that? They'd start trying to score points off each other and the truth would disappear and all you'd be left with would be a couple of egos, battling for supremacy. And that was the last thing any of them needed.

So she pinned a smile to her lips and, to her surprise, her answer came easily. 'Yes, Kadir,' she said softly. 'I will marry you.'

'Good.' For a long moment he studied her before rising up from behind the desk and walking over to the window, where he floated down the blinds, just as he had done once before. 'I believe it is tradition at this stage to kiss,' he said softly as he began to move towards her and she could feel an instant rush of heat.

His lips were hard but his kiss was sweet and with very few preliminaries he was rucking up her tunic with hands which were trembling—but weren't hers trembling, too? He trickled his fingertip over the goosebumps which iced her thighs and as Caitlin squirmed ecstatically, he kissed her again. Seamlessly, he slid down her panties and laid her on the silken surface of the Persian carpet and it felt like a dream. The most delicious dream she'd ever had. Chandeliers and golden vaulted ceilings shimmered above them as Kadir lifted his robes to straddle her.

Yet despite being more turned on than she could ever remember, Caitlin felt a rush of emotion as she looked up into his shuttered face and lifted her trembling fingertips to the rough shadow at his jaw. Her body clenched around him as he made that first thrust and she breathed out a sigh of pleasure as he began to move. He was so big and so powerful—and the feeling was so incredible that for a moment she felt dangerously close to tears.

And right then all her wasted emotions were replaced by pure sensation as he silenced her cries of pleasure with his lips. Her orgasm was spiralling up inside her—so fast and perfect and inevitable. It slammed through her with such force that her head fell back against the rug and then Kadir began to come himself, his shuddered words soft, yet fractured.

For a long while afterwards she didn't speak. She didn't want to shatter the magic of the moment. But then dark realisation intruded and, insistently, she shook his shoulder. 'Kadir. Don't go to sleep.'

He opened his eyes. 'What is it?'

'You didn't use any protection.'

'No,' he said, frowning. 'There wasn't time and I wasn't thinking straight. Neither were you, or you would have reminded me.'

She sat up, raking her fingers through her tousled hair. 'And that's all it was—a momentary lapse caused by passion?'

Kadir considered her words. She had insisted that lies were a waste of time, and surely one of the perks of a situation like theirs was that you could afford to be honest. They weren't pretending to be in love. They weren't striving for the impossible goals which people chased and then felt short-changed when they didn't materialise.

'No, maybe that's not all,' he admitted slowly. 'You are going to be my wife and I want the wedding to happen as soon as possible. Would it really make a big difference if you fell pregnant in the meantime?'

'If I *fell pregnant in the meantime*?' she echoed. Furiously, she reached for her discarded underwear. 'We haven't even *discussed* having another baby!'

'But the main purpose of marriage is for procreation, surely. You want to give Cameron brothers and sisters, don't you, Caitlin?'

'That's not the point!' she hissed.

'Why not?'

'*Why not?*' She jumped to her feet, slithering back into her panties. 'You bang on about me being an independent woman—but you're only paying lip service to it, aren't you, Kadir? You say I can "do some work" for the Xulhabian tourist board, yet at the first opportunity you forget to use a condom!' She drew in a deep breath. 'Admittedly, I got carried away myself, and therefore I'm as much to blame as you for what just happened, but even so—you can't just make out like it doesn't *matter*.'

'Caitlin—' he said, rising to his feet.

'Don't you "Caitlin" me! Either you can see that

what we just did was a big mistake, or already we're in trouble.'

He drew in a deep breath, wishing he could brush the subject aside, but he recognised that she had a point. And it might be sensible to acknowledge that.

'I was wrong,' he admitted bluntly. 'My actions were not premeditated and I wasn't thinking straight. But in future I will make no such assumptions and we will add to our family only after mutual agreement, if at all. Does that satisfy you?'

'I suppose so.'

'So why don't we turn our attention to something which is guaranteed to make you smile again?'

'What is it?' she questioned, not bothering to keep the sulk from her voice.

He picked up a previously unnoticed small leather box which was lying on his desk, flipping it open to reveal a huge diamond ring resting against a bed of dark velvet. The stone's many facets sent out astonishing rays of rainbow light and it was undoubtedly the brightest thing in an already bright room. 'Go on,' he said, handing it to her. 'Try it on.'

Caitlin lifted the ring from the box. She could tell he was making an effort and he was looking at her with an expression of quiet satisfaction, as though no woman could fail to love such an enormous rock. But all she could feel was the heavy weight of the cold stone. It was too big for her finger. Too big for any finger, really. It occurred to her that she might have liked it better if he'd slipped it on her hand himself. 'It's beautiful,' she said dutifully.

'It's thirty-two carats,' he murmured.

To Caitlin this piece of information meant precisely nothing. The only carrot she was familiar with was the kind she secretly blitzed into a tomato sauce as she endeavoured to get Cameron to eat more vegetables.

And suddenly she felt an unbearable wave of nostalgia for those simple days she suddenly realised would never come again.

CHAPTER TWELVE

SHE HAD A crown containing the biggest emerald in the world.

She wore glittering diamonds in her hair.

And a fitted golden wedding dress embroidered with thousands of tiny seed pearls, which gleamed milky and soft beneath the fretwork of lights in the palace ballroom. In fact, Caitlin was wearing so much precious finery she could barely move, and each time she did something jangled, leaving her feeling a bit like Tinkerbell. Thank goodness the bride's walk towards the groom was traditionally slow, because she certainly couldn't have managed it any faster. Yet, despite the circumstances which had brought her to this place, her stately passage towards her future husband had felt bright and magical and full of possibilities. Since the royal announcement of their wedding had ricocheted around the globe, Caitlin had clung to those feelings of hope and joy, holding them close to her like a talisman.

'You look beautiful, Mama.'

The voice of her son butted into her thoughts and Caitlin looked down at a barely recognisable Cameron, clad in matching cloth of gold for his role as attendant to the bride. Some time during the last couple of weeks he had started substituting 'Mummy' and 'Daddy' with 'Mama' and 'Papa', and she wondered if he'd learnt to do that during one of the royalty etiquette classes he had shared with his father.

'Just like a queen!' Cameron added, with a gap-toothed grin.

'That's because your mother *is* a queen now,' said Kadir softly. 'And you, my son, are a prince of the desert.'

'*Am* I?'

'You most certainly are. And when Mama and I have returned from our honeymoon in the desert, you and I are going riding together as all princes should.'

'On my new horse?'

Kadir smiled. 'On your new horse, yes. So you must think about what you'd like to call him and be very good for Morag while we're away. Will you promise me you'll do that?'

'Oh, yes, Papa. I will.'

On cue, Morag stepped forward to take Cameron's hand and as Caitlin watched him trotting away happily at his nanny's side, she felt a weird twist of emotion—realising that this was the first time she'd ever spent a night apart from her little boy. Knowing that this was the first of many partings as the years took him towards adulthood. As he disappeared from view, she looked up to find Kadir's black eyes studying her.

'You'll miss him?' he questioned.

His perception startled her. 'Yes.'

'You're a good mother, Caitlin,' he said suddenly.

And that felt like the greatest compliment he could

ever pay her. Better than telling her that her lips were soft or her hair like fire. Full of unexpressed emotion, she nodded. 'Thank you.'

She was glad the day was almost over. There had been so many things to organise in this new country which was now her home. Fittings for her elaborate gown and rubber-stamping the carefully worded statements which had been sent out by Kadir's office to the world's press. She'd been asked to approve menus and decide on flowers. And then had come the long ceremony involving much feasting and intricate musical performances, before the culmination of the event when they had recited solemn vows in Xulhabian, which had required a lot of heavy-duty prepping on her part. Now her hennaed finger sported a heavy wedding band of glittering emeralds and sapphires—the colours of the Xulhabian flag.

She'd even been having lessons in camel-riding— their intended mode of transport for the honeymoon. And then last night, when her nerves had been at their most frayed and she had longed for Kadir's embrace, tradition had reigned supreme and they had spent the night in separate beds, leaving her feeling slightly divorced from reality.

Divorce.

That was a word she probably shouldn't be using— not in any sense. Because she had been made to understand that any formal dissolution of the marriage would be highly undesirable. Kadir had said as much soon after she had accepted his proposal.

'I cannot fail this time, Caitlin.' His words had been

heavy. 'And I cannot be seen to fail. The future of my country depends on stability and continuity.'

'Neither of us will fail at this.' Her own response had been fervent. She had meant every word. 'This is too important. For both of us. And for our son.'

The train of camels which was taking them to their desert destination was a throwback to earlier times, when such a mode of transport had been the only one available. She and Kadir each had a camel—hers was called Lutfi—with two bodyguards riding in front and behind. Servants had already been dispatched to the oasis where a camp had been set up and, just as the sun was sinking, they rode into the clearing, where a huge Bedouin tent awaited them. Outside, glowing lamps were already lit and, in the distance, someone was playing a musical instrument she didn't recognise, which sounded magical and enchanting.

In the distance, lush palm trees fringed a space of water and Caitlin sucked in a disbelieving breath as Kadir helped her down from her camel, as she witnessed the most stunning sunset she had ever seen. Celestial fire and flame were turning the sand blood-red and she could see touches of indigo and saffron bruising the edges of the sky.

'Oh, but it's beautiful,' she exclaimed.

And so was she, thought Kadir, as he watched her delicate features light up. He felt almost…*elated*— something rare enough to be remarkable. He had been taken aback by the fleeting sense of joy which had clutched at his heart during the ceremony—a strange reaction for someone who had vowed never to marry again. But he had put his reaction down to Cameron's presence by his mother's side and the pleasing fact that his country's succession was now assured. He'd convinced himself that his continuing contentment was due to nothing more complicated than paternal satisfaction and a sense of having got his own way—as well as anticipation about the wedding night ahead.

He glanced across at his bride.

Freed of her wedding attire, her fiery hair accentuated by the setting sun and her tunic billowing in the faint desert breeze, she looked almost at one with the land. Wild and carefree, her appearance touched something unknown and deep at the very core of him, which made his blood begin to pulse with honeyed sweetness. Breaking into a stream of rapid Xulhabian, he spoke to all the attendant staff—bodyguards included—who quickly began moving away from the proximity of the Bedouin tent.

'What did you say to them?' Caitlin asked, once they had all disappeared.

He lifted her up into his arms then, her hair flame-bright against the pale silk which covered his chest. 'I told them I wished to be alone with my new bride and they should not come near us again until I summon them,' he growled. 'Later, I will show you the stars in the heavens, which will be brighter than any stars you have ever seen. But in the meantime, I believe it is another of your British traditions to be carried over the threshold.'

'I believe it is,' she said, a smile curving her lips as he pushed back the canvas flap and dipped his head to carry her inside.

But to his pleasure—and his relief, for he was unbearably turned on—Caitlin didn't make any predictable comments about how deceptively large the tent was, nor did she coo or swoon over the luxurious brocades and silks which were scattered over the divans. She didn't even notice the large, beribboned box which sat on a small table beside the widest divan. Instead she was eagerly lifting her head for his kiss, her hands clutching at his shoulders as if she were feeling his body for the first time. And suddenly his hands were moving over her with equal impatience, as if it were an eternity since he had been intimate with her, rather than a single night. Their robes pooled to the ground and at last they were naked, their bodies illuminated by the fretwork flicker of the intricate lights which dangled from the ceiling.

Kadir gave a soft groan as he cupped the swell of her breast, revelling in the dark contrast of his fingers against her fair skin. 'I want you, my Queen,' he said, unsteadily. 'I wonder if you have any idea just how much?'

'K-Kadir.'

He didn't like it when she said his name like that—yet he liked it way too much. It sounded... He shook his head. It was hard to define because nobody had ever spoken to him that way before. As if his name were a prayer. Or a plea. But words didn't matter—not when she was doing something far more distracting. His mouth dried to dust because suddenly Caitlin was sliding to her knees before him, almost as if she were supplicating herself to him. But she wasn't. She was reaching between his thighs and curling her fingers around his arousal—an erotic and possessive cradling of his manhood. With her other hand she had begun playing with his balls and the sensation was so good it was almost unbearable…

'Caitlin!' He shuddered as she lowered her head onto his aching shaft, her tongue tantalising him with feather-light licks before she took him fully into her mouth. He clenched his fists and resisted the desire to close his eyes. It was certainly easier not to orgasm without any visual stimuli but it was also intensely erotic to watch the bobbing movement of her bright hair as she sucked on him. He wanted to tell her to stop and he wanted her to keep doing exactly what she was doing, but it was all pretty academic anyway because, no matter how long he tried to ward off the inevitable, he was soon jerking helplessly into her mouth, his fingers tangled in her hair as his seed spilled onto her lips.

For a long moment he felt completely defenceless—a sensation so disturbing that it threatened to eclipse the last sweet echoes of his orgasm. But as she raised her flushed face to his, he reasserted his mastery by lifting her up and carrying her over to the divan.

'That was…unexpected,' he observed, once she was prone on the golden sheet.

'I wanted to do something special for you.' She hesitated as he brushed his lips over her neck. 'To take the initiative for once, if you like. I mean, I know I've been involved in all the wedding planning, but sometimes this week I've felt a bit…'

The progress of his lips halted. 'A bit what?'

'Passive, I guess,' she admitted. 'As if I have no control over what is happening to me.'

'But isn't it sometimes a good thing, to feel passive?'

he mused, his voice now muffled as he moved his mouth towards her belly. 'Like now, for example?'

'Oh, Kadir,' she breathed.

'You like that?'

'No, I'm hating every second of it. Can't you tell?'

He thought about tasting *her* until she was crying out beneath the quick flick of his tongue. But his current need was more basic than that. He just wanted to be inside her—and something about the elemental urgency of that need disturbed him.

This time there were plenty of condoms to hand and when he entered her—feeling as hard as he could ever remember—she came almost immediately, as if she had been teetering on the brink for too long. As her body spasmed around him Kadir felt the instant pump of his seed. And this time his orgasm seemed as if it were never going to end.

For a while they lay in silence until the hard pound of his heart slowed. Until the sweat which sheened his brow had begun to cool. He opened his eyes to find her looking at him and suddenly he wanted—no, *needed*—to assert his mastery. To feel more like the man he usually was, rather than someone who he was beginning not to recognise. Shaking off his inertia, he stirred.

'I've bought you a present,' he said. 'Look. It's right beside you.'

She turned her head and for the first time appeared to notice the fancy beribboned box lying there. 'Gosh,' she said, blinking very rapidly.

'Well, don't just stare at it. Open it.'

Caitlin began to untie the ribbon and pulled out a box from within the fancy paper. Inside was a camera.

The kind of camera she'd always dreamed of owning but had never imagined she would. Top of the range and eye-wateringly expensive, she turned it round and round in her hands as if she couldn't quite believe she was holding it. But the gratitude which rushed over her was nothing to do with the money he must have spent— because when had anyone ever bought her a gift which felt so *right*? She felt the sudden unexpected prick of tears at the backs of her eyes. So *thoughtful*?

'Do you like it?'

Still overcome, she nodded.

'There's a printer to go with it back at the palace.'

She put the camera down and touched her fingers to the rough graze of his jaw. 'Thank you.'

'Just let one of my aides know if you need any more accessories and they can get them for you.' He flickered her an indecipherable stare. 'Like I said, you'll need something to do alongside your charity work. Something which keeps you from getting bored, or from feeling quite so *passive*.'

She told herself it was only gentle mockery. That nobody would give you a beautiful gift one minute, then turn around and make a veiled criticism the next. But Caitlin realised that Kadir was doing that thing he always did straight after they'd had sex.

He was distancing himself.

CHAPTER THIRTEEN

COLD DREAD WAS mounting inside him as the plane began its final descent and Kadir stared out of the porthole window without really seeing anything.

He should be experiencing a sensation of quiet satisfaction. The honeymoon had been a success. Not even he, the world's greatest cynic, could deny that. It had been easy—ridiculously so. By day, he had shown his new bride the desert he knew so well, and by night they had enjoyed long feasts of the senses which had blown his mind. Caitlin had been thrilled by his wedding gift of a new camera, and he had watched her busily snapping images of the stark terrain whenever time allowed.

But now the honeymoon was over. He'd sent his servants back by camel train, while he and Caitlin had commandeered the royal flight. Any minute now they would be touching down at the royal palace and seeing their son after a week's absence. He couldn't have asked for a better outcome to the marriage he had so carefully engineered, and yet...

Yet...

Now he wondered if he had been incautious. If he had given too much of himself to his new bride and fed dreams he had not intended to feed. If he had let his guard down a little too often during the preceding week.

A sigh left his lips. He had a problem. A problem which could no longer be ignored, even though he'd been loath to address it. He certainly hadn't wanted to ruin their short honeymoon and he hadn't wanted to confront it in an environment where he would be unable to escape from his new wife.

A wife he suspected was falling in love with him.

He felt his mouth twist as familiar faint echoes of fear and cynicism washed over him in a dark tide. His own experience had fanned his determination to never fall victim to love's capricious wiles, but he had been on the receiving end of unwanted devotion often enough to recognise the telltale signs when he saw them. The tender eyes and lingering glances. The shy biting of the lips followed by a gentle smile.

Yet because he had never been intimate with anyone before Caitlin, the problem had only ever been academic. Women had adored him from afar. He had never put himself directly in the firing line before because he hadn't had to. He'd been able to walk away.

But he couldn't walk away from his new wife and neither did he want to, because she came as part of a package and that package included his son. A son he needed to continue the Al Marara line for which he had worked so tirelessly.

His vision clearing a little, he stared down at the gleam of golden turrets as the jet circled the palace and a sense of resolve made him tighten his jaw. He liked Caitlin and enjoyed her company—he wasn't going to deny that. But that was all it could ever be. He wasn't going to start reaching for the stars, or reciting poetry to her. She was going to have to learn to manage her expectations. He didn't want her love distracting him and making demands on him. He didn't want to talk about *feelings*. He didn't want to engage in *any* kind of cloying emotional dependence. His jaw firmed. And as his wife, she needed to understand that.

'Are you looking forward to getting back?' he questioned, though from the brightness of her answering smile, you'd think he'd just lassoed the moon for her.

'Of course I am. I can't wait to see Cameron again. But I'm going to miss those nights, alone in the desert with you. And the days, come to think of it. I hope...' She hesitated, before reaching across to squeeze his hand. 'I hope things won't be terribly different when we're back at the palace.'

'I think it will be difficult to maintain that same level of intimacy,' he said, carefully removing his hand from hers. 'The nature of my work is such that I cannot guarantee being available for you with such frequency.'

'Oh.'

He flicked her a glance. 'But you understand what it's like, don't you, Caitlin? You understand the demands of my role?'

Caitlin forced herself to nod, telling herself that was what an understanding wife would do and that was what she was determined to be. The words she had spoken before and during the marriage ceremony she'd meant from the bottom of her heart. More than anything, she wanted to make this marriage of theirs work and the honeymoon had given her hope that such a thing was possible. A honeymoon which had been...

She leaned back against the comfy airline seat and sighed.

It had been magical; there was no other way to describe it. Totally and utterly magical. She had seen a much softer side to Kadir than he'd ever revealed to her before. During those hot, desert days and icy-cold nights some of the unremitting layers which could make him seem so unapproachable had been peeled away. Beneath a huge and silvery moon, she had caught glimpses of the man who had first stolen her heart.

He had taken her riding on one of the hardy Akhal-Teke horses which had accompanied them on the trip— just the two of them—his bodyguards keeping a discreet distance. He had shown her some of the secrets of the desert and the life which hummed beneath the seemingly unforgiving landscape. She had been remarkably un-spooked by the zig-zagging track of a sidewinder snake and had captured the slow progress of a desert tortoise with her camera. She remembered marvelling at the incredible *baswa* tree, which survived the barren conditions against all the odds, whose leaves could be boiled to make an invigorating tea and whose sap produced a delicious syrup.

And by night… Her heart pounded with erotic recall. Kadir was the most amazing lover—she'd known that before, of course, but somehow their marriage seemed to have strengthened the bond between them. At least, it had from her point of view. Sometimes when he was deep inside her, she wanted to cry because it was so beautiful. It was just like all those romantic novels and corny songs. It was like the first time she'd met him, only more so—because this time she knew him.

And she had fallen in love with him.

Was that so wrong? She stared down at her giant diamond ring, still glinting rather aggressively on her finger. How could it possibly be wrong, when he was her only lover and the father of her child? It wasn't as if she were demanding he love her back, because Kadir had told her he could never do that. But she was convinced she could be contented with things as they stood, because she'd never felt this happy before. As if she were floating on air. As if she could conquer the world, if only the world would let her!

She turned to look at him, her gaze resting on his hawklike profile and the jet-darkness of his thick lashes. My husband, she thought lovingly. My brave and beautiful husband. 'Shall we have dinner tonight, as a family?' she asked.

He turned his head to meet her eyes and Caitlin wondered if she had imagined the sudden steely glint which had penetrated his his black gaze. For a minute he had looked... Her heart began to race with something which felt like fear. It was almost as if he were looking *through* her, rather than *at* her. As if the powerful connection which had existed between them all week had suddenly been snapped.

'I'm afraid that won't be possible,' he said, his apologetic shrug seeming a little half-hearted.

Caitlin was unable to keep the disappointment from her voice. 'Oh?'

'I must meet with my advisors after so long away. Naturally, I'll come and say hello to Cameron as soon as we arrive and spend some time with him, but after that you will have to excuse me.'

She waited for the placating kiss, for the smile which would reassure her that nothing had changed, but neither of these things happened and as the plane touched down she couldn't shake off her faint feeling of panic.

And wasn't it funny how panic could grow? A bit like a blemish on your face which nobody else could really see, only you kept touching it and touching it until suddenly it was livid and red and enormous. Because that was how it was with them. That was what her relationship with Kadir suddenly became. One minute she'd been kissing him beneath a canopy of stars—and the next she was left wondering whether the whole honeymoon had been as insubstantial as a desert mirage.

She tried her best to be pragmatic. She told herself that maybe her expectations had been unrealistically heightened by the emotion of the wedding, and she must be prepared to accept a less heady lifestyle now they were back in the palace. But even before their honeymoon, Kadir used to spend every night in her bed, even if he *had* slipped away before the rest of the palace had woken up. Whereas now he was absent for one, sometimes two nights in a row. He'd been busy with work, he said. He was making up for lost time, he said. And there was plenty of space for him to sleep in his office. Even though they had their own enormous section of the palace, she sometimes awoke in the lonely hours before dawn to find the space beside her still empty.

She tried to reassure herself about that too—because when he *was* in bed with her, it was as heart-stoppingly good as it had been before. And if she thought that sometimes he was only pretending to be asleep—well, that was just her imagination, wasn't it?

Wasn't it?

At least the Sheikh's attentions towards their son remained constant and Caitlin was able to derive comfort from that. Each morning she joined them in the stables and watched as their son grew more confident on his new pony—now called Bunni, which apparently meant brown and had nothing to do with rabbits.

With her new camera, she took hundreds of photos of Cameron with his father but she captured plenty of other images, too. Arty pictures of gilded arches, the misty blur of a fountain glimpsed through a curtain of flowers—and the snow-capped peaks of the Zeitian mountains. One shot she was particularly proud of— taken of Kadir as he walked through the wide palace corridors, his shoulders appearing to carry the weight of his destiny.

But these creative endeavours only went so far in providing her with a feeling of satisfaction, before her thoughts inevitably ran into the brick wall of fear. With each day that passed, it became harder to deny the sense of being the outsider in this gilded new home of hers. She became more and more certain that Kadir was pushing her away from him and one morning, her worst fears were confirmed.

Imagining her husband to still be occupied with the visiting Maraban Ambassador, Caitlin had been in her husband's office, a room to which, as Queen, she now had unfettered access. The light in there was particularly good and she wanted a shot of the rose garden before the sun was too high.

She wasn't snooping. Most definitely she wasn't snooping. She just happened to be walking past his

desk. And what would anyone else do in the circumstances if they saw their own name on a sheet of paper,
which was lying right next to a golden-framed photo
of Cameron?

Without touching it, she quickly scanned the handwritten note, which had the name of a London legal
firm embellished on the top. She remembered Kadir
once telling her that all legal matters were conducted
in English, because that meant they could be enshrined
in international law and also because not many people spoke Xulhabian. It had made perfect sense at the
time and Caitlin supposed she should be glad of it now
because it meant she could understand what she was
reading, but she almost wished she *didn't* understand.
Her disbelieving mind skated past the formal greeting
of 'Majesty' as she tried to absorb some of the letter's
contents, because it was about her. Or, more specifically, it was about Cameron. Her throat felt raw and
her eyes burned as one sentence branded itself on her
brain and, despite its stuffy legal phraseology, it was
easy to understand.

*The marriage obviously confers legitimacy and
inheritance rights on the young Prince, but also
the mother will now be unable legally to remove
the child from Xulhabi without your consent.*

Suddenly it all made sense. The softening of Kadir's
attitude towards her and the clever wooing. The way
he'd made her *feel* stuff she'd never been expecting to
feel. The sense that something tangible and wonderful had been within her reach, only to have it snatched

away at the last moment. Caitlin's fingers tightened around her new camera. She wanted to hurl the expensive piece of kit to the ground and smash her foot down on it, but that would be the behaviour of a hysteric and she needed to be calm. Because everything she held dear depended on staying in control. She sank down on the window seat as she forced herself to focus on one single, comforting fact.

She wasn't going mad.

She wasn't imagining things which weren't really happening. She *was* being excluded! She had served her purpose by marrying the powerful Sheikh and, in so doing, had relinquished all her maternal authority, without her knowledge. How sneaky and cruel was that? Was that why he was pushing her further away from him—so that she could quietly be siphoned out of royal life? Perhaps that was the reason he'd been so keen to make their family bigger—also without her permission—so she could become some little breeding machine in the corner of the palace, quietly giving birth to heirs and spares.

And all the time she had been falling in love with him. Deeper and deeper and deeper. Did that make her as foolish as her poor mother had been? A deluded woman who had clung to the futile hope her married lover would one day leave his wife—and who had wasted so much time in pursuit of her own desires she had made her and Caitlin's lives a misery.

But she had been guilty of something similar. She had craved love from a man who had told her right from the beginning that he was unable to provide it. She had allowed her own romantic fantasies to blind her to a truth she had refused to recognise, which was that she was simply a means to an end. She'd been so grateful to him for providing her with security and for legitimising their son that she hadn't stopped to realise that she was never intended to be anywhere except on the sidelines.

As the sun rose higher in the sky behind her, she sat on the window seat and waited, her heart pounding a fast and steady beat as a feeling of doom threatened to envelop her.

She shook her head when a servant entered and enquired whether she required refreshments and she was equally negative when Makim appeared at the door to ask whether she was okay.

'I'm waiting for…' she nearly said *my husband*, until a small voice in her head suggested she might want to start recalibrating her mindset '…the Sheikh,' she finished, unable to keep a note of venom from her voice as she looked up defiantly at Kadir's aide.

'But have you not consulted with his diary, My Queen?' He seemed perplexed. 'His Serene Majesty has meetings until early this afternoon.'

'I don't mind. I'll wait.'

Had Kadir been alerted to this display of his wife's stubborn tenure? Was that why he appeared within minutes with an expression of irritation he didn't bother to hide.

'I'm assuming this is important?' he questioned.

For a moment Caitlin felt almost awestruck by his arrogance until she remembered that he was a master of battle—and didn't people say the best form of defence was attack? Well, maybe she would take their advice.

She got up from the seat and walked over to his desk, plucking up the lawyer's letter which was lying there.

'I've just read this!'

'Oh?' His features remained implacable. 'Have you been spying on me, Caitlin?'

'Don't you dare try to turn this round!' She sucked in a furious breath, waving the letter in front of him. 'Instead, why don't you try explaining *this*?'

It occurred to Kadir that never had anyone addressed him quite so insolently just as it occurred to him that maybe, in some mysterious way, he was relieved this had happened. At least now matters could be brought to a head and there could be no misunderstanding. 'What you read is nothing but the truth, Caitlin. There is really no need to distress yourself,' he said. 'You must have known deep down that such a clause would exist. Are there not laws in place in most countries, to prevent one parent fleeing with a child without permission? And when that child is a prince, it becomes even more important.'

'You think that's what I might do?'

Kadir met her eyes and suddenly the atmosphere between them changed. He felt the first fraught dark charge of something he didn't recognise and realised too late that, by bringing matters to a head, he was going to have to face the very truth he had been seeking to avoid. 'I don't know what you might do, Caitlin,' he answered quietly. 'I've always found women extremely unpredictable.'

She nodded as she stared into his eyes and then she began to speak.

'I thought I could be happy here,' she said slowly.

'Because there's pretty much everything here a person could ever want. I liked the way Cameron settled in here and I liked the way you interacted with him. I still do. And I like Xulhabi. The desert and the palace and the rose gardens. The capital city is buzzy and vibrant—what little I've seen of it—and I was looking forward to exploring more of the country as your Queen and taking on some charities of my own.'

'So there's no problem?' he said, coolly clipping out the words as if he were in a meeting with one of his diplomats.

She gave him a look—a look of such pain that it made him want to turn away. But he couldn't. He had to face this head-on because he owed it to her. And he owed it to Cameron, too.

'I think you'll find there is,' she said quietly. 'And you know exactly what it is.'

He knew what she meant. Of course he did. But surely it was her place to admit it, rather than his to accuse. Yet the very terms he was using disturbed him. *Admit. Accuse.* Weren't those words frequently used in a court of law? Not those usually associated with the subject they were talking about, even though neither of them had had the guts to mention it. Until now.

'You're in love with me?' he suggested.

Caitlin met the gleam of his black eyes without flinching, wishing she could deny his words, but she couldn't. And what would be the point of adding a layer of lies to this already heartbreaking situation?

'Yes, I'm in love with you,' she burst out. 'I know it's irrational and a complete waste of time, but there's nothing I can seem to do about it. I tried to forget you right from the start, but I couldn't. And when you found us, I tried to hate you for kidnapping us and bringing us here, but the terrible truth is that I actually liked it. In some warped kind of way I felt protected for the first time in my life. And I liked being with you again—'

'Caitlin—'

'No,' she interrupted fiercely. 'Let me finish this—because you were the one who asked the question and you are the one who needs to hear my answer. Maybe I'm one of those sad women who are programmed to care only for men who are cruel, just like my mother. Except that sometimes—when you forget to erect all those barriers around you—you aren't cruel at all. You're funny and clever and perceptive—which goes some way towards cancelling out your arrogance and high-handedness. I know. I should have had the courage to say all this to you before, but I didn't.' She gave a bitter laugh. 'Because when you asked me to marry you, I felt hope—I'm not going to deny that. I thought that, despite everything you'd said, you might be open to change. And then I thought we'd grown super-close over our honeymoon and we might continue to do so. I thought you might be willing to give us a chance—to see if that bond between us could grow.'

'Despite the fact I expressly told you that would never happen?' he demanded.

'Yes, despite all that,' she agreed. 'Delusional of me, I know—but hope can be an annoying thing and you can't always quash it, no matter how much you might try. But you began to do the exact opposite of getting closer, didn't you, Kadir? You began to push me away and that made me re-examine my own intentions. I'd been so sure that I could be contented with the very minimum of what most people ask in a marriage. But I've discovered I can't do that,' she finished huskily. 'I can't pretend things I don't feel, and I don't want my son to grow up in an atmosphere where he's afraid to show love, brought up by parents who are cold and distant with each other. If we do that, aren't we only perpetrating the kind of dysfunctional behaviour which made your own childhood so unhappy?'

'So what are you telling me, Caitlin?' he questioned harshly. 'What is your conclusion to this astonishing list of insights?'

Perhaps if he'd been a little kinder towards her, then Caitlin might have backtracked a little. Might have suggested that maybe they should give it a month or two and see how things progressed. But the condemnation which glittered from his black eyes told her more than she could bear. And if he didn't love her now, in this early stage of their marriage, wasn't it inevitable that his feelings for her would turn at best to indifference and at worst to hate?

'I want to take Cameron back to Scotland with me,' she said, resolutely ignoring his hissed intake of breath. 'I know it won't be easy and I'm happy to take any recommendations you may have regarding security aspects—'

'Oh, *are* you?'

'He can come out here on a regular basis and, whenever you come to the UK, you can see him,' she continued. 'Because I will never deny you access.'

He met her eyes. 'But you are now aware that you cannot remove our son from the country without my permission,' he said quietly.

'Yes, I'm aware of that. But I'm hoping that you will be big enough to disregard that clause. You can have Cameron as often as is possible, but I'm asking you to let me take him back to Scotland. Please. Don't trap me here as if I were a butterfly in a jam jar.'

For a moment there was silence. A silence so fragile yet so hefty that it seemed to bear down on Kadir like the crushing of a thousand trees on his shoulders. He saw her lips trembling, but for once they were not trembling with desire, but with apprehension. He knew he could insist that she stay and that the law was on his side. Given time, he might even be able to kiss her into something approaching submission—but that would be despicable. Because he had been honest with her, yes, but that honesty had destroyed something between them, and that something was trust. She was looking at him now with such wariness and disappointment in her eyes that he felt as if he had taken something very beautiful within the palm of his hand and crushed it. The pain inside him built and built. Any minute now and it would fell him completely.

'Take him,' he said heavily. 'Take Cameron back to Cronarty, but do it as quickly as possible. And now go, Caitlin. Leave me—not in peace, no—but at least with the time to compose myself before my next meeting.'

CHAPTER FOURTEEN

THE PAIN WAS still intense. Like an iron fist clamped around a raw and bloody heart, and Kadir had never known pain like it. Not during the many battles he had fought for his country, when his lifeblood had turned the sand rusty, or the witnessing of his friend's death. Not even during his mother's early rejection, or the subsequent discovery of his first wife's hopeless addiction. Because this pain was different. This was something else.

Standing in the palace courtyard, he stared up at the cloudless sky and watched the blue and green royal jet as it headed westward—towards Scotland and a tiny rain-lashed island. He bit down hard on his lip in an attempt to distract himself from the confusion of his thoughts and the disorientating feeling that his world was spinning out of control. He told himself that of *course* he would feel something when, just an hour earlier, he had said goodbye to his wife and son. But stupidly—and infuriatingly—he found himself having to blink back tears. Tears! He who had never cried in his life. Not even over Rasim. But then he'd never had to endure a farewell quite like this before.

Cameron had clung to him as if he never wanted to let him go, but children were capricious beings and one murmured mention from Morag about the pet hamster which awaited him back in Scotland had been enough to ensure an instant gap-toothed smile.

'I will come and meet Hamish very soon,' Kadir had said gravely.

'When, Papa?'

Kadir's eyes had met Caitlin's over their son's head and he had found himself wondering when those wide blue orbs had become such cold, pale ice. He had wanted to reach for her then and to hold her against the painful acceleration of his heart, but she had turned away, her expression tight and unmoving.

'As soon as it can be arranged,' he had replied, with forced jollity.

And now he was alone. Alone with his thoughts and all the freedom he had once craved. Freedom from the unrealistic and claustrophobic demands of something he had never asked for. He did not want her love—a love he was incapable of returning. And when she had told him she could not live that way he had let her go.

He had done the right thing by them all.

It was better this way.

He went to his office, but instead of distracting himself with the stack of paperwork which awaited his attention he found himself staring at the gold-framed photograph of his son, which Caitlin had taken. It had been shot soon after they had named Cameron's pony and it had been his son's first ride on Bunni. He had been beaming with pride and achievement and the look he had slanted at him had been all for his father. A look

which had been conspiratorial and full of comrade-
ship. And love.

And that was the photo which Caitlin had printed off
and given to him in this golden frame. 'This is *my* wedding gift to *you*,' she had announced shyly.

He had felt choked—he wasn't going to deny that.
And yet he had resented the way she'd forced him to
feel that emotion. Had it been that which had made him
nod his thanks and turn away in a manner which some
people might have described as churlish?

Turning away from the window, he began to pace
the room, wondering how he could bear to endure what
he alone had orchestrated. Yet this was all for the best.
Those were the words he kept repeating, like a mantra.
If he kept telling himself it would be better for Caitlin
and Cameron in the long run, then wouldn't that make
his pain easier to bear?

But first he had to start believing it himself.

Sitting down behind his desk, he picked up his pen
and pulled a sheet of paper towards him, not lifting his
head or turning around to acknowledge the soft sound
of the door opening behind him. Makim would quickly
infer from his forbidding demeanour that he was not
in the mood for conversation, or interruption. The way
he felt right then, he couldn't imagine talking to anyone ever again.

He heard the sound of the door closing and still he
ignored it.

'Kadir?'

It was a soft voice. A familiar voice. The voice which
had murmured softly into his ear or cried out his name
more times than he could bear to remember and Kadir

cursed the tricks the mind could play. But he would not be haunted by her memory. He could not let himself do so—for that way lay madness.

'Kadir?'

The voice was a little louder now and Kadir froze, then turned round to see Caitlin standing there, still wearing the tweed skirt and blouse she had changed into before leaving for her flight.

Alarmed, he dropped his pen and rose to his feet, black fears like crows crowding swiftly into his mind. 'What's wrong?'

'Nothing's wrong.'

'Then…' He tensed, his eyes narrowing as he studied her face for clues. 'Why are you here?'

Why was she here? It was a question Caitlin had asked herself over and over during the drive back here and she still wasn't sure if she had come up with the right answer. The only thing she *had* known was that she couldn't go through with taking a sobbing little boy all the way back to Scotland. A little boy who had spent the entire journey to the airfield asking for 'Papa'. This might not be the best course of action—for her—but it was certainly the right thing for Cameron and she needed to cling on to that.

'I couldn't go through with it. I couldn't go back,' she said. 'Cameron was missing you so badly already. He didn't want to leave.'

'He didn't?'

The look of surprise and relief in his eyes was so raw that to see it felt as if she were invading a part of him he had never intended to show. And Caitlin realised then, as she had suspected all along, that Kadir *could* feel emotion. Just not for her. 'Mothers are supposed to put their children first,' she said. 'That's something my own mother never did for me, nor yours for you—and maybe it's time to redress that balance. I have to think about what Cameron needs—which is to stay here and grow up with you.'

'But I saw the royal jet flying westward.'

'I dispatched Makim to bring his hamster back here. The air-conditioning in the palace means he should be fine.'

He was shaking his head. 'I don't understand.'

She could see that. It seemed she was going to have to spell it out for him.

'You told me you didn't do love, or, rather, that you *couldn't* do love. At first I didn't want to believe it because it didn't suit me, but gradually I came to accept that what you said was true. How could I fail to? You went out of your way to show me that you meant it. You made sure you pushed me away and kept me at arm's length. You rejected all my attempts to grow closer. After our honeymoon, it was like you shut down completely.'

'That much is true,' he said flatly.

It was a blank admission and one which sounded devoid of regret, but Caitlin hid her unrealistic sense of disappointment and continued.

'But you do love your son, don't you, Kadir? You love him so much that it's a gift to watch you together—it's *wondrous*. Yet you were prepared to let him go. You were prepared to sacrifice your own feelings to do what you felt was the best thing for Cameron—and me. And sacrifice is a form of love. In fact, it's possibly the greatest form of love there is, because it's totally lacking in ego, or self-interest.'

She swallowed back the tears which were welling up at the back of her eyes, because she didn't want to break down in front of him. There would be plenty of time for tears later.

'And that's why I've brought Cameron back to you.'

There was silence for a moment and his gaze was steady, as if he were giving her time to retract her statement, but when she said nothing, he spoke at last. 'And you?' he questioned heavily. 'What will you do?'

She shrugged. 'I will stay, because I have no choice other than to stay. I cannot deprive Cameron of a mother, any more than I can deprive him of a father. I will become the best Queen I can possibly be. I will accept and enjoy what is, and not yearn for things which are not mine to have. I will not ask you for love, Kadir, because one-sided love never really works—I saw that with my mother. And in time my feelings for you will fade—that's inevitable…a bit like the flowers in a hot summer garden wilting if they don't get enough water. All I ask is that you treat me with respect and set our son a good example of what an amicable relationship can be, so it doesn't put him off love and marriage when he is of an age to want those things for himself.' She forced a smile, which felt as if it were slicing her face in two. 'Let's do our best not to warp his perception about human relationships, shall we?'

Kadir closed his eyes, realising that she had condemned him with her words. That her generosity of spirit and good heart were making him feel like the most contemptible of men—and with good reason. He was not worthy of her. Perhaps he would never be worthy of her. But he had to show that he could try to be, if only she would give him one last chance. She had to. Because this was one battle he could not afford to lose. Unless it was already too late.

He opened his eyes and knew that he was responsible for the desperately sad expression she was doing her best to hide and a feeling of self-contempt made his blood run cold. What kind of brute was he? What *kind*?

He clenched his fists. 'Caitlin, I need to tell you something—'

'You don't—'

'Please. Hear me out, as I did you.' He sucked in a ragged breath. 'What I felt for you, all those years ago, was like a bolt of lightning to my heart. But my guilt about Adiya allowed me to convince myself it was nothing but the pent-up lust of a man who'd never had sex before, which had finally spilled over. Even when I returned to Scotland to find you again, I was certain that what I felt was nothing but carnal desire, and the anger I experienced when I found out about Cameron gave me permission to dislike you. But I couldn't dislike you. The more time I spent with you, the more I saw your humour and softness, which had so attracted me in the first place. I discovered what a good person you were—as well as being a remarkable mother to our son. And that frightened me.'

For the first time, her face lost some of its tight, pinched expression. 'Frightened you? You don't strike me as the kind of man who would be frightened of anything.'

'Everyone feels fear, Caitlin,' he said, and as he spoke

he realised he was being truly honest with himself. 'It's just that some of us are better at hiding it than others. I never opened up to the pain I'd felt when I was a child. I'd never shown anyone how much my mother's treatment of me wounded me. I think I was trying to protect my father from any more suffering. He already had her betrayal to contend with—I think if he'd known of my heartbreak, it would have finished him.' He sucked in a shuddered sigh. 'Just like I never showed the pain I felt when Rasim died, for it felt like a kind of weakness to do so. I still had a country to repair after the ravages of war, and a people who were looking to me for guidance.'

'So you buried all those feelings deep inside you,' she said slowly. 'Which only made it worse. Because things which are buried just get more and more rotten.'

He gave a bitter laugh. 'You could say that.'

'But why are you telling me all this, Kadir?' she said, her voice sounding very precise, as if she was picking out each word with care. 'And why now?'

Had he wanted her to guess at his reasons without having to articulate them? Of course he had. Because that would have been easier. Easier for him, certainly. But not for her. And he owed her this. He owed her so much, but this more than anything. 'Because the pain of not having you in my life is far greater than any other pain I could ever contemplate,' he husked. 'It eclipses everything—even the fear of rejection and of becoming too reliant on another human being and opening myself up to hurt again. I've discovered that holding back from you and pushing you away doesn't make me happy. Having you beside me does—but I've been fighting those feelings for so long.

'I fought them at the beginning and I did the same when I brought you here. I fought them on our honeymoon—the single most blissful week of my life. And now I fear it may be too late. That you may have given up on me. But I love you, Caitlin. I love you so much.' He slapped his hand over his heart and let it lie there. 'Believe me when I tell you that.'

Had he been hoping for instant capitulation? For her to fling herself into his arms and forgive him? Yes, he probably had. But she didn't move. She just stood there surveying him, with that same wary look in her eyes.

'You don't have to say all this stuff to seal the deal, you know, Kadir,' she said stiffly. 'Cameron is coming to live here, no matter what.'

He shook his head. 'I'm not trying to seal the deal,' he said simply. 'I'm trying to heal the deal.'

Maybe it was the break in his voice which swung it—that or the transparent brightness of his gaze. Because suddenly she was hurling herself across the office as she had done once before on a plane high above the Alps. But this time she was not brandishing a jewelled paper knife above her head and threatening to do him harm. This time she was in his arms and covering his face with kiss after fervent kiss and telling him she loved him, that she had loved him from the first time she'd ever seen him and that she would never stop loving him.

And for the first time in Kadir's life he knew peace. Real peace. Solid and rich and beautiful. Because he didn't just love Caitlin—he believed her and he *trusted* her. And right now, that felt like the most profound gift he had ever received.

EPILOGUE

'MAGNIFICENT.'

'Superbly captured.'

'What talent! Honestly, I had no idea.'

Caitlin smiled. Some of the praise was in English and some in Xulhabian, but she couldn't fail to be aware that the reaction to her photographic exhibition remained heart-warmingly positive. It had been open for a month now but its sell-out status showed no sign of abating.

'If it was anyone else reaping this kind of praise, I'd be worried that their ego might start over-inflating,' Kadir murmured and she looked up to see a smile playing around the edges of his lips. 'But since it's you, my darling Caitlin, I don't think there's any danger of that.'

She gave a sigh of pleasure as she acknowledged his approval, and looked around the vast gallery space in Azraq which Kadir had commissioned to mount her debut photographic exhibition. At first she'd been worried that such a move might be seen as nepotism, but then a prestigious visiting dealer had seen it and asked if she would consider transferring it to London's Mayfair. There was even talk of turning it into a touring exhibition, for the Xulhabian Tourist Board were eager to show the world a different side of the country which had been so faithfully recorded by their young Queen.

Blown up and magnified were images from their honeymoon—almost two years ago now. Dramatic sunrises, star-spangled skies and a desert tortoise basking in the sand, beneath the shade of a *baswa* tree. There were arty shots taken around the palace, showing areas which the public never usually got to see. Much interest had been generated by her early portrait of Kadir, walking through the wide marble corridors with his robes flowing around him and, seemingly, the weight of his destiny hanging heavy on his shoulders. Yet the most recent photo was of him and Cameron on their horses, looking into each other's eyes and laughing. It showed a different side of the desert Sheikh—the more *human* side, as the international press were fond of putting it.

But pride of place went to a candid study of their son, holding the hamster previously known as Hamish. To Cameron's delight, the much-loved pet had been flown from Cronarty to Xulhabi, and then surprised them all by producing a litter of seven pups. And so Hamish had been renamed Hasina and her offspring had all been found caring homes.

Even Morag had found her own happy ending, for she had quietly married Ghassan, the head groom, in a simple and loving ceremony which would have melted the most indifferent heart. The middle-aged couple had been given their own small section of the royal palace and the Scottish nanny was able to continue to help care for Cameron—the little boy and future king who was thriving with each day that passed.

Caitlin sighed as she looked up at her husband. Her

beloved husband who was now her greatest friend and advocate. 'I have you to thank for letting me show my work here, my darling,' she said softly.

'And I have you to thank for bringing so much light and love into my world and transforming it completely. And although I can never thank you enough, my flame-haired temptress, I can but try.' His black eyes glinted as his voice dipped into a provocative whisper. 'Maybe we should go home right now so that I can demonstrate exactly what I mean.'

Caitlin expelled a slow breath of excitement. Who-ever would have thought that an illegitimate girl from Cronarty would have ended up thinking of a palace as her home? But she did. Yet she knew that if the world changed tomorrow and she had to go and live with Kadir and Cameron in that small croft on Cronarty—which they sometimes visited, unannounced—they would be just as happy. Because life wasn't about jew-els and palaces, or ruling a huge country. It was about the relationships you had with the people around you—and hers were just the best.

When they got back to the palace, they would retire to their beautiful sandalwood-scented suite and undress each other at leisure. Her fingers would explore the honed muscle beneath Kadir's satin skin and he would make her gasp as he put his sensual lips to good use. She would enjoy his body—and he hers—as they'd done every time they'd made love. Which had been a dizzy-ing and spectacular amount of times.

And later, when she was lying satisfied and replete in the warm circle of his arms, she would announce her news. Actually, she would make sure that most of the lamps were still lit, because she wanted to see his face when she told him he was going to be a father again. She wanted to capture his joy and keep it in her mind for ever, fixed there as permanently as any photograph. This time he would see her carry their unborn child and this time he would watch her giving birth.

A ripple of gratitude flickered over her skin as she nodded her head in reply to his question.

'Yes, my darling Kadir,' she murmured. 'Let's go home.'

* * * * *

CLAIMING HIS OUT-OF-BOUNDS BRIDE

ANNIE WEST

This book is dedicated to all the people,
professionals and especially volunteers,
who risk their lives fighting to save Australia
from deadly bushfires.
Thank you!

CHAPTER ONE

'IT'S COMING TOGETHER.' Sonia surveyed the fall of Olivia's full-length dress while another seamstress knelt between them, adjusting the hem. 'We're almost there.'

Olivia suppressed a sigh of relief. This was the last fitting and it seemed like she'd stood for hours being prodded, pinned and examined.

But the dress had to be perfect.

Next week Olivia would be here in Venice at the centre of a celebration that would spark worldwide attention. Her gown had to be one of a kind. It was expected by the public, the press and, above all, her family.

More importantly, if all went as she hoped, this dress would be visible proof to her conservative family and a risk-averse company board that she, and her proposals, had merit. Public interest in this gown would spearhead the new venture she'd put so much effort into planning.

She'd done everything her family required of her and more. Soon she'd have the opportunity to prove herself and fulfil her dreams. She'd actually have a say in running the company she'd worked so hard to be accepted into.

Olivia glimpsed her reflection in the enormous gilt-framed mirror that caught the light from the Grand Canal spilling into the *palazzo*'s salon.

The woman in the antique mirror didn't look like Olivia Jennings. Even the Olivia Jennings who'd learned, eventually, how to hold her own amongst Europe's wealthy elite. To look stylish and poised.

This dress turned her into someone else.

At a distance the chiffon and silk looked cream, but they held a warmth that came from the fact they were actually a pale blush colour. Fitted at the bodice and falling in soft folds to her feet, the dress was decorated with a multitude of tiny appliquéd chiffon flowers, each studded at the centre with a crystal. The bodice was encrusted with them and a few were sprinkled across the top of her skirt and sheer chiffon sleeves. When she moved miniature petals stirred and crystals caught the light from the windows and the antique Venetian chandelier.

'It's beautiful,' the seamstress said as she sat back on her heels, beaming. 'You look like you've stepped out of a fairy tale.'

'Which is exactly the effect we want.' Sonia nodded. 'Every woman wants to look like a fairy-tale princess at least once in her life.'

Not every woman.

It was a long time since Olivia had believed in fairy tales.

Early tragedy had robbed her of a comfortable belief in happy endings. Then, in her eighteenth year, any lingering romantic fantasies had been snuffed out for good.

But just because her hopes and dreams weren't the traditional fantasies didn't mean others didn't have them.

She looked in the mirror again, saw the delicate flowers rise and flutter with her deep breath and felt a strange tug of yearning.

There'd been a man. Just one man in the last nine years, who'd made her wonder for a few scant moments about instant attraction and soulmates.

It had been a crazy aberration. A moment that had felt like recognition, like a lightning bolt soldering her feet to the floor and making her heart dance to a strange, wonderful new harmony.

Of course it had led nowhere.

He didn't even like her.

And she...well, she'd done what she'd learned to do so well. Olivia had buried her disappointment and moved on.

Her grandparents were right. She was better off without fantasies of romance.

The flowers on her dress danced as she dragged in a fortifying breath.

Olivia smiled at both women. 'You've done a fabulous job. The dress is gorgeous and we'll have customers beating down the doors.'

'If you can persuade the board,' Sonia added, the hint of a frown at odds with the excitement in her eyes.

Olivia nodded. 'Leave that to me. I have my strategy worked out.' In a couple of weeks, when she finally took her promotion and her promised place on the board, she'd have the chance she'd worked for all these years. She was fully prepared.

'Twirl for me,' the junior seamstress said, scrutinising the hem.

Olivia pivoted on her handmade, crystal-trimmed high heels. Silk swished around her legs like a whisper. Hopefully there'd be lots of whispers from women eager to buy their own unique gown from the same source.

The seamstress got up. 'Perfect. You're going to steal the groom's breath when you walk down the aisle.'

Olivia curved her lips into the expected smile. 'Thank you.' No point explaining how unlikely that was. She and Carlo were friends, not lovers. Theirs would be a marriage of convenience.

It mightn't be every woman's dream, but, from what she knew of romance, Olivia was happy to avoid that trap. Mutual respect and friendship made a solid foundation for a good marriage.

It had worked for her grandparents.

It would work for her and Carlo.

Sonia leaned close to examine Olivia's sleeve as a knock sounded on the door.

'Would you mind seeing who it is?' Olivia asked the seamstress. 'I'm not expecting anyone.'

Her grandparents weren't even in Venice. Olivia had come ahead to check the arrangements for next week's wedding.

'Stand still a moment longer,' Sonia said, frowning at a flower that wasn't sitting right.

'There's a man here.' The younger woman scurried back, her eyes round, her hand smoothing her already smooth hair. 'It's *il signor* Sartori. He wants to talk with you.'

Carlo, here? He wasn't due till next week.

Sophia spoke. 'Can he wait five minutes? Tell him it's bad luck for the groom to see the bride's dress before the ceremony.'

'I'm afraid it can't wait.' A deep voice spoke from the doorway and all three women froze.

Olivia knew that voice. As usual it was clipped to the point of brusqueness, yet it held something more than impatience. Something that sent a trickle of heat spilling through her.

She closed her eyes for a second, regrouping.

She should be used to him by now. There was no reason for this unwanted response. They were politely distant, she and her soon-to-be brother-in-law.

That was exactly how she wanted to stay—distant.

Opening her eyes, she saw Sonia's wide stare and her assistant surreptitiously straighten her top.

Alessandro Sartori had that effect on women.

Carlo did too. But half her fiancé's attraction was in his smiling good humour. His older brother was more the strong, silent type. Except in his case it was distant and disapproving.

Olivia sucked in a breath and turned.

His straight shoulders filled the doorway. His lean frame was elegant yet powerful, as if his urbane air concealed a man far grittier and dangerous than his suave tailoring suggested.

As usual he wore a perfectly fitted suit. She'd never seen

him in anything else. He was a walking advertisement for Sartori, the firm whose exclusive menswear was renowned and coveted the world over.

Olivia wondered why the advertising gurus at Sartori hadn't suggested capitalising on their CEO's aura of leashed sexual power as a marketing tool.

His hair was like ebony, short around the back and sides and longer on top. It shone, glossy in the light from the chandelier. That same light revealed strong, even features, hooded dark eyes, a sculpted jaw and a sensual mouth that right now was set tight.

No surprise there. Alessandro Sartori always looked like that when she was around.

She wondered what she, or Carlo, had done now to annoy him. Surely with the wedding next week everything was going precisely as he wanted.

A spark of annoyance flared. Annoyance that her marriage had been concocted as part of a deal to combine the Sartori and Dell'Orto commercial empires. Concocted by her grandparents and this man.

Olivia released her breath in a calming flow.

It wasn't as if she hankered after a love match. The marriage and the merger would give her and Carlo the opportunities they'd worked so hard for.

No, it was a shadow of residual annoyance at having her life managed. *Again.*

From now on *she'd* be the one making decisions, taking control of her life.

'Alessandro. This is a surprise.' She'd hoped not to see him until the ceremony and have as little to do with him then as possible, though he'd be best man. 'I'm afraid none of the family are here and, as you know, Carlo is away.'

He must be looking for her grandparents. Alessandro Sartori's discussions with Olivia had been limited to passing pleasantries. As if she didn't have the brains or experience to understand business. The inference that she wasn't worth engaging in meaningful conversation rankled, especially as, soon, they'd be on the same management team.

'It's you I came to see.'

Just that. No explanation. No smile. Just that unwavering gaze.

Surprise held Olivia silent for a moment. He wanted to speak to *her*? It couldn't be about the wedding. He had no role in the preparations. It couldn't be business. Alessandro didn't discuss commercial matters outside the office, except with company executives. She didn't qualify...yet.

Her grandparents? Fear bubbled at the idea that something had happened to one of them. Except, if that were the case, it wouldn't be Alessandro Sartori passing on the news.

'We need to speak. Now.'

Typical of the man to expect her to drop everything the moment he arrived.

Olivia wanted to refuse, to suggest he make an appointment, since her schedule was fully booked.

She'd love to see his face if she did. He'd probably never had anyone refuse him anything. According to Carlo he'd always been the family favourite, the one who did no wrong, held up as a model to his younger brother.

A pity he hadn't learned a little humility along the way.

Yet she found herself turning to Sonia. 'I apologise for the interruption. But could you give us ten minutes?'

Sonia nodded. 'Of course. We'll go to the kitchen and grab a coffee. Call when you're ready.'

The two women left the room. Only then did Alessandro snick the door closed and cross the inlaid marble floor.

Strange how different the room felt without the other women here. Despite the salon's lofty ceilings, gilded antique furniture and vast space, it had seemed almost cosy as they chatted and worked on her wedding dress. Now the atmosphere chilled.

Maybe it was because of Alessandro's continuing silence, or his purposeful stride. As if some weighty matter brought him here.

Despite her high heels Olivia had to tip her chin up to meet his stare. He stood so near she saw tiny grooves at the corners of his mouth. They seemed to carve deeper as she watched.

'What can I do for you, Alessandro?'

It struck her suddenly that this was the first time they'd been alone together.

Olivia's heartbeat throbbed faster, banging against her ribcage.

'I have some news.' He looked past her towards a priceless but uncomfortable sofa. 'You might like to sit.'

Without thought she reached out and grabbed his sleeve. Her fingers clutched fine wool over reassuringly solid muscle and bone.

'Is it my grandparents? Has something happened to them?' They weren't a close family and the old couple weren't demonstrative in their affections, but they loved her in their own way. The thought of losing them made something inside her dip and heave.

'No, no. Nothing like that. Everyone is well.'

He lifted his other hand, as if to cover hers, then dropped it to his side.

Instantly Olivia let him go. She felt the *keep off* vibes as clearly as if he'd held up a sign. She looked away, feeling foolish.

'Come, you might as well be comfortable.'

'I can't. Not in this dress.' A sweeping gesture encompassed the beautiful concoction. 'I don't dare wrinkle it.'

'It can be ironed.'

Olivia didn't bother to answer. The comment showed his complete lack of appreciation of the delicate materials and exquisite, handmade details. Or an absence of sympathy for the poor seamstress who'd have the onerous task of making it pristine again without damaging it.

'I can stand and listen. What's this news?'

For a beat of her pulse he said nothing. 'Have you heard from Carlo lately?'

Olivia frowned. 'Of course. We're in regular contact.' Not as regular as if they were lovers, counting the hours till their reunion, but they kept in touch. He was in the States, wrapping up some business for his brother and catching up with friends.

'Today?'

Icy fingers gripped the back of her neck. 'Is he okay? Has something happened to him?'

'As far as I can tell he's physically fine. But I'd suggest you check your messages.' The glitter in Alessandro's eyes and the way he spoke, as if through gritted teeth, amplified her disquiet.

There had been a message from Carlo earlier. It had gone to voicemail when she had her phone on silent during a meeting with the caterer. Since then there'd been one thing after another. She hadn't had a chance to listen to it.

Olivia whirled away, the dress swishing around her. But her phone wasn't here. It was in the next room with her clothes. She swung back, nerves stretching as she saw a pulse throb in Alessandro's throat. A sense of urgency gripped her. Something momentous had happened.

'Just tell me! What's wrong?'

For an instant he hesitated, then Alessandro nodded.

'Carlo has jilted you. He's run off with another woman.'

CHAPTER TWO

OLIVIA FELT HER eyes bulge as she stared up into that stern face.

Jilted? It wasn't possible.

Carlo and she were in this together. They'd talked it through in detail, agreed they'd make the most of this marriage. They trusted each other.

Didn't they?

She swallowed hard, her hand pressed high against her suddenly arid throat.

'He wouldn't,' she whispered.

This wedding meant too much to both of them. And there was no other woman in Carlo's life. Not any more.

But she saw the truth in Alessandro's dark eyes. His lips twisted in something approximating a grimace.

Because he was forced to be the bearer of bad news? Or because he feared she'd collapse in a sobbing heap?

Olivia felt the air expel from her lungs then immediately rush back in as she tried and failed to take in enough oxygen. Diamond sparkles whirled before her eyes and the watered silk wallcoverings of *eau de nil* shimmered like an undulating wave rushing in to drown her.

She listed on her heels till a pair of large hands clamped around her elbows.

'Breathe. Slowly.'

Olivia blinked up into espresso-dark eyes that gleamed with an expression she couldn't decipher.

The swimming sensation eased and she stepped back, tugging free.

'You don't have to…' She shook her head. 'I'm fine.'

Yet she wasn't.

Everything seemed telescoped and odd. She hadn't felt this strange sense of dislocation for a long, long time.

For one thing, even though he'd released her, Olivia still felt the imprint of Alessandro's long fingers like a brand. She looked down, wondering if somehow the fabric of her sleeves had torn.

Of course it hadn't. Alessandro's touch had been supportive. Almost gentle. Crystal-studded flowers winked up at her. A reminder of the wedding scheduled for next week.

Olivia's stomach curdled.

'Are you absolutely sure?' Her voice was hoarse.

'Do you think I'd come here if I weren't sure?'

She sighed and reluctantly lifted her head. Alessandro looked grimmer even than usual, his nostrils flared as if in distaste at the news he had to impart.

No, Alessandro Sartori wasn't the sort to panic at a rumour. He'd be absolutely certain of his facts. Olivia had never met a more methodical, controlled man.

Sometimes she imagined Alessandro had been born clutching a fistful of company reports and scowling because the profits weren't better.

Olivia bit her lip, horrified at the way her brain meandered from the point.

Because this news was too horrible to confront.

She needed to *focus*.

'What, exactly, did he say?' Maybe Carlo only wanted to delay the ceremony. Maybe Alessandro had jumped to conclusions about there being another woman.

Yet, looking up into that serious face, she knew she was grasping at straws.

'Never mind. I'll find out myself.' Olivia spun away. She didn't want to hear about this second-hand. She needed to hear Carlo's explanation.

And she needed privacy, away from Alessandro's dour scrutiny.

Lifting her voluminous skirts, she marched down the

full length of the salon, past another set of sofas and gilded chairs. Past an enormous carved marble fireplace and four tall windows with views of the Grand Canal.

She should have kept her phone with her. Should have checked her messages earlier.

Normally Olivia would have, but today her patience had finally frayed. She'd needed a break from her grandparents' constant efforts to second-guess and query every aspect of the wedding arrangements. She'd decided she'd get through so much more if she had a few hours without interruption.

Palm against the massively tall door, Olivia pushed it open and hurried across the much smaller room she'd been using as an office while in Venice. She'd left her phone here.

Olivia's breath expelled as she found Carlo's message, put the phone to her ear and heard his voice. *Apologising.*

Her heart sank. Despite knowing Alessandro wouldn't come here without good reason, she'd hoped…

It was a long message. Carlo's tone varied between apologetic and excited.

He was genuinely sorry. He knew how much this marriage and the merger meant to them both. He didn't want to leave her in the lurch. But something wonderful had happened.

He'd met Hannah again, the American he'd fallen for while doing his postgraduate year in the States. The woman who'd broken his heart twelve months ago, refusing to leave home and move to Europe where his career was.

They loved each other—still, more than ever. This time they'd agreed a compromise. He'd live in the States for a year and work there, even if it meant giving up his prospects at Sartori, because he knew now that Hannah was more important to him than the family business. After that they'd spend a year in Europe to see how she coped living abroad. Then they'd decide where they'd settle. But they were committed to making this work. They were so happy. He regretted letting Olivia down but…

Olivia reached out and grabbed the back of a chair. Her fingers curled against the intricate wood carving, hard beneath her flesh.

The blood rushed in her ears, loud and harsh.

The fitted bodice that had been comfortable ten minutes ago now felt like a corset, cramping her breath.

No wedding meant no merger. Her grandparents had insisted on the marriage as insurance for the Dell'Orto family in the merged enterprise.

Which meant no seat on the board for Olivia. No permanent place in the company. Those too had been their conditions, despite years of exemplary work. Her grandparents might be business-savvy but they belonged to another era. An era when a woman, no matter how talented and well-educated, had to have a man at her side.

Olivia could have taken a position in another company. She'd had offers. But her heart was set on taking up her birthright. It was her dream.

Her family wanted her married. Not for love, but to maintain and expand the family fortunes. That was the way things had been done in the Dell'Orto family for generations. The exception had been Olivia's mother, who'd married for the mirage of romantic love, and look how that had turned out.

Olivia swallowed, trying to get rid of the sour taste on her tongue.

After all her work. All her dedication. Her endless forbearance with her grandparents' antiquated ways, all for nothing.

How soon before her family started scoping out a new husband for her?

For a fleeting moment she wished she could be like Carlo, falling in love. It sounded so easy. Even if the chances were it would end disastrously.

Olivia's vision blurred. All her hopes were shattered with this news. She couldn't even begin to imagine how she was going to pick up the pieces and move forward. For her family this was a business catastrophe and media nightmare. But for Olivia it was a personal disaster.

Alessandro cursed his brother silently and vehemently as the jilted bride sagged against an antique chair, her phone pressed between heaving breasts.

Her face leached to white, even her lips bloodless. She was bereft of colour except for bruised eyes that looked muddy with pain and her wheat-blonde hair in an elegant twist.

Instinct told him to go to her. She needed comforting.

He kept his feet planted where they were.

Better to keep his distance. Even now a phantom tingle teased his palms where he'd held her arms. It was a trick his mind played when he was around Olivia. He thought he'd eradicated the phenomenon through sheer determination.

Until now.

He didn't need this complication today of all days.

But Alessandro always rose to a challenge. The more impossible, the greater the eventual triumph. Not because he deliberately chose a tough course, but because life played out that way.

This didn't feel like triumph or challenge. It was an unmitigated disaster.

How could Carlo do this?

Alessandro ground his teeth, his fingers flexing. Trust Carlo to message him from America. He didn't dare face him in person.

Wasn't that like his family? Always putting themselves first, never considering how their actions affected others.

These last couple of years Alessandro had convinced himself Carlo had changed. His flighty younger brother hadn't seemed nearly so irresponsible. He'd matured, done well in his studies and at work. Alessandro had believed him ready to shoulder a bigger role in the company. He'd looked forward to sharing the load, working with his brother in tandem instead of being a stand-in parent as well as boss and mentor.

Now, with one appalling action, Carlo had destroyed the deal Alessandro had worked towards for two solid years. The deal that would see their company leap to another level.

Carlo had also left his bride reeling and distraught.

Alessandro's chest tightened as he watched Olivia. Her fingers were white-knuckled, her breathing erratic, and, for the first time he could recall, her shoulders slumped, as if she couldn't support the weight of disappointment.

He'd never seen her anything but upbeat or at least confident.

Did she love his brother? Had it been, for her at least, more than a marriage of convenience?

Alessandro grimaced.

It was a question he hadn't let himself dwell on. A Sartori-Dell'Orto marriage was required and Carlo had stepped up to the plate. That was all that mattered. Alessandro never let his thoughts stray to what Olivia and Carlo did in private.

Ever.

The pair were definitely close. From the first Alessandro had seen the ease between them that spoke of intimacy. Their heads tilted together as they laughed and Olivia's eyes sparkled when she looked at Carlo.

It was why Alessandro, despite being the elder brother, hadn't suggested being the one to marry the Dell'Orto heiress.

Carlo's surprising alacrity when the idea of marriage was raised had confirmed Alessandro's suspicion that there was already something between the pair.

Now Alessandro watched Olivia's mouth twist in pain and a fresh rush of fury engulfed him. Whatever their relationship, this news devastated her.

If Carlo had broken her heart on top of everything else...

Alessandro's hands clenched so hard they shook.

It was as well his brother was too cowardly to break the news in person. Alessandro would happily mar his pretty-boy looks with a punch to the nose. He, who'd never raised his hand to his kid brother in his life! Who prided himself on always being rational and calm.

Breathing deep, Alessandro shoved his hands in his trouser pockets and searched for his usual sangfroid.

His heart thudded too hard and too fast.

He assured himself it was simply because a heartbroken bride would be a nightmare to deal with.

'You heard from Carlo?' From her reaction she must have but Alessandro needed to be sure.

Her eyes turned to him. They looked glassy and dazed, as if she couldn't focus. Then she blinked and a frown formed on her face as if the sight of him pained her. Not surprising, given it was his brother who'd dumped her.

'Yes, he left a message.' She bit out the words as if she'd like to bite on him. Or perhaps Carlo.

Alessandro had broad shoulders; he could cope with her temper. It was justified.

'On behalf of my family I extend my deepest apology, Olivia. Carlo's action is reprehensible. Utterly inexcusable and—'

'He's already apologised. Several times.'

It was clear from her bitter tone and the twist of her lips that his brother's apologies didn't help. Even for Carlo at his most thoughtless this was a new low.

So much for Alessandro's belief that Carlo had matured during his year in America. Alessandro had put the change down to Olivia's influence steadying him, since they'd studied the same course. But clearly her example couldn't counteract the Sartori taint of heedless selfishness.

'He's done you a serious wrong, Olivia.' Alessandro found herself slowing on her name. 'He's also dishonoured our family name.'

'You'll understand if right now I'm not particularly worried about the impact on the Sartori name.'

Alessandro inclined his head, pleased to watch her stand straighter. Now she looked more like the woman he was familiar with.

Yet the way she clutched her phone to her breasts, as if holding in the ache of a broken heart, discomfited him. He wasn't used to tiptoeing around tender feelings. As a child he'd rarely known tenderness, and as an adult, well, he was wise enough to understand that sex and genuine caring were separate things.

'Of course. The trouble is that Carlo's actions won't only impact on our name.'

'No.' She turned away as if taking comfort in the view of Venice through the window. 'He's hurt us all, hasn't he?'

Yet despite her annoyance and distress, Alessandro didn't hear hatred in her voice. Where was the sharp lash of a woman scorned? Was it possible she cared so much for Carlo that even now she couldn't bring herself to despise him?

Alessandro's mind raced, trying to figure out whether that would make what he had to do easier or impossible.

'He has, and we need to discuss that.'

She swung back towards him, eyes huge in a too-pale face that seemed to have been pared back to the bone. Her oval face looked narrower, her pretty mouth tighter, and for once as she held her head high he saw not confidence but a desperate effort not to reveal distress.

'Do we? Surely this is something Carlo and I need to talk about?'

The hauteur in her tone eased some of Alessandro's tension. That was better. He'd rather deal with a woman who was cranky and offended than one who was hurt.

'Even though Carlo is in America, too craven to tell you his news face to face?'

Such behaviour was more than dishonourable. It was

pure insult. To Olivia. To her family. And to Alessandro, who'd persuaded them all to trust in him.

Now it was up to Alessandro to rectify the situation.

'That's hardly my fault.'

'Of course not. But talking with Carlo won't solve anything. He's adamant he's staying there. With another woman.' Tact should have prevented him mentioning the other woman. But Alessandro didn't have the luxury of prevaricating. He had to ensure Olivia understood the situation completely and was ready to deal with it. He couldn't let her hope for something that wouldn't happen, like Carlo returning.

She opened her mouth, presumably to object again, but Alessandro forestalled her.

'You've had a terrible shock. If I could, I'd leave now and give you time to come to terms with the news.' The last thing he wanted was to be here, having this conversation. 'But we don't have the luxury of time. We need to decide what happens next.'

He paused, watching her digest that.

She looked down, one hand drifting across a spray of jewelled flowers on her skirt.

'This merger is a juggernaut,' he added when she said nothing. 'If it doesn't go ahead the momentum will lead to a crash of unthinkable proportions. Neither of our companies or families will come out unscathed.'

'Okay.' Olivia let out her breath in a reluctant sigh. 'Let's talk.'

The idea of having Alessandro Sartori of all people picking over the bones of her thwarted marriage was about as appealing as root-canal therapy. But he was right. Damage control was vital.

Though what they could do she had no idea.

The one thing she was certain of was that her grandparents wouldn't proceed with the merger without her marriage, bringing the two families together on an equal footing. No merger meant not only years of wasted work, but also humiliation on a huge scale as the two companies drew apart. Public disquiet would go deeper than gossip on the social pages. There would be serious reservations about the competence and viability of both companies. The damage to reputation…

Alessandro gestured to one of the straight-backed chairs, inviting her to sit.

Olivia shook her head. 'Give me five minutes to get out of this dress.'

It wasn't just about preserving the dress in pristine condition. With its tight sleeves and closely fitted bodice, the gown was making her claustrophobic. Olivia wanted to rip it off rather than continue wearing a symbol of a marriage that wouldn't happen. Carlo had made a laughing stock of her and this gown was an all too physical reminder. The thought of wearing it any longer made her skin crawl. Maybe in putting on her own clothes she'd also recover her ability to think. Right now her mind was dazed and blank.

As for her chances of kick-starting a strong new venture with this dress, they were now at zero.

Alessandro was turning away when she stopped him. 'Wait.' She paused, slicking her tongue along dry lips. 'Could you help with the catch?'

Ridiculous to feel nervous. It was a simple task. But she couldn't wait till Sonia came back upstairs.

She watched one straight dark eyebrow rise on Alessandro's forehead, then flatten as he frowned.

As if she'd asked him for an unsecured business loan instead of help with a fastening. What was the guy's problem?

But he'd always had a problem with her. Right from that first day. Which showed how skewed her instincts had been regarding Alessandro.

She'd been at a party when her eyes locked on the handsome stranger on the far side of the room. She could have sworn that something primitive and powerful passed between them. Something that made the crowd's noise fade and her heart thump to an eager new beat as excitement fizzed in her blood. Then the crowd closed in and she lost sight of him.

Soon after, chatting with Carlo, she'd sensed she was being scrutinised. Only to find her heart-stopping stranger had morphed into Mr Tall, Dark and Dismissive. He'd scowled at them as if the sight of two friends talking was in some way repugnant.

Or as if she was. Olivia sensed it was the latter. Though his manners were impeccable, Carlo's brother always arranged it so they were never seated near each other. He was never alone with her. Was her presence so trying?

She suppressed a bitter huff of laughter. Carlo's news really was momentous. It had brought Alessandro to her. Would wonders never cease?

Her spurt of humour faded as he stepped behind her, close enough that she was conscious of his tall frame centimetres away. Warmth invaded her. From him? Or from something inside herself?

'Where's the catch?' He spoke softly yet his voice hit a disturbingly low note that she felt deep within. His breath expelled across her hair, piled up in a chignon, and down her neck, as if he inclined his head to investigate the dress.

Her breath snagged, breasts rising, and to her mortification Olivia's nipples beaded.

Choking down the urge to tell him it didn't matter, she lifted a hand to the neckline at the back of the dress, feeling for the first tiny catch.

'It's very delicate. There are a couple of fastenings.' The first she could manage but the next one was difficult.

'I see them.'

Olivia felt his fingers move against the fabric. He seemed in no hurry but soon she felt a whisper of air as he parted both the first and second fastening.

'I'll lower the zip a little, shall I, to get it started?'

She was about to tell him she'd manage when she felt it slide to her shoulder blades then stop. His hand lifted and she realised he'd been careful not to come into contact with her flesh. Nor had he dragged the zip too low. Clearly she didn't have to worry he'd take advantage of the situation. Proof, if she'd needed it, that Alessandro was anything but interested in her as a woman.

Unfortunately Olivia couldn't claim the same level of disinterest. Her nostrils twitched as she inhaled a hint of citrusy bergamot and—was that leather? It was a warm, summer's scent, with a depth that she guessed came from Alessandro himself, and it made her tingle all over.

She swallowed and tried to pretend her interest was purely professional. Because she hoped one day to steer the company towards creating designer fragrances.

If they could bottle Alessandro's scent...

Olivia pressed a palm to her bodice, though it wasn't in danger of falling, and looked over her shoulder. He stood so close they almost touched. Something snapped hard in her chest.

'Thank you. I'll meet you in the salon in a few minutes.'

'I'll ring for drinks.' He moved to the door, the frown back on his face as if the sight of her worried him. 'Coffee or something else?'

Brandy to revive her after the shock?

Her nose wrinkled. She felt like ordering a double vodka just to see his expression. It sounded the sort of thing you'd have when your world crumbled. Except she'd probably choke on the neat spirit and feel more gauche than she already did.

'Coffee is fine.'

He left the room. Only when the door shut did Olivia let her shoulders drop. She felt like she'd carried an unseen weight since she got Carlo's message.

She looked again at the phone. But what was the point

of listening to the message again? Alessandro was right. There was no time to rehash what was already done. They needed a plan. No matter how wobbly she felt or how unprepared to meet with Carlo's brother in the hopes of salvaging something from this mess.

Five minutes later, wearing a slim-fitting skirt and silk shirt, Olivia stepped into a pair of high heels and slicked on a bright lipstick.

Armour to face Alessandro?

The idea was laughable. He'd already seen her at her weakest. Besides, he wasn't her enemy precisely. Only a man who made her very uncomfortable.

Her laugh was a snort of self-derision. As if anything could make her more uncomfortable than today's news!

All her plans, her hopes, gone to glory.

Straightening her backbone, she turned the doorknob and entered the salon.

Alessandro stood by a long window. Not looking at the iconic view, but scowling down at his phone, texting.

It struck her that she'd never seen him relaxing, even at social events. He was always networking, discussing business opportunities, making every moment count.

Except the evening they'd first met. Then, for a brief time, it had felt as if all his attention was totally, irrevocably focused on *her,* not on business.

Hastily Olivia buried the thought. It was nonsense. Something she'd imagined. Even if it weren't, that moment had passed long ago.

She crossed the room, trying come up with some strategy to save the day. Some coup that would divert the disaster that loomed. But her brain ran in circles.

Except for the part of her mind fixed on Alessandro. The light slanting through the windows cast shadows that emphasised his aggressively masculine yet disturbingly sensual features. He wasn't a comfortable man to be around. She always felt on edge when he was near, as if one unwary step or word might end with…what? She'd never worked it out, just knew he made her tense.

But Alessandro was the driving force behind Sartori. His business acumen was phenomenal. If anyone could come up with a plan to lessen the fallout from this disaster, it was he.

Instead of going straight to him, Olivia headed for the tray on a nearby table. His untouched espresso was there and a milky coffee for her.

Had he noticed that, though half-Italian, she'd never developed the taste for strong coffee? She frowned and picked up her cup. As if! This was the housekeeper's doing.

When she looked back Alessandro was watching her. He'd turned towards her and with the sun behind him she couldn't read his expression. Yet tiny pinpricks pinched her skin. She knew his scrutiny was intense.

Looking for signs she was going to turn hysterical?

She picked up the tiny espresso cup and held it out to him, grateful when he moved to take it. The silence was thick with tension.

Olivia waited but still he didn't say anything. The nape of her neck pinched as if nipped by phantom fingers.

'I presume you're here because you've got a plan, Alessandro.'

Why else would he stay? He'd already delivered the apology on behalf of his family.

He lifted the tiny cup to his mouth and swallowed, then put it back on its saucer with a decisive click. Only then did he answer.

'I have.'

Olivia started. She'd thrown out the words more in hope than expectation.

'Why don't you sit before you spill that?' he added.

His words reminded her of earlier, when he'd come here to tell her she'd been jilted. But, she reassured herself, nothing he could say now could cap that. She'd had her earth-shattering news for the day.

So she ignored the warning premonition feathering her senses and sank onto a chair. That was better. Her legs were still too shaky.

'So.' She looked up to where he still stood, unmoving. 'What's your idea?'

'Simple. The wedding goes ahead.'

Olivia scowled. 'Even you couldn't force your brother back here to marry me when he doesn't want to.'

So much for believing Alessandro had a solution.

'Ah, but it won't be Carlo marrying you.' He paused, as if assessing her reaction. 'It will be me.'

CHAPTER THREE

ALESSANDRO DIDN'T THINK himself a vain man. He was pragmatic and understood that many of the women who vied for his attention and a place in his bed were drawn as much by the Sartori name and money as by him personally.

His brother accused him of being a dour workaholic. But Alessandro had known that, unless someone took responsibility, their dwindling family fortune would be gone before his parents knew they'd run out of champagne. That someone had been him.

Yet, watching Olivia's jaw drop and her cup rattle precariously on its saucer, he felt annoyance surge.

'I realise the idea comes as a shock.'

Still she said nothing. Just put her coffee down with shaking hands and stared at him with something that looked like horror. If she'd been pale before, now her pallor turned dead white.

Impatience rose. And something else. Something like disappointment, yet starker and unpalatable.

He'd expected surprise. But this? This was pure insult, though she said not a word. Her gaping dismay spoke volumes.

Anger rose, a searing flashpoint.

Olivia Jennings had been happy to marry his flighty brother, even though, from what he'd observed, she was more serious and sensible than Carlo.

True, Alessandro didn't have his brother's playboy charisma that made him the life and soul of every celebration. But Alessandro hadn't had the luxury of partying in his teens and twenties. He'd been too busy saving the family business from his parents' depredations.

But nor was he a gargoyle whose looks scared women away.

It's because she cares for Carlo. Maybe even loves him. Even now, despite what he's done.

He felt a hard, dropping sensation in his chest, as if something inside had come unmoored.

Could it be true?

How would it feel to be loved like that?

It wasn't something Alessandro had thought about before. He didn't waste time pondering circumstances that were unlikely to occur.

As a child the closest he'd come to love was his nanny's affection. As an adult there'd been women who'd claimed to love him but he hadn't believed them. Love was an easy word, usually an excuse for grabbing what you wanted, like sex or security. He suspected the reason his parents' marriage survived wasn't love but a mutual passion for indulgence.

'Olivia?' He kept his tone even, refusing to reveal his bruised ego.

Though he did take a moment to imagine how it would be if, no, *when* Olivia turned to him instead of away.

This deal had begun as a business necessity but now it was more. Alessandro would marry her because it was the only answer to the problems bearing down on them.

But he refused to have a wife who shunned him.

There'd be enormous satisfaction in watching that horror change to pleasure, to eagerness. For him. Not his good-for-nothing brother, but him, Alessandro Sartori.

Didn't he deserve some compensation for his labours?

Olivia with her alluring smiles, quick intellect and enticing body would provide just that.

'You're not serious!'

Alessandro flattened his lips. He never joked about business.

'You *are* serious.' She sat back in her chair, her expression changing from horror to concentration. 'But…' She shook her head and a tiny lock of hair wafted around her neck. It must have come loose when she changed. 'It's impossible. I'm to marry Carlo. The paperwork is done, the legalities…'

For the first time since he'd announced his plan Alessandro felt a flush of satisfaction. Because the bride's first objection wasn't personal but pragmatic. The paperwork was for Carlo Sartori to marry, not Alessandro. Surely if she and Carlo were in a serious personal relationship, her first thought wouldn't be legal forms.

'Leave that to me. The paperwork will be correct.'

She opened her mouth as if to object, then snapped it shut.

Alessandro watched that teasing lock of blonde hair swirl near her pale pink lips, her slim neck, then across her blouse of khaki silk that made her eyes glow more green than brown.

Even too pale, even distracted and distraught, Olivia drew him. She had from the start. Too much.

Finally she spoke, her voice strained. 'We barely know each other. You can't want…' She stopped, shaking her head as if in bewilderment.

His gaze skated her body, noting the stylish yet conservative skirt and blouse that signalled business. Then down slim legs to black stilettos that issued a completely different message.

Heat eddied low in his body.

Oh, he wanted, all right. Had wanted from the first.

It was a relief to acknowledge it. He hadn't allowed himself to think about it. Because she was the woman destined to be his brother's wife.

All that had changed.

Now they played by a completely different set of rules.

Now, finally, Alessandro let himself recognise the sharp hunger gnawing at his belly. A hunger that had nothing to do with food and everything to do with the woman sitting demurely across from him.

Yet for now it was best kept locked away. Till the time was right.

'This marriage has always been driven by the need to unite our families and businesses. It was never about personal wants.'

Alessandro watched her closely as he spoke, searching for some sign of agreement.

'Unless you're telling me you agreed to marry because you want Carlo? That it wasn't just business?'

His words surprised him. As if by even raising the possibility he urged her to agree that was the case.

Yet, even for the sake of the huge opportunities unlocked by this deal, he refused to take as his wife a woman who was actually in love with his brother.

She liked Carlo, obviously. They got on well together. They might even have been in a sexual relationship.

That thought evoked a familiar bitter taste on his tongue and a snarling bite of jealousy in his gut.

But there was a huge difference between sex and love. If Olivia was going to spend the next few decades sighing over some romantic dream—

'No.' Frowning eyes met his. 'The marriage was always about business. It was my grandparents' idea, not mine.'

He nodded. The Dell'Ortos' insistence on a marriage to seal the company merger was outdated, not the suggestion of a twenty-seven-year-old. Especially one who'd spent her formative years on the other side of the world, far from her grandparents and their antiquated notions. Families like theirs hoarded their wealth through generations of arranged unions. Why should it be different now?

And he, modern man as he was, had seen the positives

of the merger. Why not marry to benefit the company and the family's interests?

'So you're not in love with my brother?'

Alessandro gritted his teeth as the words escaped. Did they make him sound needy for reassurance? Or simply like a man clarifying the ground rules?

Olivia's neat chin lifted, her eyebrows contracting in a tight frown. 'No. Carlo and I were never in love.'

Olivia's heart thumped as she met that penetrating stare. For some reason Alessandro Sartori always had the ability to make her feel as if he saw right through the shell she'd built around herself to the woman beneath.

She told herself that was impossible. No one understood how she'd struggled to turn herself into a woman who could hold her own in the cut and thrust sphere of international business and the rarefied world of Europe's privileged wealthy. She might be a descendent of the Dell'Orto family but they'd made it clear from the day she arrived in Italy at age thirteen that she lacked the gloss, elegance and social skills required of her.

Now she fought to suppress a blush at the idea of discussing love with Alessandro Sartori of all people.

Romantic love wasn't on her agenda. Hadn't been since she was eighteen, gullible and badly let down. Which made the immediate, inexplicable tug of awareness she'd felt the first time she met Alessandro so disturbing. And made her even less comfortable discussing feelings with this man.

That didn't seem to bother him. He gave a curt nod as if satisfied. 'Good. If you don't love him, then you'll have no objection to becoming my wife. The principle is the same.'

Olivia felt herself goggle. The principle might be the same but the man definitely wasn't. Where Carlo was sunshine and optimism his brother was dark skies with a hint of thunder in the distance. He made her skin prickle just by walking into the same room.

'But I don't know you.'

One sleek black eyebrow lifted.

'Marriage will remedy that.'

His deliberate, audacious refusal to understand her reservations grated, firing her anger. Olivia's lungs swelled on an in-caught breath.

For a nanosecond she could have sworn his glittering stare dropped to her heaving breasts. But logic told her she imagined things. Alessandro didn't see her as a woman but as a pawn to be moved on the chessboard of his contract negotiations.

Was there ever a more frustrating, annoying, *arrogant* man?

Between them the Sartori brothers seemed determined to make her life hell.

Now she regretted not asking for that double vodka instead of coffee. Maybe it would have inured her to the shocks of this conversation. This whole discussion felt surreal.

'I can't believe you're seriously suggesting that I marry you next week.'

'Why? I think it's an excellent solution.'

He leaned back in his seat, stretching out his long legs and crossing one ankle over the other, the picture of ease.

Olivia felt her blood sizzle at his air of sophisticated boredom. As if he hadn't lobbed one hand grenade after another into her life. First Carlo's desertion at the eleventh hour. Then to suggest marriage with the casual insouciance of a man ordering a pre-dinner aperitif!

As if *she* were available for the ordering!

'Hmm, let me think.' She sat straighter, her chin lifting. 'Maybe because all the guests, not to mention the press and the world at large, expect to see Carlo put a ring on my finger, not you?' Her breath snared at the sudden, vivid picture filling her brain. Because she was so furious, she assured herself. 'What on earth would we say? What reasonable explanation could we give?'

'We'd say nothing. It's no one's business but ours.' His gaze didn't waver. 'Never explain. Never give excuses.'

She shook her head. 'But your friends and family wouldn't understand.'

Her grandparents wouldn't object. On the contrary they'd be happier, seeing her yoked to the CEO of the company, not his younger sibling. As for her friends, she'd realised in drawing up the invitation list that she didn't have any truly close friends any more. She'd lost touch with her close friends from her student days when she returned to Italy and devoted herself to the family business. Now her 'friends' were people vetted and approved by her grandparents. People she was content to socialise with but no one with whom she'd share her thoughts or concerns.

It wasn't a comforting realisation. Even for a woman used to relying only on herself.

Alessandro's deep voice interrupted her thoughts. 'My family knows the reason for this marriage. As for other guests,' the shrug of those broad shoulders was eloquently dismissive, 'they're attending to see the wedding of the decade. They'll recover soon enough from the surprise.' He paused, eyes gleaming. 'In fact the change of groom at the last minute will increase publicity surrounding the event, especially if no one but us knows the real story. That can only be a good thing.'

Olivia stared, dumbfounded at the sheer arrogance of the man. Not even to offer any sort of explanation? To have people arrive at the wedding expecting one brother and discovering the other?

It was outrageous. Audacious. Impossibly high-handed.

So typical of Alessandro Sartori.

Yet he was right.

The businesswoman in her knew it.

Her heart thudded a discordant rhythm as she realised the sheer effrontery of his suggestion might work.

Speculation would be rife, adding an extra, titillating spice that would keep focus on the wedding, and their businesses, well after the rose petals and rice had washed away in the next Venetian high tide.

Catching and holding the public's attention was the name of the game.

The wedding she'd planned was no small gathering of intimate friends. It would be an event with a capital E, showcasing the best of both the Dell'Orto and Sartori businesses. Sartori was a byword for exclusive men's fashion, and for generations Dell'Orto had been at the pinnacle of Italian style for women. The event would be packed with a who's who of international style and glamour, including a sprinkling of gorgeous models wearing previously unseen designs by both houses. Invitations were hotly sought and serious security was planned to keep out gatecrashers, though the press would get their photo opportunities.

Add a whiff of mystery and a hint of potential scandal and the world would be wild with curiosity. Every move the bridal couple made, and, more importantly, every new commercial launch from their merged companies, would instantly be headline material.

His suggestion would turn a disaster into a PR coup of phenomenal value.

Yet still it meant marrying Alessandro Sartori.

Her hands tightened on the arms of her chair and her stomach lurched.

'Nevertheless—'

'Instead of throwing up objections, think about the implications if the wedding doesn't go ahead.'

He sat straighter, all trace of lazy disinterest gone.

'No wedding means no deal.' His voice was remorseless. 'No merger. No chance to pursue all those opportunities both companies have already identified. Opportunities we both *need*, if we're to hold our own, much less stay at the top commercially.'

He paused, his eyes locking on hers, and a jolt of energy slammed into her. She had no doubt that Alessandro was as concerned as she to find a way out of this mess.

Olivia wished she could find comfort in that. But despite their apparent joint purpose, she sensed he played by his own rules. There was no guarantee their interests would continue to align. In which case, she might end up as collateral damage.

'From what I know of your grandparents, they'd pull out of the deal, even at this late stage, if there's no marriage.' All insouciance had disappeared. The man staring at her was grim-faced.

Alessandro was right. Her grandparents believed a wedding would reinforce their family's equal participation in the merger, even though it had been agreed that Alessandro would chair the board.

No deal meant no spot on the board for Olivia. No chance to push her ideas for new directions. The management position that had been promised at the end of her years of on-the-job training and development would vanish. Or be deferred for even more years. Because Dell'Orto Enterprises would need to regroup in order to cope with the aftershocks that would flow from reneging on this deal.

Alessandro might have read her mind.

'Don't think that both companies would simply return to their earlier status quo. Not after coming to the brink of amalgamation then parting ways. There'd be a loss of trust in management and incalculable damage to each brand.'

His mouth turned down at the corners in a look of such distaste that Olivia understood, if she hadn't before, how much his company and its reputation meant to him.

It was the most animated she'd seen this stern, self-controlled man.

She drew in a shuddering breath. He was right. Again.

Such a sudden and complete change in direction would affect confidence in both companies. Business was difficult enough without that.

'I see you understand the gravity of the situation.'

She met his hooded scrutiny. 'Of course I understand. *I* wasn't the one to pull out of the deal.'

Yet she would be the one to pay the price.

'All the more reason to embrace my alternative.'

Did Olivia imagine an emphasis on the word 'embrace'?

The idea that on some level Alessandro was enjoying this made her hackles rise.

Something else rose too. Something that shimmered and skipped in her blood as she took in those imposing shoulders and his air of barely leashed masculinity.

She didn't know how he did it. Or if it was a figment of her wayward imaginings. Alessandro Sartori's brooding presence always signalled a wholly male energy that made every other man seem insignificant.

No, no, no. Don't go there.

Olivia didn't even like the man. He was cold and disdainful. For all her drive and focus on work, she preferred people who could relax. Who could think about something other than business occasionally. Who smiled.

Like Carlo? He was affable, charming and sociable.

And he'd created this mess.

'Can you think of a better option?' Alessandro's voice yanked her attention back. He regarded her with a steady, unblinking gaze that pinned her to her seat.

Frantically she scrambled to conjure an alternative solution.

Because the thought of marrying this man...

'It's one thing to marry a man I know and—' She swallowed.

Respect wasn't a word she could easily use about Carlo any more. His betrayal cut deep, even knowing the reason for his actions. Why hadn't he and Hannah mended their relationship ten months ago instead of now, when it was too late to turn around the merger and wedding?

Olivia held Alessandro's eyes. 'But you and I...we don't even like each other.'

For a second his only response was to lift one eyebrow, making her feel wrong-footed. Even though it was true. Even though what he suggested was completely outrageous. Even though she suspected nothing she said or did could ever dent his monumental ego.

'So you actively dislike me?'

'I...' Stupidly Olivia's mouth dried.

He annoyed her. Intrigued her. Repelled her with his ability to make her feel like she was beneath his notice even while maintaining an air of apparent cordiality.

Alessandro reminded her that she was, at heart, an outsider, despite her years of hard work, learning and adapting to the social mores of her Italian family's rarefied world.

'I see.' His mouth flattened.

Olivia repressed a squiggle of discomfort and guilt. If he didn't like the truth it was because he wasn't getting his own way.

'My point is that we don't know each other. We have nothing in common.'

'We have a business enterprise in common.' His eyes narrowed. 'Or were you merely pretending an interest in the company?'

That almost drew Olivia out of her chair. She sat forward, hands clutching the seat arms to stop herself catapulting across the space between them.

Not a good idea.

She'd learned to keep her distance from this man. He disturbed her too much.

Her nostrils flared as she dragged in a calming breath. Except that, by some fluke of draught, or maybe her imagination, she caught the scent of bergamot and warm male and a shudder went through her.

'If you talk to anyone at Dell'Orto you'll know I take my work there very seriously. I'm good at it too and I intend to make it my future.' She didn't attempt to conceal her pride or her determination.

It was more than a job to Olivia. It was the career, the aspirations and dreams, she'd built her life around.

'Consider this, Olivia.' He stretched out the syllables of her name as if they didn't sit well on his tongue. 'You may have no future if this merger founders.'

It was all too true!

Alessandro steepled his fingers under his chin, elbows on the arms of his chair, in an attitude of contemplation. Of waiting.

The ball was in her court.

Bizarre as his proposal was, she didn't have an alternative.

Proposal!

There was a word.

Olivia's mouth hardened. Twice now the suggestion had been made that she marry. Yet in neither case had she received anything approximating a proposal of marriage. The first time her *nonno* had sat her down before his desk and told her a union had been arranged between her and Carlo. Now Carlo's brother made not an offer but an ultimatum. Marry him or irrevocably damage the company she loved and that her family had worked for generations to build.

It had been a long time since she'd yearned for romance or for a man in her life. Yet, despite her learned pragmatism, something inside rebelled at being used as a bargaining chip, a means to secure a profit.

Some deep-buried part of her protested that surely she deserved a proper proposal. Made by a man who wanted her for herself.

Olivia shied away from the idea, knowing it for a weakness. Yet her disgruntlement remained. Surely any man with a modicum of sensitivity would at least *ask*. Not assume.

Yet one look at Alessandro Sartori reminded her this was a man who probably never had to ask a woman for anything. He was handsome and darkly sexy with that brooding air of his. He'd have women eagerly offering whatever he wanted. She'd seen them, flocking like moths to a dark flame, at various social events.

Olivia might be caught between a rock and a hard place but it wasn't her role to make things easy for him.

'My point, Alessandro,' she drew out the syllables of his name as he'd done hers, 'is that if we marry we'll be expected to *live* together. Yet I know nothing of you except for your work. I don't know what sort of man you are. What your character's like.' Apart from disapproving. 'Yet you ask me to enter into a lifelong contract with you.'

Shrewd eyes held hers. She couldn't work out if that was approval in his gaze or annoyance.

Finally he spoke. 'The one thing you need to know is that I'm an honest man. I'm sure your family will vouch for that, and anyone else you care to query. I always keep my word. You can trust me.'

That was true. His reputation was renowned. He was viewed as hard but honourable. Olivia wouldn't be sitting here if that weren't the case. But she needed more.

'I keep my word. So you don't have to worry whether I'll be waiting at the end of the aisle for you.'

Olivia's breath snagged, hearing the steel-hard undercurrent in his voice. How Carlo's behaviour must rankle with this man. For it meant that now he had to marry the Dell'Orto heiress against his own inclinations.

Then he gave another of those fluid shrugs. 'As for getting to know me... That will come with time.'

'This isn't like your average corporate agreement. You're expecting me to *live* with you in the same house, even if not in the same bedroom.' Olivia paused to make sure that sank in. 'Yet I know little about you personally, the way you behave.'

Something flared in those deep-set eyes, making her wonder if she'd actually managed to puncture his phenomenal smugness. But it was a passing illusion.

'You're worried about my bad habits?' He paused, his gaze laser-sharp. 'Or is it more than that? Are you afraid I might force myself on you?'

The words hung between them like a dark cloud.

Olivia refused to look away. It wasn't something she actually suspected of him but it was a valid question.

'Ask anyone you like, and I can give you the names of some previous lovers. I can assure you that I'm not a violent man and I detest bullies. I'd never force a woman. You have my word on that.'

Alessandro's words were calm, almost soft, and his expression hadn't altered, but the air around them shimmered with heightened tension. Olivia felt she'd crossed a boundary. That whatever his original reason for disliking her, she'd just exacerbated his disdain.

Too bad. This was her life. Her future.

'Thank you for that assurance.' She inclined her head. 'And I do trust your word.' Even Carlo, who occasionally complained of his older brother's stern ways, respected him. Alessandro's mention of bullying had also reminded her of something she'd forgotten. Carlo had said once that his big brother had saved him from a bunch of school bullies.

Maybe, behind that closed-off air, Alessandro was a man who cared. Not about her, of course, but his family.

Alessandro inclined his head. 'Given the circumstances, there's no time for getting to know each other better before the wedding. I have to leave Venice in an hour and won't return till next week. But let me assure you that you'll be quite safe living with me.'

No mistaking it now. She recognised wounded pride when she heard it. In Alessandro's case it made him sound more distant than ever.

'Obviously, as far as the world is concerned, we'll live

as a couple. In fact, while the press interest lasts, we should aim to appear as the ideal couple.' His mouth lifted at one side in what could have been a hint of derision. 'But as for our personal lives, there'll be no need to live in each other's pockets.'

Olivia nodded. That made sense. And it was good to know he didn't expect to impinge on her independence in private. As for not living in each other's pockets—no doubt Alessandro would need his privacy to pursue discreet relationships with other women.

Once more it felt like he'd read her thoughts.

'The main thing is that we both behave in a way that won't taint the firm or our reputations. Beyond that, I'm sure we can come to an accommodation that will work for us both.'

His dark eyes fixed on her in a way that was stern rather than encouraging. A reminder that her behaviour would be scrutinised and assessed?

Annoyance rose like steam in her veins.

All her adolescence and adulthood had been devoted to doing the right thing, appearing in the right way, being careful of her behaviour so as to live up to Dell'Orto standards. Occasionally Olivia wanted to lash out and live impulsively. Not do anything wildly radical but maybe tear off her carefully chosen fashion-forward shoes and hitch up her tailored skirt and dance barefoot in a fountain, just to enjoy the cool water on a hot day.

Was she exchanging her grandparents' close scrutiny and demands that she live up to their expectations for someone else's?

Olivia looked away to the watered silk covering the walls. Its soft green was like the lagoon outside rising around her. Rising to submerge her and hold her down till she gave up struggling.

No one had forced her into the engagement with Carlo. She'd agreed to the marriage.

Yet, despite her dismay at being jilted, and horror at the problems they'd face without the wedding, she'd begun to feel a sneaking relief at the idea of being free again.

Part of her, the laid-back Australian side that her grandparents so disliked, had resented tying herself into a business deal marriage. Resented turning herself into a commercial asset rather than an individual. A woman.

But this was the world she lived in. The world she'd chosen.

What choice did she have?

Holding back a sigh, she turned to Alessandro Sartori. The man who wanted to be her husband.

No. The steely gleam in his eyes reminded her he had no desire for that. What he wanted was the deal, the company, the ever-increasing profits that would come with the merger.

The realisation both repelled and reassured her.

'I accept, Alessandro. I'll see you at the wedding.'

CHAPTER FOUR

THE SOUND FROM the waiting crowd rose several notches as Alessandro and his best man entered. Heads craned and one or two people stood to get a better view. Desultory conversation became a rampant buzz of speculation when it became clear Carlo Sartori, the expected groom, was nowhere to be seen.

Alessandro nodded at familiar faces and ignored the patent surprise he saw reflected back. There were corporate and political leaders, film and sporting stars, artists and designers, even some royals. It was a who's who of the world's fashionable, powerful and glamorous, here as much to be seen as to witness the wedding.

Just as well the *palazzo*'s chapel was huge. Its high ceiling of cerulean blue was festooned with cherubs and it seemed that every sort of baroque excess, from twisted spiralling marble columns and fanciful plasterwork, adorned the place. Even in Venice, a treasury of antique art, the place would make an art historian salivate.

It made Alessandro slightly nauseous. Not from nerves but from its blowsy ebullience. Why add one decoration when sixteen would do? Alessandro was firmly of the 'less is more' group. But he recognised that the gilt, marble and painted panels made a perfect backdrop for such a significant wedding.

The chapel was a reminder of Dell'Orto wealth and social status even more than it was a place of worship. His own family were nouveau riche who'd rocketed to wealth only a few generations ago. His great-grandfather had been a tailor, though a supremely talented one, and the family was named for his trade, Sartori meaning tailor.

Not that they had anything to prove. In fact it was the

aristocratic Dell'Ortos who were so eager to join the two families.

On that thought he crossed to the front pew and greeted the bride's grandparents. As usual they were the epitome of old-school reserve and elegant manners. Their air of refinement set them apart from many in the gossiping crowd.

He knew they were pleased at the prospect of the wedding, even more pleased to snare him as a grandson-in-law than Carlo. Yet their smiles were cool, as if any show of emotion, particularly satisfaction or pleasure, was too vulgar to be tolerated.

For a flicker of a moment he wondered how it would be, born into such a family.

Imagine the calm. The peace. The lack of histrionics.

People called Alessandro reserved. But it was as much a defence mechanism as an innate trait. With two passionate parents, both addicted to excessive self-indulgence and over-the-top displays of emotion, retreating to an inner world of calm had been a survival instinct.

The quiet relief of his own ordered mind had kept him sane through the ups and downs of life with parents who had no filter between mind and mouth, at least where their wants, disappointments and disagreements were concerned. Fortunately paid staff, then boarding school, had provided a barrier between himself and them.

Yet meeting the cool gaze of Olivia's grandmother, hearing her speak of a recent blip on the stock market, he wondered for the first time how Olivia had fitted into the Dell'Ortos' world.

On the surface she was calm and socially adept, at ease in any social setting. But when he'd talked with her last week he'd sensed a fizzing effervescence of emotion, like a shaken bottle of champagne about to explode.

Granted, she'd been under extraordinary pressure. Even so she'd handled the shock better than he'd expected.

But he wasn't thinking of her surprise. He was recalling the heated glow in her eyes as she'd told him she didn't know him well enough to trust him. When she'd refused simply to nod and acquiesce to his scheme.

He'd been annoyed, yet at the same time fascinated. There'd been a spark in her that drew him. Like the spark he'd sensed the first time he saw her.

Then he recalled the look in her eyes as she agreed to marry him.

No spark then. Just a blankness that curiously had made him feel hot and uncomfortable. As if he'd done the wrong thing.

Yet he was the one, as usual, coming to the rescue when his family turned its back on responsibility.

Nevertheless, as he nodded to her grandparents and turned to wait on the other side of the aisle, it wasn't the over-decorated church he saw. It was the memory of Olivia's flat stare. The defeated downturn of her ripe lips.

Damn Carlo for hurting her!

Damn himself for noticing. For wanting more from her. For wanting to see that flare of emotion burn brighter in her eyes, not from anger but pleasure.

The organist began another piece of music, as intricate and triumphant as the chapel itself. There was a spike in the conversation behind him then a hush. His best man turned towards the entrance then stopped, his jaw sagging.

As the music swelled and filled the space, Alessandro sensed movement behind him. It wasn't possible but he almost fancied he heard the swish of long skirts on the ancient marble floor. A tingling began at his nape and spread out across his shoulders.

Slowly he turned. Something in his chest rolled over as he saw the veiled woman walking alone down the aisle. The light was behind her, a brilliant glow like a sunburst radiating behind one of the chapel's painted saints.

As she neared he was struck by how ethereal she looked in that gauzy gown. The top of it sat just above her breasts, leaving her shoulders and a creamy expanse of skin below her collarbone bare. She wore no jewellery. She didn't need it with the hundreds of delicate, crystal-studded flowers decorating her long sleeves and slender curves. The effect was opulent but refined. A concoction so light and elegant she might have stepped out of an old fable about princesses and magic spells.

Did that make him Prince Charming?

Or the devouring dragon come to ravish her?

The flight of fancy pulled Alessandro up short.

Heat ignited low in his body as he thought of Olivia bearing his name. Sharing his life, his home. His bed. For, though he'd never bully her into consummating their marriage, he had every intention of persuading her.

He could be very persuasive.

Alessandro swallowed and discovered his throat was suddenly dry.

He hadn't admitted it before, even to himself, but he looked forward to this marriage. Maybe not every aspect of it. He was a loner and that suited him. Having a wife would take adjustment. Yet he experienced none of the discomfort he'd expected at getting married. Instead he'd been surprised to discover he felt…eager.

He dragged his thoughts back to the present, finally registering that Olivia walked alone. There were no bridesmaids and no one to give her away.

Her elderly grandfather had said they'd decided he'd best not walk her down the aisle as he was recuperating from a severe ankle injury. But surely someone could have accompanied her? An uncle or old friend?

Despite his anticipation, Alessandro was disturbed by a sense of—could it be guilt at how alone Olivia looked? How fragile and vulnerable.

Olivia walked down the long aisle, aware of faces turned towards her, the sigh of whispers as she passed. But it was the man waiting at the front of the crowd who captured her attention.

The darkly handsome groom who outshone every other man.

The man currently scowling at her.

Her nervous stomach squeezed and she had to concentrate on slowing her breaths and keeping her pace regular.

It had taken all her resolve to do this. For the last week the endless preparations had kept her busy. Till this morning, when she'd discovered she had nothing to distract her from the ceremony looming ahead. Olivia had known uncharacteristic panic. Had actually started plotting the route she'd take out of Venice if she turned her back on Alessandro Sartori and ran away.

Except there was nowhere to run. Wherever she went she'd still need to confront her family's outrage and disappointment, and the repercussions wouldn't stop there.

A shiver began at her nape and trickled like iced water down her spine as she looked at Alessandro's disapproving face.

What was his problem? She was here, wasn't she? And she'd signed the all-important prenuptial agreement without cavil.

Her chin lifted as she approached. Whatever his problem he'd better look happier than he did now if he was going to convince people he wanted this marriage.

She stopped at the front pew and her grandfather got to his feet, leaning heavily on a stick. His injury had been fortuitous in one way. It had stopped any argument about him walking down the aisle to give her away. Olivia already felt enough like a chattel being traded. She preferred to do this alone, reinforcing, if only to herself, that this was her choice.

Nonno lifted her veil back over her head and kissed her on the cheek, a rare smile on his papery lips. With a few murmured words of encouragement he turned back to his seat, leaving Olivia to walk to Alessandro's side.

To her surprise Alessandro moved to meet her, his earlier scowl replaced by a look she couldn't decipher as he caught her hand and lifted it to his mouth.

'Exquisite,' he said, his breath hot on her bare fingers. 'Utterly ravishing.' His voice was just loud enough for people in the front rows to hear. Undoubtedly he'd spoken for their benefit.

Olivia was amazed to feel herself react to his praise. As if it wasn't for the dress others had designed and laboured over. Or for the fantasy image the pair of them projected for their audience. As if that glow in his eyes, that sizzle she imagined in the air between them, were for her.

As if he really admired her.

Her pulse quickened and her lungs went on strike as he held her eyes.

Slowly he bent his head and she felt a whisper like silk on her flesh as his lips caressed her knuckles in fleeting salutation. Tingles darted and spread across her skin from the point of contact.

Was it the first time Alessandro had touched her? It felt like it. Actually, it felt overwhelming and that frightened her. Usually he made a point of not getting too close. It was insulting, really, as if she carried some invisible taint.

Which made her shivery response to his touch both embarrassing and worrying.

He must have seen something in her expression, for his grip tightened as he lowered their clasped hands between them.

'You're all right?' This time his words were for her alone and she could almost believe he was really concerned for her.

Of course he is. He doesn't want you running for the hills or fainting dead at his feet. At least till the ceremony is over.

The thought stiffened her unsteady knees. Even the fluttery sensation in her stomach eased.

She'd been through the arguments in her head so often.

There was only one way forward and that was to marry Alessandro.

'Never better,' she lied with a smile, conscious of the stares trained on them.

But as she turned to face the priest, she was conscious only of Alessandro's regard. The way she *felt* the weight of his dark stare. And the clasp of his long fingers wrapping around hers, his hold easy but, she sensed, unbreakable.

The wedding was a triumph.

Alessandro's smile wasn't in the least forced as he received congratulations and parried questions about the change of bridegroom. Most of the time all it took was a comment about the bride finally choosing the right brother, accompanied by a melting look at Olivia, or, even better, a kiss to her wrist, and those around them were satisfied. For now, at least.

To his surprise he rather enjoyed himself. The ceremony went without a hitch and the reception in the vast mirrored ballroom was a huge success. As a PR exercise this was gold. The invitees were having a wonderful time, pleased to be included in such an exclusive event, and delighted to be the first to see the new fashions worn by the models who attended. As for having Olivia at his side, Alessandro discovered that was a particular pleasure.

For so long he'd avoided being alone with her, or getting too close. Because from the moment he'd seen her and his brother together he'd understood it was Carlo she'd marry. Which made the disturbing awareness Alessandro harboured for the Dell'Orto heiress totally inappropriate. He'd tried to obliterate it and when he hadn't completely succeeded, had kept it as his shameful secret.

Because lusting after your brother's intended bride broke every rule.

The sound of music and voices drifted from inside the ballroom. Out here, on the *palazzo*'s private jetty with its poles of striped crimson and white topped with gold, the air was cool. But the light was perfect for the sunset pictures the photographer wanted. As those photos would be part of a massive PR push by their soon-to-be-joined companies, Alessandro was happy to cooperate.

Especially when most of the photos involved standing very close to his blushing bride. Often with his arms around her.

Olivia's blush surprised him. He'd seen it in the chapel when he'd bent his head and offered her a chaste kiss on the lips, suppressing the impulse to lean in and ravage her mouth. Then later through the afternoon when he wrapped his arm around her waist and drew her close he'd seen colour tint her cheeks.

As if his nearness affected her.

His ruthlessly logical brain told him that was unlikely. It was Carlo she cared for.

Maybe it was just a reaction to the warmth of two bodies pressed close to each other.

He surveyed her, standing near the water's edge, a light breeze lifting the veil behind her. She looked soulfully romantic and beautiful. As attractive in her own way as any of the models sashaying through the crowd inside. And, unless he was mistaken, cold. Was that a shiver?

Alessandro strode across the wooden planks, shrugging out of his tailored jacket. Ignoring the photographer peering into the massive camera, he walked up to his wife.

His pulse gave an exaggerated thump. His wife. That would take some getting used to.

'Are you cold, Olivia?'

She looked up, hazel eyes seeming to grow in her face as they locked on his. Alessandro felt that familiar tug.

'A bit. This wind is chilly.'

He put his jacket around her shoulders and her mouth opened as if on a sigh of surprise.

Alessandro was hard-pressed not to take that as an invitation.

He wanted to wrap an arm around her waist and plunge his other hand into the mass of her shining blonde hair to discover if it was as soft as he imagined. Above all, he wanted to press another kiss to her lips. Not a chaste one this time but something much more carnal.

Recklessness filled him. An unfamiliar urge to throw caution to the winds and act spontaneously. He knew the paparazzi and tourists would love it.

Every vantage point across the canal was crammed and boats clogged the waterway, earning the ire of gondoliers as the photographers on board vied for the perfect, saleable shot.

That was why he didn't succumb to temptation.

Because it *was* temptation driving him. Alessandro made it his policy never to act rashly, driven by emotion. There was too much of that behaviour in his family and he worked hard to be the exception to the rule. He had no intention of giving in to weakness now, with all the world watching.

'Thank you.' Her voice sounded curiously breathless. 'But this isn't the shot the photographer wanted.'

Yet her hand fastened on the lapel of his jacket and she didn't take it off. She must be cold indeed. Why hadn't he noticed earlier?

'She's taken enough shots of you by the water.' He swung his head around to tell the photographer they were finished out here, only to find the woman with the camera nodding approvingly. She gestured as if encouraging him to continue.

But continue what? He couldn't succumb to that feral urge to ravish his bride. But no doubt the photographer saw what he did, that Olivia, with her hair ever so slightly mussed, with a couple of tendrils loose in the breeze, and wearing his dark jacket over that ultra-feminine dress, looked impossibly, gut-wrenchingly alluring.

In the apricot glow of sunset, with the light gilding the grand *palazzos* behind her across the canal, Olivia could grace any high-fashion magazine.

So instead of leading her inside, he leaned towards her with one hand propped on the striped pole behind her. Telling himself he did this only for the photos which would be so good for business.

The evocative scent of orange blossom teased his nostrils, familiar now from when he'd kissed her after the ceremony. He'd assumed it came from the flowers she carried. But now she was empty-handed, the bridal bouquet over near the photographer.

The scent settled inside him and Alessandro felt something within him ease. As if being with Olivia was exactly where he wanted to be.

'Surely she's almost finished,' Olivia said under her breath. Yet she played her part, tilting her head up towards him, for all the world as if she thought of nothing but him.

Alessandro enjoyed it, though he knew it was an illusion.

Standing so near, he saw her eyes looked more brown now than green. From fatigue? Or was that their natural colour? He was intrigued, looking forward to discovering more.

'Can you bear a few more minutes before we call an end to the session?'

For answer she stood straighter and nodded.

'Excellent.' He slid his arm around her waist, leaning close.

For the benefit of the camera.

'I was surprised,' she murmured as he bent towards her, 'that none of your family is here today.'

That pulled Alessandro up short. He hadn't given his family a thought for hours.

He managed a shrug. 'You wouldn't expect Carlo here, would you?'

It still stung that his brother hadn't contacted him since

that message saying he was staying in the States. Alessandro had rung back but Carlo's phone was switched off. All he could do was leave a message asking him to call back. There'd been resounding silence since. It hurt to acknowledge it, but even after what Carlo had done Alessandro had expected better.

'Of course not.' Olivia's gaze clouded and he mentally kicked himself for mentioning his faithless brother. Whenever he stood close to her today he forgot Carlo. After all, she was *his* bride now, not his little brother's. But he wasn't callow enough to believe she was over Carlo.

What he couldn't determine was whether she still felt... tenderness for his brother, or just hurt.

'Can you imagine if he had attended? That would *really* have got the gossips working.'

Her mouth twisted in a rueful downward turn that made his belly grow taut. Those lips...

'But what about your parents? I'd have thought they'd be here.'

Alessandro felt his facial muscles tighten around his smile and wondered if the camera would pick up the change in expression.

'They had other commitments.'

'Other than their son's wedding?' A line appeared on Olivia's forehead and he wanted to tell her that frowning would spoil the photos, except he guessed she wouldn't be sidetracked. Besides, they were married now. She had a right to know what to expect.

He glanced over his shoulder, making sure the photographer was still some distance away.

'They're in the middle of a polo party in Argentina.'

'A polo party?' Olivia shook her head. 'I don't understand.'

Alessandro wasn't surprised. Her grandparents might be old-school and rigidly unbending, but they felt strongly about family. His parents felt strongly only about themselves.

'Three solid weeks of polo matches and related celebrations. They go every year. It's one of their favourite A-list events.'

'And they chose that instead of attending your wedding?' She angled her head as if to get a better view of him. As if his parents' behaviour could be understood by reading his face.

He wished her luck with that. Alessandro had taught himself as a kid not to reveal hurt or disappointment at his parents' thoughtlessness. Now the habit was ingrained, or maybe he was inured after so many years, but he no longer felt even a scintilla of regret over their actions. He'd learned they could only be depended on to be undependable.

'They know it's a marriage of convenience,' he said quietly. As if that made a difference. He could have declared he was marrying the woman of his dreams and they wouldn't have interrupted their partying.

The only thing that would stop them was when their bodies finally succumbed to the ravages of decades of decadent self-indulgence.

'I...see.' She blinked then turned towards the photographer before lowering her voice. 'So I'm not to expect them to accept me as part of the family?'

Alessandro frowned. He couldn't put his finger on it. Olivia's voice was calm, lacking any obvious emotion, her face ditto. Yet he knew something was awry. He *felt* it. As if disappointment—or was it hurt?—radiated from her.

The sensation, like a phantom pain, drove a spike of regret straight through his chest.

It seemed his parents still had the ability to hurt people, even at a distance. It hadn't occurred to him that Olivia might need protecting from them.

Alessandro raised his hand to her cheek, brushing the velvet softness with his knuckles, aware only of the need to ease her hurt.

'This isn't to do with you, or our marriage. It's nothing personal.' His voice was a husky whisper. 'So don't feel bad.' He even managed a smile, though it felt drawn too tight.

'I don't understand.'

He leaned in so his words feathered her ear. 'They treat me and Carlo the same way. They always have. They're just not interested.' He almost, for Olivia's sake, felt a stab of regret. Then a twist of self-derision saved him. 'Welcome to the Sartori family, such as it is.'

Through the rest of the celebrations Olivia kept remembering her new husband's expression when he spoke of his parents. Most of the time Alessandro was difficult to read beyond an air of impressive self-confidence. But for those few moments she saw, or thought she saw, something else in those dark eyes. Something turbulent. It didn't look like love, but how could she tell?

She merely sensed that behind the deliberately self-mocking tone and his casual air was something potent. Something that stirred his emotions.

That fascinated her. It made Alessandro seem, for the first time, more human. Subject, like the rest of them, to forces and feelings beyond his control.

Of course he was. He was simply a man.

But in her mind she'd grown accustomed to thinking of him as inaccessible, unbending, almost unfeeling.

He didn't give that impression now.

As he swept them through the crowd of well-wishers with the adroitness of a man used to mixing with the rich and privileged, he was charming, drawing people. Everyone was eager for his attention, even some guests who were famed for their self-absorption.

Whenever Alessandro turned to her, the façade he created of eager tenderness might have fooled even her if she hadn't known the real reason for their wedding. If he didn't have his arm around her, he was holding her hand. Olivia felt like she was plugged into an electric socket, with little tremors constantly racing across her skin.

Now though, with a final wave, and a resounding cheer from the guests, they were alone, turning their backs on the gilded ballroom and heading for the wide marble staircase that led upstairs.

Neither spoke and Olivia was preternaturally aware of the rustle of silk and chiffon and the quickened thud of her pulse.

Alessandro's arm was around her waist.

She understood why he stayed glued to her side, because it was possible a stray guest might see them. Yet, as they ascended the stairs, Olivia wished they could walk separately. She was acutely aware of the size and heat of his tall body right beside her.

Belatedly she realised she'd have been happier to spend tonight elsewhere. Somewhere totally private where they didn't have to maintain the pretence of affection.

But the *palazzo* was the best choice, for commercial reasons. It would imprint in the public's mind the connection between their families and rarefied luxury.

The place had been in her mother's family for generations. Its grandeur made it one of the family's most prized possessions, even though they didn't live here now. It was used for major events, product launches and celebrations, even let out to the city sometimes for exhibitions. But a number of suites were maintained for family should they stay in Venice.

Which meant that tonight she and Alessandro would share a sumptuous suite well away from the last of the revelry downstairs.

They passed more security staff, stationed to ensure the private floors were totally private, and still Alessandro didn't remove his arm from around her waist.

Finally they reached the imposing double doors at the end of the corridor.

Olivia drew a breath to say something then realised she'd run out of small talk.

It felt like the day had used up her store of easy chat, along with her ability to dissemble.

She felt disturbingly, alarmingly unprepared. As if she'd put all her energies into dealing with the wedding arrangements instead of letting herself think of the reality that would follow—being married to Alessandro.

Nerves fluttered through her middle on the thought.

Still silent, he opened the door and Olivia wondered if, like she, he'd found the day, and the constant need to keep up the charade of being a happy couple, taxing. She swept into the room, relief filling her that he hadn't decided to take the masquerade so far as to carry her over the threshold.

But her relief disappeared as she slammed to a halt.

Someone had turned the twin room she'd organised into a romantic dream of a bridal suite.

As she stood, gaping, Olivia heard the click of the lock snicking behind her.

CHAPTER FIVE

ALESSANDRO TURNED THE key in the massive door and immediately heard Olivia speak, though it didn't sound like her.

'What are you doing?' Her voice spiked high.

'Making sure we're not interrupted by a guest with a camera who claims to have got lost. Despite all the security on the two lower levels, I won't feel completely private till the last guest has gone and...'

He stopped as he turned and took in Olivia's frown.

Then he registered the view beyond her and forgot what he was saying.

The room was grandiose. High-ceilinged, decorated in a style that was popular a few centuries ago. The furniture and artworks probably belonged in a museum, though the glimpse he had of a bathroom through an open door spoke of modern luxury.

Yet it wasn't the opulence of the room that surprised him. It was the preparations that had been made for tonight.

Centred on one wall was the biggest bed he'd ever seen, crowned by a canopy of silver gilt brocade and acres of softer, filmy draperies. On a side table stood an ice bucket complete with a foil-topped bottle on fresh ice. Alessandro recognised the wine as one of the world's best champagnes. Beside it stood a pair of crystal glasses. On the other side of the vast bed rested an elegant water jug and more glasses. On a larger table was a platter of fruit and chocolates, another of cheeses and a third with caviar on ice.

The air was delicately scented from the masses of fresh flowers placed around the room and, despite the enor-

mous chandelier overhead, the light came from hundreds
of candles.

Alessandro's belly contracted as he took in the ambience.
It screamed intimacy.

Especially the turned-back covers on the bed, scattered
with rose petals.

And the lacy nightgown spread lovingly across one corner. He could make out scarlet petals beneath it, proof that
it was virtually see-through.

The heat in his belly exploded out into his veins, shooting through his body in a rush of fire.

He'd told himself he needed to tread carefully with his
new wife. That trust and seduction would take time.

Had he misjudged Olivia?

'Did you arrange this?' His voice had a hoarse edge,
echoing strangely in his ears. His breath stalled back in
his lungs. Of all the things he'd expected tonight, it wasn't
this. A woman he'd wanted since the moment he saw her.
A room staged for seduction...

Eager thoughts filled his mind till he turned and looked
again at Olivia. She was whey-faced, her features almost
paler than her gown.

'No! No, I didn't.' She stepped hurriedly away. Her shoulders were hunched high and her chest rose and fell with her
rapid breathing.

'I see.' If she hadn't planned this it was a surprise to her
too. Not a pleasant one, given her reaction.

Alessandro fought to find the familiar stoicism he
needed. It was harder now after that moment of incredu-
lous excitement when it had seemed as if his demure bride
had set the scene for seduction.

Strange how much more difficult it was to resist something when for a moment it had seemed within your reach.
All those months of determined distance he'd set between
them had been obliterated for a couple of vibrant seconds.

Now resurrecting that protective wall seemed so much harder.

But he'd done more difficult things in his life than resist a woman.

He just couldn't recall at the moment what they were.

Abruptly Alessandro turned his back on the bed, and Olivia, his mouth tight. With one decisive move he switched on the chandelier.

Was that a sigh of relief he heard?

Despite everything he felt annoyance stir. Did Olivia really find him so unattractive?

With brutal force he slashed through that line of thought. Not now. Not here.

He swung to face her. 'Clearly someone has been busy.' It was a shame it had backfired. He fought not to notice the weighted tension in his groin.

As he spoke she moved to pick up a card propped on the table beside the food. Alessandro heard the swish of her long skirts and wondered how the soft fabric would feel against his palms if he bunched it high in his hands to reveal her slender legs. Would they be bare or was she wearing silky stockings?

Wrenching his mind back onto the straight and narrow, he busied himself blowing out a couple of nearby candles.

'Who's it from?' he said when she remained silent, her head bent.

Slowly she turned, not quite meeting his eyes. Her mouth was turned down in a curious twist that looked somewhere between delight and regret.

'The events team from Dell'Orto. Rather than hiring a wedding planner I organised today myself, with help from the team.'

That surprised him. The whole thing had been a mammoth undertaking. He'd assumed she'd bought in the services of a top-notch wedding specialist. Everything had been done with an attention to detail and professionalism that had relieved the last of his doubts. For, though he'd acceded to the Dell'Orto insistence that they, as the bride's family, arrange everything, Alessandro was accustomed to his own staff taking charge. Especially of an event so crucial to both brands.

'And so?' That didn't explain the expression he now deciphered as wistful.

Olivia lifted her shoulders in an angular shrug. 'The team was concerned that I'd focused all my attention on the ceremony and reception but not what came after. I just asked someone to inform Housekeeping that we'd use this suite.' Her cheeks were already pink-tinged, so he couldn't tell if she blushed harder.

Alessandro closed the distance between them with a couple of strides. She handed over the card and immediately turned away to snuff out an array of candles near the fireplace.

As if standing close to him made her nervous. But that couldn't be. They'd spent the day side by side and she'd displayed no sign of discomfort.

Alessandro scanned the card, reading the handwritten comments. To say they were enthusiastic was an understatement. These were the sort of remarks made by friends rather than employees. All wishing her, them, well. All upbeat and clearly heartfelt.

'They wanted to give you a special surprise.'

'Well, they managed that.' Her clipped voice held a sour edge and he didn't have to look up to know she moved with the restive energy of a caged animal. The click of her high heels on the floor was like staccato bites.

What fascinated Alessandro wasn't his bride's discomfort at the misunderstanding that this would be a night of romance. It was what the gesture—which would have taken so much time and effort to organise—and those playful, delighted comments in the card revealed.

The team members she'd worked with respected and liked her. They didn't view her just as part of the executive echelon of the company but as someone they could relate to. They were willing to go the extra mile to provide a wonderful treat for her. Those comments weren't from people sucking up to their boss's granddaughter. They were genuine.

Alessandro tried and failed to imagine anyone at Sartori doing this for Carlo.

Or for himself. Though, to be fair, there were a few, the members of his loyal executive team, who would, if they could imagine him marrying for love.

'The events team. You've worked with them before or just on this?'

Olivia paused in the act of snuffing out huge pillar candles. 'Why?' Her eyes, narrowed in query, met his and he felt that thud of awareness he'd been aiming to ignore all afternoon. It got tougher by the hour.

'Just curious.'

'Last year I was placed there for six months.'

'Placed?' Alessandro hadn't been given much detail about her work for Dell'Orto, and he hadn't pushed for more. It was something he'd get to when the deal went through. But now he was curious.

'You don't know?' Her eyebrows lifted. 'I thought with the merger...'

She pursed her mouth. Oddly, instead of it making her mouth look tight, the effect was a pout that did devastating things to Alessandro's good intentions. To give her time and space to get acclimatised to having him rather than Carlo in her life.

'I joined the company as a junior after school and during my business degree. I've worked on rotation in almost every area of the business since. My family prides itself on understanding every aspect of the company.'

The Dell'Orto heiress had learnt the ropes of the business from the bottom up? He'd imagined her like Carlo, more interested in the socialising that was part of their luxury-end business than the actual work.

Her hands found her hips and her chin rose. 'You have a problem with that?'

'Not at all.' He wished he'd been able to persuade his brother to do something similar. In the last twelve months he thought he'd succeeded. Till Carlo left them all in the lurch. 'I think it's laudable.'

'If I'm going to take my place on the board, and in the company, I need to know what I'm doing.'

Alessandro nodded. It had worried him, the idea of an untried young woman on the executive team, but he'd assumed she'd be easily managed. Now he wondered what else he didn't know about her.

As he watched she marched across to the bed, light winking off the delicate crystals on her dress. Alessandro couldn't take his eyes off her. She was usually graceful and poised but now there was something more vital in her movements.

It called to him, making him wonder about that other side to her. The spontaneous, vivid side that he'd merely glimpsed when she laughed with Carlo or spun in his brother's arms on the dance floor at a charity ball.

'I thought so.' She lifted the coverlet at the foot of the bed then let it drop.

'Thought what?' He moved closer, but not too near. She'd looked spooked when they'd entered the room, as if she expected him to jump her. And she'd moved away as soon as she'd passed him the card.

Olivia shook her head. 'There used to be two big, *separate* beds in here. With a large space between. That's why I asked Housekeeping to make it up for us. We couldn't have separate bedrooms tonight and maintain the fiction of a real marriage.'

Alessandro was about to correct her, reminding her this *was* a real marriage. But he bit back the words.

'The team have pushed the mattresses together and created this...' She waved her hand to take in the enormous bed and soft draperies.

'Bower?' he offered, his gaze skimming the vast, petal-strewn surface.

It took all his determination not to picture Olivia lying there wearing that blatantly erotic nightgown. Or in her ultra-feminine dress, with a cloud of bridal skirts rucked up to her hips and him moving between her bare thighs.

He gritted his jaw and looked away.

'They must have had the sheets and coverlet made especially. Nothing else would fit.' Her expression was an intriguing mix of admiration and annoyance. 'But now we're stuck here. I can't sneak out and make up a bed in another room.'

Alessandro took her point. The situation wasn't ideal if they were to spend a celibate night together.

Especially when awareness of this woman was a hum of heat vibrating up from the base of his spine and clutching at his vitals.

'We'll cope,' he said decisively. There was no alternative. 'The bed is enormous.' He caught and held her gaze, doing his utmost to look reassuring. Olivia needn't know his mouth was watering at the sight of her framed against the massive bed. 'I've already told you I'm not interested in sex with an unwilling woman.'

She said nothing, but her tension was obvious in the sharpened line of cheek and jaw and the darkened flare of her eyes.

Something, a silent pulse in the thickened air, beat against and through him.

Did she feel it too? This *awareness*?

Or was he kidding himself? Ascribing his own feelings to her?

Alessandro drew himself up, corralling his wayward thoughts. Of course she didn't reciprocate his desire.

Not yet.

It was too soon. She was still acclimatising to marrying him instead of his charming younger brother.

Alessandro's jaw clenched as he encompassed the almost impossibly wide bed with one sweeping gesture.

'There's no chance of us accidentally rolling together in a bed that size. I'll get in one side and you can get in the other and I guarantee there'll be no touching in the night.'

His gaze bored into hers, willing her to trust him.

'You're right,' she said at last with a tiny movement of her lips that he thought was an attempt at a smile. 'I don't know what's got into me. That bed's almost as big as the piazza outside. And,' she gave a small nod, 'I do trust you, Alessandro. I know you're not going to try taking advantage.'

If Olivia knew how much he wished the situation were different, how delighted he'd been for those few moments when he thought she'd planned a proper wedding night, she wouldn't be so sanguine now.

'You've had a shock. It's unsettled you.' His nod encompassed the romantic trappings surrounding them.

'Plus you're tired.' For the first time he noticed tiny smudges beneath her eyes that he was sure hadn't been there before. It had been a long, arduous day and she was probably stressed about projecting the image of an enraptured bride.

Not to mention marrying the wrong Sartori brother.

'It's been a mammoth job putting together this wedding. I had no idea you'd led the team to do it.' He paused, letting his words sink in. 'I have to congratulate you, Olivia. You did a stunning job. The event was the perfect showcase for our companies and it will be talked about for years to come. My own staff couldn't have done better.'

Her lips curved in a real smile this time. One that lit her eyes and punched a fireball straight to his belly.

The impact slammed his breath back into his lungs.

For once he wasn't on the outside looking in, watching Olivia enchant others.

She'd smiled at Alessandro all afternoon and evening. Smiles for their guests and for the cameras. This was different. For the first time he was the recipient of a genuine smile from Olivia. One that wasn't a politeness or a masquerade.

Even in the chapel, when he'd told her how ravishing she was, his bride hadn't looked at him with such a glow of delight.

Not because he'd complimented her on her looks but because he appreciated her work.

That was a revelation. A fascinating one.

Alessandro filed it away for close consideration.

'Come, sit down. Have something to eat.' He gestured to the table groaning with delicacies. 'You barely touched the food at the reception. You'll feel better with something in your stomach.'

She stared at him, clearly surprised.

Because he'd noticed her lack of appetite? He noticed a lot about Olivia, but now wasn't the time to mention it.

'You're right. I'm never good when my blood sugar gets low.'

She moved across to the table and sank onto the chair he held out for her. But instead of reaching immediately for food, she lifted her skirts, baring her feet and calves as she leaned down to take off her shoes. They were totally unique, delicate, covered in pale silk and decorated with crystals. But it wasn't the shoes that held Alessandro's attention. It was her ankles and the smooth line of her bare legs.

Naked. No stockings.

He swallowed hard and turned away, surprised to discover how that revelation jumbled his thoughts, making it difficult to recall what they were discussing. Instead that fantasy was back. Olivia lying in disarray on that wide mattress and he lying between her legs.

Alessandro strode across to the ice bucket and lifted the bottle, deftly removing the foil and then the cork with a muted pop. Liquid hissed into the flutes and the scent of fruit filled his nostrils as he poured the fine wine.

'What are you doing?'

He didn't answer till he'd poured two glasses, then took them across to her.

'We may not have a traditional wedding night but we still have something to celebrate.' He handed her a glass then clinked his against it. 'To a successful wedding, a successful merger and a successful marriage.'

Though this was a marriage of convenience, it was binding. It behoved them both to make it work.

Olivia nodded and raised her glass before drinking.

He paused, watching her swallow and feeling a familiar tightness in his groin. For so long he'd cursed his reaction to her, ashamed to feel attraction for the woman who was destined to be his brother's bride.

Now she was his. Or would be soon.

Alessandro lifted the glass to his lips and made another toast, silent this time.

To my gorgeous bride. And to our getting to know each other much better.

Satisfied at the prospect, and his own ability to give the appearance of disinterest, while everything urged him that patience was overrated, he drew out a chair from the small table. He'd barely eaten at the reception either. He'd been too busy playing host and networking.

'Before you sit down…' Olivia paused, her brow puckering.

'Yes?' he said when she didn't continue.

She shrugged, her gaze not quite meeting his. 'Would you mind undoing those catches at the back of my dress? You know where they are. I'd like to change into something else.'

Only with a phenomenal effort did Alessandro stop his glance going to the lacy bit of nothing displayed on the bed. Olivia had made it abundantly clear she didn't want sex tonight. But soon...

'Sure.' He put his glass down and moved behind her. 'It will be easier if I take off the veil too.'

'Please.'

Finally Alessandro had his wish. His hands went to the glorious shimmer of her hair. His jaw clenched as he fought the impulse to stroke it, instead working to locate the concealed hairpins that kept it in place.

One by one he dropped them onto the table, working slowly, enjoying the mass of softness against his hands. In the process he managed to half undo the tidy chignon that kept her hair up off her face and shoulders. Tantalising locks of blonde hair uncoiled across his hands and he breathed deep, again absorbing the scent of orange blossom. Was it sewn into the veil?

Carefully he put the fragile fabric onto the bed and turned back to the woman sitting so stiffly before him.

His fingers flexed at the thought of touching her again. With those couple of trailing tresses coiling past her shoulders she looked even more inviting. As if a lover, not a mere convenient husband, had run his hands through her hair, making it dishevelled.

Out of the blue, anger pierced him. It shot, an ice-hot arrow, from his chest to his gut.

Alessandro intended to make the best of this marriage, in every way possible. He just needed time. Yet it was a bitter thing to know his new wife held herself still and tense because *he* was here, instead of his feckless, selfish brother. That it was Carlo she'd been drawn to from the start.

That the searing lightning bolt of attraction that had cemented Alessandro's feet to the floor and stopped his lungs the moment he first saw Olivia hadn't struck her too.

With a grim twist to his mouth he stepped close again, his hands going to the tiny, hidden fastening.

He felt her stiffen, shoulders rising and her back coming away from the chair. Deliberately he paused. Olivia had to get used to his presence and, more, his touch. Starting now.

After a long moment she eased back in her seat and her shoulders dropped. He could almost hear her slow exhale, as if she forced herself to be still and endure this.

Once more that anger stirred. This time nibbling through his belly, teasing him towards acting importunely. But he bided his time.

Slowly, deftly, he undid the first fastening then paused, his knuckles resting against the velvet-soft flesh of her back.

'Are you having trouble?' Her voice sounded breathless. Alessandro told himself that one day soon she'd sound that way not from nerves, but from excitement and longing.

'No. I think I've got it.'

He undid the next catch and then the next, gradually revealing a V of creamy skin that glowed golden in the light.

Finally he lifted his hands, his heart hammering in his ears and his whole body racked with suppressed arousal.

Interesting that she didn't instantly shoot up from her chair but sat immobile. As if waiting.

A second later she proved him wrong, rising with an evocative rustle of soft fabric that tightened his groin. He could only be thankful she didn't turn around to thank him and see his tented trousers.

'Thank you, Alessandro.' Even the sound of his name in that husky voice felt like a caress.

She moved away to her suitcase on the other side of the room, then the bathroom.

Alessandro stood, unmoving, even when he heard the sound of water running in the next room. Because he needed to master the urge to do something stupid, like march in and claim his bride.

She'd be his eventually. He was a patient man, and confident. He looked forward to seducing her.

There was only one glitch in his plans. Being with her, touching her, inhaling the scent of her skin, seeing her smile, ratcheted up the hunger he'd suppressed so long. He was already in torment and he had yet to survive a night chastely sharing her bed.

Alessandro could only hope his patience held out.

CHAPTER SIX

THEY LEFT THE autostrada east of Milan and headed north for Alessandro's house in the foothills beyond the city.

It had been a surprisingly relaxed trip, once they'd left the *palazzo* and faced the good wishes of the staff who'd gathered to see them off.

Of course, they hadn't left unnoticed. The paparazzi had taken up residence around the *palazzo*, camera lenses raised as soon as the newlyweds stepped into the sunshine.

Alessandro had suggested they give the photographers what they wanted. So they posed for photos on the private pier, their custom-made Dell'Orto luggage stacked beside them and their motor launch bobbing on the canal, its polished wood gleaming. The 'perfect' couple advertising two of the world's best-known luxury firms. Olivia had worn a teal dress that she knew would photograph well and found her nerves at facing the press weren't as bad as usual. Probably because her attention was on Alessandro, devastatingly handsome in another tailored suit.

Her breath snagged as she stared blindly at the passing landscape through the window of the sports car.

She'd thought him suavely stunning in a suit. Now she knew he looked even better without. He slept bare-chested and the sight of his taut, muscled body had teased her well after she should have been sleeping.

Nor did he have to be half naked to arouse her. She recalled him yesterday in shirtsleeves as he leaned nonchalantly towards her, one hand resting on a mooring post outside the *palazzo*. Those impossibly broad shoulders had hemmed her in and she'd been aware of little but his imposing masculinity. His warmth and vitality blanketed her and not simply because he'd draped his jacket around her shoulders. The air around her seemed thick with the force of all that casually controlled maleness.

Everything inside her had jittered with excitement. At his thoughtfulness in noticing she was cold and later putting an end to the interminable photo session. But more specifically because something deeply feminine and *aware* shuddered into life as he'd leaned close.

Nor had it retreated again. Instead it lingered, growing stronger as the hours passed and he remained glued to her side.

All those disturbing longings that she'd stoically told herself were figments of her imagination crowded closer than ever.

Till they'd entered the bridal suite and all she could take in was Alessandro, so powerful and so near, and the giant bed.

His behaviour then had made a mockery of her concerns. As if he had any interest in bedding the bride he'd married solely for commercial reasons!

Though she'd clarified in advance that it was to be a hands-off marriage, being in that suite, she'd felt nervous as never before.

His thoughtfulness had confounded her. Not what she'd expected from the man who'd shunned her for so long, choosing always to talk with her grandparents or anyone else in the vicinity except her.

That had changed yesterday. It had to so they could play the part of a happy couple.

Yet the change in him wasn't just for show. Last night he hadn't avoided her. Nor had he laughed at her sudden attack of nerves in the bridal chamber. Instead he'd ascribed that to stress and lack of food, easing her embarrassment with an aplomb that left her grateful.

Once or twice she'd even imagined his attention lingered on her with warmth. There'd been moments when it seemed like he responded to *her*, and not because of their contractual obligations.

When he'd unfastened the top of her gown… Even now her breath clogged as if she felt his phantom touch. She'd been so aware of Alessandro as a man, her whole body coming to tingling life at the merest touch. She'd been almost certain he felt something too. His voice had taken on a curious quality, and surely his hands had lingered?

Heat flooded her cheeks and she shifted in the car seat. She'd imagined it. He hadn't made a move on her, or even hinted he was interested. She was totally safe from unwanted sexual attention.

Strange that thought didn't provide the relief it should.

'Here we are.' Alessandro's voice broke across her thoughts as he turned smoothly between a pair of tall gateposts and down a long drive. The car purred between two rows of trees then finally swept around a rise, out of sight from the road.

Inured though she was to the luxuries that money could buy, Olivia found herself delighted at the scene before her.

In the distance rose the blue-tinted hills that surrounded the lakes for which the area was renowned. But it was the villa before her that commanded her attention. Two storeys high, the terracotta-roofed building was a soft sand colour with dark shutters bracketing each long window. At ground level the main façade had a series of arches forming a graceful colonnade providing shade. At either end two wings projected forward. They created a wide paved courtyard that on its open side faced not only the driveway but also an exquisite formal parterre garden with low-growing topiary surrounding whimsical fountains.

'You like it?'

Alessandro's voice dragged her gaze to him. Surprisingly it sounded as if he cared what she thought of his home. A bizarre idea, given the nature of their marriage.

Olivia nodded. 'It's beautiful. I like the way it sits in the landscape.' To the sides of the villa she saw lawns and clustering trees, creating a peaceful, park-like setting.

Her grandparents preferred to live in the city. And, despite the thick walls and heavy security, their place didn't have the peace she sensed here. With a preponderance of dark furniture and heavily decorated antiques, their home had a slightly stultifying air.

Olivia pressed a button to lower her window. A soft breeze flirted across her cheek, bringing the scent of cut grass and sun-drenched roses.

She breathed deep, her gaze searching for and finding a pergola laden with pale blossom.

'The scent reminds me of home.' The words slipped out unbidden.

'Your grandparents are gardeners?'

Olivia kept her gaze turned towards the bounty of full pink roses, feeling the sudden slip and shift inside as buried memories stirred.

'No,' she said slowly. 'My father. He grew roses for my mother.'

Strange how she'd forgotten that. Now it came back to her. The warmth of a summer's afternoon, the perfume of roses and freshly mown grass and the sound of her father grumbling about pests while her mother laughed and assured him the roses were perfect, despite the fact the parrots had been nibbling the buds.

A rush of warmth filled Olivia.

What surprised her most was the realisation of how *happy* they'd been. Life had seemed idyllic then.

Later events had blotted that from her mind.

How long since she'd thought of those days?

After her parents died and the disruption that followed, such memories had retreated further and further away as she had no one to share them with. Especially when she moved to Italy, where her grandparents made it clear they hadn't approved of their son-in-law or their daughter's marriage and preferred not to discuss either.

Olivia blinked, disorientated to discover her eyes prickling.

'He sounds like a romantic.'

She blinked again. The observation was so at odds with what she knew of her parents' marriage that it pulled her up short.

Except, she realised, examining that memory again, there'd definitely been a sense of romance between her parents that day. The realisation confounded her.

Ignoring the implied question, she changed the subject. She didn't want to talk about her parents. 'Did you design the garden?'

Alessandro's laugh was a deep, rich sound that she'd never heard before. It slid through her, like a weft thread slipping up and under her thoughts, creating a new pattern in her brain. A pattern that spoke of friendliness and a man willing to laugh at himself.

Who was this new Alessandro Sartori? He was so different to the stern, self-contained man she'd come to expect.

Surely she couldn't have misjudged him for the last year?

'I'm afraid I can't claim responsibility for the garden, or the roses. That's Guido's department.'

'Guido?'

'He came with the house. He's looked after the grounds for more than forty years and he has strong views about any plans to change them.'

Olivia turned to find Alessandro regarding her with something almost like a smile. It altered his features totally. Instead of brooding, he looked merely thoughtful. And far too attractive.

Tiny pinpricks of sensation exploded across her skin, drawing it tight.

'Let me guess,' she said, striving for an easy tone. 'You wanted to rip out this garden and put in a pool?'

He shook his head, his eyes never leaving hers.

Olivia told herself the wash of heat across her throat and cheeks was from the summer sun and the old, strangely unsettling memories this place conjured.

'I wouldn't dare. Besides, the pool is out the back. I did, however, suggest adding some new hybrid varieties to the plantings.' Alessandro's lips twitched and it was as if he tugged a wire inside her. 'He wasn't impressed.'

'He wouldn't do what you wanted?' Olivia was intrigued by the idea of anyone telling Alessandro no. He was a man so patently used to command.

He lifted his shoulders. 'Let's say we're still in negotiation.' Another tiny curve of his lips, making his mouth ruck up at one side.

It was ridiculously, appallingly attractive.

'I have to meet this man. He sounds like a force to be reckoned with.'

Anyone who could hold Alessandro at bay and in a state of prolonged negotiation must be impressive. Alessandro had a way of persuading people to see things his way and achieving whatever he set his sights on.

The way he'd persuaded her into marriage, less than an hour after informing her she'd been jilted, was a case in point.

No wonder her grandparents were eager to combine forces with Sartori. With Alessandro at the helm the company had gone from strength to strength.

Olivia thought of the vivid memory that had filled her mind mere moments ago. Of the happiness and warm companionship she'd sensed between her parents that day. Her grandparents hadn't wanted that for her. Instead they'd bartered her in a calculated negotiation.

No, that was unfair. She knew her grandparents didn't believe in marrying for love. The disastrous end to Olivia's parents' marriage bore that out. It hadn't ended in sunshine and roses but in raised voices and—

'I'll introduce you to him later. First you'll want to unpack.' He opened his door and got out, moving around to her side of the car, but she was already out, taking in the tranquillity of the place.

This wasn't what she'd expected. If anything she'd been nervous about moving from her city apartment to Alessandro's home. In her mind it represented a loss of independence, even if the change brought the career opportunities she'd worked so hard for.

Yet rather than feeling on edge, she felt expectant, eager to explore.

That was in no small part due to Alessandro. Last night and today he'd let her see a different side to him. One she could relate to, even begin to relax with.

Olivia hoped this was a glimpse of the real Alessandro Sartori and not a mirage.

His hand at the small of her back stopped her thoughts. So much for relaxing! He only had to touch her and she tensed as if a current of energy hummed from his hand to her body.

'Come on in.'

Silently she nodded, moving forward to the front door, where the housekeeper waited to greet them.

Instead of touring the house they made straight for the master suite.

Olivia's heart thudded down to her sandals as Alessandro pushed open a door into what was clearly his bedroom. Hadn't they already sorted out their separate sleeping arrangements?

She stopped in the doorway, taking in the colour scheme of grey, pewter and white with occasional indigo accents. It would have been a relaxing space, except that the wide bed filled her gaze.

'This is me,' he said, his voice feathering her hair, making her hyper-aware of his proximity. No other man affected her like this, making her both excited and horrified at his nearness. Her shoulders tightened and rose as tension filled her.

It struck her like a bolt out of a blue sky that perhaps this convenient marriage promised complications she'd never imagined.

Rubbing her arms, Olivia opened her mouth to demand a separate room, but he was turning away.

'And this is you.' The words trailed him as he strode down the passage to the next door. When she caught him up his eyes gleamed with an expression that was hard to identify.

Again that tiny stroke of awareness fluttered across her skin. Awareness of Alessandro as a man, not a contracted partner.

'The staff here can be trusted not to relay private information about us, but it's best to have neighbouring rooms. Future guests might find it odd if we sleep at opposite ends of the villa.'

Because as far as the world was concerned theirs was a real marriage.

Olivia inclined her head in agreement. The last thing she wanted was rumour and innuendo about them not being a real couple. It had been bad enough facing down the speculation yesterday because the original bridegroom had been replaced by his brother. Fortunately only a very few had persisted in quizzing them about that and Olivia had been grateful to leave answering to Alessandro. His responses didn't give much away and he didn't lie, but he somehow implied they'd been swept off their feet by true love.

He pushed the door open and stood back for her to precede him.

Like the suite next door, it was spacious and bright, the furnishings modern but sympathetic to the graceful lines of the old villa. The colour scheme of rich creams, old gold and bronze made it a welcoming space, despite the trademark elegance she saw everywhere.

A low bowl of tawny roses edging to pink gave off a delicate scent and she felt her stiff shoulders drop.

'I hope you'll be comfortable here, Olivia.'

Instantly guilt hit. She'd misjudged Alessandro. Of course he hadn't assumed she'd share his bed. Not once had he indicated any such interest in her.

A quiver of something that might have been hurt trembled through her. How perverse!

Could she really want him to be physically attracted when she had no interest in consummating their marriage?

No interest?

The voice of honesty began to protest but Olivia shut it down. She turned to Alessandro with what she hoped was an easy smile.

'Thank you. It's lovely. I'm sure I'll be comfortable here.'

'Good. I'll leave you to get settled in. Your luggage has already been unpacked, but if you need any help rearranging it, or anything else, pick up the phone. It will connect to the housekeeper.' He moved towards the door. 'I'll see you later.'

Later was much later.

Once or twice, feeling that thrill trip across her skin at Alessandro's nearness, or seeing what looked inexplicably like heat in his eyes, Olivia imagined her new husband experienced the same hyper-awareness she did. As if their bodies communicated in arcane signals she couldn't read but felt.

Yet when she came downstairs Alessandro was nowhere to be seen. The housekeeper said he was in his study on a conference call.

It shouldn't surprise her. Though they'd agreed to spend a week away from the limelight and the office, ostensibly on honeymoon, there was a lot of work to be done in light of the merger.

It was just that she'd thought, for reasons she couldn't

explain, that Alessandro would show her around his home himself.

Olivia bit back unreasonable disappointment. She wasn't in danger of falling for the PR image, was she? They weren't a besotted couple. Even if her new husband—her mind stumbled on the word—had been considerate and even friendly, it didn't mean she should fall for the story they'd spun.

So Olivia accepted the housekeeper's offer of afternoon tea in the courtyard. To her delight it really was tea. Proper tea, made the way she liked it.

When she thanked the housekeeper enthusiastically the woman stunned her by revealing Alessandro had given her a list of Olivia's preferences, including the fact she drank tea or milky coffee.

Olivia's eyes widened at the idea Alessandro had set someone to discover what she liked.

In business he had a reputation for not missing the smallest detail. But it stunned her that he'd taken such trouble to make her feel at home.

Migrating from Australia to Italy at thirteen, she'd already developed a taste for tea and had never been able to stomach the aromatic yet super-strong espresso her grandparents sipped from tiny cups. Nothing had been said but her choice of beverage always set her apart, emphasising the foreign ways they tried so hard to eradicate in her.

Olivia spent the afternoon alone, exploring the house, which, despite its aristocratic lines and luxury furnishings, felt like a home not a showpiece. She ventured into the gardens, first the formal parterre section, then the sunken rose garden and the kitchen garden, full of the scent of herbs. Beyond that were rambling, park-like grounds.

She'd breathed deep, enjoying the clean air after so many years living in cities. The villa was an easy commute to Milan yet it was a different world.

Maybe that was why shreds of memories kept surfacing.

Nothing major. Just snippets of the days when she'd lived with her parents in a house surrounded by roses and the sound of raucous, colourful birds.

Perhaps that accounted for her unusual mood as she shared an evening meal with Alessandro. This place might embody comfort but it also set her on edge, making her thoughts stray down unfamiliar paths.

To half-forgotten childhood memories. To the breath-stealing effect of Alessandro wearing a casual shirt that clung to wide shoulders and made him look even more vital, more quintessentially male than before.

Or maybe it was due to the change in him. Where was the brusque businessman who'd never had time for her? Who preferred anyone's company to hers, leaving her to wonder what she'd done to offend or bore him? Since yesterday's wedding he was a changed man.

'Your video conference was successful?' Olivia's voice had a husky edge that horrified her. She busied herself picking up her dessert spoon. It gave her an excuse not to look into his hooded eyes.

Normally Olivia didn't eat dessert. In the years after her parents' death she'd been dogged by puppy fat, partly because she took consolation in sweet treats. She still recalled the horror of her elegant, reed-thin *nonna* when she'd seen a teenage Olivia struggle to find something to wear that wouldn't make her look like a baby elephant. Her size was another of the many things that set her apart from her peers at her exclusive boarding school. Now she'd passed those chubby years, but she was ever-conscious of the need to look good as a representative of the family brand.

'Which conference?' Alessandro's tone held a thread of humour. 'There were several.' Then he shrugged and dug his spoon into his zabaglione. 'Actually, yes. Significant progress and no major problems.'

'A good day, then.' She scooped a little of the dessert

onto her spoon and into her mouth, closing her eyes for a second at the deliciousness of it.

'Hmm?'

She looked across to find Alessandro staring, his spoon halfway to his mouth.

Heat drenched her at the lambent fire in his eyes. Could it be that he…?

No. She imagined things. See, his expression was as bland as ever.

Yet Olivia put her spoon down. His scrutiny made her tense, even though she knew his interest wasn't sexual. He made her too aware of her body drawing tight and achy.

'Have you had any contact with Carlo?'

What made her ask, she didn't know, apart from the urgent need to fill the silence.

From what she understood of the brothers' relationship she guessed Carlo would lie low as long as possible. He'd grown up in his elder brother's shadow and she suspected, despite his bravado, he hated disappointing Alessandro more than he'd ever cared about incurring their parents' disapproval.

'No.' The single word was terse. Alessandro's brows drew into a frown that was instantly familiar. It was the look he'd given her time and again from across a room as she chatted with Carlo. As if something about her irked him.

She should have known better than to expect a leopard to change his spots. Her new husband—she swallowed on the word—had obviously been on his best behaviour for the last day and a half but it didn't take much for him to revert to type.

Deliberately she broke his gaze, shoving a large spoonful of creamy dessert into her mouth. She wanted to ask what she'd ever done to make him regard her that way. But to ask would reveal that his disapproval bothered her, even had the power to hurt.

'Why? Were you expecting him to call?'

'No, I—'

'Because, knowing my brother, he's too busy enjoying his latest conquest to spare a thought for the woman he left behind.' Alessandro's voice dripped with scorn. 'If you're pining for him you're a fool.'

Olivia dropped her spoon with a clatter, the sweetness on her tongue turning to acid at the disdain on her companion's face.

'I'm not pining. I'm just enquiring. Because whatever you think, at some stage we're going to have to talk with him and—'

'I prefer not to discuss this.'

Across the table his eyes were as dark and unforgiving as obsidian. Alessandro's mouth turned down and his nostrils flared as if in disgust at some noxious odour.

Did he think to shut her down simply because he preferred not to talk about Carlo?

The man sitting across from her now was all autocrat, his features carved in emphatic lines.

Yet something tangled and hot stirred within Olivia.

Madness! That's what it was. To feel attracted to such a man.

Carefully Olivia folded her napkin and put it on the table. She pushed her chair back.

'Excuse me, Alessandro. I've had enough. I'm suddenly tired. I'll see you tomorrow.'

CHAPTER SEVEN

ALESSANDRO PACED THE length of his study, anger twisting his thoughts. Anger at himself.

How could he have been so stupid? In one second he'd undone any good he'd achieved with Olivia.

As if he were an untried youth who couldn't control his tongue.

As if just the mention of his brother's name unravelled all his caution.

As if he were jealous.

He rocked to a stop at the window, hands shoved deep into pockets and shoulders taut as he stared across the lawn to a grove of trees and the mountains in the distance. Usually this view soothed him, but not today.

He'd jumped down Olivia's throat for asking about Carlo. She'd looked at him with wounded eyes till that expression had been replaced with a glitter of indignation and reproach. She hadn't thawed since.

He might be perfectly correct about his brother, but he should have kept silent.

All he'd managed to do was get Olivia's back up.

And prove that Carlo's appalling behaviour hadn't severed his bond with Olivia.

She'd retreated behind a wall of frigid politeness, keeping Alessandro at arm's length.

His jaw clamped in mingled fury and determination. He needed a circuit breaker. Something to distract her into relaxing her guard and letting Alessandro in. Something they could share.

His mouth kicked up in a self-derisive smile. He could

think of several things he'd like to share but he doubted she'd agree to them. Not yet.

That was what had got him into this mess, thinking about Olivia and sex.

He'd sat across the candlelit table from her, watching her eat dessert, and all his tact had disintegrated in the rush of blood from his brain to his groin. The woman turned eating into foreplay. The way her eyes fluttered shut in sensual ecstasy as she closed her mouth around the spoon and sucked—

Alessandro's trousers grew tight as he recalled the spontaneous hedonism of her pleasure. He'd wanted to reach out and touch her, invite her to ditch the zabaglione and consume him instead.

He'd known there was something special about Olivia from the moment he saw her. The ground had shifted beneath his feet and longing exploded deep inside, instantaneous and devastating.

He'd been crossing the crowded room to her when he'd been waylaid by a senior government minister, wanting to discuss new legislation that would affect industry. By the time Alessandro had excused himself, Olivia was no longer alone but having a *tête-à-tête* with Carlo. Reading their body language, their teasing laughter, he'd halted midstride. It was obvious they were intimates, an assessment borne out later.

Since then, to Alessandro's chagrin, he'd found no pleasure with other women. Even when he'd told himself the best cure for what ailed him was to get laid.

The trouble was none of them was her, the woman he'd connected to and craved from the first moment.

The woman destined to marry his brother.

Alessandro uncurled his fists and withdrew them from his pockets.

She wasn't Carlo's now. She was Alessandro's and he intended to make her his wife in far more than name.

He spun on his heel and stalked to the door. Waiting for her to get over her hurt hadn't worked. It was time to act.

He found her on the terrace, in the shade of an umbrella. She wasn't aware of him, too intent on the screen before her. Papers littered the table and a thick notebook lay beside them. He wondered what absorbed her attention.

Finally she must have heard his footsteps, for she looked up. He saw a flash of something in her eyes that made his heart pound quicker, then the shutters descended. Her expression turned bland and questioning as she closed the screen.

'Alessandro.'

It wasn't a greeting, just an acknowledgement of his presence. As if he were a pesky interruption to something far more important. Her attitude stoked his annoyance, but he stifled it. It was his fault she'd retreated from him. Just because he'd spoken the truth didn't mean it was palatable for her.

'Olivia.' He smiled and watched her eyes widen.

He realised that around her he rarely smiled. In the past he'd put distance between them so as not to feed the compulsion to monopolise her. He'd been in a constant state of hyper-awareness and vigilance, determined not to betray his feelings. Now he could relax, so long as he was cautious.

Alessandro drew out a chair beside her, deliberately looking away from her dazzled stare to her scattered papers. Satisfaction stirred. His wife might be annoyed but she wasn't indifferent to him.

'What are you working on? A new project?'

She hesitated so long he thought she might not answer. 'Yes, something new.'

He turned to survey her. There was something in her tone he couldn't identify. Challenge? Doubt? Bravado?

'Is there something you want?'

As if he needed a reason to be here with his wife.

'Actually, there is. I need your help.'

Was that astonishment on her face?

'*My* help?'

'Absolutely.' He leaned back and smiled again, willing her to relax. 'I was impressed at the wedding with your eye for detail and your style. You created something that was magic for the photographer as well as for the guests. It's a gift few people have, even in our industry.'

'I... Thank you. It's kind of you to say so.'

Her mouth curved in a tiny smile but, because he didn't miss anything about her, Alessandro also registered the faint pucker on her brow, as if she were confused. As if she weren't used to receiving praise. Surely that was impossible. She was the Dell'Orto heiress. He imagined her grandparents cossetted her. Unlike his own family he knew hers took a close interest.

'I'm not known for kindness but frankness.'

She hesitated just a beat.

'What is it you want me to help with?' She turned to face him a little more and Alessandro felt triumph surge as she leaned forward.

Not just triumph but pleasure too. Because he craved her attention. Her interest. Her approval.

Alessandro didn't pause to think about what that said about him. He'd given up repressing his need for Olivia.

'The success of the wedding got me thinking. We're merging two companies that are synonymous with luxury and the sort of lifestyle millions aspire to. Yet so far we've only planned the mechanics of the amalgamation and the launch of next season's designs. We haven't planned a celebration.'

Olivia's brow wrinkled. 'Surely that's what the wedding was. A celebration that would be the anchor of our new releases.'

Alessandro nodded. 'Of course. The press coverage and careful use of the photos over coming months will feed into product launches. But I was thinking of something more.

Something even more exclusive that builds on that initial spike of interest. Something focused on our core clientele rather than the mass media.'

The idea had occurred to him this morning when he'd searched for a way to break the ice wall Olivia had erected. The more he considered it the more he liked what he'd come up with.

'What do you think of a party here? In our home.' Alessandro paused on the word *home*, savouring the fact that from now on Olivia would live here with him.

'But you *never* host events in your home. You're famous for your privacy.'

'Exactly.' He watched her eyes narrow in concentration then grow round as she assessed the implications.

'You'd really do that? Open up your house?'

He shrugged. 'To a very, very select few. I had in mind a private event for only our most loyal and prestigious customers. That will make them feel special and make others wish they'd been invited. It would be extravagant, of course, but elegant. Something a bit different.'

'A masked ball!'

'Sorry?'

Olivia leaned in, every shadow banished from a face now bright with enthusiasm. Her eyes glowed as they met his and something in Alessandro's chest rolled over. 'The ballroom here is divine. It would be a perfect venue for a formal ball.'

Alessandro considered the idea. 'It might work.'

'Of course it would work.' She waved one hand expansively. 'Guests can spread onto the terrace and the gardens. They'll adore the chance to see a little of the place where you live—'

'*We* live.'

Olivia blinked then slowly nodded as if, for a moment, she'd forgotten the fact this was now her home.

'In fact,' she continued, 'if it's a success, it could become an annual event. A one-off occasion is okay, but if it's going to be glamorous and super-exclusive it will have even more impact if people are hoping for future invitations. It could become a must-attend event in their social calendar.'

Like his parents' polo week in Argentina.

Where the sour thought came from, Alessandro didn't know. Maybe it was because, while he was rich, he was an outsider to the sybaritic party scene. He didn't indulge in long Caribbean yachting holidays with a bevy of naked models or après-skiing parties in the Alps. When he skied it was for the snow and the speed, and any sex romp was strictly private.

'You don't like the idea of an annual event?'

Alessandro saw Olivia frown and realised he hadn't answered. 'I do. If the first one is a success.'

She nodded. 'A ball would make a real splash. The setting is perfect for one and it would set the party apart from the usual. And if it were a masked ball...' Olivia shrugged and spread her hands. 'It has that extra touch of panache, don't you think? I suspect invitees will go all out to impress with gorgeous costumes, which will feed into your plan to set it apart.'

'You could be right.'

Olivia's raised eyebrows told him she knew she was right.

Alessandro's mouth twitched. He'd wanted to break down the barrier between them. He'd never guessed it would be so easy. Even if the change in Olivia was merely temporary, he basked in her enthusiasm.

'We should invite the members of the new combined company board,' Alessandro said. They were a disparate group and corralling them into working effectively would have its challenges.

'That could be interesting. I'm not sure they'd all warm to the idea of dressing up.' At his stare she shrugged. 'Some are a little...set in their ways.'

Alessandro nodded. 'It's time to see if we can introduce them to change, one step at a time.'

'Perhaps tie the event to a charity initiative? That might persuade them to participate. If they were to be seen to contribute to something worthy.'

Alessandro was fascinated, both by the idea and Olivia's perceptiveness.

'You're right. A charity link is an excellent idea.'

Alessandro leaned back in his seat, his mind buzzing with possibilities. Discussing this with Olivia wasn't just a way to melt the barrier between them, it was incredibly productive. His initial idea had been good but now it promised far more than he'd anticipated.

Sometimes he brainstormed with his team, but most of the time it was he alone, assessing expert advice and approving company strategies. It felt satisfying to bounce thoughts off someone else. Once he'd hoped he'd do that with Carlo. He'd never expected to be plotting strategy with Olivia.

He really needed to find out about her previous experience. The Dell'Orto management team had made it sound as if her work experience was peripheral and he'd assumed that, like Carlo, she'd enjoyed spending the family company's profits instead of building them.

'Does Sartori have any favoured charities?'

Alessandro shook his head. 'We make a sizeable amount of charitable donations but each year we support different entities. I understand Dell'Orto does the same.'

'It does. But…'

'But?' He watched her sit back, shoulders squaring as if she marshalled her defences.

'There's a programme I'd like to see us support.' Olivia looked down to where she twisted her wedding ring on her finger. Gone was the solitaire diamond Carlo had bought for her with company money. In its place she wore the emerald engagement ring Alessandro had purchased for her.

His money, his ring, his woman.

The sight of it, and the wedding band, on her slim finger gave him a fillip of possessive pleasure.

'Go on.'

She looked up and he caught enthusiasm in her excitement. 'It's all about promoting a healthy body image to young women.' She paused, her brows twitching together as if she waited for him to protest. When he simply nodded she went on. 'It's aimed at school-age girls and there is a range of initiatives. Given our work in the fashion industry, promoting saleable images of beautiful people, the least we can do is help people understand that looking good isn't all about being built like a stick insect.'

Her stare was pure challenge, as was the angle of her chin. Plus there was an edge to Olivia's voice he hadn't heard before.

Here was passion. Not the sort of passion he'd looked for, but he found it compelling and appealing. This mattered to her.

'That's an interesting idea.'

Olivia's chin tilted. 'Is *interesting* code for something you wouldn't touch with a bargepole?' One fine eyebrow arched high in a look that reminded him she was descended from a line of aristocrats while he was of working-class stock.

Yet instead of creating distance between them that stare merely amplified his determination to bridge the gulf. He looked forward to having his blue-blooded bride rumpled and flushed beneath him. Panting for his touch...

'I don't speak in code, Olivia.' He paused, enjoying the sound of her name on his tongue. 'I admit, it's not something I've thought about, since up to this point Sartori has been all about men's fashion. But why wouldn't I be interested?'

As he watched, her straight shoulders lowered a fraction. He realised how defensive she'd been.

'I mentioned the idea within Dell'Orto and it didn't go down well.'

'Ah.' Now he understood her reference to people living in the past. 'So you put it to the company executive?'

'No. Just one of them. My manager at the time. He wasn't

supportive, said it would be counterproductive, so it was shelved.'

'And you'd like to resurrect it?'

'Why not?' She met his stare. 'It's a sound programme that does a lot of good. Plus it relates directly to the fashion industry. We could hopefully help a lot of girls and women.' She looked down at the rings she twisted around her finger. 'Too many people in the industry have no concept of the damage that can be done to young lives through the pressure to look good.'

Alessandro nodded, intrigued. The way she spoke made him wonder if someone she knew had been affected, perhaps with an eating disorder.

'Have you prepared a full proposal for consideration?'

Her head jerked up. 'No. I'd begun to but when the idea was scotched I let it lapse. But I could.'

'Excellent. When it's ready, give it to me. I'll ensure it's assessed with all the other suggestions for charitable spending.'

'Just like that?'

'I'm not promising it will get approved, Olivia. But it seems to have merit and deserves consideration.'

Suddenly there it was. The sunny smile he'd seen directed at Carlo but never at him. Alessandro felt her grin like a punch of heat to his middle. It warmed him from the core, tendrils of fire radiating through him till he wanted to rip off his shirt and fan himself.

It intrigued him that Olivia was so grateful over such a straightforward thing. Because her ideas weren't valued in her home company, or because her track record wasn't good? He'd soon find out.

Meanwhile he wanted far more from her than gratitude.

Olivia grinned back with unfettered enthusiasm. At Alessandro Sartori of all people.

Who'd have thought?

After last night's cutting words she'd determined to shield herself from his barbed comments. But today he was different. Not the man who'd snapped at her last night. Someone more like the one who'd been pleasant and considerate in the days since their wedding.

Maybe he was doing what she should, extending an olive branch in the hope of making this partnership work. That's what they were now, partners in a convenient marriage.

Strange that the idea didn't send cold shivers through her as it had a week before.

Perhaps it was the mellow warmth of the day but the shiver tracking her spine held no chill.

Alessandro treated her as an equal, which was more than she'd experienced from some of the hidebound executives in Dell'Orto. He was interested in her input.

But the warmth within had as much to do with the sight of her husband as anything else.

Her *husband*. The word settled, both a promise and a taunt in her brain.

Alessandro had always been the most striking, devastatingly handsome man she'd met. Now, wearing jeans, loafers and a casual shirt that left a V of olive flesh bare at his collarbone, Olivia found him breathtakingly vital. It was all she could do to keep her attention on his face instead of roving that athletic body as he sauntered towards her.

Her heartbeat quickened and there was a shimmy of something she didn't want to put a name to deep inside.

She'd wondered if he ever wore anything apart from tailored suits. Now she had the answer and couldn't look away.

Concentrate on business, not Alessandro.

'About the party.' She stopped, realising she'd spoken at random to divert her thoughts.

'Yes, you have an idea?'

Olivia nodded. Strangely, given how Alessandro distracted her, sitting so close and leaning towards her as if hanging on her words, she did have ideas.

'Yes, but first we need to clarify something.'

'Go on.'

Olivia stared into hooded eyes that looked almost lazy. But she wasn't fooled. She knew his sharp intellect. Her nerves jangled because increasingly she wondered how Alessandro would look at her if they really were man and wife, not just on paper but in every other way.

Sex.

That's what she thought of when she met his gleaming eyes.

That's what she'd thought about as they lay on opposite sides of that wide bridal bed. And even last night as she lay alone, her anger had been underscored by physical awareness of the man. Even when he infuriated her!

Now she couldn't completely concentrate on their discussion because part of her was busy undressing him in her head.

'We need to be clear, Alessandro.' She strove for a calm tone but her words emerged too stridently.

Olivia took a second to swallow and regroup. 'I'm happy to work with you to design a celebration here. I'm happy to put in as many hours as it takes to make it a success. But I won't be sidetracked into becoming nothing but a part-time party planner. I have every intention of doing meaningful work in the company.'

For a long time Alessandro regarded her, his expression frustratingly enigmatic. Olivia's heart pounded against her ribs. She'd worked too long and hard to be sidelined now.

'You suspect my motives?'

She shrugged. 'I don't know you well enough to guess your motives, Alessandro. I thought it good to be upfront about this.' She folded her hands in her lap and held his gaze. 'I've been promised a seat on the board and a senior position in the company instead of more temporary placements. I intend to work, not be some,' she waved one hand, 'adornment.'

'Attractive as you are, *cara*, I've never thought of you as an adornment.'

Olivia refused to dwell on the fact he found her attractive. The jittery feeling in her stomach wasn't pleasure. It was probably hunger. She might be attracted but she wasn't the sort of woman to be swayed by sexual desire. Experience had taught her better than that.

'Then how do you see me?'

As soon as the words were out she regretted them. Did she really want to know? But that thought only hovered for a moment. She wasn't a shy, overweight teenager. She was a capable woman who knew what she wanted and intended to get it, even if she found herself in the bizarre situation of being married to a man she barely knew.

Alessandro's eyebrows rose but he didn't look discomfited.

'I see a charming, enthusiastic woman who can negotiate our social sphere with ease.'

Olivia's heart sank. He sounded like her *nonno*, who wanted her to be decorative. Who still doubted her abilities despite her qualifications.

'Plus I see someone who has an incredible eye for detail and a talent for planning, who's hard-working, adaptable, and can think on her feet.'

Olivia's eyes widened as he inclined his head as if in response to an unspoken question. 'Your work on the wedding proved all that, and our discussion this morning. Plus Carlo has sung your praises.'

Perplexed, she stared at Alessandro. Last night the mention of his brother had put him in a temper.

'You trust Carlo's judgement?'

Alessandro lifted his shoulders and spread his hands. 'His observations were backed up by others.'

Olivia wondered who those others were.

'Plus,' his eyes glinted, 'you're a beautiful woman, Olivia. Sexy and appealing.'

That stopped whatever words she'd been about to form. Alessandro found her sexy?

Warmth swarmed through her, making her skin tingle and, she could feel, her cheeks glow.

She'd always assumed she wasn't his type. Surely the way he'd looked at her during the wedding and the celebration that followed had been purely for show?

It was far more likely that he was telling her what he thought she wanted to hear.

The thought reassured her. There was no way even Alessandro could guess at her teenage trauma when she struggled to fit an image of beauty and grace that always felt far beyond her reach.

'I fully expect you to take up your position in the company, Olivia.' His words hauled her back to the present. 'I asked for your input because I want to hear your thoughts, not to keep you away from the office.'

'That's good to hear.' She nodded briskly as if her mind wasn't whirling.

'While we're on the subject...' He paused and raised his eyebrows. 'Your thoughts on me?'

Olivia's breath snagged. Her heart raced as she thought of all the things she refused to say. That he was too distracting, with an air of sensuality beneath that often stern façade that intrigued far too much.

'Clever, ruthless, unwilling to put up with people who don't pull their weight.' Carlo had complained of that more than once. 'Honest.' She paused. 'Contained. Controlled. I was surprised when you asked my views on this party. I assumed you'd be more likely simply to decide and proceed.'

'Not a team player, you mean?' He tilted his head as if considering. 'You could be right. Though there are times when I'm very willing to cooperate with the right partner.'

Alessandro's expression didn't alter. He was talking about work. But as Olivia met those liquid dark eyes all she could think of was sex. Of Alessandro naked in bed, cooperating very efficiently—

'Anything else?'

Olivia blinked and focused. 'You're handsome and you always draw female attention. But you know that.'

She threw the words out almost as a challenge, but his expression remained unchanged, as if he were reading her instead of reacting to her words. It was unsettling.

'About the party. I have another idea.' She needed to get off the personal, back to the pragmatic.

For a second he didn't speak and Olivia felt a strange thickening of the air around her. Did he realise how uncomfortable she was?

'I'd like to hear it.'

Relief sighed in her lungs. 'I thought perhaps a midwinter ball. We could have silver and crystal themed decorations, ice sculptures, of course, and braziers outside if guests want to venture into the gardens. Possibly even an artificially cooled ice rink out in the grounds. Even if the guests don't skate I'm sure we could bring in some expert skaters in costume—'

'I like it. It would definitely set the event apart. Why don't you open your computer and we can make some notes? I had another thought too...'

For a while longer they brainstormed ideas for the celebration and how to make best use of the event from a PR perspective.

Olivia felt energised and excited. She forgot the need to watch her words as they piggy-backed ideas off each other and debated the merits of each suggestion. It was companionable and productive.

By the time they adjourned she felt more positive that this unconventional marriage might work.

Only one thing bothered her.

Her intense awareness of Alessandro as a desirable man. The heat of his body and that tantalising scent distracted her when he leaned near. And, though she tried to concentrate on the notes they were creating, she was conscious of every shift of his tall frame, every brush of his arm or knee against hers.

Because she wanted her husband.

Her breath stalled on the admission, the static white noise of shock filling her ears.

Olivia wanted him with a longing that defied caution, pride and the fact this was a marriage foisted on them by circumstance. None of that could squash the longing fluttering to life in her dormant body.

This wasn't in the marriage contract.

Yet hadn't she battled this feeling from the very first? From the day she'd looked up at a crowded party in Rome and seen Alessandro watching her across the room with those sexy, heavy-lidded eyes. One look and heat had juddered through her. Connection. Interest. Desire.

All the things she'd told herself she'd never feel again for a man. Not after her first lover had lacerated her heart and her confidence at the age of eighteen.

Yet this wasn't a teenage fantasy. It was all too real.

It had survived despite his earlier apparent disapproval of her and her own best efforts to quell what she saw as weakness.

It was inconvenient and profoundly unsettling.

The question was, what would she do about it?

CHAPTER EIGHT

AFTER FIVE DAYS of marriage Olivia felt ridiculously restless on her first day alone. She and Alessandro had stayed at the villa, ostensibly having a very private honeymoon.

Not a traditional honeymoon.

Instead of spending their time in bed, they mainly worked.

Of course, Olivia didn't mind, she assured herself as she sat in the shade of a loggia, scrutinising a screen full of wedding photos.

She wasn't dissatisfied that Alessandro had gone out and left her alone for the day. She was just...

Edgy. Unsettled. Finding it hard to concentrate.

This feeling was unfamiliar. Most of her life she'd been essentially alone. She'd built up reserves of inner strength and a determination to succeed. Plus she had enough work to keep her very busy.

Yet she'd grown used to Alessandro. Despite that current of awareness that dragged through her belly and tightened her nipples when their eyes caught and held. Then she almost imagined he saw her as something other than a contracted partner.

When had they moved from being wary colleagues in a convenient marriage to companions?

They shared mealtimes, worked together on ideas for the winter ball and even relaxed together. Last night they'd watched a new-release film in the cinema room, chatting afterwards about the merits of various directors. Early each morning they rode together, exploring the estate and beyond.

Olivia had been delighted to discover Alessandro kept

stables. He'd even brought in a mare especially for her when she mentioned she loved riding. It was one of the few things she'd enjoyed about her exclusive boarding school, the chance to commune with horses instead of snobby trust-fund teenagers determined to make her life hell because she wasn't like them.

Olivia looked up from her screen to gaze across the gardens.

It wasn't only the riding she enjoyed. Or the films. She liked being with Alessandro.

This morning, when he'd excused himself to attend a meeting of senior staff, she'd actually been disappointed. Though she understood the need to be fully prepared for tomorrow's first board meeting for the newly amalgamated company.

How crazy was that? She wasn't some adolescent, unable to occupy her time or desperate for attention.

She'd spent the morning finishing the presentation she'd make to the board tomorrow. The presentation Alessandro had put on the agenda, to consider her proposal to establish a permanent bridal-wear arm of the company.

In the past Dell'Orto had produced bridal dresses only for runway shows. Olivia wanted to create an exclusive bridal boutique service, catering not just for brides but entire wedding parties, right down to the shoes and accessories they wore and the luggage they used. It would meld the strength of Sartori menswear and Dell'Orto feminine fashion, tapping into the universal desire to mark a wedding as special and memorable.

In time, she hoped to expand into providing a range of off-the-rack bridal gowns at the less exclusive end of the market as well, under a label linked to but separate from the original luxury brand names.

Olivia was torn between excitement and trepidation. This was her chance, finally, to push one of her own initiatives.

One she was convinced would be creatively and financially worthwhile.

She had Alessandro to thank for that. He'd listened to her idea, asking incisive questions then agreeing to list it for consideration, noting it was prudent to put such a major change in direction to the board, especially so soon after the amalgamation.

It was further than Olivia had got in Dell'Orto. In the past her suggestions had been quashed. She wasn't sure if the managers she'd worked with had been set in their ways and unwilling to put up a radical proposal lest it reflect badly on them. Or whether they resented her coming in, a favoured member of the family, when some of them had worked in the company for decades.

If only they knew. Far from her being favoured, her grandparents set higher standards for her than for anyone else. They expected her to be dedicated and knowledgeable, to learn every aspect of the business from the ground up as well as excel in her business degree.

She was never allowed to forget she was a Dell'Orto. She had to be elegant, poised, charming and vivacious, able to hold her own with princes and politicians.

Yet they'd delayed giving her a full role in the company.

Till now. Tomorrow she'd finally take her place there.

Excitement rippled through her and she wished Alessandro were here. They could chat over a glass of wine before dinner about business or films. She could lose herself in that curious sensation of warmth and approval she felt with him.

Her husband was the perfect antidote to the gnawing edge of nerves grabbing at her stomach when she thought about tomorrow.

Her husband.

The word didn't seem as strange or difficult after a week of marriage.

Shaking herself, Olivia turned to the screen. The initial

tranche of wedding photos had arrived with recommendations of lead images for their media campaign.

They were excellent, even better than expected. The photographer had captured the light and made the most of the
venue and the bridal gown's delicate beauty.

Suddenly Olivia's thoughts frayed and her smile faded.

The screen filled with a photo taken outside the *palazzo*.

A blonde woman stood on the pier. She should have
looked odd wearing a delicate gown with a man's formal
jacket draped around her shoulders. Instead the incongruity
of her clothes looked impossibly romantic. Partly because
of the late sun gilding the iconic Venetian scene. Partly because of the man standing close, one arm propped possessively near as he leaned in, impressive shoulders and narrow
hips the epitome of maleness. But the effect was mainly because of the bride's expression.

Olivia swallowed, unnerved. In the photo her hair was
slightly dishevelled, a few stray strands glistening golden
against the dark jacket. Her eyes glowed enormous and her
lips were parted as she looked up into the darkly compelling features of her groom.

She looked like a woman besotted.

A woman lost in the spell woven by a man who'd showed
her the simple kindness of a warm jacket against the gathering chill. Of a kind word and a little encouragement.

Olivia's hand went to her throat.

Was that all it took for Alessandro to break down her
barriers? A little consideration?

She breathed deep, telling herself it was a trick of the
light, the photographer's art.

Yet her ribs tightened as if corseted.

Had Alessandro seen what she saw?

The thought sent a shudder of nerves through her.

Then her chin lifted. If there was one thing she'd learned
it was how to project an image. It was a skill she'd forged
with blood, sweat and tears. It would come to her aid now.

Alessandro would think she'd acted for the camera. All she had to do was keep her cool and she'd be fine. She hoped.

'That's it, ladies and gentlemen. Thank you for your attendance and your input.' Alessandro looked around the long table, catching the eye of every member of the newly formed board.

Every eye but one. Olivia was tapping onto her tablet. Everyone else was closing folders of notes and easing back, tired after a long, productive meeting.

Alessandro's gaze lingered on his wife, her upright posture a contrast to the weariness of other board members.

He knew she'd been energised, even nervous about today, yet the meeting was over. Surely she could relax? Something about her body language sent a tickle of warning through him.

Alessandro stood. 'Now that our business is over, I hope you'll all join me in the salon next door for refreshments and to toast our future success.'

He was surrounded by people eager to congratulate him on the results of the meeting, and the way the merger was working out on the ground.

Yet Olivia didn't look his way.

Alessandro had grown used to her warm looks as she relaxed more with him. The sparkle in her hazel eyes had an addictive quality. Despite the undercurrent of sexual urgency that ran beneath all his dealings with his wife, Alessandro had discovered the simple joy of sharing time with her.

Had he grown so accustomed to her smiles that he actually sought her approval? Simply because he'd brought this first, potentially fraught board meeting to a successful conclusion?

Surely not. Alessandro didn't need anyone's approval. He'd shouldered the burden of leadership a lifetime ago and was secure in his own decision-making.

In the salon he took a glass of wine and waited till the other board members had glasses in their hands. Still Olivia didn't approach.

A twitch of annoyance rose. He wanted her here beside him. Then he saw her hemmed in on the far side of the room by her grandparents and another executive from Dell'Orto. Mentally he shrugged. They'd be together soon enough, driving back to the villa.

He grew restive at the slow pace of his plan to seduce her. Because Alessandro refused to rush and jeopardise the progress he'd made.

But soon, very soon.

The thought brought a smile to his face as he lifted his glass and called for the group's attention, making a toast to their new enterprise.

There was an air of excitement in the room and a smatter of applause. Then, at last, he felt Olivia's eyes on him.

It was a sensation he recognised instantly. A skewer of heat straight to the vitals.

From the first, even in the days when he'd avoided her because he knew she was destined to marry his brother, he'd *felt* Olivia's gaze as surely as if she'd reached out and touched him.

Alessandro turned to meet her glittering stare and every sense clicked onto high alert.

Something was wrong.

Swiftly he surveyed her, trying to catalogue the source of his conviction. Outwardly she looked fine. More than fine. She wore a slim-fitting suit in a colour between blue and purple that looked fabulous against her pale skin. Her blonde hair was swept up in a style that emphasised the purity of her features and revealed the blue-black pearl studs in her earlobes.

She looked coolly elegant and subtly sexy. A feathering of tension deep in his groin signalled his response.

But her lips, glimmering moist from the wine, were tight at the corners.

Until a young executive approached her and she smiled, her face turning radiant.

Another jab to Alessandro's belly. This time not of awareness but of jealousy.

Because his wife smiled at another man, not him. He put his glass down and started towards her, but a hand on his arm waylaid him. Two new board members wanted to speak to him and his priority was business, wasn't it? Casting one last glance at Olivia, now apparently at ease, he reluctantly turned to the pair before him.

Later he'd find out what bothered Olivia, for something certainly did.

Except later, when finally the board members left, she'd disappeared. She and the handsome guy she'd been chatting with so animatedly.

'Have you seen my wife?' Alessandro turned to his assistant, his voice carefully casual.

'She left. She said she'd call you.' At Alessandro's hard stare he hurried on. 'I heard her mention a taxi to Paolo.'

Taxi? Surely not all the way out to the villa. And Paolo was the man who'd stuck like glue to her side for the last half-hour. Had they left together?

Shock blasted through him, rocking him back on his feet.

He recalled Olivia talking about the need for discretion and privacy to ensure this marriage worked. His stomach curdled.

She'd better not be looking for privacy with Paolo!

Alessandro gritted his teeth. Olivia would never do anything so crass as to leave the meeting with a lover. She'd always been discretion personified. Besides, if she had a lover, surely it was Carlo, his brother. Nothing about Olivia hinted that she hopped from bed to bed.

Yet that didn't stop Alessandro spinning on his heel and striding away, a far more primitive impulse than logic speeding his steps. Something was up and he intended to find out what. Why would Olivia call him later? Why hadn't she spoken to him before leaving?

In the foyer he found her gone, but the doorman had heard the address she'd given the driver.

Minutes later Alessandro was on his way, uncaring of the work he'd planned to complete before leaving the office. For once he didn't stop to think. He simply followed the instinct urging him towards Olivia.

For a week he'd held back, tempered his desire for her, gone at her pace. But if she'd gone off with another man...

Logical, cool-headed Alessandro said he leapt to conclusions. There was a perfectly simple explanation.

She'd just smiled at the guy.

And let him monopolise her.

And left the building without explaining or apologising.

Alessandro breathed deep, searching for calm, but instead found only stirring anger at what he'd become because of her. Alessandro didn't do jealousy. Not till Olivia. All these years and his love life had been satisfying and uncomplicated. Now he tied himself in knots over a woman who wasn't even his lover!

But it felt like she was. At a deep, visceral level Olivia felt like *his* woman.

The taxi pulled up and Alessandro got out before a handsome apartment block. He'd make sure she was okay. He didn't really believe she was with another guy. He was concerned about her, that was all.

Reading the names against the apartment numbers, he headed for the third floor.

She took her time opening the door. Which gave Alessandro time to wrestle his temper under control. He'd spent his life learning *not* to give in to emotion.

His parents, with their fads and enthusiasms, their easy emotions, their *feelings* always on display, had been examples of what he refused to be—uncontrolled, inconsistent and driven by emotion.

The door opened. She'd shed her jacket and shoes and stood in stockinged feet, hair dishevelled as if she'd begun to let it down.

Or as if someone had run their hands through it.

Her chin jerked high and Alessandro told himself it was because of their height difference, emphasised now she was barefoot. But that didn't account for the febrile glitter in her hazel eyes or her pinched mouth.

She didn't want him here.

Alessandro looked past her into a wide hall, spying her discarded shoes lying haphazardly where she'd kicked them off.

As if she'd been in a hurry to undress.

'What are you doing here, Alessandro?' Her grip on the door looked talon-tight and the flare of her nostrils spoke of displeasure.

He told himself it wasn't because she was entertaining a man in her apartment. Yet he slid one foot forward, inserting it in the doorway, and drew himself up to his full height.

'We need to talk.'

He hadn't even finished speaking when she shook her head, wheat-blonde tresses swirling over the delicate top she'd worn beneath her jacket. His fingers itched to thread through her hair, then slide down over the subtle sheen of silk to cover her breast.

Alessandro's breath stalled as desire slammed straight to his belly.

'Not now, Alessandro. It's not a good time. I'll see you later.'

Not a good time because she was busy with Paolo? It wasn't going to happen.

'This can't wait.' He kept his tone even but her expression said she read his obstinacy. Narrowed eyes rested on his then swept over his palm, planted flat on the door, and down to his gleaming shoe, blocking it open.

'We agreed that we were each entitled to some privacy.'

The skin at his nape and shoulders prickled in a chill that galloped down his spine and froze his gut. 'Privacy' meaning time with a lover? A sick sensation roiled through him and something else, a feeling that he lurched to the brink of some terrible catastrophe.

'This won't take long.'

Because it would take mere moments to eject Paolo. And if he wasn't here, Alessandro could get straight to the bottom of Olivia's strange mood.

Without a word, but with a supremely dismissive shrug, Olivia turned and stalked down the hall, leaving Alessandro to appreciate the way her fitted skirt turned her annoyed march into a treat for any red-blooded male.

His body's response underscored the intensity of her effect on him. Which in turn undermined his vaunted control.

She waited, standing arms akimbo in a comfortable, elegant sitting room. She didn't invite him to sit.

'What is it, Alessandro? What's so urgent I can't have an hour to myself?'

He swept the room with a quick glance. 'Are we alone, Olivia?'

'Sorry?' She looked genuinely perplexed.

'Is Paolo here?'

'Paolo? Paolo Benetti? Why didn't you say so?'

His stomach nosedived and something sharp cleaved to his tongue.

'Where is he?' Alessandro had crossed the room before he finished speaking, striding into first a sleek kitchen then a bedroom, bathroom—

'What are you doing? He's not here!'

Her voice came from behind him but Alessandro didn't stop. He flung open a final door and slammed to a halt, taking in the room before him.

It was beautiful, with only a few pieces of furniture and no overcrowded decorations, yet it was the bedroom of an utter romantic. A swathe of gauze draped from an antique brass fitting high above the bed. The ivory satin bedcover was exquisitely quilted, and the few pieces of art on the walls evoked the fantasy of an earlier, more elegant age.

This was where Olivia slept? The woman who, he'd now discovered through discreet enquiries and his own observations, had the makings of one of the most pragmatic members of the new management team. Where others in Dell'Orto clung to tradition, she'd urged change with the clear-sightedness of a savvy businesswoman.

Nothing could be further from the image she projected.

'What do you think you're doing?' Hazel eyes speared his as she stepped in front of him, hands once more on her hips. 'You've got no right to invade my privacy. And why would you think Paolo was here…?'

Her words petered out and he saw the moment she put two and two together. She seemed to swell with outrage, fire burning across her cheeks as if she'd been slapped.

Alessandro saw his mistake and cursed his unfamiliar neediness. How could he have let suspicion drive him so far?

'You thought Paolo and I came here for sex?' Olivia watched her husband wince at her words.

Nausea churned through her stomach and she thought she might lose her lunch. She shook her head, her breath stolen by the sheer effrontery of the man.

When he opened his mouth to speak she shoved up her hand, palm out. 'Don't answer that. It's clear you did.' Her shoulders twitched as a shiver scuttled through her. Alessandro's suspicion made her feel dirty.

Here in her own home!

Wasn't it bad enough that today had gone as it had? That he'd allowed, no, *encouraged* her to put so much effort into her presentation, only to refuse to back her when she needed him?

She'd begun to trust him. To hope they'd find a way of working together, even making this marriage a success. Yet all the time he'd been…what? Keeping her busy and out of his hair with a proposal he knew would be rejected?

Olivia ground her teeth. She didn't know what hurt more. The way he'd deliberately set her up to fail at the meeting or that he now stormed in here pretending he cared what she did!

'If I were having sex with Paolo, it would be none of your business.' She prodded Alessandro's chest so hard a lesser man would have fallen back. 'However, despite what you think of me, I have more respect for myself and you than to go straight from our workplace to bed with a lover right under the eyes of our colleagues.'

How could he think it of her? As well as anger, she felt a ripping sensation deep within as hurt tore through her. It had been a long time since she'd hurt so much.

Because she'd begun to open herself up to Alessandro and let him in and now learned he thought so little of her?

She should have kept herself to herself as she'd learned. Not giving anyone the power to hurt her.

'Paolo and I went downstairs together but he caught another taxi.' She folded her arms against her heaving chest. 'I suggest you go after him to discuss whatever it is you need him for so urgently.' She paced to the door, ostentatiously gesturing for him to leave. Every muscle twanged with tension as she drew herself up to her full height.

'I don't want to talk with him. It's you I want.'

Olivia inhaled sharply at the irony of his words. Alessandro didn't want her at all. He was playing some possessive macho game but it wasn't really about her.

'Too bad. I'm not in the mood for you, Alessandro, with your high-handed ways and your insults.' To her horror her voice wobbled on the last word. Only because she was utterly furious at his distrust.

'I'm sorry, Olivia.' He spread his hands in an age-old gesture of placation. 'I didn't really believe it. I just—'

'Don't lie. Of course you did. You stormed in here like a vengeful husband.' Indignation made her heart pound so high it felt like it reached her throat.

'I am your husband. But I apolo—'

'Not like that. This is a paper marriage. You don't own me.' Her chest heaved with pain and short breaths that didn't fill her lungs.

Once more he spread his hands wide. 'Of course I don't own you. But I was worried about you.'

'Worried? I don't believe it!'

'I really was worried.' His deep voice ground so low she felt it like a subterranean rumble. 'I got distracted when I thought you'd brought Paolo here, and for that I apologise. But I wanted to talk to you because I was concerned about you. You weren't yourself after the meeting. I know there's something wrong.'

Olivia shook her head at the gall of the man. 'Something wrong? Of course there's something wrong. Did you really think I'd be simpering up at you like those other toadies after what you did?'

The injustice of it rankled. Worse, because she'd been there before, believed she had a chance to contribute fully, only to be shot down by executives who said one thing to her face and another to their peers.

'What did I do?'

His raised brows and questioning look were too much. She flung away from the door and stalked across the room, needing to move, needing some outlet for the fury and disappointment bubbling inside.

'You made me think you'd support me.' She tugged the last of the pins from her hair and threw them on the bedside table. 'You *played* me, and I was stupid enough to fall for it because I wanted to believe that, despite what I knew of you, you were genuine.' She huffed out a bitter laugh. 'You betrayed my trust.'

'Now, hold on—'

'No, you hold on.' She pivoted to find he'd crossed the room to stand before her, taller and more heartbreakingly handsome than ever. The fact she noticed was the last straw. 'I married you in good faith. I didn't expect miracles but I did expect fair dealing and,' she swallowed, 'trust. You should have told me you weren't going to support my initiative.'

'This is about the *meeting*?'

'What else?' As if she hadn't put her heart and soul into her proposal. As if she hadn't basked in his enthusiasm and encouragement.

Alessandro shoved his hands in his pockets and rocked back on his heels. 'You're flying off the handle because you're disappointed at the way the meeting went?' He made her sound like a child having a temper tantrum.

'No, I'm forcefully expressing my contempt and disappointment. You're the one who stormed in here, accusing me of sordid behaviour. Of course I'm angry.' She drew a massive breath, seeking control of the urge to go and beat his big chest with her fists. Or—madness—kiss him till he gave up on that perplexed air and she'd worked off some of her desperate feelings.

'You didn't only agree to put my proposal for a bridal collection on the agenda, you led me to believe you'd support it. Instead you sat there letting people talk it down. You gave them more airtime than you gave me to rebut their arguments. Then you cut off discussion without a decision. You *buried* it, Alessandro. Despite everything you said in private about it being innovative and full of potential.'

'I didn't bury it, *cara*. I gave the naysayers the chance to be heard, and allowed everyone to hear the potential negatives and positives. I only put it to the board as a courtesy while we all get used to each other, and so they feel fully informed. This is a decision for the CEO—me—and I've already decided to go with it. I thought I'd made that clear to you. A memo about it will circulate next week.'

Olivia blinked up into eyes that for once didn't seem shuttered but open and honest.

'Then why didn't you tell me? Why make me think…?'

His expression shifted and she almost imagined she read discomfort there.

'I'm used to making things happen. Not sharing. I thought you understood.' He sighed and suddenly he looked not like the indomitable, forceful man she knew but one carrying a heavy burden. 'We spent a lot of time at the meeting poring over details that in future will be handled outside meetings. Because this is a settling-in period and I know some members,' his pointed stare made her think of those who'd objected to her suggestion, 'find this merger more difficult than others.' He paused. 'I'm sorry for not bringing you into my confidence. I honestly didn't think of it.'

All the furious words she'd wanted to fling at him disintegrated.

Maybe she'd been naïve about how the board meeting would work. She'd never presented to one before. Her expectations and her nerves had been so high.

Elation rose, a sizzle in her blood. Alessandro would implement her suggestion. Her plans for a bridal portfolio would go ahead! Wait till she told Sonia.

'And the suspicion about me and Paolo?' That still grated unbearably.

'Ah.' He forked his fingers back through glossy hair. 'I regret that.'

'But why would you behave that way?'

Olivia couldn't fathom it. She'd done nothing to create such suspicions. The look on Alessandro's face as he'd loomed in the doorway, as if no one and nothing was going to shift him…

'You really don't know?'

Had he moved nearer? Suddenly she had to tilt her head to hold his stare. Her insides trembled as she inhaled his distinctive scent of bergamot, leather and warm male skin.

'No. I really don't know.'

Yet her stomach turned in jittery flips as those dark eyes held hers and the space between them shrank.

'Then let me explain.'

One moment he was standing there, holding her spell-bound with that gleaming gaze. The next his hands were on her upper arms and his mouth was on hers.

CHAPTER NINE

HIS MOUTH WAS GENTLE, but there was nothing tentative about the way his long fingers curled around her arms. His touch was easy, assured and very, very possessive.

Olivia told herself that wasn't a thrill racing through her body. That the strange soft feeling in her middle wasn't her insides melting into a puddle. Yet her eyelids fluttered shut as their lips met.

She didn't kiss him back but stood, mesmerised, as her brain played catch-up with her revelling senses. He covered her mouth then planted tiny kisses along the seam of her lips that made her yearn all the more.

She'd known this was coming at some subliminal level. Or maybe she'd wondered about it so long it felt like it was inevitable. For too long Alessandro Sartori had played havoc with her thoughts and even her dreams, inserting himself where he wasn't wanted.

But that was the trouble. He *was* wanted. Since the wedding she'd battled a losing fight to keep her hormones under control, reminding herself her husband wasn't interested in her. That she had more self-respect than to offer herself to a man who didn't like her.

Except there *had* been liking and more too, or so she'd believed.

Olivia arched her back, pulling away while she pushed at his chest. She didn't let herself think about the pinpricks of pleasure tickling her palms at the feel of that solid chest beneath her touch.

'That's enough.' Unfortunately her reedy voice held a breathless edge that betrayed her.

'You really think so?'

She read the spark of humour in his ebony gaze and a flash of searing heat that short-circuited her thoughts. Alessandro teasing? That did strange things to her. Things she didn't like to think about. Not when she fought a last-ditch battle against her own traitorous self.

'Just because we signed legal papers—'

'Because we *married*,' he corrected, his voice impossibly smug.

She snatched a quick breath, unfortunately redolent with sexy male. Olivia prayed for control.

'Doesn't mean you have the right to storm in here throwing accusations. Or to kiss me.' She set her jaw and told herself she'd be fine as soon as he let her go and stepped away.

Except she didn't want to be fine. She wanted to be with Alessandro. Slaking the terrible, tormenting need for him that had swamped her from the first.

'I apologise about my suspicion. I overreacted. I saw you smiling at him and felt...'

Alessandro shook his head as if words failed him, but she felt the quick tattoo of his heart beneath her hand.

'You were *jealous*?'

Olivia boggled up at him.

She should be outraged. Instead a new feeling bloomed behind her ribcage. A rising fullness that made her breath turn shallow.

His mouth, the mouth that for seconds had caressed hers so sweetly, compressed. A fierce light shone in his eyes.

'I want you, Olivia. So, yes. I was jealous. Needy. Half out of my mind thinking you'd turned to another man instead of me.'

Despite the ecstatic jig going on inside her, Olivia frowned. 'Because you see me as a possession now we're married?'

Then Alessandro did something that shattered her final defences. He lifted one corner of his mouth in a crooked smile that bore no resemblance to any of his smiles she'd seen before. It spoke of wry self-knowledge, of amusement at his own expense.

'I've never thought in terms of owning a woman, Olivia. I've never been that interested. Plus I have too much respect for your feistiness to go down that path.'

His amusement faded, replaced by an intensity that drilled right through her. 'But yes, I want to possess you, physically.' His words slowed as if to ensure she understood every syllable. She did. Every cell in her body shimmied in eagerness. 'I want to take you and have you take me till neither of us can think of anyone or anything else. It's driving me insane trying to keep my distance.'

Olivia expelled a shuddering sigh.

How was she to resist when he put into words exactly how she felt? Yet old habits died dreadfully hard.

'You want me because you thought someone else had me.' She knew what it was like to be wanted as a trophy rather than for herself.

A warm finger curled beneath her chin, tilting it so there was no escape from his laser-sharp stare. 'I wanted you the first moment I saw you. This has nothing to do with anyone but you and me.'

The first moment I saw you.

Could it be he'd felt that lightning bolt too?

Tremors ran through her as she held herself away from him, trying to resist the seduction of his words, the images he conjured. But how could she ever know if she could trust him? All she could do was walk away—a sheer impossibility. Or succumb, knowing that it was what she wanted.

'From the first? You didn't even like me!'

His eyebrows rose but his gaze didn't waver. 'Wrong, Olivia.' The way he said her name, in that husky velvet voice, turned it into something precious. The sound wove through her, seductive and enchanting. 'It's you who didn't like me.'

'I…' She'd all but admitted it in Venice, when he'd persuaded her to marry him then asked what she thought of him. At the time she hadn't found the right words or wanted to. Olivia stared back into those mesmerising eyes and felt the truth drawn from her. 'I thought you didn't approve of me.'

Once more his mouth twisted in that self-deprecating smile that tugged at her heart. It turned him into a different man. One she wanted, desperately, to know.

'You were wrong. I approve of you. Very much.'

His hand moved from her chin, feathering along her jawline and up, long fingers flirting with the sensitive skin of her neck and earlobe, then channelling through her loose hair. Olivia's eyelids flickered at the whorls of sensation created by his circling fingertips.

'We'll be very, very good together, Olivia.'

He spoke with such certainty, as if there were no question that they'd become lovers.

He also spoke with the voice of experience. Whereas she had so little. But that didn't prevent her yearning.

Olivia was tired of being cautious. Of watching every step she took. What could it hurt to enjoy sex with the one man who'd reawakened her libido? With her husband, the man who, despite her best efforts, had always affected her.

She shifted her palms across his chest, feeling the solid contours that spoke of masculine strength.

She was so close she saw the pulse at Alessandro's throat throb fast, as if triggered by the movement. She liked the sense of power that came from his body's reaction to her. For the first time it felt like she wasn't playing catch-up with Alessandro, second-guessing his thoughts or feelings. He'd laid those bare with a startling honesty that still unsettled her.

I wanted you the first moment I saw you.

How was she to resist when she felt exactly the same? When in this, at least, they were equals?

His hands were still possessively clamped around her

upper arms. But she didn't want him to let her go. Instead she wanted, so badly, to possess Alessandro too.

Suddenly desire was a compulsion she could no longer resist.

Stretching up, Olivia slid her hands around his neck and tugged, but he was already bending towards her. She had an impression of eyes glittering like shards of obsidian, of powerful arms encircling her, then their lips met. This time her thoughts frayed completely. There was no questioning or worrying, just the luscious delight of being in Alessandro's embrace, glorying in his kiss.

Yet again he was gentle, tender, and Olivia marvelled at his restraint. The feelings welling within her were so urgent she needed more than the light graze of his lips along hers.

Angling her head for better access, she bit down on his lower lip, feeling the succulent cushion give, then laving it with her tongue.

It was as if she'd woken a sleeping giant.

No, not sleeping. There was nothing dozy about Alessandro. Those half-lidded looks he'd given her had been all about sexual awareness. Now she unleashed the firestorm.

A low growl rumbled in her ears and through her body where she pressed against him. His mouth closed on hers, nipping this time, sending darts of fire scudding to her breasts and womb, making her shiver and cling. And his hands, those big, capable hands, slid down to her buttocks and drew her higher against him. Close enough to feel the hard rod of his arousal push against her. Where moments ago there'd been caution, now there was urgency.

Olivia cradled his skull, fingers anchored in his hair, as she answered his delving kiss with a desperate response. Mouths fused, tongues dancing, she felt the heat pour from his body into hers, swamping her.

Another hungry sound from the back of his throat made the hair at her nape stand up and her body quiver in anticipation.

Her need was every bit as untamed as Alessandro sounded. So when he shaped his hands lower around her backside and hauled her up his body she could have cheered.

Except that would mean lifting her mouth from his, and nothing short of death would make her do that. Alessandro's mouth on hers elicited the most wondrous sensations. Better than anything she'd experienced or even dreamed of experiencing.

For a second her severely limited sexual experience worried her. Would she be able to give him anything like the pleasure he was giving her? Then he pressed her right up against his impressive erection and she stopped worrying. No doubt he had enough experience for them both.

Olivia wrapped her arms over his shoulders and lifted her knees. With some help from him, shoving her skirt high, she found purchase to wrap her legs around his narrow hips.

The feel of him there, right at her core, while his tongue thrust hungrily into her mouth, sent erotic excitement shuddering through her.

Had anything, ever, felt like this? They were still clothed, yet Olivia was impossibly aroused. As if just thinking about sex with Alessandro might send her over the edge.

She tilted her hips, greedily increasing the friction between them, and heard a rough sound. A moan, raw and aching, just as she ached for more. It took long seconds before she realised the sound came from her own throat.

Their kiss grew from urgent to frantic.

Olivia felt movement. A rush of air, but even that didn't still their hungry mouths, and it was only when Alessandro rolled and she found herself sandwiched between his hard frame and the mattress that she realised he'd fallen back onto the bed with her in his arms.

Excellent. Sharing a bed with Alessandro was exactly what she wanted. Her hands scrabbled to grip his back, till she realised he wore a suit. He must have had the same thought, that there were too many clothes between them.

For abruptly he levered himself up on his hands, breaking their kiss.

Olivia's chest seared as she dragged oxygen into air-starved lungs.

Her gaze collided with Alessandro's.

The look on his face, the expression of raw, unvarnished hunger, made her heart flip and her stomach squirm in delight.

This was what she wanted.

This, she realised, was what she'd wanted a year ago when she'd looked across that crowded party straight into fathomless eyes that promised everything she'd never dared let herself dream of.

After her first, awful foray into passion, she'd been too cautious to covet any man. Too scared.

She wasn't scared now. She felt bold and powerful. Sexy and desirable as never before.

And impossibly needy.

Her hands went to his discreetly patterned silk tie and wrenched it undone, tugging it free.

'You're wearing too many clothes.' Her voice was almost inaudible since she was short of breath, but Alessandro's feral smile told her he agreed as he grabbed her hand and put it to his top shirt button. He shrugged out of his jacket and tossed it as she began unbuttoning.

'So are you.' His hands went to her waist, pulling up her top, then, when it caught on her skirt zipper, giving up and moving instead to grasp her scoop neckline.

Olivia shivered in excitement as his warm fingers curled around the edge of the fabric, his knuckles touching the upper slope of her breast and sending delight skittering through her.

Olivia's heart pounded in her ears as he raised one questioning eyebrow.

She gave a curt nod and instantly felt the material lift from her body. She heard the silk tear and air wafted across her breasts as Alessandro pulled the remains of her top away and flung it to one side.

Her breath stoppered and her breasts rose, budding against constricting lace in flagrant excitement.

This was ravishment and she revelled in it.

She adored Alessandro's single-mindedness and the wild glint in his dark eyes. In her peripheral vision she saw her shredded silk caught on the edge of her bedside table. The sight tugged a line of heat through her belly right down to that achy, empty place between her legs.

Olivia only got halfway down his shirt buttons before the hot, satiny flesh of his torso tempted her to spread the fine cotton wide and splay her fingers, moulding solid muscle. Delight coursed through her, reaction to the friction of chest hair against her palms.

She exhaled, torn between momentary relief at finally being able to touch his body and impatience.

He must have felt the same, for in a couple of swift moves he pushed her skirt up to her hips. His glittering gaze spoke of approval and excitement, burning even brighter as she dropped her hands to his belt.

'Hurry,' she murmured.

He needed no more urging. One swift movement and he had his wallet out of his back pocket. By the time she'd undone his belt he'd extracted a condom.

Was there anything more arousing than watching Alessandro tear the foil packet with his teeth while his fevered gaze held hers?

She undid the fastening of his trousers by touch alone. Then the zip. Her skin tightened in anticipation as her knuckles grazed his erection and his eyes shut. She saw a shudder pass through him and her inner muscles clenched.

She needed him. Now.

'Olivia.' His voice was hoarse, proof his need matched hers. 'I want you so badly. I can't promise to take it slow.'

Crazy that, out of the fog of desire, she identified vulnerability in his strong features and even in the powerful body looming over her.

It should be impossible, yet she was sure it was real. And it drew hard at something within her. Something that was more than lust. Something tender and wondrous.

Olivia refused to heed the voice saying she imagined things, trying to turn Alessandro into someone he wasn't.

Instead she smiled and lifted her hips, hands going to the waistband of her tights to drag them and her underwear down in one sharp tug.

'I don't want slow. I just want you.'

The next sixty seconds were a blur of urgent movement. Olivia struggled to roll off her tights while Alessandro rolled on the condom, each hampered by the sight of the other. She'd never forget the look in his eyes, approval and desire in an earthy, glorious mix that made her feel impossibly desirable.

For the first time she understood exactly what was meant by a devouring stare. Alessandro looked like he wanted to eat her up, one mouthful at a time. If she'd had the energy she'd have crowed in delight.

Then there was the sight of his arousal, powerfully erect and ready for her, that simultaneously dried her throat and moistened other places ready for his loving.

Finally, after a few desperate tugs, she was naked from the waist down and Alessandro was between her thighs, positioning himself where she needed him most.

For a second he held still, watching her, then with a single slow, sure movement he glided right to her core.

Olivia's breath shuddered in a husky rasp of shock.

She'd thought she remembered how sex felt, but her memory was nothing like this.

This was indescribable, the weight and fullness of him, now part of her, filling her right up to where her heart beat a staggering new, triumphal rhythm. The gleam of awareness and appreciation in his eyes matched what she knew must be in hers. Feathery ripples of arousal burgeoned from where their bodies met.

Alessandro's hair was rumpled, his shirt half-undone and shoved low across one shoulder.

He'd never looked more wonderful.

He moved and she gasped. Gossamer strands of delight wove more strongly through tightening muscles.

She tilted her pelvis to him and there it was again, wonderful tension pulling harder.

Her hands went to his shoulders, fingers digging into the pads of muscle as she arched her back to his next thrust and the world began to spin.

Then Alessandro's head lowered, his mouth taking hers in a hungry caress that matched the quickening rhythm of their bodies. His hand clamped her breast through the lace cup, eliciting more shudders of pleasure that arrowed to her womb.

Olivia's hands slid to his head, fingers channelling through thick hair, holding tight as each arch of their bodies wove that thread of connection tighter, turning the rhythm of their movements into a pattern of give and take as beautiful as anything she'd ever known.

But it didn't last long. Already she felt the sparks of lightning exploding.

She tried to withstand it because this was too wonderful to give up. But the surge of ecstasy was on her, taking her to a place she'd never been.

Alessandro threw back his head, his proud features transformed into a mask of tension and incandescent joy. A joy Olivia felt as their gazes meshed and they fell, jolting and burning, into the flames.

Later, much later, as Olivia snuggled against Alessandro's chest, she wondered at how quickly she'd morphed from the poised, sophisticated woman she'd striven to become. Had it been her heightened emotions of anger, mistrust and finally relief that had tipped her over the edge? Had they alone turned her into a woman she didn't recognise?

Or had it been Alessandro himself? Since the evening she first saw him, Olivia had felt there was something significant between them. Unfinished business. Business she hadn't let herself start. Till now.

Today she'd revelled in the primal power of passion. It had been primitive and untrammelled and profoundly real. More real than anything she'd ever experienced. Enough to make her question her perception of herself and Alessandro. For she had no doubt this magnificence wasn't simply about sex. She'd had sex before and magnificent it wasn't. This was about her and Alessandro together.

Even now, lying boneless and weightless in his embrace, she felt changed. Had he done that to her, or had she, by opening the Pandora's box of desire?

Losing herself in Alessandro's caresses, she'd felt more true to herself than ever before.

Her heart danced as she thought about him. Not merely his sexual allure and stunning physical power. Or the tenderness he'd shown, the initial reluctance to proceed when he knew he couldn't hold back.

Olivia's pulse thudded faster, her body reawakening at the memory.

She'd crossed a boundary with her husband. If she were utterly truthful it was a boundary she'd wanted to cross from the first. But where did that leave her?

More precisely, where did it leave *them*?

CHAPTER TEN

ALESSANDRO STARED AT the ceiling, heart still pounding and a smile splitting his face.

He'd known they'd be good together. But that had been better than good. His instincts were right, the chemistry between him and Olivia outstripped anything he'd known. And they'd only just begun.

His mind turned to that day a couple of weeks ago when he'd told Olivia they'd marry. She'd been understandably surprised. But her expression had revealed something more like horror than shock. Alessandro had told himself it didn't matter, yet it had felt like a body blow. He'd had no idea she actually disliked him. She'd passed it off by saying her reservations were because she didn't know him. Yet at a deep, primal level, that had hurt.

Only now did he allow himself to ponder that. To wonder at this woman's ability to bruise his ego when no other person could. Alessandro had spent a lifetime shoring up his defences against his family's self-absorption and there'd been no woman whose opinion mattered that much to him.

Until now.

Just as well Olivia had dozed off. He needed time to come to grips with what had happened.

He drew a deep breath, conscious of her weight on him, her head nestled on his chest, hair splayed like rippling satin across his skin, her arm flung across his waist as if to prevent him rising.

Satisfaction stirred.

She may not have liked him initially but that wasn't the case now. Yes, she'd been fiery with rage when she thought he'd tricked and betrayed her, but that had died quickly.

Her temper was fascinating, given the aura of poised calm she usually projected. Over the last week he'd seen behind that, discovering a woman of strong feelings who was even more enticing than he'd initially thought.

Whatever she felt for him now, it wasn't dislike. He'd tracked the change in her. The way she relaxed with him more. Smiled at him. Enjoyed being with him.

That wasn't feigned.

If she'd disliked him, would she have been so frantic to share her body with him?

Alessandro breathed deep. That hadn't been angry sex. It had been desperate and profoundly satisfying, but there'd been no edge of fury. It had felt as if they both, finally, surrendered to forces too strong to resist.

Absently he stroked the blonde tresses spilling across his shoulder.

He thought of that wedding photo on the Grand Canal. He'd stood, canted towards Olivia, his stance one of utter possessiveness, and she'd looked up at him with shining eyes and parted lips, like a woman smitten.

When he'd seen it Alessandro had stamped down on the thrill of excitement that snaked through him, telling himself she'd played at being a starry-eyed bride.

But was Olivia such a good actress? Had she felt something for him then? Despite her dislike?

Instinct told him she had. Surely this afternoon's events proved it.

Satisfaction flooded him, and relief.

His wife wanted him, physically at least. She'd been utterly abandoned and glorious, so sexy and alluring he'd barely managed to remember a condom, much less give her the sort of loving he wanted to.

His mouth curved in another smile.

Though there was a lot to be said for hard, fast and bone-meltingly satisfying. Sex with his wife made him want to beat his chest and shout his triumph.

And have her again.

His loins tightened.

With an effort Alessandro concentrated on his marriage. Olivia wasn't indifferent. She was attracted. She enjoyed being with him. Every morning on those early rides across the estate her eyes shone and there'd been no hint of constraint. Nor at any other time since they'd moved to the villa.

He could work with that.

Alessandro might not be looking for love but he wanted Olivia in ways he'd never wanted anyone else. He wanted her as his wife in every sense, and not just now, while the merger was fresh. He wanted her long-term.

She was his and he intended to keep her.

Deliberately he deepened the stroke of his hand as he caressed her, curving his palm and fingers across her bare shoulder, down to the line of the bra she still wore. She arched, stretching against his touch, and the feel of her moving against his bare chest was enough to make him hard.

He huffed a disbelieving laugh.

'What's so funny?' Was that frozen note wariness or disapproval?

Alessandro moved to one side, tilting her chin till their eyes met.

Olivia's glowed more green than brown, as if decorated with shards of peridot. He'd thought he'd imagined that— the way their colour changed as she reached her climax.

Oh, yes, he had a lot to work with.

Except he read something else in her furrowed brow and the crimped corners of her lush mouth. Did she think he was laughing at her?

'*I* am.'

The tightness around her mouth eased. 'You? I don't understand.'

'I'm lying here with my arms still in my shirt, my shoes and socks on and my trousers around my ankles. Hardly the suave, cosmopolitan look.' He paused, watching her absorb that, feeling the moment when she relaxed.

'Does it matter?'

'Maybe not. But generally a man likes to make a good impression on a woman he wants to seduce.'

'We already did the seduction.'

Fascinated, Alessandro watched a hint of colour tinge her cheeks. Was Olivia embarrassed?

He hadn't expected a shy, retiring flower. He'd expected she'd be experienced. His mind had shied from the possibility that some of that experience might have been with Carlo.

But looking at her now, her gaze shifting from him and the colour in her face intensifying, she didn't seem as sophisticated and nonchalant as he'd anticipated. The word *vulnerable* came to mind. That surely explained her wariness, the way she seemed to expect something negative in his words. Alessandro was tempted to add the word *innocent*, with those downcast eyes and flushed cheeks, but that was ridiculous. This was the temptress who'd ordered him to take her.

But despite her earlier desperation there was definitely something intriguing here.

Wariness often went hand in hand with past hurt. As he knew from childhood experience.

Alessandro filed that idea away for later. She wouldn't appreciate him probing now.

'Alessandro?' She watched him now, gaze steady. He felt his response like a line of fire running straight to his groin.

His lips curved up in an appreciative smile. With her hair in loose waves around her shoulders, her grave expression and that lacy white bra, she looked like a fantasy seductress, all innocence on the surface, but all hot, wondrous woman beneath.

Oh, how he wanted her.

'You don't think we're finished, do you? That was a taste, a starter.'

Fascinated, he watched her swallow, her gaze flicking down towards his burgeoning shaft.

'You look shocked.' He hadn't meant to say it. Alessandro wasn't a garrulous man, he watched what he said, but here, now, with Olivia, his usual caution frayed.

The tint of pink on her cheeks turned bright and when her gaze caught his he saw what looked like embarrassment as well as challenge in her expression.

'I didn't think you could be…ready again so soon.'

He hadn't expected it either. Yet her words reinforced that impression he had of innocence, or at least inexperience. He surveyed her intently. Alessandro wanted to know her so much better.

In the meantime, her words, accompanied by another sidelong look at his groin, only encouraged his body's eager response.

He'd work on finding out more about his wife later. Now his focus was elsewhere.

'For you, *cara*, I'll rise to the occasion.'

To his fascinated delight she rolled her eyes, shaking her head at his terrible pun, a giggle escaping her kiss-swollen lips.

Alessandro couldn't remember ever joking with a lover. Strangely it seemed as intimate as sex itself. And, loner though he was, he liked it. Liked the unfamiliar warmth spreading around his heart.

Olivia's fingers trawled across his chest, making it rise on a sudden breath, then followed a meandering trail down his torso.

'You're sure you're not too worn out?' Her delectable pout was pure invitation.

'One thing you'll learn about me, Olivia, is that I never leave anything important unfinished.'

Propping herself higher above him, she met his gaze squarely. 'Unfinished? After that amazing orgasm?'

Pure male pride filled him. He'd watched her come, felt her climax, yet to hear her call it amazing...

'Unfinished because we both want more, don't we?' He waited till she nodded. 'And important. Very important.'

If this was his best way of tying Olivia to him, then he'd take every opportunity to do that. As if sex with his gorgeous wife wasn't exactly what he wanted!

He began undoing his cufflinks. 'Only this time I suggest we both get fully naked.'

For a moment she didn't move, then abruptly she slid off him. Alessandro stifled a groan at the loss of her body against his, but then she was at the foot of the bed, in a sexy bra and crumpled skirt, wearing a smile he'd almost describe as cheeky. Before he knew what she was doing she dropped down low and he felt her nimble fingers on his shoelaces. The trouble was that his brain computed the sight of Olivia crouching between his knees and imagined her doing far more than undressing him.

Alessandro suppressed a groan as his erection surged more strongly. Setting his jaw, he flung the cufflinks aside and sat up, reefing the shirt from his back and onto the floor.

Glowing hazel eyes looked up, meeting his as she peeled off the last of his clothes. Jagged heat ripped through Alessandro's belly. He wanted his wife so badly he could barely contain himself.

Dim thoughts filtered into his brain about showering, but then Olivia rose to her feet and unzipped her skirt, letting it drop to the floor.

It hurt to swallow. Alessandro's throat seared as if he swallowed fire. She was exquisite. The delicious curve of waist and hips, the triangle of dark gold hair above long, smooth legs.

She lifted her hands behind her back and the lacy nothing of a bra fell.

'You're beautiful, *tesoro*. Perfect.' He didn't recognise

his voice. But he did recognise the frown crinkling her forehead.

'You don't have to flatter me, Alessandro.'

He shook his head, trying to find enough brain cells still working for him to hold a conversation. Forcibly he yanked his gaze up from the contours of her gorgeous breasts.

'It's not flattery.' He met a stare that looked almost mutinous.

'No one's perfect.'

You are. For me.

It was crazy. But in that moment Alessandro felt the truth of it resonate through him.

He didn't know her as well as he wanted. They were acquaintances brought together by business and by the most powerful sexual attraction he'd ever experienced. Yet there was more. That *coup de foudre,* the lightning bolt of attraction he'd felt the moment he laid eyes on her, meant something. Not love at first sight—he barely believed in love—but something. An instant knowledge that this woman was special.

She crossed her arms over her breasts and he wanted to drag them down so he could look his fill.

'Let me rephrase. You're sensuous and exciting. Beautiful, especially when your skin flushes and your eyes shine at me like gems and you take me into your lush body and let me share myself with you.'

That flush was back, not just in her cheeks, but down her throat and across her breasts.

She was so delectable he wanted to eat her all up. Slowly. His skin tightened as desire ratcheted up unbearably.

'Come here.'

He'd meant to ask, not order. Definitely not to sound gruff. But it was amazing he could push words out of his mouth, form thoughts in a brain shrinking as another part of him expanded.

She stepped closer and he grabbed her hand, expelling

a sigh of relief. Dimly Alessandro felt shocked by his desperation, as if he'd die if he didn't touch her again, but his thoughts were already racing ahead.

He raised her hand to his mouth, kissing the back of it then turning it over to press kisses to her wrist and palm, feeling her pulse thundering like his.

His other hand lifted to the satiny skin of her belly, weaving long strokes that made her shiver.

'Straddle me.' Another order.

'Sorry?' Her hand stiffened in his and he looked up into wide hazel eyes the colour of a spring forest.

Gently he tugged her closer. 'Sit on my lap.'

A deep breath made those sweet breasts jiggle, then slowly she put her hands on his shoulders and knelt astride him.

'Like this?' Once more he caught hesitation in her tone but there was no time to dwell on it.

'Perfect,' he growled as he skimmed his hand across the juncture of her thighs. He was rewarded with a stifled gasp and a shiver of her glorious body. 'Good?'

'More than good.' She pressed closer and Alessandro's chest tightened. They were so attuned.

'It gets better,' he murmured, urging her down, hands on her hips, till her warmth enveloped him.

There. Like that. Just…there. She sank a little lower and gasped as she slid around the tip of his erection.

A shudder started in Alessandro's groin and shot up his spine to the back of his head then around to clamp his jaw closed. He wanted to encourage her, soothe her, but no words came. Instead he lifted one hand to cup the back of her head and draw it towards him, kissing her with everything he felt. The lush sensuality and the urgency. The hunger and the soul-lifting tenderness.

Olivia moaned against his mouth and wrapped her arms around his shoulders as she sank down on him.

The sensation was amazing. More erotic, surely, than

anything he'd known. Alessandro didn't stop to query that but thrust up, learning again the slick, tight heat that was Olivia. The soft, undulating body. The little whimpers of encouragement and delight.

He'd told himself that first coupling had been intense because it had been so long delayed. It felt like he'd waited for ever to possess Olivia. But this, now, gave the lie to his thinking.

Once again there was no time for delay, for taking time. Already Alessandro felt the rolling wave of excitement thundering towards him as her grip tightened on him and her whimpers turned into a moan. And all the time their bodies strained together, faster, hungry, desperate.

'Alessandro!' It was a gasp of shock and awe as her eyes snapped open, bright and wondering, to stare at him as if she'd never seen him before.

The quick, rhythmic clench of her muscles around him and the sound of her voice as she quivered on the brink of ecstasy sent him over the edge.

He thrust like a wild man, jerky and uncontrolled. Felt the sheer wonder of Olivia's soft body and softening gaze, then rapture enveloped him. At first it was sharp and shattering, then a soaring sensation that took him beyond himself into burnished brightness and indescribable delight.

For the first time in his life Alessandro felt the urge for post-coital conversation.

They hadn't managed to leave the bed yet except for his quick trip to dispose of the condom, and he held Olivia in his embrace. Which meant more sex was possible.

His mouth curved. Not possible. Probable. Definite. He had plans for his wife. Plans that involved sex and plenty of it. Because it helped break down her barriers. And because at this moment he couldn't imagine ever wanting to let her go.

She was like fire in his blood. A craving that grew stronger instead of weaker.

But just as strong was the need to understand her, to secure her with ties that didn't rely on the physical or a legal contract.

'Can I ask a question?' Better to move slowly, given how ready she'd been to suspect his motives.

'It depends what it is.' Her hand stopped its tiny circular caress across his hip and he drew a slow breath, surprised at how much he wanted her to continue.

'Why didn't you like it when I used the word *perfect*?'

Of all the things he wanted to ask, that seemed the most innocuous, but as she stiffened he wondered.

'Does it matter?' With her head on his shoulder he couldn't read her face, but he heard her defensiveness.

'I want to know you better, Olivia. You're my wife. The more we understand each other the better our relationship will be.'

There was silence for a moment then she pushed up to prop herself on her arm beside him. Wide eyes surveyed him as if searching for the truth in his face. It seemed that, instead of asking an easy question, he'd managed to choose something of real significance to her.

Finally she shrugged. 'Fair enough.'

Alessandro waited, sure now that this was something he needed to know. Once he'd imagined Olivia to be straightforward, a poised, pampered, attractive woman who for some reason got under his skin. Now he knew there was much more to her.

'When I came to Italy I had trouble fitting in, for lots of reasons. Plus there was pressure from my Italian grandparents to be perfect.' She grimaced. 'No, that's not right. They never used the word, but that's how it felt. Everything I did, even the way I looked, was wrong. I never measured up.'

'It must have been a huge change, coming to live in Italy.

And,' he paused, choosing his words, 'your grandparents aren't exactly an ordinary Italian family.'

Olivia laughed. 'You can say that again. You couldn't imagine anyone more different to my Australian grandma.'

The warm glow on her face diverted him.

'Tell me about her.'

'About my gran?'

He nodded. She never wore that expression when she mentioned her Italian grandparents.

'She was lovely. Warm and cuddly and encouraging. She taught me to bake when I lived with her. Chocolate cake was her speciality, and lamingtons. She always had a treat waiting for me after school.'

Alessandro remembered when he was very young, before boarding school, coming home to a snack and questions about his day. Not from his parents but one of their paid staff.

'You lived with her?' His brow wrinkled. 'I thought it was your Italian grandparents you lived with.'

She nodded. 'Them too.' After a pause she spoke again. 'I lived with my parents in Australia till I was eight. When they died in an accident, I went to live with my father's mother. She said it was important we look after each other.'

No mistaking the wistfulness in her voice.

'You miss her.'

Olivia looked away. 'She was special. She helped the pain go away. But then she packed me off to Italy when I was thirteen, said it was time I knew my mother's family.'

Olivia's voice was even, almost unnaturally so, yet he sensed undercurrents. As if that memory cut deep.

'You didn't want to go?'

She shrugged. 'I was a kid. I didn't want to leave her but I was excited to travel overseas. I thought I was only going for a visit to meet more family.' At his questioning look she added, 'They'd never visited us and my parents never went to Italy.' She looked down to where her index finger traced tiny spirals across his ribs. 'Nonno and Nonna didn't approve of my mother's marriage. They thought she'd turned her back on their wishes. That she'd been swept off her feet and it wouldn't last. They thought it would end in tears.'

She swallowed hard and Alessandro wanted to wrap his arm around her and hold her to him. But he didn't want to interrupt the flow of confidences. Who knew when or if she'd feel like sharing this stuff again?

He suspected phenomenal sex had led to this feeling of closeness and her willingness to open up.

'So they kept their distance, even from their orphaned granddaughter?'

Once more Alessandro found himself blurting out his thoughts instead of considering each word carefully.

Hazel eyes met his. He noticed they seemed more brown now than green. Was it possible they changed colour with her mood, or was it a trick of the light?

'They cared, in their own way. I discovered later that they'd wanted to adopt me when my parents died but the authorities decided it was better for me to live in an environment I already knew with someone I loved.'

So the decision had been made by the authorities, not the family. That sounded like there'd been a tug of war over who'd raise Olivia.

'But you didn't go back to Australia?' Alessandro wished he'd found out more of this earlier. He'd had no idea her life had been so difficult. Orphaned at eight—

'I couldn't.' Again that abnormally even tone. 'What Gran didn't tell me when she sent me away was that she'd been diagnosed with an aggressive cancer. I got a letter from her, delivered after her death, explaining that she didn't want me to see her suffer, and that it was time I became part of my other family.'

Alessandro opened his mouth to say something. But he could think of nothing. Orphaned twice. Sent to a foreign country to people she didn't know.

'Tell me you at least spoke Italian.'

Her gaze met his and her mouth twisted wryly. 'I learned how to say the days of the week, some basic greetings and *torta al cioccolato* on the flight.'

'Chocolate cake? Why?'

Her smile flattened and died. She shrugged. 'I was thirteen. I thought it would be good if I could ask for my favourite food.'

Her tone made him suspect it hadn't worked out that way. 'They must have been pleased you'd made the effort.'

Olivia nodded. 'They were. But appalled that was all I knew. And that I was unprepared for my life as a Dell'Orto.'

Alessandro was good at concealing his thoughts but this time she read him easily—a disturbing phenomenon.

'Oh, they didn't say that to my face. But over time I heard snippets of conversation and it was pretty obvious.'

Once more she concentrated on the feather-light circling caress of his torso that was sending him slowly towards breaking point. He wanted, needed to hear this, yet at the same time his body had another agenda. He'd never known anything like this insatiable greed for a woman.

'It wasn't just that I didn't speak the language. I was a working-class kid from Australia. I understood nothing about their world, so they set about improving my understanding, my manners, deportment, how I looked—'

'You needed braces or something?' He tried to imagine her with wire on her teeth and maybe long plaits.

Olivia shook her head. 'I was chubby. Gran said everyone in her family was the same till they grew out of it in their teens. It didn't help that I comfort ate when I was stressed, and there'd been a lot of stress.'

'So you didn't get your chocolate cake?'

She laughed and relief skittered through him. She'd looked so sombre mere moments ago. 'Never. Sweets were banned. Even when I went to boarding school I wasn't allowed to indulge. Not that I wanted to. The place was full of stuck-up girls who thought I was a fat yokel. You don't know how desperate I was to conform.'

'To look *perfect*?' Now he thought he understood.

Their eyes met. 'Absolutely. I was too young to know there's no such thing. It took a long while to learn to make the most of what I am and be happy with that.'

Which possibly also explained Olivia's determination to support a charity that helped girls maintain positive self-belief.

Something swelled in Alessandro's chest, warm and strong. Pride. Admiration.

'What you are is impressive.'

Her eyebrows arched high. 'You think so?'

'I know it. You've got a good head for business, you're an original thinker and you make things happen.' His hand curled around hers, stopping that distracting caress against his skin, and giving him the chance to touch her.

'People like you too, because you value them and treat them as equals.'

'They are equals. I'm not better than anyone else because of my family's name.'

Alessandro nodded, forcibly reminded of his parents' dismissive attitude to the people who served them.

'Plus you're sexy and passionate.' He lifted her hand to his mouth. 'I find you incredibly attractive, perfect or not.'

Her revelations only made him appreciate her more. There were so many layers to this woman. She was tough to have survived and thrived, yet at the same time he'd discovered a softness about her that he sensed few knew about.

'Alessandro...' Her voice was a husk of sound, yet it wound his body tight as if she bound him with rope.

He pressed his finger to her lips.

'Thank you, *cara*, for telling me about your family, and your past.' There was so much more he wanted to know but he wouldn't push her now. 'I'm honoured you shared that with me.'

She lifted her shoulders in a tiny shrug, yet he knew how lucky he was that she'd given him these insights.

What struck him most, apart from melancholy at the sadness she'd endured, was the similarity between them. He hadn't been orphaned but his parents had left him and Carlo to their own devices. Alessandro had turned to the family company in order to save it and now it was the most important thing in his life. He saw Olivia's fire to succeed in business and read in it a desperation borne of her struggle to fit in and excel in her new life. It seemed that for her, too, career was everything.

They had that in common.

Yet, as her lips softened around his finger and that flare of connection sparked once again, it wasn't business they were thinking of.

His gaze dropped to her nipples, pebbling as he dragged his hand around to cup the back of her head and draw her close.

Alessandro struggled to concentrate. He had a plan, hadn't he? To understand Olivia and bind her to him. Yet as she leaned in and he inhaled that scent of orange blossom leavened with the musky scent of sex, anything like a plan disappeared from his brain.

He'd think about it later. For now all that mattered was Olivia. Here. Now. His.

CHAPTER ELEVEN

'YOU'RE LOOKING WELL, OLIVIA. Very well.'

Her *nonna* cast an approving look over her and Olivia was glad she'd worn the new dress of rich mulberry Sonia had designed. Glad too that Alessandro had seen her dithering this morning over what to wear and said casually that the shade complemented her complexion.

Sartori might be known for its menswear but her husband had an unerring eye for women's fashion. Not that he ever suggested what she should wear. But when he told her she looked good, she believed him. Though usually he used words like beautiful, gorgeous, sexy. The thought sent a thrill of heat scudding through her.

Surprisingly, with him, Olivia felt all those things.

Surprising because, though she'd worked hard to develop her image as a representative of Dell'Orto Fashion, she sometimes felt like she pretended to be someone she wasn't. Someone poised and pretty instead of ordinary.

Not that she had concerns about her professional capacity. It was on the personal level that doubts assailed her.

'You look…happy. Marriage suits you.'

Her *nonna*'s assessing gaze met hers. Around them the muted sounds of lunch in the chic Milan restaurant continued, but their table was set a little apart. For privacy?

'Thank you. I'm…content.'

Such a blank-sounding word to describe her extraordinary relationship with Alessandro. Their marriage was nothing like she'd imagined it would be.

In public they were a sophisticated couple. Attending society events, being seen in the right places. At work they focused on business, which was busier than ever. But at home—strange that after a mere six weeks she thought of Alessandro's villa as home—they were…well, they were like honeymooners. *Real* honeymooners.

Olivia's skin heated as memories flooded her mind. Alessandro waking her from sleep with one of his trademark breath-stealing kisses that turned her not to putty but into a wild woman desperate for his loving.

Alessandro and she in his study, poring over mock-ups for a new ad campaign, till one inadvertent touch led to a caress, then another. Then she was leaning over the wide desk, legs splayed, while Alessandro took her from behind, his hand between her legs and the deep, rhythmic thrusts of his body sending her to heaven and back.

She felt her skin tingle and reached for her mineral water. Now wasn't the time to think about Alessandro, with her *nonna* so sharp-eyed.

'Content is good. We'd hoped you and Alessandro would deal well together.'

'Yet you pushed me to marry Carlo.' Strange how that rankled.

She hadn't complained at the time, had she? She'd gone along with her family's scheme.

Yet now, from the perspective of her relationship with Alessandro, Olivia looked back on what might have been with something like horror.

Imagine being married to Carlo! She'd thought him a friend but he'd let her down. Instead she had Alessandro, a man who appreciated her. Made her feel special and valued. A man who'd introduced her to a world of erotic passion she hadn't had a clue about.

Her one previous foray into sex had been at eighteen, with a guy she was crazy for. Only to learn he'd been interested in her family connections rather than her. That he found her unexciting and unsophisticated but still a trophy worth bragging about.

That blow had almost shattered her. Until she resolved to

take all her hurt and use it to fuel her single-minded pursuit of excellence. If she couldn't be desired for herself, she'd prove to everyone that she was a worthy inheritor of the Dell'Orto name and business.

'Olivia?'

She blinked and focused. 'Sorry?'

'Naturally we wanted you to marry Alessandro, but he made it clear at the start that any union would be with Carlo. That wasn't up for negotiation.'

Olivia blinked. It shouldn't come as a surprise. Hadn't she guessed as much? But somehow she'd let herself believe it was her grandparents who'd suggested Carlo as her husband, since he and Olivia were friends.

The fact Alessandro hadn't wanted to marry her didn't change what they had now. She hadn't wanted to marry him either.

Yet hurt grazed, leaving her unexpectedly raw.

'Is something wrong?'

Olivia met her *nonna*'s shrewd gaze. 'No. Everything's fine.' Yet it rubbed some of the gloss off her glow of happiness.

'Alessandro has the character to make a fine husband. Hard-working, loyal, with excellent business acumen. With him you can build a solid partnership.'

She made it sound like they were business partners. As if there were no tenderness between them. No rush of delirious pleasure. No heady delight.

As if there were no point craving anything more, like companionship, or fun. Or even love.

Where had that come from? Olivia hadn't thought in terms of romantic love since she was eighteen. Yet she couldn't squash the feeling that there should be *more* between a woman and her husband.

'Is that what drew you to Nonno? His business acumen?'

Finely shaped eyebrows shot high. Her grandparents

loved her, she knew that, but they had a deep store of reserve and avoided discussing emotions.

'He was chosen by my parents, and they picked well.'
A glimmer of a smile lit her fine-boned features. 'I was
young and if it had been left to me I'd have chosen a flashy
charmer instead of a good man I can depend on.'

A charmer like my father.

Olivia didn't say it. She knew her grandparents' view
of her dad. They'd never approved of her mother going to
Australia with a man she'd only known a couple of months.
They'd been determined Olivia would never make the mistake of marrying for the illusion of romantic love.

'Now, tell me how you're going with the new bridal-
boutique plans.' Her *nonna* turned to her meal. Clearly the
discussion of marriage and husbands was over.

Olivia hesitated. She wanted, badly, to talk with someone. To share the wonder and joy she'd found in her marriage. To dissect the whys and wherefores and make sense
of her feelings for Alessandro. And his for her.

No matter how often she reminded herself that great sex
was just great sex, part of her was convinced there was more
to it. That what she shared with Alessandro was special.

But Nonna would never be that confidante. Maybe if her
mother had lived, or Gran...

Straightening her spine, Olivia pushed such thoughts
aside and began talking. Business. This she could do. It
was what she lived for.

Yet as they discussed the initiative that was so dear to
her heart, dissatisfaction niggled.

Surely there should be more to life than business?

Another childhood memory surfaced. There'd been more
and more of them lately. This time they were on the beach,
she and her parents. Olivia looked up from her sandcastle
to see her father carrying her mother out into the shallow
waves, the sound of their laughter bright as golden sunlight.
They sounded like a couple in love.

As opposed to a couple in an arranged marriage.

A solid partnership.

Something inside her rebelled at having her future mapped out as a 'solid partnership'. It sounded soulless. Like marrying a man for his *business acumen.*

Which was what she'd done. Yet now it felt like there was more, tantalisingly just beyond her reach.

What it was, Olivia didn't know, but she wanted to find out. She wanted to reach out and grab it, hold it tight and never relinquish it.

'It' meaning Alessandro.

Her description of Sonia's design flair faltered as realisation hit. She had to pause and reach for her mineral water while she regrouped.

Her feelings for Alessandro were…

She looked up into her *nonna*'s questioning gaze and forced herself to think about business. Costings. Competition. Projected sales.

But Olivia knew that behind her professionalism something fundamental had altered. *She'd* altered. Because of Alessandro.

She wanted more than her family expected from this marriage. More than she'd ever dared hope for.

The knowledge petrified her.

'Here, let me.'

Olivia's nostrils twitched appreciatively as Alessandro's scent of bergamot, leather and healthy male vied with the horsey smell of the stables. He lifted her saddle down as he did every morning, despite her assurance that she was more than capable, and turned to carry it and his own away.

Olivia's gaze lingered on his long-limbed, narrow-hipped walk. The easy way he hefted both saddles, the straight line of his shoulders and the bunch of taut glutes against worn denim as he strode off.

She swallowed hard as something caught in her ribs, a

deep-seated yearning. Quickly she turned back to her horse, curry comb in hand, and began grooming, fighting the yen to run after Alessandro and…

What? Tackle him to the ground and make passionate love to him?

Spill the fact she felt more for him than she'd ever expected and wait for him to admit he felt the same about her?

Her skin shrank against her bones as she imagined his shocked response. Feelings had never been part of their bargain. Yet, since yesterday's lunch with Nonna, Olivia couldn't ignore the fact that feelings were front and centre of her marriage to Alessandro. For her this was about more than business, convenience or stupendous sex.

The realisation left her restless and edgy.

Because now she understood her happiness wasn't just satisfaction at finally being an acknowledged part of the company or excitement to be working on the new enterprise she'd championed. *Alessandro* made her happy.

From the next stall came the murmur of his deep voice, crooning to his mount. The sound ran straight through Olivia, curling around her middle and softening her knees.

She rested her head against her bay mare and breathed deep, searching for calm. But there was no escaping these feelings. The realisation she was happier than she could remember being, here with Alessandro. And with it, the fear her happiness couldn't last. Experience had taught her never to count on anything good continuing.

Yet she couldn't bottle up her feelings. Or her desperation to know how he felt about her.

'Alessandro?'

'Hmm?'

'What did you mean when you said you'd wanted me from the first?' She'd longed to ask ever since he said it. But she'd told herself she'd rather not know if he'd exaggerated in the heat of passion. Now she *needed* to know.

Silence from the next stall, except for the restless stamp of a hoof.

Olivia busied herself with long strokes of the curry comb, till the skin at her nape tightened and she turned. Alessandro was watching her from over the divider between the stalls.

'Surely that's obvious.'

She shrugged, trying to ignore the frantic hammer beat of her pulse as she met that enigmatic stare.

'You spoke in the heat of the moment.'

'You think I didn't mean it?' One eyebrow shot up and she was reminded of the dour, aloof man she'd so disliked before she married him.

Except she hadn't disliked him. Not really. She'd disliked the way he avoided her. But always, despite herself, she'd been drawn to him, always aware of his presence, watching him when his attention was elsewhere.

Because Alessandro had fascinated her even then.

'When it came to organising a Sartori-Dell'Orto marriage you told my grandparents Carlo would be the groom. That it wasn't up for negotiation.'

That shouldn't hurt. It had been a mere business arrangement. Then. But things had altered.

'You're complaining about that?' His brow crinkled in a frown.

'I'm trying to make sense of both facts.' She kept her chin up as if she didn't want to cringe back and not hear his answer. 'If you'd wanted me—'

'Oh, I wanted, Olivia. Make no mistake about that.' His voice dropped to that shivery deep note she sometimes heard during sex. Now, as then, it reduced her to smouldering weakness.

'Then why arrange for me to marry your brother?' She folded her arms across her chest, holding in her unevenly beating heart.

To her surprise Alessandro forked his hand through his hair. A sign, she'd learned, of frustration or stress.

'Because I saw you together and knew you and he were close. How could I step between my brother and the woman he cared for?'

Alessandro heard the words fade into silence and clenched his jaw. He'd revealed too much, left himself open to pity or even ridicule. He watched Olivia's eyes widen. In shock or rejection?

He'd avoided referring to Carlo in front of her because he didn't want to think about his wife and his brother.

Did she still hold a torch for Carlo, despite his desertion? Did she fret over marrying the wrong brother?

It didn't feel like it. He'd begun to feel that Olivia was happy with him. Those smiles of hers, her eagerness for sex...

Yet if she was happy, why drag this up now?

Alessandro's body tightened, each sinew and muscle ready for action as adrenalin pumped through his blood.

'You were looking out for *Carlo*?'

'He's my brother. Mine isn't a close family but I have *some* standards. Loyalty being one of them.' Alessandro saw Olivia stiffen and realised his voice had turned icy, an instinctive mask for turbulent emotions.

He hurried on, needing to distract her. 'Carlo's only a few years younger than me but I spent a lot of time looking out for him, filling the gap our parents left.'

Wary hazel eyes met his over the wooden divider. 'Because they weren't there?'

Alessandro shrugged. It was no secret, though he preferred not talking about his childhood or parents. 'Not much.' Not ever. 'We were left with nannies and later sent to boarding school. I wasn't much of a parent substitute but I did what I could.'

Not enough. He'd tried to give his younger brother stability and a sense of family but maybe Carlo's inability to settle to one thing came of pushing him too hard. Alessandro had tried to ensure he didn't turn out like their careless, hedonistic parents.

'I'm sure you did.' She stepped away from her horse, towards him, looking up with what seemed like sympathy in her hazel gaze. 'It must have been hard on you, as the eldest.'

Once Alessandro would have spurned any woman's sympathy. He didn't need it. He was perfectly fine as he was. Yet he felt the crackling tension inside ease at Olivia's expression.

'I was okay. Our parents' lack of interest had a positive side. My father didn't care about the business, just spending the profits, so he didn't mind when I said I wanted to be part of it.' He'd been just twenty and resolved to save the company generations of his family had built, though he had little more than determination on his side. 'That's how I got started at Sartori.'

'And eventually turned it around.' It wasn't a question. Olivia had done her homework. 'People say you were a prodigy, breathing new life into a dying company after only a few short years.'

He shrugged. 'I had a lot to learn and I made mistakes, but I was determined.' He couldn't bear the thought of his family's achievement collapsing due to neglect. He'd fought tooth and nail so he and Carlo could inherit their birthright, a premier company, not a morass of debts. Even now, with success assured, Alessandro was always seeking out ways to do better, shoring up long-term profitability. Hence the drive to merge with Dell'Orto. 'I care about it, very much.'

'And you care about Carlo.'

His heart plummeted at the way she kept bringing the conversation back to his brother.

'Alessandro? You still care, don't you? Even though he made you angry?'

He raked his hand across his scalp. 'Of course I care!' Though he'd gladly shake his brother for hurting Olivia.

Yet if Carlo hadn't jilted her, Alessandro wouldn't have her. Hell, what a tangle.

'Good. Because one day soon you'll need to talk with him and—'

'What about you, Olivia?' He planted his arms on the top of the dividing wall and leaned towards her. 'How do you feel about Carlo?'

It was the answer he'd alternately been desperate to ask and desperate to avoid. His breath sucked in hard and his heart seemed to hesitate as he waited for her answer.

'He let you down badly.' Alessandro realised he was trying to lead her into giving an answer he wanted and forced himself to stop.

'That's not as important as your relationship with him. You're his brother.'

'It's important to me.' He paused and drew a calming breath, yet when he continued his voice was an urgent burst. 'I need to know. What's your relationship with my brother?'

'We're friends, or we were. I admit that the way he dumped me right before the wedding cooled my affection though.'

'Affection? So you were…intimate friends?'

It was as he'd thought. Alessandro told himself that was in the past. What mattered was the future. And yet…

'Intimate?' She shook her head. 'We were good mates. He's great company and he made that postgraduate degree in the States fun instead of all work. But we were never *intimate.*'

Olivia felt her cheeks warm as she stared into Alessandro's narrowed eyes. He believed she and Carlo were lovers!

Her heart jumped as her brain processed it.

Could that really be why he'd held back from her all that time? Because he didn't want to poach his brother's woman?

It put a whole different complexion on things.

'Carlo and I have only ever been friends. Nothing more.'

'Truly?'

She nodded. 'Truly. He's fun but he's not my type.' How could he be when it was this man alone who'd awoken not only her body but also her long-dormant emotions?

There it was, the sign she'd sought. A flash of emotion in Alessandro's taut features. Remarkably it looked like relief.

He really did care!

He'd wanted her in the beginning and he wanted her now.

Maybe not in the ways she wanted him, but it was a start, a far better start than she'd imagined that day he'd strode into the *palazzo* and basically ordered her to marry him.

He was attracted and he cared. Surely, over time, they could build on that?

For Olivia had learned something significant from their short marriage. Business-minded she may be, but when it came to her personal life she wasn't interested in just a *solid partnership*.

Of course she wanted constancy and respect but she craved tenderness too, excitement and passion. The hallmarks, she realised, of her parents' marriage.

For years she'd seen their relationship through the prism of her grandparents' disapproval. And it was true that last day there'd been tension between her parents. Their bickering as they walked to the car was the last thing she'd heard of them, till news arrived of their crash. She'd let that and her grandparents' prejudice colour her recollections, especially as there was no one left with whom to share happy reminiscences.

But lately other memories had come back. Of laughter and warmth. The way they'd been a family, bonded by love.

That's what she wanted. Love.

She gazed up into that glittering dark stare and understood with a silent wave of emotion that it was what she already felt.

Love for Alessandro. A man she was only beginning to understand.

Yet in some ways she felt as if she'd known him from the moment her eyes caught his across that room in Rome.

The realisation was thrilling, nerve-racking, yet profoundly satisfying.

So what if the odds were against her? She had a track record of fighting for what she wanted.

It sounded like Alessandro had little experience of love, at least from his family. And, yes, he was a lone wolf, with a reputation for being ruthless and self-contained.

But that wasn't the side he showed her. He wasn't the distant autocrat she'd believed him to be. He made her feel good about herself. Special.

Maybe, eventually…

'Do you have plans for the next hour?' She put down the curry comb with a clatter.

Alessandro shrugged. 'Nothing urgent, though I had another thought about the masquerade ball.'

Olivia nodded. It was Saturday morning and there was no rush to leave the villa. She moved out of the stall, shutting the door behind her. Alessandro did the same, emerging to stand before her.

'Why? Have you got something in mind?'

'I have.' She took his hand, so large and powerful in her smaller one, and drew him towards an empty stall at the end of the stable block.

They had the place completely to themselves. Excitement rose at the thought of taking advantage of that. Of sharing her feelings with the man she loved even if, for now, she wouldn't spell them out loud.

'Olivia?'

'Alessandro.' Her voice sounded throaty and thick, choked by the enormity of her emotions. A tremor started up inside her, a tiny trace of anxiety, but she ignored it. It was too late to be nervous. Her feelings were engaged.

Leading him into the empty stall, she turned and pressed her palms against his hard chest. Instantly those lovely big hands clasped her hips. Beneath her palm his heart beat strong and even, perhaps, a little fast? She smiled as she pushed him back towards the wall.

His eyebrows rose but he complied.

Her kiss erased any doubt of her intentions. She stretched up on her toes, deliberately sliding her hips and breasts against his tall form, letting her weight sink into his, and heard a groan of appreciation that vibrated straight to her core. Olivia lifted her hands over his shoulders to bracket the back of his skull and tilted his head down to her hungry mouth.

The knowing heat in his eyes went straight to her bones and then, as their lips and tongues touched and fused, heat exploded right through her. From her scalp to her soles and at every erogenous point in between.

This wasn't a simple kiss of the lips. It was body on body, urgent hands roving, cupping, squeezing, stroking. It was a hungry tilt to the pelvis, friction of flesh against denim against eager flesh, and above all the luscious, decadently arousing language of their mouths mating.

Alessandro hauled her even higher up his body, supporting her with wide-splayed hands that cupped her backside and held her hard against his thrusting groin.

Olivia nuzzled his neck, and the smells of horse and hay faded. Instead she could imagine herself in a sunbathed citrus orchard, made perfect by the heady base note of aroused male, the most wonderful aroma she'd ever known.

She bit down on his flesh, right where the strong cords of muscle rose towards his neck, and his hands clenched convulsively. His responsiveness made her heart soar. *She* made him feel this way.

'I need you, *tesoro*. Now.' Alessandro's voice was gruff, almost unrecognisable, and she smiled.

'I need you too.'

'But not here.' Against her breasts his chest rose and fell on a mighty breath. 'Even with the straw the floor's uncomfortable.' He swallowed hard. 'Hang on and I'll carry you inside.'

'No.'

'Olivia?' His head reared back so he could see her face. His own looked starkly sculpted, as if the flesh drew tight across his bones. His eyes, impossibly, appeared black rather than just dark.

He looked elemental and utterly gorgeous and she wanted him so badly she thought she'd shatter if she couldn't make love to him. She didn't want to wait to reach the house. This was too urgent.

'Put me down.' She softened her sharp command with a thumb pressed to his bottom lip.

In response he sucked her thumb into his mouth, slow and hard, drawing the powerful thread of arousal tight within her.

He shook his head. 'Let me look after you, Olivia. I want to make this good for you.'

Typical of Alessandro. From the first he'd taken charge. It was how he operated. Even when he was tender and passionate, he felt the need to protect her. As if she were his responsibility. Just as he carried her saddle despite her protests that she could manage.

Olivia revelled in his consideration. She adored that he looked out for her. But she wanted the care and responsibility to be mutual.

'It will be good. More than good. Put me down.'

Still he didn't move, except for the heavy pound of his heart against hers and the fine tremor of arousal across his skin.

'Alessandro.' She cupped his face in her hands, delighting in the texture of hot, yet-to-be-shaved skin. 'I love sex with you. It's magnificent.' Her heart gave a little shimmy of excitement at the word *love*. One day, hopefully soon, when she was sure of his feelings, she'd tell him she loved him. 'But making it good isn't just your responsibility. How about letting me take the lead this time?'

It wasn't only about sex. It was about feeling an equal partner, a starting point, surely, for the sort of marriage she wanted.

Those glinting eyes held hers. Then slowly, so slowly it was exquisite torture, Alessandro lowered her, sliding her down his body.

Spot fires ignited in her breasts, belly and pelvis at the contact. Olivia's eyelids drooped to half-mast at the sensuous assault on her body.

Then she was on her feet, swaying slightly.

A sliver of doubt pierced her. She was a novice in the sensual arts. Her first experience of sex had been flatly disappointing and quick. Everything she'd learned had been from Alessandro. She'd learned a lot, but was it enough?

Then she met his ebony eyes, read the tension in his carefully restrained body and relaxed. She was worrying about nothing. All she had to do was follow her instinct. Show him all the love she felt for him.

Swiftly she rose on tiptoe and pressed a kiss to the corner of his mouth as her hands worked his belt undone.

'Thank you, Alessandro.'

Back on solid ground, she unsnapped his jeans and tugged down the zip, her hand brushing his burgeoning erection.

Then, with a smile and a surge of excitement, she shoved his jeans and underpants down and dropped to her knees before him.

CHAPTER TWELVE

ALESSANDRO PAUSED IN the early-morning shadows of the loggia, his gaze on the woman who'd changed his life so profoundly.

'How about letting me take the lead?' she'd said.

'Making it good isn't just your responsibility,' she'd said.

She'd persuaded him with those earnest hazel eyes and pouting lips to cede control, even though it had taken a superhuman effort not to stride into the house and throw her onto the bed and take charge.

He'd let her have her way with him and a day later he was still in a daze of shocked delight.

She'd loved him with her mouth, her hands, her whole body, and he'd never known anything like it.

Even now, shoulder propped against a supporting pillar, he felt weak at the knees, recalling what they'd done together in the stables. Better than any erotic dream. Headier than anything he'd ever imagined.

Nor was it just about what they'd done with their bodies.

There was something more, at least for him. There'd been an affection, a tenderness, even at one point a bubbling sense of shared amusement, he'd never experienced with another lover.

Alessandro's chest contracted in urgent spasm and he tried to recall if anyone in the family had a history of heart disease. His breath came in short bursts and his pulse thumped erratically.

Then Olivia moved, reaching across the table for a notepad, and the early-morning light gilded the sweet curve of her breast.

His thoughts shattered.

Something rose up inside him. A powerful force that clogged his brain and banished any passing concern about his health. For his heart beat strong and true once more as he watched her frown at her notes.

She worked too hard. She'd work every waking hour if he didn't distract her now and then. People had accused him of being a workaholic, but she was worse. As if she feared what might happen if she stopped.

Because she'd had to work so hard to be accepted by her family? And to win a permanent place for herself in the company?

It was easier to focus on Olivia than the foreign emotions inside him. Alessandro had been aware of them for weeks but managed to suppress them. Till yesterday. This vast, burgeoning sensation, as if he were full of feelings that kept expanding, was now unstoppable.

Abruptly Alessandro stepped out of the shadows, needing to yank himself free of his thoughts.

Instantly Olivia lifted her head, her gaze colliding with his and clinging.

There it was again, that punch of heated delight in his belly.

And more. Tenderness. A warmth that wasn't sexual but was every bit as real as the hormones charging around his body.

'What are you up to?'

He loved the way her eyes ate him up as he approached, leaving him in no doubt that she was as eager for his company as he was for hers.

'Checking our release timelines and the Paris contract.'

Alessandro stopped beside her, his hand going to her shining hair, unbound across her shoulders, the way he liked it. Had she left it down for him? His glow of wellbeing became a blaze.

'Those have already been checked.'

She shrugged. 'I wanted to be sure. This is important.'

He stroked her hair, soft against his palm, and she tilted her head into his touch. That full feeling in his chest was back again, stronger than ever.

'I understand, *cara*. It's the launch of your initiative.' A chance to prove herself. He'd discovered how precious that was to her. 'But you and your team have it covered. You need to take a break. You work too hard.'

She huffed out a laugh. 'Isn't that the pot calling the kettle black?'

Alessandro shook his head. 'Once, yes, in the early days, when the business was floundering and I had to learn fast to turn it around. Then…' He paused, his thoughts slowing as he considered his lifestyle. 'Yes, you're right. I've lived for my work.'

But not now.

For Alessandro realised with sudden certainty that he wanted more in his life than constant work, long hours and nothing but commercial triumphs and ever-increasing profits.

He wanted…more.

Everything in Alessandro stilled, even that strange feeling that his chest grew too tight to contain his emotions. Instead he experienced a moment of complete calm as everything clicked into place.

A smile curled his mouth at the vision in his head. A sense of absolute rightness filled him.

'Alessandro?' Olivia's fingers threaded through his, drawing his hand to her cheek. 'Are you okay?'

'Never better, *cara*. What do you say to a day off? A day completely away from work? There's somewhere I'd like to take you.'

He had his answer in the instant gleam in her eyes, yet she hesitated, her teeth worrying her plump bottom lip and threatening to undo his good intentions—not to go straight back to bed with her.

'I'd love to. But…' She looked down at the schedule and notes spread before her.

'Then how about this? We work together to check whatever is bothering you. The pair of us will get it done faster. Then I take you out for the day.'

'Thank you, Alessandro. I'd like that so much.'

Olivia's husky voice wove a trail of pleasure through him. Her smile was the best thing he'd ever seen. Better than any profit report or business accolade.

And it got even better when she reached up, curling her hand around the back of his neck, and pulled him down for a swift but thorough kiss.

He fell into it, wallowing once more in the hot, bright, *rightness* of him and her together.

Then he sat down beside her and tried to concentrate on her paperwork. It took a while for his brain to slip into gear because he was so wrapped up in the significance of what had just happened.

For the first time Olivia had reached for him and kissed him. Not because they were making love. Not because she was aroused. But as an expression of affection and thanks.

His pounding heart and prickling nape proved how much that meant. To be appreciated for himself. Not just in bed…

Previous lovers had been very appreciative because he was generous during sex. No one, ever, had made him feel wanted for himself. Even his relationship with Carlo was coloured by the fact he relied on Alessandro to help him out of every bind he'd got himself into.

It felt, for the first time he could remember, that someone appreciated him, the real man. It was a shockingly powerful idea.

The speedboat whipped along the deep blue lake waters but for once Alessandro wasn't in charge. Federico from the marina was steering, delighted at the chance to handle the craft, while Alessandro faced the rear, keeping an eye on Olivia.

From here he could see the grin that split her face. He wore a matching smile, delighted at her delight.

She looked like a water sprite, with that peridot-green one-piece clinging to her curves and her hair, saturated to a dark gold, plastered to her head.

He'd never seen her look so free and vibrant, except in his arms.

She'd never been water skiing and, as they'd driven to Lake Como, had murmured about her lack of sporting ability, doubting her ability to ski. As if she was going to be judged on how good she was!

Alessandro had had to bite his tongue rather than ask who'd made her so doubtful of herself and so wary of not living up to expectations. He guessed her grandparents' pressure to adapt to their world was part of that. And, from something Olivia had let slip, an unfortunate peer group at school.

He wouldn't have cared if she never got the hang of skiing, except that she'd miss out on the thrill of speeding across the water.

Seeing her happiness was magic. Better even than the pleasure he got from skiing himself.

The engine slowed as they approached the end of their run. Olivia almost made it right to the end, but at the last minute wobbled and lost control. A second later the tow rope trailed loose as Olivia, with her life jacket and skis, sank into the water.

Alessandro shouted to Federico and instantly they were slowing, circling back to where she bobbed in the blue depths.

As they approached and came to a standstill, he dived in, coming up to tread water beside Olivia. Even now her smile was brilliant.

'You enjoyed it?'

'It was brilliant! Absolutely amazing. I don't know why I didn't try it years ago.'

'Ah, but then you didn't have me to persuade you.' He swam up to her, pushing her wet hair back off her face.

Something in her expression changed. Her smile was still there but the glow in her eyes intensified.

His own smile stalled and he swallowed hard.

'I'm so glad you did, Alessandro. Thank you.' Her hand cupped his neck and despite the water's chill heat bloomed inside him. 'I—'

Federico's voice interrupted them and Alessandro saw one of the skis floating away.

He didn't care. All he cared about was Olivia and what she'd been going to say. But the moment had gone. She was already twisting towards the wayward ski.

'Let me.' He took a stroke towards it, easily securing it.

'You didn't need to dive in,' she said as he passed the skis up into the boat. 'I could have managed.'

'I know.' He couldn't resist nuzzling her damp cheek before helping her up into the boat. He refused to explain that he'd seen her smile and wanted to bask in it up close. Her pleasure did that to him every time. 'But this is quicker. We've got a lunch reservation waiting for us.'

A late lunch, followed by a siesta in the premier suite of an exclusive waterfront hotel. He couldn't wait.

Olivia should be working yet instead found her gaze lifting from her emails to the photos gracing her office wall. The series showcased past Dell'Orto designs. Usually it inspired her. Today they, and even Sonia's updated bridal designs, couldn't hold her attention.

Her mind was full of Alessandro.

The way he'd dived into the water to help her out, his hunky yet streamlined body all raw masculinity.

The fact he'd taken time to share a favourite pastime with her. To ensure she enjoyed it. When had anyone, ever, focused solely on her and what she might like? She'd felt pampered and treasured. Something she hadn't experienced since childhood. He'd fussed over her like a hen with a single chick before letting her ski. As if a hen could ever look as mouth-wateringly gorgeous as her husband!

She blinked at her circling thoughts.

Always they came back to Alessandro.

The delicious late lunch he'd organised not at some grand restaurant but in a little, character-filled place that served the best food she'd ever tasted. The hotel they'd adjourned to later *was* grand, but its elegance had been wasted on her. All she'd been interested in was Alessandro and the magic of his loving.

She was so distracted it took her a while to realise her phone was ringing.

Putting it to her ear, she heard a familiar voice.

'Olivia. Is that you?'

She blinked, astonished, and sat straighter. 'Carlo?'

'Yes, it's me.' He paused and in the silence she found herself wrestling anger and curiosity, plus a hefty dollop of hurt. She'd counted him as her friend but he'd abandoned her.

'What do you want, Carlo?' Her voice was sharp.

'You automatically think I want something? You sound like my brother.'

Anger surged. Apart from that first day when he'd been utterly furious at his brother's behaviour, Alessandro rarely mentioned Carlo. But Olivia wasn't fooled. She understood enough now about the man she'd married to realise how badly disappointed and hurt he'd been by Carlo's actions. She'd also learned, mainly from others, that Carlo hadn't pulled his weight at work, relying on his family connection and brother's goodwill to see him through.

'Don't you? Or were you ringing, finally, to apologise in person?' Olivia knew she'd had a lucky escape marrying Alessandro, not Carlo, yet Carlo still hadn't bothered to talk to her properly. 'I thought we were friends!'

'We were. We are. I'm sorry, Olivia. It was bad timing.

I should have flown over to break the news to you face to face, but the truth is I was scared it was all too good to be true. That Hannah might change her mind about us staying together if I left.'

It didn't sound like a very sound relationship if it couldn't withstand a couple of days apart. But Olivia said nothing.

'And it's worked out for the best, hasn't it? Hannah and I are happy together, and it looks like you and Alessandro are getting on like a house on fire.'

'How would you know? You're in America.'

'Oh, I keep my ear to the ground. There's a lot in the press about you both. I have to say in the photos you look like a doting couple.'

He paused as if waiting for her comment but she had no intention of discussing her marriage with Carlo. Even if she spent most of her time these days wondering what Alessandro felt about her.

She sighed and leaned back in her seat, eyes closing.

'Why are you ringing, Carlo? Just to apologise?' They'd been friends and she knew he'd been heartbroken when Hannah ended their relationship. She didn't like the position he'd put her in but what was done was done.

'Well, I did actually want to ask you something else as well. But whatever you do, don't tell Alessandro I called you. That would wreck everything.'

'Why? What's going on?'

'Nothing! I just…well, I wondered if you'd put in a good word with him for me, but it has to be at the right moment. It's really important, Olivia.' For once there was no light-heartedness in his tone. Carlo actually sounded grim. 'I'm desperate and you're the only one who can help me. Otherwise I wouldn't—'

A sound nearby made her eyes snap open.

There was Alessandro, poised in the open doorway, hand raised to knock.

'I'm sorry, I can't talk now.' Her voice sounded strangled.

'Call me another time.' Before Carlo could speak again, she ended the call.

'You didn't have to hang up because of me.' Alessandro surveyed her with an unreadable expression.

'It wasn't important.' Her gaze ducked from her husband's and she felt heat rise in her cheeks. Olivia drew a slow breath, willing the colour to recede.

She felt ridiculously as if she'd done something wrong. For a second she imagined blurting out that it had been Carlo. But there'd been real worry in his tone. Something she'd never heard from Carlo. She'd at least wait to find out what the problem was before sharing it with Alessandro.

'Good,' he said finally. 'I was going to invite you to lunch before my next meeting. If you have time?'

Was it imagination that his gaze turned piercing?

Olivia's flesh drew tight under that scrutiny and she silently cursed Carlo for putting her in this position. If only he hadn't seemed so worried.

'I'd like that. Thank you.' Yet her words sounded stilted and her smile hung heavy on her lips.

Alessandro felt sick to the stomach. For more than twenty-four hours he'd waited for Olivia to confide in him. To tell him the truth about that phone call.

She'd said nothing. Even in the aftermath of a night of ardent loving there'd been no explanation, no pillow-talk confession as she lay, sated, in his embrace.

With every passing hour his fears solidified into an ice-cold lump in the pit of his belly.

It hadn't taken his wife's blush signalling guilt to put him in the picture. Carlo's voice, always carrying, had risen with what sounded like emotion. Alessandro had recognised the sound of it instantly, though he couldn't make out the actual words.

All he knew for sure was that his brother, who'd always been so close to Olivia, had rung her and she'd sat back in her chair, eyes closed, as if lapping up every syllable. And that, when asked, she'd hidden the truth from him.

Alessandro swallowed hard, pain scraping his throat at the stiff movement. Hurt radiated through him.

Was that all it took? One call from Carlo?

Or had there been more? Maybe that call wasn't the first.

He shook his head, thrusting down the bitter stew of distrust. Olivia wasn't like that. She wouldn't carry on with his own brother behind his back. She had too much integrity.

Then why doesn't she tell you she's spoken to him?

At dinner tonight he'd deliberately wondered aloud how Carlo was getting on in America. It was the perfect opening for her to mention he'd been in contact. Instead she'd all but buried her face in her *spaghetti alla vongole*, refusing to meet Alessandro's eyes. She'd left the table soon after, saying she had calls to make.

Calls to his brother?

Alessandro told himself Olivia wouldn't go behind his back. There had to be some reasonable explanation, as there'd been that day she'd left the office with Paolo Benetti. He shouldn't jump to conclusions.

But it was hard not to. Especially when, unbidden, images filled his mind, of Olivia and Carlo together, heads inclined towards each other, laughing over some shared joke. Despite the instant thunderclap of connection he'd felt to Olivia, for too long he'd been on the outside looking in, seeing her and his brother close.

They'd never been lovers, though. She'd told him so.

Alessandro blocked out the inner voice of suspicion. Olivia had told him and he believed her, didn't he?

But he couldn't take any more of this doubt. Waiting for her to confide in him hadn't worked. He'd simply ask her outright. He should have done that in the first place.

And the reason he hadn't?

His jaw clenched as he moved to the door. The reason was that his plan to seduce his wife into caring for him had

had unexpected consequences. He cared for her in ways he'd never thought possible. In ways that meant her betrayal would gut him. He cared so much he was *scared* of what she might reveal.

A bitter laugh escaped him as he loped up the stairs. He'd wanted her and been determined to keep her, and all the while he'd been oblivious about why.

After the childhood pain of his parents' complete lack of interest Alessandro had never let anyone matter enough to hurt him. Except Carlo, but even then he'd learned to shore up his defences by expecting the worst. Besides, Carlo's affection was partly because he relied on his older brother.

In Alessandro's whole life no one had ever cared enough to stay with him.

It had never mattered before. He'd enjoyed the freedom of being his own man, of pleasing only himself.

Until Olivia.

He paused with his hand on the bedroom doorknob, breath rasping in aching lungs. Fear welled but he ignored it. One thing he wasn't and that was a coward.

He opened the door and stepped in. The bedroom was empty, but the clothes Olivia had worn were draped over the end of the bed. His gaze went to the closed bathroom door. Maybe she was having a soak in the bath.

Alessandro thought of other nights when they'd shared that oversized tub. Usually he preferred a quick shower, but with Olivia a long, hot bath took on a whole new fascination.

He marched across the room, flinging his jacket onto the bed and wrenching off his tie, tossing it in the same direction.

Almost at the door, he heard a phone ring. Not his but Olivia's. It sat on her bedside table.

Alessandro covered the distance in a single stride, drawn by a force he couldn't resist.

The ringtone was insistent, drawing his gaze down despite his telling himself not to look.

The digital display revealed a single word: Carlo.

Alessandro sank onto the bed, eyes on the phone as on a venomous snake.

Yet that didn't stop him reaching for it, closing his fingers around it as if to prove that what he saw was real.

The ringtone pealed again, insistent. His fingers tightened. He didn't want to accept the call, despite the fact he'd waited too long to hear from his brother. That he'd actually begun to worry about him.

His stomach curdled as he thought of Carlo calling his wife, not him. All too easily memories stirred, of Carlo and Olivia, and—

'What are you doing with my phone?'

Olivia stood before him. Her feet were bare and it was obvious she wore nothing beneath the aqua silk robe cinched around her waist. With her glorious wheaten hair loose around her shoulders and her breasts rising high against the fragile fabric, she should be impossibly alluring.

Except her face was drawn tight in a way he'd never seen before. It looked almost angular, her mouth a flat line, tension turning her into a stranger.

How well did he really know his wife?

Alessandro's heart dipped, and deep within something tore wider and wider till it felt like there was a yawning chasm of hurt inside.

Had he made the biggest mistake of his life?

CHAPTER THIRTEEN

THE PHONE STOPPED ringing but in its place was a silence that stretched so long it shredded Olivia's nerves to breaking point.

Guilt hummed through her.

And anger. She hadn't wanted Carlo to call her! Yet every instinct said it had been him. Again.

She'd ignored the call as long as she could. She'd told Carlo earlier not to ring her till he'd sorted out his problems with his brother. She hated that he'd put her in the position of hiding something from Alessandro, even as a favour to an old friend. It hadn't felt right.

But Carlo's insistence on caution, coupled with her own doubts about how Alessandro would react to Carlo ringing her, had decided her to keep quiet about his calls. Carlo had been his usual persuasive self, trying to get her to approach his brother on his behalf till eventually, when he'd refused to take her advice and speak to Alessandro himself, she'd hung up on him.

Now she wished she'd turned the phone off. Then she wouldn't be watching her husband stare at her as if he didn't recognise her.

The sight sent a thrill of disquiet skating along her bones. Her stomach twisted with the curl of his lip and for a second she thought she might lose her meal.

'Carlo rang.' His voice was devoid of emotion.

Alessandro's eyes looked darker, more impenetrable than ever, yet they glittered with a fierce heat that did nothing to warm her suddenly chilled body.

Olivia remembered that blaze of possessiveness when he thought she'd been with Paolo Benetti. His fury had been white-hot and she'd barely been able to get a word in as he ranted.

How much more daunting was this? She sensed his turbulent emotions, felt the radiating heat from his tall body, yet the fact he said so little, and in that preternaturally composed voice, made him seem more menacing.

Could he really believe there was something between her and Carlo? Even after her assurances?

She folded her arms as if to ward off the waves of tension rolling from him.

He dropped the phone onto the bedside table and shot to his feet, towering above her.

'What were you doing with my phone, Alessandro? I didn't give you permission to touch it.'

'No, you didn't.' He bunched his shoulders, shoving his hands into his trouser pockets, and she noticed his jacket and tie flung across the bed.

Had he been coming to join her in the bathroom? Olivia pushed the thought aside.

'That's private property.' His dark eyebrows rose imperiously. 'I don't snoop at your phone.' Which only managed to make her sound petty.

The sudden stillness in him was palpable. 'But then, I have nothing to hide from you, *cara*.' The way he said the endearment, flat and unfeeling, was so different to the way he usually spoke to her, she felt it like a blow. 'I'm not keeping secrets.' He paused, his gaze slicing through her. 'But I'm sorry for touching your phone. You don't know how sorry.'

The air between them thickened, making it difficult to breathe.

'It's not what you think,' she blurted out.

'No? And what is it I think?'

That was obvious.

'That there's something between me and Carlo.' She drew herself up to her full height, her hands falling to her sides.

'There isn't. There never has been. It's just that he wants to talk with you.'

'Then why doesn't he? He has my number.'

Olivia waved her hand in a frustrated gesture. 'That's exactly what I've said to him.'

To her dismay, Alessandro's expression turned more wooden by the moment. As they spoke the fierce glow in his eyes dimmed till he resembled the remote, unreachable man he'd seemed for so long.

It was like watching him turn to stone before her eyes and it carved a gash right through her heart.

Alessandro hadn't looked at her that way in a long, long time. She'd thought he never would.

How that hurt, watching him retreat from her.

'You have to believe me, Alessandro. He's not interested in me. He's deliriously happy with Hannah. But he's scared that in pulling out of the wedding the way he did he's gone so far that you won't forgive him. You're the one person he really respects. Your opinion matters to him.'

Her words seemed to have no impact on her husband.

Husband! He looked like a disapproving stranger.

'And Carlo matters to you?' He leaned forward the tiniest bit and crazily Olivia wanted to reach up and smooth the furrows from his brow. Kiss him into relaxing and turning once more into the caring man she'd known these past weeks.

'No! Yes.' She shook her head. 'He's a friend. But it's more than that. I want the two of you to make it up. I see that you miss him, that you worry about him, and—'

'And so you make secret calls for *my* sake?' His tone was clipped, yet for a moment she thought she saw something change in that midnight-dark stare.

Something that sent a jolt of dismay through her.

'I didn't make any calls. He rang me.'

But that was prevaricating. She'd lied to her husband, by omission at least. She should have told Alessandro that

Carlo had called and wanted to talk, despite Carlo's insistence on planning the perfect moment.

Didn't he believe her? Olivia's hands found her hips and a rush of righteous indignation buoyed her. Did Alessandro really think she was having an affair? It seemed impossible after all they'd been to each other.

'I see.'

Which was all right for him. For Olivia didn't see at all. Alessandro looked so remote, so unfamiliar, she hadn't a clue what he was thinking. He didn't look at all like the man who held her in his arms each night. The man she loved.

Distress filled her. And fear. Had a couple of phone calls wrecked their fragile relationship? Surely it was stronger than that.

But Alessandro made no move towards her.

Because he doesn't believe you.

Pride came to her rescue.

'In the circumstances,' she hefted a breath shaky from her adrenaline rush, 'maybe we both need some space. I'd prefer to sleep alone tonight.'

After a fraught moment Alessandro nodded, his mouth looking even grimmer than before. 'If you feel that way, then of course.'

Yet neither of them moved. It was as if the force keeping them apart was matched by an equally potent force, yoking them together. As if any move would shatter the fragile equilibrium.

Finally he spoke. 'I'll see you in the morning.'

Then he left, closing the door quietly behind him. Leaving her feeling as if he'd sucked all the warmth out of the room.

Next morning over breakfast Alessandro informed her there were teething problems with the new Far Eastern flagship store and that he'd decided to go and check out the issues in person. He had a flight booked that morning.

He made no mention of her accompanying him.

Of course, it wasn't possible. Not at the moment, with so much to do on the new bridal venture. But that didn't stop Olivia wishing he'd invited her. Or at least that he'd tried to bridge the gap last night's argument had created.

Not that it had been an argument. More a confrontation, during which Alessandro had turned again into that withdrawn, judgemental stranger he'd once been.

Olivia's heart ached at the memory. She should have reached out to him, made him listen as she reiterated that there was nothing untoward between her and Carlo. But she was hurting, upset that the man she loved was willing to believe the worst of her. So she'd shrugged and wished him a good trip. Now three nights away had turned into five, and still no sign of him.

Every night he'd emailed, giving her a brief update on business, asking if all was well there, and if she was.

She'd lied and answered that everything was fine, when everything *wasn't* fine. She felt shaky with emotion, getting upset more than once over insignificant things.

All because her relationship with Alessandro had plummeted from wonderful to dysfunctional.

Even if he'd stormed at her the way he had ages ago in her Milan flat, then she'd have responded in kind and they'd probably have ended up making love and sorting out their differences on the spot.

Or was that wishful thinking?

And was it really making love as far as Alessandro was concerned? She'd hoped he'd begun to care for her. Surely his tenderness and thoughtfulness signified his feelings were engaged.

But the night he'd discovered Carlo ringing her there'd been no flash of possessiveness as there'd been over Paolo Benetti. Instead her husband had retreated into the remote figure he'd been before they married.

She couldn't bear it.

At least she had work to keep her busy. She strode down the office corridor early that Monday but slammed to a halt outside her room.

Because it wasn't her name on the door any more.

Confused, she looked over her shoulder, counting doorways. But she had the right one. Frowning, she pushed the door open and her heart kicked into a quickened beat. Gone were her desk and bright red ergonomic chair. Gone the fern she kept in one corner and, she realised as she stepped further inside, gone were the photos of past Dell'Orto designs. A new desk sat where hers used to.

What...?

'Sorry, Olivia. We weren't expecting you so early.'

She swung round to find Alessandro's assistant in the doorway, looking flustered.

'What's going on? Where's my stuff?'

'Ah. Sorry. Alessandro hoped to speak with you before you came in and—'

'Alessandro's here?' She'd thought him still in Asia.

'Just arrived.'

Olivia swallowed hard. She shouldn't be surprised that his PA knew he was back in the country before she did. Yet still it hurt.

'So what's happening here?'

'Alessandro wants the new head of PR in here. It's convenient for—'

'He does, does he? And where is my stuff? Further down the corridor?' Away from the conference room and the access to the next floor, where Alessandro's office was situated.

'Er...no.' The PA looked more than flustered now. He looked embarrassed. At her stare he hurried on. 'Alessandro didn't want you on this floor any more...'

He said something garbled about office moves from which all she really took in was the fact she apparently didn't belong here any more, before his words petered out.

Alessandro was moving her from the floor where all the company's senior managers worked.

Demoting her?

She rocked back on her heels as the walls swayed around her.

She'd known he was upset about the calls from Carlo but surely not that upset. Did he really think he could kick her off the executive floor, and, no doubt, off the executive team? She'd never thought petty vengeance was his style. But the evidence of her eyes was irrefutable.

Alessandro had a reputation for ruthless efficiency in business. Was she now seeing his ruthless side? Had his earlier tenderness, his warmth, been a façade employed to make their marriage of convenience more pleasant?

Every instinct screamed it wasn't so. Alessandro cared for her.

But how could she reconcile this action with a man who genuinely cared?

Olivia spun on her heel and marched back the way she'd come, ignoring the PA's protests. After her circling emotions of the last few days, regret and guilt as much as annoyance and hurt, this surge of clear, bright fury was liberating.

She was too het up to take the lift. Instead she stomped up the stairs, the click of her heels giving voice to the ire building inside.

She'd worked so hard to build her career and be taken seriously. If Alessandro thought he could rob her of all that he had yet to learn what she was made of.

Stalking across the reception area, she headed for the CEO's office, only to stop as the door opened and Alessandro emerged. He wore another exquisitely tailored dark suit and her heart did that silly, familiar cartwheel. Because he was everything she wanted in a man. Or so she'd believed until today.

She blinked hard, that wellspring of emotion too close to the surface, making her vulnerable.

While he was away she'd vowed she'd forget her pride and try to bridge the gulf between them. She wanted their marriage like it had been.

But that was before he'd tried to cut her out of her own company. Even now she couldn't quite believe it. But what other explanation could there be?

He knew how she felt about her career. To play games with it because he was annoyed about Carlo…

'It's okay, Marco.' He spoke to someone behind her and she realised his PA had come up in the lift. 'Olivia and I have things to discuss. Why don't you get a coffee down the street?'

Olivia heard the lift doors close with a hiss. They were alone.

'Hello, Olivia. It's good to see you.' He had the temerity to smile.

To her horror, her stomach twisted in knots like a puppy wriggling in delight, waiting to be patted.

She set her jaw and fought the impulse to rush across and tell him she'd missed him. How dared he smile as if nothing was wrong when he'd betrayed her?

'What's going on, Alessandro? I've been to my office.'

'Ah.' His eyebrows twitched in a frown and she had the impression he was disconcerted. 'I'd meant to talk with you first.'

'I bet you did. What were you going to say?' She folded her arms, feeling her heart pounding too quick, too hard. 'How dare you make such a change? Without even talking to me?'

'I know it's a shock but it's for the best—'

'For the best?' She stalked across to stand before him. Toe to toe. So close she inhaled the heady scent of bergamot and Alessandro that even now beckoned her. It was the last straw. 'I've given everything to my career. You *know* that. You'll never find anyone more dedicated than me and yet you want to kick me off the executive team over a spat about your brother! It's outrageous. It's—'

'No one's kicking you off the executive team.' Alessandro's hand closed around her elbow and she realised she was shaking with the force of the emotions raging through her. 'What on earth did Marco say?'

Olivia frowned. 'That you hadn't wanted me to find out before you spoke to me. That I didn't belong on the executive floor any more.'

To her horror her throat closed on the words. It brought back ancient memories of crying over her parents' death and then her grandma's. She'd never cried since, not even through years of being bullied and baited at school. She wasn't about to start now.

She swallowed and looked clear-eyed into Alessandro's drawn face. Now she looked properly he didn't appear as confident as he'd seemed at first glance.

'What's going on?'

'Sit down.' He urged her towards a chair.

'I don't want to sit.' She yanked free of his hold but didn't move away. 'Just tell me what's going on. Is this about Carlo's call?'

'In a way.'

Her insides shrivelled. She'd been right. He hadn't believed her.

'So sacking me is your retribution?'

'No!' His eyes rounded. 'How can you think I'd sack you?'

'Demotion, then.' She crossed her arms, ignoring the way they brushed his suit. She wasn't backing down now.

'You've got this all wrong. What sort of man do you think me?'

'What sort of woman do you think me, when you accuse me of having an affair with your brother?'

'I never accused you—'

'But you thought it, didn't you?'

As she watched, the stern lines of his face carved deeper and his mouth twisted down.

'I told myself it wasn't possible. That such a betrayal would be repugnant to you. Then I saw Carlo's name on your phone and for a split second it seemed too real. Because how could you genuinely care in the way I wanted you to about someone you'd been forced to marry? It wasn't reasonable to expect it.'

The way he wanted?

Those words lodged in her brain and wouldn't shift.

'So, yes, for a single moment I doubted. Then you appeared and...'

To Olivia's amazement his words failed. She watched him swallow, his strong throat working in a jerky movement as if he felt the same constriction she did.

'I realised how it looked to you. You'd seen me in a jealous rage once and now you saw me sneaking a look at your phone. It made me feel paltry. Like some insecure loser whose self-esteem is so low he can't even trust the word of the most genuine person he's ever met.'

'Genuine?' Her head spun as she grappled to take all this in.

'What else? When you explained about Carlo calling you because he was frightened to make contact with me direct, I felt like some ogre. How could he actually fear calling me? And to learn you went along with it for my sake, because you cared about me and my relationship with my brother...' He shook his head. 'I was ashamed.'

'Alessandro?' She peered up into that stark, proud face and suddenly it wasn't in the least bit remote. She realised the taut angles and newly etched lines spoke of strong emotion. Pain and regret and maybe even fear.

She knew those feelings so well. She'd lived with them herself since the night of their confrontation.

A muscle in his tight jaw worked. 'I'm not used to dealing with emotions, Olivia. It's a weakness of mine.' His lips moved into a twist of a smile. 'I used to think that a strength. All those years learning not to mind that my parents weren't around. That they dumped little Carlo on me. That they didn't care about us. It taught me to distance myself from emotion because caring hurt.'

He shook his head and suddenly he was holding her upper arms, his touch so gentle she could break it if she wanted. But she didn't want to. She wanted to lean into him but didn't because she needed to hear more. She let her arms fall to her sides.

'I'm not looking for sympathy, just explaining. All my life I did what I could for the family and the family company. I didn't expect thanks for salvaging it and didn't get any. That's now how my family works. As for relationships with women, I never expected more than sex and casual companionship because that's all I was comfortable with. I knew they wanted me for what my money could buy.'

And because he was sexy, intriguing, passionate and caring. But Olivia kept that to herself.

'Then along you came and suddenly everything I knew flew out the window. I was bombarded with...*feelings*.'

'You make that sound bad,' she whispered as a maelstrom of feelings bombarded *her*. Hope wrestled with disbelief.

Dark eyes held hers and the sinews in her legs softened.

'I didn't know how to handle them. I didn't know how to handle *you*.'

'You could have fooled me.'

'That's just it. I projected the façade of a man in control when I felt totally out of control.' He dragged in a deep breath and Olivia suddenly realised how on-edge he was. Almost as much as her? 'I felt too much.'

'What did you feel, Alessandro?' She gave in to the need welling inside and planted her hand on his chest. Instantly the pound of his heartbeat thrummed through her. It matched her own.

'Lust. That came first.' His brows twitched. 'No, not just

lust. Connection. Something I can't name. Elation, maybe. Then savage disappointment when I saw you with Carlo. I'd never felt so bad.'

Olivia's own emotions see-sawed with each revelation.

'Then later, concern. I wanted to protect you. And pride.' His lips tilted in a tiny smile that played havoc with her emotions. 'You really are good at what you do.'

'We have that in common.'

Alessandro shrugged as if his commercial abilities meant nothing. 'The more time we spent together, the more I felt for you, Olivia. I did everything I could think of to make you happy so you wouldn't think of leaving.'

Leaving? Where had that come from? Then she remembered what he'd said about his absentee parents and short-term girlfriends.

'I was grappling with my feelings when Carlo rang you. Suddenly I realised how much I had to lose and for the first time I can remember I was truly afraid.

'Far from betraying me, you were trying to help, because you *cared* about me. It was wonderful news but terrifying too, because the way you looked at me that night, I knew I was in danger of losing you.'

Olivia drank in each word, amazed to hear fear tint Alessandro's voice.

'When you said you wanted to sleep alone I jumped at the chance. I needed to regroup to sort out my feelings and decide what to do about them. I had to make things right and knew I couldn't afford to make another mistake. I couldn't lose you.'

She heard his raw emotion, felt it in the pit of her stomach. A great trembling started up inside. She was shaky as a newborn lamb, rocky on its feet. The way he spoke…

'For a man not used to facing his feelings you're doing a good job.' Her voice wobbled perilously. She wanted to wrap her arms around him but she had to hear everything.

'Only because I vowed I'd be completely honest with

you. Olivia…' He paused and her pulse seemed to stop till he continued. 'I love you. I love you so much the idea of being without you fills me with dread.'

His words exactly matched her feelings, matched the words she'd never dared say aloud, because she'd thought she alone felt this way.

Was it possible?

The abrupt surge of emotion was so powerful she couldn't tell if it was elation or disbelief or even fear that this wasn't real. She swallowed hard, trying to find her voice, trying to convince herself it was true.

Her husband *loved her.*

'Oh, Alessandro.' She leaned into him, looking up into blazing dark eyes. Life had never been so utterly glorious. 'I'm not going anywhere. You're stuck with me. I love you too. I think I've been in love with you from the moment I saw you at that first party. I told myself it was crazy and then I tried to hate you because you disapproved of me.'

'I never disapproved of you.' His hand went to her cheek, stroking tenderly. 'I couldn't bear to see you and Carlo together and knew I couldn't take you from him.'

'Silly man. Carlo and I—'

'Were never an item. I know.'

'Do you?'

Alessandro's thumb swiped across her bottom lip in a caress that made her whole being hum with yearning. Could this really be happening?

'I'll invite him to stay at the villa, shall I?'

Olivia breathed a sigh of relief and delight. He meant it. Suddenly the world seemed a brighter place. Joy rose, incandescent. She felt as if her bloodstream sparkled with sunshine. 'If you like, but only for a short visit. I like our privacy.'

Her husband's mouth turned up in a slow smile that turned her knees weak. He caught her close as she sagged and Olivia felt that she was exactly where she wanted to be.

'Tell me more about loving me. I want to hear everything.' Alessandro's voice was stronger now and there was no sign of doubt in that strong, beloved face. In fact, he looked smug.

Olivia was glad. She never wanted him to experience that dreadful anxiety again, for she knew how it felt.

'In a minute.' She frowned, remembering. 'First tell me what's going on with my office.'

Instead of looking guilty, Alessandro smiled, an exultant grin she couldn't help responding to, since it curled like a warm embrace around her.

'Ah, that's one of my better ideas.'

'Really?'

'Really.' He bent his head and pressed a lingering kiss to her lips. She was melting into it when he withdrew, breathing hard through his nose. 'Soon. Very soon. You need to see this first.'

To Olivia's surprise he shepherded her through the door to his office. They stopped in a new anteroom that hadn't been there last week. Before them were two offices, separated by a wall of glass. In one was Alessandro's desk and visitors' chairs clustered around a table. In the other was a familiar red chair, wide desk and a fern in a brass pot. On one wall was a collection of fashion plates.

'You don't belong downstairs,' Alessandro said, his words riffling the top of her hair as he stood, embracing her from behind. 'You belong up here with me. I'm making you joint CEO.'

'You're *what*?' She spun round in his arms. 'What are you talking about?'

'I want you at my side, Olivia. And you deserve to be. Don't forget, this new company is as much Dell'Orto as it is Sartori.'

'But I…' Words failed her. It was too unexpected. Too preposterous. Except the gleam in Alessandro's eyes told her he meant it. 'But I'm not CEO material. I've got so much to learn.'

'You *are* CEO material. Yes, you have a lot to learn, but I had to learn very young when I took control of Sartori. I made mistakes but we survived. Don't forget I'm here to help you. Besides,' he paused, eyes locked on hers, 'sharing the load means more time away from business. Time for *us*. I want to build a future with you, Olivia.'

'You really mean it!' Alessandro didn't joke about business but it was his expression that convinced her, that look of pride, tenderness and love, clear now for her to see. Olivia's heart squeezed.

'Don't fret. You're not going to break anything. We'll work together. How does that sound?'

She goggled up at him, her heart filling her throat and a mad rush of adrenaline catapulting through her body. It felt like falling in love all over again.

Or realising that the man she adored really did love her.

'It sounds scary and absolutely wonderful.'

'Let's concentrate on the wonderful.' Alessandro's eyes danced as he pushed shut the door to the outer office.

A laugh bubbled in Olivia's chest and spilled out. That laugh didn't sound like the voice of a CEO. Or even a serious, successful executive. She didn't care.

Olivia reached for her husband, pulling his head down to hers, and smiled boldly into that smoky hot stare. 'Yes, let's do just that.'

EPILOGUE

'IT'S A TRIUMPH. I knew it would be.' Alessandro's voice was warm with approval.

Olivia looked up into her husband's handsome face, disguised by a small mask that matched his silver-embroidered black velvet coat. He was resplendent in the costume of an eighteenth-century aristocrat, from his snowy neckcloth to his form-fitting breeches. If she'd known he'd look so good she'd have locked him in their suite. There'd been too many women ogling him.

'You say that now, but I wasn't sure until today.' Despite the best plans there'd been a couple of glitches.

She breathed deep, feeling the clasp of her tight bodice and suppressing a smile as Alessandro's gaze dropped to her décolletage.

'Earth to Alessandro!' She waved her fingers before his face.

'I was listening, but I was looking too. You're magnificent tonight, *amore mio*. Let's have a masked ball every year.'

He raised her hand to his mouth and kissed her wrist, sending a bevy of butterflies cascading through her.

Olivia smiled. She knew she looked good in the antique-style crimson ball dress. It cinched in her waist and plumped up her breasts and made her feel more feminine than ever before. Or perhaps it was Alessandro's gaze, like hot syrup, glazing her skin.

'I knew it would be a success,' he murmured against her flesh, sending delicious shivers up her arm and down to her womb. 'I have every confidence in you.'

The teasing light disappeared from his eyes and Olivia's heart dipped as she met her beloved's gaze full on.

It had been an amazing six months. Frantically busy as she learned her new role. Wonderfully fulfilling as she discovered what it was to love and be loved by a man such as Alessandro. A man who was proud yet tender, infinitely patient despite his passionate nature.

Oh, that passionate nature.

There'd been disagreements and there would be more. But by common consent they discussed them up front, leaving no festering resentment behind.

And as she acclimatised to her role of joint CEO they had more time together away from the business. She had hopes that private time would increase with the plan to give Carlo more responsibility when he and Hannah moved from the States. Already he'd proved his value in troubleshooting problems in the US stores.

And if they had more private time maybe one day they'd start a family. It wasn't something she'd thought about much before, but now, so happy and secure with Alessandro, she found her thoughts turning to a family of their own. Others managed a work-life balance. Surely they could too.

'When you look at me that way I'm tempted to sweep you away from all this and back to our room.'

'But it's still early!' Yet her protest wasn't vehement. Olivia wanted nothing more than to be alone with her husband. 'The guests...'

'Let Carlo and Hannah look after them. And your grandparents. They're revelling in this.'

It was true. Her grandparents were in their element in this exclusive, elegant celebration.

'Besides,' Alessandro dropped his voice to a note that burred across her skin and turned her bones liquid, 'I want to talk to you about a proposal.'

'Another proposal?' She grinned. 'Be careful. Last time you did that you ended up with a bride.'

He pulled her flush against him and her hormones rioted

at the feel of his hard body. 'Precisely. It worked perfectly last time. I got exactly what I wanted. You.'

Olivia pretended to frown to cover her delighted smile. 'And what is it you want now?'

Alessandro ducked his head and whispered in her ear. Her teasing laughter faded as her heart swelled. It seemed she wasn't the only one thinking about a family.

'Olivia?' He lifted his head, those liquid dark eyes capturing hers. 'Is it too soon? We can wait.'

Her hand on his mouth stopped him. 'Not too soon at all.'

'No?' A slow smile creased his face and she forgot to breathe. Her husband was the most gorgeous, sexy man alive.

'No.' He had to bend close to hear the whispered word. But then Olivia realised he'd bent close to curve an arm behind her legs and scoop her up against his chest.

'Alessandro! We can't!' She turned to look across the glittering room, where guests danced and chatted in a froth of colour, jewels and goodwill.

'We can. No one will miss us if we slip out for an hour or two.'

Without a backward glance he strode away, his arms strong around her.

Olivia looked up at that obstinate jaw and satisfied smile and knew her husband for a proud, masterful man. But against her ear she felt the quick, erratic thud of his heart and knew him for a man in love.

She sighed. She wouldn't change her beloved Alessandro for anything.

* * * * *

COMING SOON!

We really hope you enjoyed reading this book. If you're looking for more romance, be sure to head to the shops when new books are available on

Thursday 6th August

To see which titles are coming soon, please visit
millsandboon.co.uk/nextmonth

MILLS & BOON

Coming next month

CONFESSIONS OF AN ITALIAN MARRIAGE
Dani Collins

"Get in," Giovanni said.

The sight of him struck like a gong, leaving her quivering. He had a shaggy black beard and dark glasses, and his black hoodie was pulled up to hide all but his familiar cheekbones, but his legs stopped above the knees and she recognized the tense line of his mouth.

Alive. Her heart soared so high, it should have shattered the sky.

At the same time, a thousand furies invaded her like a swarm of killer bees. There was no triumph in learning she was right. There was only a crippling heartbreak that he had abandoned her. If he'd been truly dead, she would have been angry, but she wouldn't have blamed him.

This, though? He had put her through horrifying hours of actually believing he was gone. She had endured his gut-wrenching funeral, convinced it was a sham. Then, two short weeks later, she'd suffered another unbearable loss that would never heal.

He'd forced her to go through all of that alone.

For every minute that had passed since that awful day, she had longed for him to reveal himself, but now her feet only carried her forward so she could bitterly hiss, "Go to hell."

"Where do you think I've been?" he growled.

"I'm calling the police!" Teresina yelled from deep in the alley. Two of Teresina's employees were recording everything on their phones.

A man in a suit was running toward her. She instinctively moved closer to Giovanni, heart jamming with fear.

Giovanni's hard arm looped around her and he dragged her into the back of the car. He clutched the door for leverage, but his strength was as annoyingly effortless as always.

She didn't fight him. In fact, once he grabbed her out of her stasis, she helped, kicking against the edge of the door to thrust herself inside, desperate for whatever sanctuary he offered.

They wound up in a heap on the back seat while the man who was chasing her came up to the open door and reached for her leg.

She screamed and kicked at him with her sharp heels. He dodged her shoes and threw the yards of silk in after her, then slammed the door before he leaped into the passenger seat in front of Giovanni.

"Go," Giovanni said to the driver, and he pushed himself upright.

As the SUV sped into traffic, Freja rocked deeper into the seat, stunned to her toes.

Continue reading
CONFESSIONS OF AN ITALIAN MARRIAGE
Dani Collins

Available next month
www.millsandboon.co.uk

JOIN US ON SOCIAL MEDIA!

Stay up to date with our latest releases, author news and gossip, special offers and discounts, and all the behind-the-scenes action from Mills & Boon...

 millsandboon

 millsandboonuk

 millsandboon

It might just be true love...

MILLS & BOON

HEROES

At Your Service

Experience all the excitement of a
gripping thriller, with an intense romance
at its heart. Resourceful, true-to-life
women and strong, fearless men face
danger and desire - a killer combination!